All The Muscle You Need

First Edition
10-9-8-7-6-5-4-3-2-1

Spinsters/Aunt Lute Book Company
P.O. Box 410687
San Francisco, CA 94141

Cover and Text Design: Pam Wilson Design Studio
Cover Photo: Pam Wilson

Typesetting: Ruby Fowler and Comp-Type, Inc., Fort Bragg, CA

Production: Martha Davis   Cindy Lamb
              Debra DeBondt   Mary Travers
              Nancy Fishman   Kathleen Wilkinson
              Jeanette Hsu

Spinsters/Aunt Lute is an educational project of the Capp Street
Foundation.

Printed in the U.S.A.

Library of Congress Cataloging in Publication Data
     McRae, Diana, 1951-
  All the muscle you need
  I. Title.
PS3563.C68A78   1988   813'.54   88-23954
ISBN 0-933216-59-9 (pbk)
ISBN 0-933216-61-0

All The Muscle You Need

AN
ELIZA PIREX
MYSTERY

DIANA
McRAE

spinsters | *aunt lute*

SAN FRANCISCO

For Carolyn

She'll arrive at eleven. When she comes, she will come toting murder, madness, and lost time. But since she hasn't checked her baggage with me yet, I sit unencumbered in my square grey office doing bookkeeping, double-entry. I am, as always, satisfied with my accounting.

I held the job of bookkeeper before I began the incalculable series of adventures that led me to become a private investigator in Oakland, California. Oakland resonates, like L.A. did when Raymond Chandler used to stroll downtown looking for big-bosomed women and mystery. Because I am a woman, my cases don't always wax as mean as the city streets. Clients with hard-boiled problems tend to lack confidence in my slighter frame.

I often battle petty swindlers and liars. My rates compare favorably to those of the big investigative firms so I work for parties who don't think their problem warrants a major investment. I never lack for work.

When she called last week, she said, "I'm messier than most of your clients. I seem to have lost track of almost everyone I've ever met. They were penciled in my address book and I erased them. Let's not worry about that, though. I never erased Ruthie, or anyone who knew her. But I can't find her anyway. And I want her back." Eileen Goldeen, my eleven o'clock appointment, can really rattle on.

I pointed out to her that almost any person can be found by following a few simple steps. Surprisingly, considering the admitted disarray of her personal records, Eileen had already executed these steps. Eileen pursued last known address, place of work, and immediate family, with no success.

I checked the subject's name for credit record, motor vehicle information, status with the IRS, and more. I got nothing either. Possibly, Eileen Goldeen presents a suitable case for further investigation. I am a little surprised. I supposed from her telephone style that Eileen could be living in the same town as her missing person, too scattered to notice.

Eileen arrives late, quarter past eleven. She stands paralyzed with her feet planted awkwardly after we shake hands so I guide her to my comfortable client chair, the one with padded arms. I start the tape recorder spinning without Eileen knowing.

Eileen wears a subdued green drop-waist dress and elegant low-heeled leather pumps appropriate for a suburban lady's visit to a downtown Oakland office. I find the long clean lines of Eileen Goldeen's body, and her unusual face, attractive, but I would guess that the small well-molded women in the community over the hills, where Eileen lives, don't accept her as one of their own. Her height, her soft large mouth, and a conspicuous naiveté and inquisitiveness, would not appeal to that group. I put some warmth on my face, to soothe her, and lean on my elbows across the bare expanse of oak desktop.

"Have you required the services of a private investigator before?" I inquire.

"No, of course not. I don't even watch the detective shows on television. I can't tell which are the clues and I never know why they've started shooting at the detective. I would have been afraid to hire you except that when I read, 'Something plaguing you?' I thought to myself, 'Yes, there is.' It's particularly hard on my birthday. My mind wanders and I look for Ruthie to be at the party. Of course, she isn't. Because she's disappeared."

I gaze fondly at a framed camera-ready copy of the ad that Honor wrote as part of her original marketing campaign for me.

Something Plaguing You? If you're uneasy because of *uncertainties* at the workplace, *questions* about your personal life, or *troubles* from the past, you can afford peace of mind. We'll give you a low-cost estimate for any job no matter how large

(or small).

ELIZA PIREX INVESTIGATIONS
All the Muscle You Need

The italicized words humiliate me the most. This advertisement (and the embarrassing graphic accompanying), planted in give-away journals and women's newspapers, upped our annual income by $15,000 the first year we ran it.

"Tell me about you and Ruth Gold," I say. Eileen looks startled by my inclusion of herself in the question.

"We were friends at U.C. Santa Barbara, for two years. Then Ruthie transferred to Berkeley and I dropped out. My mother got sick and my grades weren't very good. I met my husband, Rich, on a vacation in Palm Springs. I'd always thought Palm Springs would be high-toned but I didn't like it." She pauses and reflects. "Except for meeting Rich," she adds.

I have now ascertained that Eileen Goldeen does not think in a linear fashion. I eye her grimly. "Was that when you lost touch with Ruth?" I ask.

"No. Rich comes from the Bay Area. He works for his dad's company, their main office is in Walnut Creek. Rich manages the company really, but his dad won't admit it."

"And Ruth?"

"Ruthie finished at U.C. Berkeley and then moved to San Francisco. Rich didn't like me seeing Ruthie because his dad thought, just because of the color Ruthie had dyed her hair when he met her, that Ruthie was disreputable. But she was my best friend until she disappeared six years ago. I wasn't her best friend actually but that was okay. Ruthie always had a lot of people."

"I gather from what you told me during our initial phone conversation that you've given a lot of thought to finding Ruth. Do you have a special reason for wanting to get in touch with her? I'm asking because many people lose touch with old friends but wouldn't consider hiring a professional to locate them."

Eileen Goldeen looks roused for the first time. Her pupils constrict. She runs her fingers through fine brown hair, undoing her pricy Orinda coiffure. "I guess I haven't told you much at all."

Eileen begins the story of a moment in Santa Barbara. They went down to an ocean which shimmered in a floating oil derrick's light. Ruthie raised her fist to the moon and swore that she would find a rich man, rich and musical, and marry him. In the cool of that night, Ruthie and Eileen pledged everlasting friendship. Eileen woke up the next morning with tar on her soles.

3
▲

Before I cut her off and ask for a less convoluted answer, Eileen interrupts herself to gasp, "What's that?"

I wonder what she means. Then I realize that I've been hearing background noise coming from the courtyard outside my office while we've been talking.

I share an office building with Sarah Frybarger, Attorney at Law (specialties, divorce and bankruptcy); Lucas Jang, Ph.D.; and his partner, Mike Woolley, MCSW, marriage and family counseling. The building used to be a small motel. It forms a square with a paved courtyard in the center. Sarah, Lucas, and Mike have spacious, plushly carpeted offices along the left and right. The reception area fronts the street. I have a studio office at the rear of the courtyard with grey-brown linoleum flooring.

I raise the blinds so that Eileen and I can peer into the courtyard. Eileen puts a timid hand over her mouth. "It's Rich! My husband. He gets irritated when he has to wait for me. He must have finished early at Ron Richter Sports. He's supposed to be trying on boots."

An over-dressed 35-year-old man imitating someone older stands arguing with Precious Harrold, our collective receptionist. We hired Precious to be pleasant but firm and she never disappoints us in either respect, although Rich Goldeen strains the first right now. Rich obviously escaped through the back door of the front office and into the courtyard.

I open the door and step out into the thin April sunshine. Eileen follows me. When I glance backward, I see Eileen scowling at the ground as she walks. I hear Precious state with authority, "No admittance to anyone without an appointment. All the professionals in this building work with clients who are sensitive about their privacy." Precious' tone indicates that she will enforce her dictum, even in the face of assault by suburban noblesse oblige.

I would swear that Rich Goldeen sees me and Eileen from out of the corner of his eye before he speaks, but he proceeds to boom, "My wife is talking to some low-cost lady detective who does errands for housewives who are too dumb to take care of their own business. What's so private about that?" He leers disagreeably at Precious.

I'm embarrassed by the rude capsulization of my career especially because I notice my neighbor, Lucas, and a weeping client, at his window observing this scene. I march forward to

4
▲

take control but Eileen hurries past me. When I catch up to her, she ceases muttering in her husband's ear and makes introductions. Precious smirks at us all. In the weak sunlight, Precious, tall, assured, and the color of night, has more presence than Eileen or Eileen's uncivil spouse.

"Eliza Pirex, I'd like you to meet my husband, Rich Goldeen." Eileen tries to conciliate. "He's used to getting his way during work hours. That's why he's being so pushy." He gives her a spiteful shrug. She throws her shoulders back and says meaningfully to her husband, "I'll only be about fifteen minutes more. We said I have until 11:45, Rich. Remember?"

"We have a real nice selection of magazines in the front óffice, sir." Precious uses her low throaty voice to make the offer sound enticing. "We subscribe to *Psychology Today, People*, and *Ellery Queen's Mystery Magazine*." I hope Precious can sell him on one.

I escort Eileen Goldeen back to my office and shut the door behind us. "He's not as rude as he seems," Eileen apologizes again. "He's more of a hypochondriac than a maniac. He yells because his stomach is bothering him."

"Since it sounds like we have only fifteen minutes," I say brightly, "let's try to assess where to go with this case." I know that I don't sound enthusiastic. My caseload for this month will keep me adequately busy without Eileen. Eileen Goldeen looked more attractive as a client before I got a look at Rich. Eileen gazes into her lap in response to my dwindling interest. Then she raises her eyes with a new seriousness.

"I haven't told you about the strange things that happened. Before Ruthie vanished, I mean. Things my husband doesn't like me to talk about."

Eileen Goldeen says solemnly and slowly, "Ruthie was important."

Eileen and I stare across the desk at each other, the first time she has made eye contact. Her eyes have an unusual lavender hue. I find Eileen more compelling silent than when she speaks. The faint traffic hum from West Grand Avenue and the thumping of other lives in the apartments behind my office recede for me now that I have focused all my attention on Eileen.

A fine sleight of hand by Eileen Goldeen, a little trick with the eyes actually, and I'm conjured into doing her bidding. I need to draw from her some concrete facts about her friend's disappearance, probably not an easy aspiration. What does she want from me and Ruth Gold?

5
▲

"Important in what way?" I ask.

"Well," Eileen speaks more carefully than she has previously, "Ruthie was never ordinary. She looked like Cleopatra. She did. She had big dark eyes and white skin and straight shiny black hair cut sharp around her face. Men and women would stare when she walked by. Sometimes, crowds would part for her." I try not to appear skeptical.

"Here," says Eileen, reverential. "Ruthie usually wouldn't let anyone take her picture but I have this one. I had an 8″ X 10″ copy made for myself. You can keep the original."

Eileen passes me a photograph that looks as though it's been folded, a coffee-colored stain floats in the sky. I am looking at a tan young Eileen Goldeen squinting into the sun with her arm around a 20-year-old woman with Semitic features whom I would describe as scrawny and tired-looking. I look closer trying to find the rare and exotic personage Eileen has described. Maybe her posture suggests a flamboyance of spirit, but then again, maybe she just wasn't trained to stand up straight.

"She looks interesting," I offer. Eileen nods, her eyes fixed on the photograph. I glance back at the photo and something smoldering there leaps out at me for a minute. Then it's gone.

"I'll do it," I say.

"What?" Eileen looks puzzled.

"I'll find her for you. I'm working now on a job for Kains College that consumes a lot of time. But I'll begin making inquiries in the Bay Area for you right away."

"Thank you," Eileen mumbles, not as grateful as I would like. "Rich said to get some references before I give you a deposit but I'm sure everything will be fine." Clearly, Eileen didn't consider the possibility that I would not take the job.

"Mrs. Goldeen, let me explain what a private investigator can do for you. I'll organize your data and then pursue other information which you might find too strenuous, or don't have the contacts, to gather for yourself."

"Call me Eileen," she replies, cowed by my spiel.

"Should the need arise, I have recourse to modern techniques of surveillance and information retrieval. I hope I can give you the current location of," I glance at my notes, "Ruth Diane Gold without investing a large number of hours. Were you hoping to receive more information about Ruth? Her financial status? Employment history?"

"I just want to know where she is," Eileen verifies, the

lavender eyes wide with the gravity of this business transaction.

I have to show clients early on that I'm going to interact with them in a professional manner even though I'm (usually) their age (in our thirties), or younger than them, and a woman. There's always the risk that I'll scare them off but it has to be done in order for me to operate and then to collect my fees.

I look up and see Rich Goldeen pacing directly in front of my office. "Eileen, I'd like to interview you further, this week. We'll want to construct a timeline including everything that happened before Ruth disappeared, any details and events that you can recall. Is Wednesday morning at 9:00 a.m. okay with you? I'd be willing to conduct the interview at your home." I invite myself to Eileen's home out of curiosity.

"I guess that would be fine. Rich will be out in the field." Good. Eileen swivels in her chair and sees Rich stalking outside. I get up and close the blinds, which leaves the office darker than I would prefer.

"As I told you on the phone," I say firmly, "I'll want you to sign a written contract outlining the extent to which you want me to pursue the case and any constraints on expenses. I'll put in writing the hourly fee, the overnight fee, and charges for expenses we talked about earlier."

Eileen isn't interested in the nitty gritty. She maintains a cultivated pose, facing me, but her eyes have glazed. I know the look. Dennis Eckenberg, with whom I apprenticed as an investigator, has a sage maxim about the moments when a client decides to reveal another piece of their hidden motive for hiring a private investigator—as opposed to the polite and superficial reason they presented initially. Dennis will be disappointed in me. I can't remember the sage maxim.

"Eileen, before you go, is there anything else you want to tell me?"

Eileen leans forward confidentially as if she has waited for this cue. "I suppose I should tell you the things that were going on before Ruthie left. She might have disappeared because of the weirdness that was going on."

"Sure. Just tell me whatever you like in the time we have left." I sit forward and put my pencil conspicuously to the worksheet upon which I am taking notes.

The prod doesn't work. Eileen mutters, "Maybe when we get together on Wednesday. Rich is going to ask me as soon as

7
▲

I get outside the office if I dramatized things. 'Don't drama-
tize,' he always tells me."

"We can wait until Wednesday," I agree, although, having
accepted this spare little case, I would have enjoyed hearing
something to warm me up more. But I don't have to wait to
hear the dirt, after all. When Eileen realizes I might consent to
postpone her opportunity to unburden herself until Wednesday, she crosses her arms over her chest and starts talking
rapidly. "I'm not normally paranoid. But I've worried ever
since my last three phone calls from Ruthie. I should have
tried harder to help her."

I ignore Eileen's concern over her liability. "What did she
say during those phone calls?" I prompt.

"Ruthie always knew people who had problems. She
never knew how to get rid of them. She'd be their girlfriend,
she'd buy them chocolate, she'd visit their grandparents with
them. She couldn't stop herself." Eileen's face grows so open
and vulnerable as she begins to level with me that I see why
Ruth Gold, with her social worker streak, once chose her for a
friend.

"The third to last time I talked with her, Ruthie was
feeling lousy. She had gotten thin. She'd faint when she had to
walk on sidewalks or go into stores but she was afraid to stay
in her apartment, too. She told me she would rather die than
have to spend her life hiding in small hot rooms. Ruthie
always had a lively way of talking about her troubles but she
had gotten sad. I think she was sucked dry by all the weird
people and the things that had been happening."

"What had been happening?"

"Her psychiatrist had started following her and playing
tricks on her. I hope you don't think badly of her but Ruthie
dated her psychiatrist while he was seeing her as a doctor.
Rich always said Ruthie didn't have a lot of discretion. The
doctor didn't sound at all professional to me, especially after
he started acting strange."

"What else was going on?" I ask quickly, forestalling a
discourse on medical ethics.

"Ruthie had been getting notes about forgetting to put
her cat out. She wasn't sure who they were from. They upset
her a lot."

"Had she been forgetting to put her cat out?" I try to
clarify.

"Certainly not. He was an inside cat. But that brings me to
the second to last phone call I ever got from Ruthie. Before

8
▲

that year, it was usually me who called her," Eileen supplies one of her tangents.

"What did you talk about during that second phone call?"

"I didn't want to tell you about Rings," Eileen chokes. I push a box of tissues across the desk and she takes one. "But I guess I have to." I wait sympathetically, expecting to hear that Ruthie had her jewelry stolen on top of everything else.

"I gave Ruthie one of my cat's kittens to keep her company," Eileen says and pauses.

"Nice," I reply and wait for Eileen to expand upon this new divergence.

Eileen begins speaking again, even more distressed. "Its mother was our purebred Egyptian Mau, Dutchess. We still have her. Dutchess sleeps with me when Rich is gone on business. Ruthie named her kitten Rings because his tail had funny bluish rings." The story doesn't involve jewelry.

"Ruthie didn't even have a houseplant before. Or she did, but she let them die. She promised me she would take good care of Rings.

"Rings was about six months old. It was pretty late when she called that night. Ruthie was screaming. She screamed, 'I'm sorry, I'm sorry.' Ruthie used to say she was sorry a lot.

"Ruthie said she'd been in bed, sound asleep, when the doorbell rang. Not the buzzer downstairs but the one on her own door. She got up and went to the door and looked out the peephole. You know, the kind where you can only see the intruder if they put their face directly in front of the hole. She didn't see anything.

"So she opened the door. Ruthie was never careful. Outside the door sat a Safeway bag gathered at the top, with a card tied on like on a present. She read the note first. It said, 'Forgot to put the cat out.'

"That was when I asked her, 'Ruthie, I thought you never let the cat out,' and she screamed, 'I don't.' She didn't appreciate my asking.

"Ruthie opened the bag after she read the card and, of course, Rings was in it. He didn't look smashed, just limp. He was dead. A piece of his fur had been shaved off. Rings had a scarab mark on him which was supposed to bring luck but the mark didn't protect him any. 'So much for superstition,' Rich said."

"It must have been hard for you," I respond. I don't worry that Eileen will elaborate upon Egyptian beetle lore or the merits of shopping at Safeway. The weight of her pain about the long-dead Rings drags her tongue straight down the rest of her story. Eileen continues.

"Yes, it was hard." She raises a tissue and presses it to her nose. "I tried to talk to her about who might have done it. She didn't think it was anyone she knew, in spite of the note. She promised me she would get a new deadbolt and be more careful about opening the door.

"Rich checked on her when he went to San Francisco later in the week. He said that she looked even sicker from the whole thing. Of course, he never thought she looked good. I think Rich was upset by seeing her. He was shaky when he got home that night."

"How was Ruthie the last time you talked to her?" I'm waiting for a climax.

"Rich doesn't like me to discuss it. He doesn't want me to involve us in criminal activity."

"Did something criminal happen?" I ask.

"Yes. The last time I talked to Ruthie she sounded dead. Oh, that's a terrible choice of words. You see, Ruthie was calling to say that her friend, Claudia Hollings, had been murdered. She was murdered in Ruthie's apartment. The police didn't know who did it.

"Ruthie wanted to know if she could stay at our house for a while to get away from her apartment. When she heard that Rich's parents were staying with us because their house was being painted, she decided to go to someone else. She'd met Rich's parents, you remember."

"Did you know Claudia Hollings, Eileen?"

"I only met her once and I didn't even remember what she looked like. Claudia Hollings worked with Ruthie at the Jazzmatazz Dance Company in Santa Cruz. Claudia was a dancer with the company. Ruthie was a piano prodigy, did I mention? She drove down to Santa Cruz twice a week to accompany the dancers at practices. Ruthie might be a famous concert pianist by now. Maybe that's what she's doing." I don't bother to write down Eileen's conjecture.

"Claudia's best friend was Ruthie's younger sister, Jane. Jane danced for the company too. Jane and Claudia lived in Santa Cruz near Jazzmatazz. I don't know why Claudia was in Ruthie's apartment in San Francisco the day she got killed.

"I asked Ruthie if I could call Jane to give her my condolences about Claudia's death. Ruthie said that Jane was gone for good. She wouldn't say anything else. I tried Janie's number anyway and the phone was disconnected, no new number. Don't you think that's strange?"

10
▲

"Strange," I echo. "I'm going to have you fill out a sheet for me detailing every fact you remember about Jane Gold. Here, have a look at the one I've been compiling about Ruth." I hand her the standard investigator's rap sheet.

As she reads, I ask her, "Did Ruth mention with whom she was thinking of staying?"

"No. I didn't ask. I figured she'd call me when she got back to San Francisco and we'd talk about everything that had happened to her. When I didn't hear from her for weeks I called her. Her landlord was in the apartment and picked up the phone.

"The landlord was rude to me. He said Ruthie had left without paying the next month's rent. I should have said I'd pay it for her. He said she was gone for a while before a neighbor reported to him that the apartment was vacant. She left a lot of her things sitting in the apartment. That was the last time I talked to anyone who knew about Ruthie."

"Did you ask the landlord if you could check the apartment? Maybe see what she took with her and what she didn't?" I ask.

"He was mad about the rent so he hung up on me. Much later I wished I had asked him more. I called over there and tried to talk to him. But he had sold the building and no one knew where he was living. I lost Ruthie completely."

We sit for a while. Eileen doesn't offer to leave. Idly, I try again to recall Dennis' maxim but I can't. Finally, she cracks.

I notice Eileen Goldeen's eyes blur with lavender tears. "I may as well tell you. There's something bad I've dreamed about ever since those last times I talked to Ruthie. I guess it's why I need to know she's all right." I wait to hear about Eileen's six-year-old chimera.

"Ruthie always slept in a shortie nightgown, blue nylon. Very pathetic-looking because her chest had gotten bony like an old woman's. In my mind, I see whoever took Rings come into Ruthie's apartment and get him out of his red plaid catbed in her bedroom.

"Ruthie liked to curl up on top of her plain white bed sheets on warm nights. I remember how she looked from when I spent the weekend with her one time. The blue nylon looked thin and wrinkled. I don't really know it happened that way, because for all I know the person grabbed Rings from the little balcony outside the apartment. But I can't stand thinking of some sick person seeing her like that before he killed her cat." Tears roll down her soft pink cheeks. The

11
▲

time has come to end this interview, I've learned enough for now.

"I'm coming for you, Ruthie," I think to myself, "whether you need me or not." I confirm that Eileen and I will meet even though we've covered more ground than I expected. Eileen gives me a deposit in cash. She doesn't want a receipt. Rich Goldeen's shadow has become fixed, straight up and down on my window blind, like the noonday arrow on a sundial. I open the door for Eileen.

decide to make a partial transcript of my interview with Eileen. I wasn't expecting the rabbits out of Eileen's hat at the end of the conversation: the shaved cat in the shopping bag, the tricky psychiatrist, the sister's murdered friend. I had anticipated a missing person case as ordinary as I assumed Eileen to be. Maybe I'll get some sport out of looking for Ruthie.

I slide the description charts and information sheets I've begun with Eileen's data into a manila folder. The folder goes into a locking file drawer. An inveterate thief of privileged information myself, I lock up my own papers whenever I'm not actively using them. With Ruthie shut away, I can postpone thinking about her until after I've eaten.

Picking up the phone, I dial Dennis Eckenberg's number by heart. To become a private investigator in California you have to work as a police officer or apprentice with a licensed private investigator for 2,000 hours. My previous training was with a political group that the State of California doesn't recognize when it comes to counting experience hours.

Dennis and I worked together 50 to 60 hours a week for a couple of years. We've sat side by side in the front seats of cars, in separate cars on different parts of the road, around the corner from each other on city streets, eyeing the scene then comparing notes. Now, years later, I wish Dennis had chosen to become an actuary. I care about him and the detective business can be dangerous.

Dennis told me his word for where ordinary people hide, below the surface of casual lives and daily events: the underplace. Anyone who needs to hire a private detective has been to the underplace. Ruthie may have gone there permanently. Dennis loves to coin a phrase and hear someone else use it, so I do. He does not, on the other hand, practice the obnoxious habit of spouting P.I. jargon like "cowboy" (unlicensed private investigator), "LKA" (last known address), and "zinger" (summons).

"Lighthouse Investigations," Dennis answers the phone himself. I can tell immediately that he's not cheerful. I'd rather have caught him on a good day. But Dennis doesn't like his moods to affect the course of things, so I proceed undaunted by his underlying tone of voice.

"Hi, Dennis, it's Eliza. We talked about having lunch today if you weren't called to Sacramento. Do you want to eat?"

"Yeah. I have a bit of news. I'll tell you when I see you. Where do you want to meet?"

"I've been thinking about Mexican. You want to meet at La Casa de los Dos Heroes?" I ask, in a voice that probably sounds overly full of joie de vivre to him.

"I want whatever you want. I can be there at 1:15." Dennis' phone starts to click, signaling another call.

Talking to Dennis even briefly gives me comfort. He knows me and approves of me. I'm an attractive woman without womanly humility, so I sometimes put people off. I have learned to appreciate Dennis more than I could ever say without making him tense.

I have an hour left for routine tasks. The paperwork I need to get in order for each of my working cases waits in my in-box for updating. One job, a security problem at a local women's college, generates a lot of paper considering I've seen no action on the job. They hired me to find a bad guy or bad guys.

Early this year, several students alleged that one, possibly two, of the four night-time college security guards had been harassing students. The students claimed that the episodes were racially motivated. The initial incidents involved black women students.

The college administration decided that hiring a woman to look into the matter would be a good tactical move. They feared a black woman investigator would be at risk, given the situation, so they commissioned me. I assume someone in the administration saw my advertisement in the college newspaper. They instructed me to spend time at the school and keep an eye on the suspects.

"Find out if any of our guys aren't acting right when the girls are around," ordered a bellicose, square-bodied woman, the Assistant Dean, 'guys' meaning college employees, and 'girls' being the students. "If those guys do something they shouldn't, you make sure you tell me first."

Four evenings a week, I put on a dingy dress and white shoes. I'm supposed to be working for the maintenance firm that the college uses, Busy Bee Building Maintenance. The job demands that I wash down floors and empty wastebaskets for six hours a night. I'd love a good excuse to quit.

I intend to hunt up an even baggier, droopier costume for tonight. One guard, Dwayne, asks me every night to share some Johnny Walker Red and a steak after we get off work. I tell him I have a family. He replies that I have to eat, don't I, and the family's bound to be asleep by now. I move back and forth from classroom to dumpster. He follows at my heels. I'm the only one I've seen harassed so far.

The other case usurping my time depresses me every time I talk to the client. I consider whether I should call her right now. I talked to her just yesterday evening, though, and on second thought, I decide I need a break.

Doris Shipley, my pitiful client, broke her ankle about a year ago. She drinks a little and carries a lot of weight on the top half of a body which narrows to inordinately small feet. I've pointed out to her, after instances when she's fallen down in my office, that she needs to remember her balance isn't good.

While Doris waited for medical assistance last year, outside the emergency room at the County Hospital, she met Brenda Coller, not Collier. She and Brenda became good friends, or so Doris thought.

Brenda started dropping by Doris' house every day for beer while Doris' ankle healed, bringing magazines and plastic containers of macaroni salad. Doris *may* have agreed to pay Brenda $150 per month for her companionship. Doris now says she agreed to no such thing.

For three months running, Doris gave Brenda her state disability checks to cash. Brenda said later that Doris instructed her to keep $150 in wages out of the cash and then bring Doris the remainder of the money. Whatever the reality, Doris brought Brenda to small claims court and told the judge that Brenda had pocketed all the money from the checks.

Brenda presented a tidier appearance to the judge and put forward a plausible story explaining Doris' confusion over their relationship and about the money. The judge not only awarded Doris none of her money, he went on to tell her that she hadn't impressed him as respectable in any way.

That's when Doris hired me to try and document Brenda's finances. Doris then decided that she would like to know the particulars of Brenda's life since the time they met. She requested that I report who Brenda sees, where she spends time, what she wears, everything. I believe in access to information, so I didn't even suggest that people in certain circles consider invasion of privacy to be bad manners.

Doris recently met a new friend while waiting for her counselor at the Employment Development Department, a depressed-looking teenager named Andy. Since Andy's arrival on the scene, Doris has lost much of her energy for the Brenda situation. But Doris hasn't given up on the case.

I get my writing tasks completed with no wasted moves. I bore easily but I pride myself on working fast when the dull stuff needs to be done. I lock the files in my cabinet. This cabinet cost more than anything else in my office or home. It's designed to be state-of-the-art burglarproof. I hope burglars recognize state-of-the-art. The digital quartz clock on my desk spells out 12:44 p.m.

I put the Eileen interview cassette tape into a manila envelope and label it. I pick up my gun. Ever since the County Sheriff awarded me a license to carry a concealed weapon, I do. I clear the blotter so that anything on the desk's surface pertains to today's business. The library table behind my desk on which I stack work in progress looks orderly, as always.

I have a grey Haeger vase in the center of the table to tone up the atmosphere. Sometimes Honor puts flowers from yards in our neighborhood, with wet napkins wrapped around the stems, on the front seat of my car. She believes that no one can own a flower. Then I have flowers in my vase.

As I lock the office door and try the handle, Sarah Frybarger comes out of her office escorting dressy-looking clients. Sarah wears a nice peach-colored jacket and pearls but the woman with her looks downright ritzy in black and white. The woman's companion wears a suit that suggests his legal problems are probably sophisticated.

Sarah waves me down and calls, "Eliza Pirex, I'd like you to meet the Bentons, Jim and Marie. I've given them your number. They have a small matter they might use you for. Jim's crazy about Spenser and Rockford, all those detective heroes. Why don't you come to lunch at the Park Boulevard Cafe and tell Jim and Marie some detective stories? It'll be on my account." Sarah looks eager for companionship. Jim and Marie must not be very amusing.

"I'm sorry, Sarah, I've got a lunch date in a few minutes. Maybe we can get together some other time." I am sorry. Not only do I like her, but Sarah's law practice gets more successful every year. She acquires referrals from all over the upper-middle class Berkeley/Oakland professional community and has a reputation for being competent and caring. She could easily throw a good bit of work my way.

I can't help enjoying the idea that Sarah finds me desirable company for her clients. Sarah waves a brave goodbye and walks away conversing with Jim and Marie. She possesses better social skills than most people I know.

In the front office, Precious' husband, Charles Harrold, lounges on an uncomfortably small stain-resistant orange armchair. Our better seat accommodates office supplies piled high. Charles is probably waiting for Precious to lock up the office at one and switch our calls to the answering service.

"Hi, Charles, where's Precious?"

"The copy machine's broken so she went up the street to Woolworth's. She's fixed the telephone so that the machine gets the calls. We all know she doesn't trust me with the phones." Charles gives me a charming smile. What we do know is that Precious thinks of Charles as worth his weight in gold even though they've been married since she was sixteen.

I go out the door on the street side of the office to get to my car. I'm still carrying the manila envelope with this morning's interview tape since I forgot to leave it at Precious' desk for transcription. I stuff the thing in my shoulder bag. Since I parked my car three blocks away in a spot where they have no meters, I have to jog or I could be late. I make sure I'm punctual for appointments, including lunch.

I see Dennis' car in the restaurant parking lot. He's always early, partly because he's a compulsive person, partly because he likes to have a drink before I get there and cramp his style.

Dennis' father holds a middling-to-high level job in the CIA. Dennis' sparse stories about his father's secrets and power both fascinate and pain me. After a childhood among his father's associates, a bland-seeming but ruthless crew, Dennis grew up and became a small-time good guy with a pinched, conscientious set to his face. The crew taught Dennis to drink, not profusely, but too much. Maybe he would have been a drinker anyway.

The air conditioning prickles my skin when I come through Los Dos Heroes' padded doors. It's too early in the year for air conditioning. A sign says "Please wait to be seated," but I hurry past hoping to avoid the high-powered hostess.

I see Dennis sitting at a table instead of at the bar. His broad shoulders make an arc over his margarita. He stares into space. Dennis thinks quickly and when he finishes with what he's thinking, you can see the unengaged wheels in his mind spinning fruitlessly. He looks like he needs new grist for the mill right now.

"Hi, Den." He looks up, heartened at seeing me.

"Good afternoon, I ordered you a margarita. I knew you'd enjoy licking the rim of the glass."

"Thanks." I slide into an upholstered swivel chair. Los Dos Heroes caters to overweight middle-aged anglos and rich Hispanics who aren't picky about their food but like to make themselves comfortable. "What's getting you down, Dennis?"

"The usual. Atmospheric conditions affecting my inner ear. Or whatever. I'll be a fun lunch date. You know I can do it." I refuse to be sidetracked.

"This schlump has all the earmarks of something rotten happening in your life," I offer a tentative guess.

"Making a couple improvements, actually. Changes take it out of me. I didn't have a great morning, though, now that you mention it."

We halt conversation when a Mexican waitress with no expression on her face and no pad and pencil asks for our orders. We order by number. I recall that the food comes up pretty fast in this place but I break down and eat some tortilla chips and green chile salsa anyway.

"What's going on?" I don't badger anyone else about their feelings the way I do Dennis. I think it has more to do with him than me.

"Remember Bingo Amory?" Dennis asks.

"The guy who had the old lady with the hats drive him around? You worked for him when I was with you," I remind him.

"I never found his son, Demarcus, who ran off with the money from his business. Guess what? Demarcus Amory was found yesterday." Dennis takes a sip from his drink and grimaces.

"But not by you," I assume.

"By Bingo. He found his son's name in a list of last month's AIDS victims. He's going to get an infected corpse back but not the money."

"Oh, dear," I commiserate.

18
▲

"Not a case where I come off looking particularly useful."

"You did everything you could," I point out. "The guy obviously spent all the cash and then disappeared to someplace where you don't need a driver's license. Now he's gone through one last big bankruptcy and come back dead." Jetsam from the underplace often resurfaces in our business.

Some businessmen stride past led by the imposing hostess. They give us a glance, pause to give me another look and then look back at Dennis. I'm polished-looking enough to make an odd contrast to Dennis. Dennis' long unruly brown hair never looks styled, even when it has been, and he habitually wears jeans and a ratty jacket. Still, the interesting, craggy features of his face and his muscular body have made more than one woman try to get close to him, after only one look. Everything about him seems dear to me. I glare aggressively at the men going by and they all look down at their shoes.

"Anyway, if you take what you've been paid and divide by the number of hours you've put in, you probably made 25 cents per hour. If you include the hours you spent worrying over Bingo, you made nothing an hour."

"You're tougher than me, Muscles," smiles Dennis. "We all acknowledge that. You never have to debate about refunds." He's determined to be bleak. "You might get a few snickers because of the ads in the ladies magazines but you do what you do without things coming out wrong." He's on a jag.

Dennis continues, "I'm working for the guy who owned Rocky's Carpet Remnants before it burned. I got a contract tighter than a carpet tack but I just figured out that the guy's going to screw me. He seemed like such a pathetic little slob, I let him add a few clauses to ease his mind.

"I'm going to show you the papers next time you're at my office," he says. I pat his hand for comfort. The waitress puts two large platters in front of us and warns us not to touch the plates because they're hot. Dennis was about to turn his plate around so that his enchiladas would be closer than the rice and beans. He jerks his hands away.

I rise to Dennis' implicit compliment of me. "I do pride myself on a certain cleverness in the creative end of my work," I say smugly. "Then there's my naturally curly hair. You're right, I've got it made.

"Before you get overly awed by my investigative skills, though," I caution, "I have to tell you that I may have taken on a loser case. I'm not sure I know how much energy I should put into it." His rough appearance to the contrary, Dennis puts together the fragile pieces of a dilemma in a daintier fashion than any other investigator I've seen at work. He gestures me to fill him in.

"I got a referral from my advertisement in the *Mt. Diablo Women's Times*. You remember, the ad that encourages clients to hire me just for clearing up any odds and ends nagging at the back of their mind. The client lives in Orinda. She's intelligent but undisciplined. She has a pompous husband who seems to run her."

"Their name Goldeen?"

"Yes." I'm startled. "How would you know? Did they try to hire you first?"

"No. The husband—Richard, right?—called me for a reference on you. He sounded like he'd just as soon his wife dropped the whole thing. She wants to track down a friend from college. Richard thinks the friend might as well stay lost." I have Precious give out references, including Dennis, but I always hope people won't call them.

"Richard sounded like a loser. But I told him you were a modern day Philip Marlowe."

"You didn't really say that, did you? Rich Goldeen wouldn't know Philip Marlowe from—you."

"I'm kidding," Dennis amends. "I cited your finest work. I told him he couldn't get more for his money than Eliza Pirex, all the muscle he needs." Dennis can't stop playing with the words from my advertisements.

"Okay, thanks for the good words." I decide not to worry over Rich Goldeen checking up on me. I make it a rule not to get disturbed while chewing my food. I look down at my two succulent chile rellenos swimming in monterey jack cheese. I've learned which of their platters Los Dos Heroes does well but Dennis never remembers. Dennis' enchiladas are filled with luke-warm grey hamburger, only the plate on which they sit comes hot. Next time, I will tell him what to order. "Do you want to hear more about Eileen Goldeen's problem?"

"It'll beat hearing about the pail and mop job at the college," he says, resigned.

I give Dennis a synopsis of Eileen's story about Ruthie. Dennis doesn't look particularly interested until I get to the death of Rings the cat, followed by Claudia Hollings' death, and Ruthie's sudden disappearance.

"Ruthie had various emotional problems," I tell him. "They're hard for me to diagnose from Eileen's account but they sound bad. Eileen makes Ruthie sound charismatic and attractive, too.

"According to Eileen," I proceed with my recap, "Ruthie had miscellaneous outstanding attributes, for example, she was a piano prodigy. Of course, Eileen's memory has been colored by time and sentiment. Who knows whether Ruthie can crank out anything except 'If A Woodchuck Could Chuck Wood' by now.

"There are two points that interest me, Dennis. For one thing, I don't understand why Eileen's husband should care whether or not she looks for Ruthie. He seems pretty hostile considering the circumstances."

"Maybe he has nothing better to worry about," Dennis suggests, his mouth full of tortilla and congealed meat and cheese.

"Maybe. You're probably thinking this sounds like a dull exercise and just what I deserve because I don't wait for legit clients who run their finger down the column of investigators in the yellow pages, like everyone else does. And don't start in on the percentage of clients you acquire by word-of-mouth," I say. "I'm proud you don't have to stoop to soliciting. Dennis, there's a second point that interests me about this case."

Dennis listens, giving me his full attention although my conversation does not interrupt his chewing. "Why did Eileen develop this interest in finding her friend after six years? Was she inspired by my ad? Or is there something else going on that she hasn't told me?"

"There's probably a not-very-interesting story behind her friend's disappearance," Dennis volunteers. "Don't you think Ruth probably moved to Milwaukee because she'd been accepted to graduate school in anthropology? Or met a hotel busboy who invited her to run away with him to the hotel's Honolulu branch? And she didn't leave a forwarding address because she hoped to avoid the final phone bill and the last month's rent?"

"I think there could be something more complicated going on. Possibly something criminal," I contradict.

"I hope you uncover an interesting kink or two," Dennis says. "I know how you get when you're bored. Your clean-up efforts at the college won't keep your juices flowing much longer." Dennis signals for another margarita. I never take it personally when he orders a third drink. Some of his friends are five or six drink conversationalists.

The first sip of his fresh drink gives Dennis a thought. "I lost touch with Chubbs Feldbar who I shared an apartment with in college. If I've ever given it any thought it's to think,

'Thank God I don't have to be around to see what kind of a mess Chubbs has made out of his adult life.'

"If I knew where to send Chubbs a Christmas card, I'd feel like I had to do it. Then he'd know where to come find me. Eileen and Ruthie must be a different story than me and Chubbs." Dennis has finished his food. He salts tortilla chips and starts eating them, corners first. "So I see your point," he concludes.

"I'll let you know if anything happens. You do want me to keep you up on this, Dennis?"

"Sure. What the hell. I've taken even less meaty cases, you know that." Dennis moves into his advisory mode. "I know you'll keep those muscles flexed. Ruthie may have had a good reason to disappear. Or Ruthie may have met a bad end in which case you could put Eileen or yourself in jeopardy by stirring things up."

I can tell that Dennis isn't over his investigative faux pas, the death of bad boy Demarcus Amory. He doesn't want me to fail likewise. But Eileen's problem doesn't parallel that of Dennis' ex-client. The world never registered Demarcus Amory's existence much. Ruthie got a lot of attention from the general populace. She seems to have had a lot of personal power in her heyday.

And then, sometimes, where Dennis would get a thorn in his side, I receive laurels, for the same kind of case because I've learned from Dennis' example. I have bottom-line ethics but I am not as good a guy. I get more satisfaction out of my endeavors because I'm not. And I sleep just as well at night. Better.

"I love a session with you," I say, to atone for what I am thinking. "While the rest of the profession leans toward the 'send me a check and I'll send you the goods' school of detection, you stand alone."

"Yes, I believe in social responsibility. And truth. I believe in truth," drones Dennis, straight-faced. He thinks he's being funny.

The waitress brings a check and puts it down. There's nothing written on it except the total. "So, how's the family?" Dennis switches tracks. His code of etiquette demands that he acknowledge the other aspect of my life.

"Jemmy's getting to be a psychologist. He goes out cruising in the neighborhood and then comes back with questions like, 'Why doesn't Mr. O'Dell say anything when Mrs. O'Dell says to come in for lunch? Why does the guy at the market want to have a dog when he keeps shaking his broom at it and

22
▲

chasing it into the street?' When Jemmy graduates from first grade, I'm going to consider taking him into the business."

Dennis doesn't enjoy a heavy dose of news about the younger set but I insist on giving my children equal billing. "Annabelle got the starring role in her class play, 'Elizabeth Blackwell, First Woman Doctor.' She doesn't have star quality but she's very driven to succeed. Lately, I have to remind her constantly not to grind her teeth, and she's only twelve."

"How's Honor?" Dennis asks with real curiosity.

"Okay. She's feeling testy because the publisher has issued a new edition of her father's book. You know how she is. Otherwise, she's great." I don't want to talk about Honor during business hours, it takes too much out of me.

We fight over whether Dennis or I get to treat for the lunch. He pays. Then we meander out to the parking lot.

"You're my best buddy, you know that?" Dennis says and punches me in the arm. I have no idea why he's kidding this way.

"What's gotten into you?" I hope he doesn't punctuate his comments physically anymore.

"Can't I get sentimental if I feel like it? I've been thinking about the old days. Remember I told you I had some news about the business?" He begins fiddling with his keys.

"What don't I know about?" I ask, alarmed. Dennis' business never prospers but he keeps his affairs in perfect order, always, and brings in a modest profit. I'm going to be shocked if he confides he's in financial distress. And Dennis operates in a way that does not invite problems with the police or hostility from clients. He seems reluctant to tell me what is going on. I freeze when I hear his first words.

"I've got a new apprentice, Sharon Clemens. You guys will really like each other. She's not you, but she has some of those great Eliza P. characteristics. Wants to fight injustice without being mean to anybody. Wants to step right up and tell everybody the secret the world's been keeping from them." He grins at me fondly.

The woman sounds really obnoxious, I think to myself, then decide that I have to trust Dennis' instinct. He pretends to enjoy everybody but he only really likes the good ones. I force a smile.

"Can I still count on you for backup, Den? Or will you be out on one-car stakeouts with another girl in my seat?"

"I'm at your disposal," replies Dennis with a gallant bow, "until somebody cripples me or breaks my righteous spirit. You know that. We're buddies—Holmes and Watson, Cagney

23
▲

and Lacey." He gives me a hug, clumsy, because we don't know what to do with each other in this instance.

"I'll talk to you at the end of the week," he promises. "We'll decide if Sharon is Lighthouse Investigations caliber. Right?" He gives me a last placating wave.

I use another investigations outfit for backup coverage as well as Dennis' firm so I'm not dependent on him professionally. There's no reason for me to begrudge Dennis an apprentice to liven things up at work. Still, I feel slightly flattened. But I'm glad that Dennis felt he needed my seal of approval on his new Sharon.

I walk to my Toyota station wagon. As I unlock the door, I notice with irritation the children's various possessions scattered across the back seat and the cargo area. I promise myself I'll march the kids out and have them take every toy and piece of clothing into the house this afternoon.

I can't find a parking spot on Service Street, my preference because it's not far from my office and has two-hour parking. I'm not going to be in the office long so I decide to look for a meter near our building and find one on West Grand about a block and a half from the office. I have to walk past doorways that lead to crummy houses and decrepit businesses. Our building, too, looks run-down from the outside but has been remodeled inside.

I saunter along considering what present the residents of our office building should chip in and give Precious and Charles Harrold for their 25th wedding anniversary next month. The Harrolds and the Beckleys, Precious' family, intend that the celebration be a gala event.

A phantom leaps at me. He grabs me from behind before I have time to register. I can't get the pistol out of my shoulder holster. Holding his gun at my back, he unzips my handbag and begins rifling through.

Some damn mugger, I think, my mind whirling under duress. I've given classes on self-defense for women. I always begin by telling women that men about to make an assault look for the right woman to hit. They pick the person whose demeanor suggests timidity or weakness. The woman who moves too quickly or looks tense, the woman who wanders as though she's not on top of what's going on around her.

Do I have any options about what to do with this gunman? I decide that I don't. I stand, limp. The mugger roots around and takes his pick of the items in my bag. Then he lets the bag fall to my side, still hanging by the strap. The thump against my side startles me. At least I won't have to buy a new purse.

I hear the mugger clear his throat. I realize that our brief interaction has taken place in silence. The "gurr gurr swallow" he just made sounds outlandish, unexpected.

Unbelievably, I hear him start to speak, this late in the game. I concentrate, not understanding what he says at first. I'm waiting to hear "Empty your pockets." But that's not what he says.

His almost unintelligible speech ends when he growls, "Stay away from Ruthie. Or else."

He pauses as if to gauge whether his admonishment came out clearly enough for me to understand. The gun's thrust into my back increases while he replays the message in his mind. He decides I heard it, then puts away his gun and seizes my shoulders.

He shoves hard. I land on my hands and knees facing up a stairway. The peels of metallic grey paint on the stairs crack under my palms and pant legs. As I hear him start to run, I crane my neck to see him flee.

Well, good, I think, feeling punchy. The guy didn't pick me out because my demeanor suggests timidity or weakness, I wasn't targeted because I was wandering or scurrying. I don't need to give up my practiced impervious strut. This guy came calling for me personally.

I push up off the steps. I dust my knees.

3

"**L**eave the office on time or you'll pay." The threat gets delivered in a silky, even tone. This assailant, unlike the last one, terrifies me absolutely.

"I'll leave ten minutes early," I swear.

"See that you do. I'm waiting for you." She hangs up. I cut phone calls short and abbreviate letters and reports. I leave one-half hour before I had planned. I hobble to the car and drive rapidly through the light commuter traffic leaving downtown Oakland.

I make a left turn onto Tahoe Avenue, no relation to the resort area, and notice fresh food wrappers in the gutter and on the sidewalk near my property. I like to park directly in front of the house but a shiny new Ford Fairmont from out of the neighborhood occupies the space behind our van. I have to leave the car across the street. Forgetting how much I love my house, I rue the day we bought a place without a real garage.

Everything adds to my deepening irritation. I notice that I've forgotten to mow the grass strip along the curb. I'm stuck with lawn mowing for life. Honor would let the grass obscure the view from the front window before she would force herself to muck with the lawn mower.

I hurry quickly across the street, under duress from Honor who mugged me and stole my heart years ago. Then I slow to a dignified pace. I try not to let Honor know how much power she has over me.

I call to mind the first time I set eyes on Honor. My deep-rooted analytical bent failed me the minute I stood within three feet of her. I didn't calculate her presentation of herself correctly until many years later.

Honor walked in, shocking the dingy room. The office in which I worked reflected our group's determination to do good for humanity without frittering any of the world's resources on such things as picture frames, carpeting, and desk organizers. The looks of our contingent's members didn't dazzle the eye any more than our interior decoration.

Honor glowed, possessing then, as now, a rare, rose-hued tint to her complexion I had formerly seen only in glossy magazines or maybe just in my mind's eye. Her subtle light brown hair hung almost waist-length then. All other women I knew had slick cropped heads.

Spaced at fortunate angles, her big green eyes gave the impression that the person behind them would be frank and unusual. Mistake number one. Honor is certainly unusual but too careful to reveal herself through her eyes, definitely not frank.

Honor paused in front of my desk and said sweetly, "I'm looking for meaningful work."

Looking for meaningful work.

'Meaningful' should have been the word that I keyed in on when Honor spoke her first sentence in my presence. Honor works very hard, sometimes. But only when she perceives the task to be meaningful.

With Honor, some odd personal standard affects every decision. We might need vacuum bags picked up, or chicken purchased, or a decision made about what summer camp to choose for our children. Most days, Honor does these things if we have assigned them to her. Some days, they don't mean enough to bother attempting. I have learned not to worry about how daily events unfold. In return, I reap Honor's unending praise for my good nature.

Work.

I focused on the word 'work,' the first time I met Honor. I felt thrilled that the exquisite person poised next to Adelle's litter-strewn desk might prove to be useful as well as lovely. I was captivated by the idea that we might employ so ornamental a person to work by my side.

Now that Honor has become central to my life, my early confusion of inflection, or semantics, impacts on me every day. I support a family of four: me, Honor, Annabelle, and Jemmy. Honor helps with finances when she acquires work in the field of commercial design which strikes her as meaningful and happens to come with monetary compensation. That happy combination doesn't occur frequently enough to budget by. In leanest times, her father deposits money in our account on behalf of his grandchildren's quality of life. I know the sum total he has invested in us over the years and it makes me shudder.

As I walk up our stairs, I realize that my knees have stiffened from the fall I took onto someone's front steps earlier this afternoon. I'm going to be mopping the Kains College floors and carting plastic garbage bags from six until twelve tonight. A hot bath before I go might get me through.

In our household, no one ever guarantees you a bath. We have one bathtub, in our downstairs bathroom. Our upstairs bathroom came equipped with one of those huge old-fashioned shower stalls only. At any moment, someone in the house may invent some crisis that involves needing a bath. I stop suddenly at the top of the front stairs and acknowledge that in fretting over bathing privileges, I am avoiding the point of real tension: Honor.

Honor will inevitably find out about the guy who grabbed me this afternoon. She may even have heard about the incident already from one of her contacts. Honor actively resents the proximity to violence that goes with my job.

Once Honor worms today's developments out of me, I risk setting her off on a tirade. She might freeze me out whenever I mention Ruthie. I would lose the luxury of keeping her up to date with the case.

Honor doesn't direct my thoughts but she provides editorial commentary. I emerge from these conversations with new directions to proceed with my work. I hope Honor will discuss Ruthie with me. If I get to soak my knees in hot water before she notices them, I have a chance to present the case in a favorable light.

I collect the mail from the box, unlock the door. Honor appears from the dining room, dogtrotting toward me. She speeds up halfway through the living room, moving steadily even though she's running on hardwood floors in bare feet. Her hair, now properly cut to shoulder length, flies behind her giving off a soft light.

She reaches me and throws her arms around my shoulders. "Crazy about you," she yells. The ominous quality of the telephone call that fetched me home early must have been due to a momentary state of desperation for my company. Honor often acts this happy to see me come home. Unbecoming as it looks in an adult, she fights the children off in order to grab me first.

The whole heaviness, the weight of my feeling for her, settles on my chest when I hold her. "Crazy about you," I reply, holding her tighter.

Honor dances around me while I look carefully at the mail and then throw it on the magazine table. Honor has no interest in mail, no matter what the source.

"There's a postcard for Annabelle and Jemmy from Warren," I tell her. Honor was married to Warren Siegel when she gave birth to Annabelle, now twelve. She left him a few months before she found out she was pregnant with Jemmy, who is seven years old this year. That first day I saw Honor, a very tiny Jemmy swam hidden inside her.

It took a few years after we got together for Annabelle to become my child as well as Honor's. But Jemmy and I have had an easy relationship ever since I saw him slide out of Honor. Warren Siegel lives abroad most of the time, conveniently enough for the integrity of our family, doing business on an international level. Honor's father managed to send him away in a generous fashion, finding him a job where his competence and decency would be amply rewarded. The children and I look forward to his visits.

Seven years after meeting Honor, I still feel twinges of astonishment that I stumbled upon such a family, Honor and our two more-than-satisfactory children. I get a superstitious feeling that I don't merit my blessings. I look to Honor's sweet demanding face for reassurance and sometimes she is reassuring. Today I feel like washing away my concerns by sitting in the bathtub and telling Honor about Eileen Goldeen's problems, instead of mine.

"Honor," I begin. She has begun picking up Lego pieces off the sofa and putting them into a wooden chest. "Remember I told you about the phone call from a woman in Orinda? You thought it sounded like a 'cute' case? Well, I met with that woman today. I'm going to take a bath. Come in and talk to me."

"Jemmy's got to bathe. He did sand play at the J.C.C. today. I sent the kids out to the backyard because I didn't want Jemmy dribbling sand all over the living room. He'll be inside any minute and we'll have to vacuum if we don't bathe him."

I feel desperate. "Please let me have a bath, Honor. Please. I promise I'll empty out Jemmy's shoes and cuffs myself." When I imitate the children begging, Honor breaks down every time. She gets whined at before I get home, she probably can't take any more.

"All right, Eliza. You have the first bath. But hurry up. I made stuffed green peppers. They weren't easy. I want everybody to sit down and eat them before you go off to work." I make for the bathroom hoping that Honor doesn't spot some minute deviation in my gait.

Honor picks up the children's postcard and begins to read, her attention momentarily diverted. Honor lost any personal interest in the fate of Warren Siegel years ago but she follows his career assiduously on behalf of her children. Once satisfied that Warren has not penned anything that seems insensitive toward her daughter and son, Honor tosses the card down and jogs to the back of the house.

I hear her shout, "Annabelle, Jem, you have a postcard from Daddy. It got here all the way from Saudi Arabia. And Eliza's home, you guys, so we're going to eat soon. Get in here when you finish the wing of the fort that you're working on."

Honor returns while I'm fetching towels. I have the water roaring and I feel the tension start to drain away at the soothing sound. "What did you do today?" I inquire on my way to the linen closet. Routine dialogue may divert her from the state of my cartilage.

"Nothing much." Honor doesn't sound distracted by my interest. Her voice diminishes and then certainty seizes her. "Eliza Pirex, what happened to you? I talked to Dennis. He said he had a nice lunch with you. Now you're *limping*. Have you been out doing something risky? What's going on?" Honor throws her arms around me as her voice rises in pitch. She's told me that she feels better screaming at me if she's clutching me to her chest at the same time.

"Honor, I'll tell you everything but you have to let me go so I can check on the water. I'll talk to you from the bathroom. I've got misery in my knees."

Honor hovers outside the bathroom while I go back and forth, dropping my clothes off in the laundry room and fetching my bathrobe from the bedroom upstairs. It's no longer any use being cautious. Honor, alert to every nuance of movement, listens with intensity as I hand in my explanation.

I give her an exacting account of the day and of the mugging so she can't reprove me for omitting details. When I finish bath preparations, I watch her in the kitchen for a minute, her radiant face propped on long finely chiseled hands. I leave the bathroom door wide open and get into the tub.

"So," she asks after I finish, "what's this Orinda woman's name?"

"Eileen Goldeen," I fill in the name. Honor doesn't deign to comment on how badly Eileen fared in marrying someone surnamed Goldeen. I wouldn't mention the name of a client to anyone except Honor, the children, or Dennis, without permission.

"Is her husband's name Rich Goldeen?" Honor asks unexpectedly. She and Dennis have both been a jump ahead of me, landing on Rich's name, and it's unnerving.

"Yes. How do you know them?" I ask. Honor grew up in an even ritzier enclave than Orinda, situated higher in the hills. She knows people who went to school in the Orinda area during the years that she lived there.

"I don't know Eileen. She probably came from somewhere else. But I dated someone in high school who was friends with Rich. We went on a double date with Rich and his girlfriend once. I remember we saw *Thoroughly Modern Milly*. The good old days." I see Honor grimace, remembering either those high school days or the Julie Andrews movie.

"We couldn't get away from Rich because we all went in one car. After that, I made sure I never got trapped in the same car with a pair of high school sweethearts again. I barely remember the awful details. I'll let you know if I think of them. Or I could phone Brendan McKenna, my date. I got his phone number at my high school reunion."

"You don't have to go that far," I assure her. "But if you remember anything interesting about Rich, let me know. Rich looks like he's an average suburban husband. His only notable feature that I've been able to ascertain so far is boorishness.

"Do you think there's any chance Rich could have paid an Oakland thug to threaten me?" I ask. "The idea seems pretty incongruous." I chatter on glibly, banking on Honor's adjustment to the fact that I was held up earlier. She replies without harassing me.

"You just told me that Rich went into his father's construction company," Honor comments. "Don't those guys in construction have ties to the criminal underworld? Or is that just on the east coast?"

"Rich looks to me like any connections of his would be pretty bland," I reply, wondering, as a professional reflex, if I'm right.

"I don't know," Honor cautions. "Those pompous types might do anything. And I'll just bet Rich's pomposity has ripened with the years. But maybe there's an explanation for the mugging that has nothing to do with Rich or Eileen. Was anything taken from your bag other than the money?" She wanders away.

I can hear Honor start folding paper at the kitchen table. She likes to master new art forms to stimulate the children's imaginations. This week she's doing paper folding. Unfortunately, she usually gets tired with each new project by the time she learns it and before she gets a chance to share her expertise. We have plentiful artwork around our house, though.

"No," I call. "The guy took his time mugging me. He got the cash out and then politely returned the wallet to my bag. The whole thing was real easy for him. And this was right out on the street." I hear the paper fold at a faster clip.

"So this guy didn't take anything out of your bag that has a connection to you or to your case, identification or checks or whatever?" I sit up in the tub so swiftly that the bathwater splashes onto the blue and yellow checked tiles of the wall and floor.

"Honor, go get my bag. Quick."

Honor runs out to the entry hall and returns to hand me the bag. I sit up straight, to keep my bag above the water level in the huge clawfoot tub. I unzip the bag but its shape gives me the information I want before I look inside. The large envelope containing the interview tape no longer rests in the side pocket.

I explain the loss to Honor.

"This is creepy. Someone knows too much about what you've been doing," Honor says, not sounding as annoyed as I might have expected. She's torn between feeling intrigued by the problem and offended by the mugging and threat of violence. Honor lapses into silence instead of scolding me.

"Why would someone go to the trouble of stealing a tape that contains mostly meaningless gibberish?" I ponder. "I mean, let's face it, Eileen Goldeen isn't the Pentagon Papers."

"Eliza," Honor commands, "you should call the police and tell them that the tape was stolen. Then maybe they'd be more interested in following up on the whole thing."

"The Oakland Police weren't interested to hear that I lost one hundred fourteen dollars and a lucky silver certificate," I tell her. "Much less would they care that I had a cassette tape, originally purchased from Payless, stolen."

This sets her off. "Eliza, I hate this. I hate you getting yourself into situations where the police won't even help you. You know I think it's good that you go out and bring back most of the money to support us. I appreciate it. But nothing makes risking yourself worthwhile. I want you to back out of this, now."

I hate not doing what Honor wants. Not only do I love her but she can make my life miserable for an extended period of time when I go against her.

"Just give me a chance to check into this thing," I ask. "Maybe when I question Eileen Goldeen, I'll find out where the mugger came from. Maybe I'll be able to locate Ruth after a few hours work, a few phone calls. Then it will all be over. Don't jump on me right this minute, okay?"

"I can't stand it when you grovel, Eliza. All right, I'll drop it for now," Honor relents. She's going to stick with me. Life with Honor can be sweet. Less than a foot below the acetic tongue, a good heart clacks and spins. "What are you going to do tomorrow?" She leans against the door frame. The face that could warm a cosmetic advertisement fixes mine. She probably wants to hear an account of my safety measures.

"I'm going into San Francisco to check around the apartment where Ruthie last lived. Maybe a tenant or a neighbor has a forwarding address. It'll be a casual investigation, no one will know I'm going to be there except you."

"Ruthie? We're very familiar, aren't we? Let's see," she begins musing. "Annabelle and Jemmy have tomorrow off for teacher's prep or whatever the excuse is this time. It would be educational for them to see how you operate in the real world. The kids and I will go to the city with you."

"Honor, we were just discussing an attack on me, an assault directly linked to this case. You and the kids can't come."

"Do you think I would put them in any jeopardy?" I have deeply offended Honor who truly does worry over every possible threat to her family's well-being. "I listened carefully enough to be sure that no one in the world could find us at the apartment building tomorrow. Annabelle and Jemmy love combing for clues," Honor continues, trying to circumvent any more objection from me. "They can look for old cigarette butts. A brand only Ruthie smokes. Or a yellowed scrap from an old letter. I may call her Ruthie?" Honor asks, now facetious.

"Ruthie hasn't been around for over six years," I point out wearily. "Any telltale clues would have to be the durable kind."

"Like postal records, or memories, or legends," reflects Honor. She seems to be in the mood for the Ruthie case, in spite of herself. I run a last shot of hot water into the bath to ease my knee joints for a few minutes more.

"You're not coming," I reiterate. I sink until my chin submerges. "Anyway, don't you have work tomorrow? The new publicity graphics for the High Sierra Company?"

"Yes. I forgot. Nancy promised to take care of the children. They don't think Nancy's much fun but I don't have time to drive them anywhere else. The H.S.C. executives get up with the sun, they're very pretentious that way. They've called the meeting for 7:30." Nancy lives next door. I wonder if she's up to this adventure in childcare. Our kids don't like being hauled out of bed before 7:00, they remain groggy until 7:30.

"Why are you smiling, Eliza? You're a recent crime victim, after all."

"I love it when you work," I tell her.

"I beg your pardon. I thought you appreciate my leisure activities more." We pause for thought. We grin at each other.

The hot water has given me a rush of optimism. "I have everything in good order in my mind," I tell Honor.

"You must have had a happy thought about your new girl, Ruthie."

She's right, I have. "If Ruthie was so deeply involved with people," I point out, "someone has to have stayed in touch. Even though the standard sources haven't turned her up, I figure this case to be a quicky. No mugger will have time to catch me again before I find Ruthie."

"This kind of brilliant deduction is what made it worth sending you to detective school. You're my hero," says Honor, fond and condescending. She thinks my ideas plebeian and my work distasteful but she's still crazy about me, I can tell.

A pummeling sound on the kitchen floor announces our children. Annabelle yells, "Eliza, I'm in," and Jemmy screams, "Mom, where are you?" Annabelle calls me Eliza but Jemmy calls me Mom. I can picture them elbowing each other to get to me, without even turning my head to see.

"Hi, kids, I don't want anybody in the bathroom with me," I raise my voice. Jemmy bursts through the door and starts petting the top of my head before I'm finished shouting. He puts a kiss on my scalp. Annabelle stamps her feet.

"I've been waiting all day to tell Eliza about my social studies report on the old days when Grandpa Pirex worked renting furniture. Mrs. Doyle said my writing was profound and moving. And she loved my table of contents and the drawings in the back, too." Annabelle runs off toward her room, obviously to fetch the actual report as evidence.

I experience a wave of satisfaction. Honor probably coached the profound and moving aspect of Annabelle's school report but I count the success of the general organization of material as evidence that I'm succeeding in my attempt to train my children to become critical thinkers. A training program sabotaged at every turn by their fantastical momma.

"Out of the bathroom, everybody," Honor orders. The children never ignore Honor when she musters them. "Eliza's going to come out and tell you about her new case. Or maybe I'll tell you about it."

Honor has the bathroom cleared in a few seconds. She makes a solo appearance to hiss at me, "Don't even allude to the mugger. I don't want Jemmy having anxiety later at bedtime." Honor can be the fiercest of mothers. I hear her in the kitchen describing the long-lost Ruthie's mysterious disappearance. She demonstrates how to put together an appetizer out of vegetables, crackers, and anchovy paste.

A few minutes later, Honor scoots back to the bathroom and sticks her head through the door, leaving the children to eat. "Eliza, I've just remembered something about Rich Goldeen. A story circulated to my high school after the time I double-dated with him."

"Yes?" I'm happy to delay getting out of the water.

"The story was that Rich went nuts when his girlfriend, Connie, or maybe Bonnie, broke up with him. He stopped going to wrestling meets. Wrestling had been his main extracurricular activity.

"He didn't just go into an adolescent funk. He kept after what's-her-face, Connie, for months. Then Connie went on a school Ski Club trip. Rich followed her to the mountains and something happened. I don't know what, but Rich was on probation until he graduated. Connie got sent off to a private school somewhere. I wish I knew more.

"Of course," adds Honor equitably, "this doesn't mean that Rich is still screwed up. Or that he hired a mugger. But he might not be a straight arrow. I'm going to get the dirt on him from someone. It'll be a present to you from me." She blows kisses and leaves.

I hear Annabelle begin quizzing Honor in the kitchen. She clearly recognizes some tension. I know Annabelle will wait until she has her mother to herself and find out that somebody had a gun in my back this afternoon. Honor does not believe in withholding reality from Annabelle. Annabelle sleeps soundly without fail.

So Rich Goldeen may be crazy. Like Ruthie was crazy. And that would mean Eileen married someone crazy. Craziness seems to be a key note in the matter of Ruthie.

I'm stiffening even though I'm in warm water, maybe I should keep floating for a while. A last injection of heat might help. Honor calls one more time, "Crazy about you."

"**W**ho was that on the phone?" I ask Jemmy the following morning. I've just caught the end of a muttered conversation.

"Grandpa. I told him how you're going to find Ruthie so Eileen Goldeen won't have to worry." I'm not happy that Newell Sutton knows names and details concerning my case. I wouldn't have confided to Newell under any circumstances but especially not when my client moves in somewhat the same circle as he.

I glance at Jemmy's bright face and say only, "What was your grandpa calling for?" I'll remind him about the rules of discretion later.

"He wants Annabelle and me to keep Momma away from Aunt Lucy and Uncle Linden."

"Why doesn't he want Honor seeing them?"

"I don't know. Grandpa probably has secrets again. Or maybe he's playing a game," postulates Jemmy. I sigh. It's no good questioning Sutton behavior. Honor arrives to comb Jemmy's fine, soft hair, a painful procedure that ends our conversation.

Honor has gotten her wish, a phenomenon which happens often. When I woke up this morning, I discovered that bending my leg at the knee brought light blue patches of pain before my eyes. My stint at the college last night caused the joint to swell and my scant hours of sleep didn't remedy it. I can't drive. Honor got to call off her crack-of-dawn meeting in order to chauffeur me today. She hums while she combs, even though Jemmy sighs in pain.

"Say goodbye to Eliza," Honor directs the children. They would never neglect to say goodbye but Honor enjoys giving direction. She leaves to walk them next door.

As soon as Honor leaves the house, I make myself a sandwich, marshmallow and milk chocolate bar between graham crackers. Within minutes, I hear three sets of footsteps return. I take one last big bite and throw the sandwich down the garbage disposal.

"Nancy's heart is beating fast," Jemmy says with glee.

"Nancy has tachycardia," Honor comes in behind him. "She tried plunging her face into ice water but it didn't help. She's going to take some valium to control her pulse rate. She gets drugged into a stupor by valium, so she won't be able to look after the children." Honor doesn't sound like she wasted much sympathy on Nancy and her condition. Honor only behaves nurselike toward Annabelle and Jemmy and then only if they can validate their physical complaint.

"I've gone over the situation," Honor tells me, satisfaction evident in her face. "There's no danger in taking Annabelle and Jemmy to the city unless someone tails us." I go over my plan for the morning, deciding whether there could be the slimmest element of risk.

"Is someone going to tail us?" asks Annabelle, joining us in the kitchen, her face alight with interest.

"No, sweetheart. I'm trained to recognize and eliminate a tail," I assure her. "And besides, I can't imagine why anyone would invest enough time and energy to tail us. So, cool out, you guys, this isn't going to be that exciting a morning."

Honor drives us to San Francisco in her van which seats everyone with room to spare. After we take off, I tell the kids some sneaky tricks I used last night to keep an eye on the security guards at the college.

Annabelle listens intently. She's probably memorizing the maneuvers in case she should ever need to do surveillance on bigoted college employees. I look at Annabelle in the rearview mirror, seeing Honor's beautiful features superimposed with earnestness instead of quirkiness on Annabelle's face.

Jemmy not only keeps up with current TV detectives but knows most of the plot lines from old rerun shows like *Barnaby Jones*. He doesn't look particularly interested in my sedentary pursuits. Then his face clouds slightly.

"Mom," he asks me when I pause, "if you find out that the guys at the college are doing bad things to women, and they get fired, I bet they keep on doing the same things. Except they won't have a job. I don't know how they're going to pay when they go to the store. Maybe you should make them a deal, that if they stop, you won't tell on them." I compliment Jemmy on his analysis and his charity. I like seeing my endeavors in the light of Jemmy's kind nature.

Honor tires of hearing about my non-exploits at the college. She highlights opportunities for the children to shine today as associate detectives.

Traffic looks snarled going through the Bay Bridge Toll Plaza. I estimate for the children how long we might be in the car until we get into the city. Then I give them a thumbnail sketch of Ruthie Gold's life in San Francisco, as I heard it from Eileen Goldeen. Traffic speeds up before we get to Treasure Island and soon we see the highrise buildings of the Emerald City appear out of the mists.

Honor tells me that she's going to take the Main Street exit, which lets us off the freeway some distance from where we want to go. "Yes, Momma," Annabelle clammers from the back seat, "take the first exit. I want to see the restaurant where Grandpa and Grandma ate when they went on their first date."

I've commemorated Newell and Lynn Sutton's first date enough times considering I know the event led to as much trouble as it did good fortune. Honor has her own motive for wanting to get off at Main Street. She likes to conduct city street tours which broaden the children's experience. Her tours feature grim introductions to seamy urban lives seen through the car window. Honor strives to provide the children with opportunities to view nostalgic points of interest. I can't count the number of times we have visited the bus terminal where clairvoyant Aunt Mauve Sutton was last seen. With that thought, I veto Annabelle's eager request, redirect Honor, and tell Jemmy to stop bobbing up and down.

"We're going straight to the Richmond District," I pronounce. "It would take ages to go through the city. I have to get into the office after lunch, guys." Honor gives up, rather gracefully. She may not actually feel like giving her city tour, perhaps just lobbied for the opportunity on principle. Since she has the wheel, I count myself lucky that Honor seems so tractable today.

We head toward the Golden Gate Bridge, exit from the freeway, and make our way through the Richmond District's relative serenity and cleanliness. I'm surprised that the charismatic Ruthie didn't live in a jazzier part of town. I remind myself that I don't know anything about Ruth Gold except Eileen Goldeen's vision of her.

41
▲

I recheck the San Francisco street map but being slave to a map doesn't bring out the best in Honor. She votes for an alternative route that she knows from memory. I insist we follow the course I have mapped out. The street names don't seem familiar to Honor. Only our arrival at 1200 Leonid Street ends Honor's protests that we should find Geary and start again from there.

Honor opens the door, leaps out, and flies around the car to the curb. No matter how accustomed to her company I become, Honor's physical presence in a new setting always generates a thrill down the center of my body. The sidewalk suddenly looks as though a movie director just added the first glamorous person to the scene and will begin shooting soon.

The weather today provides an exotic backdrop for my investigation. The San Francisco climate creates that special effect where the fog hovers above our heads. Filtered sunshine glitters from the ground to about building level as though generated by a source within the earth. The distant presence of the unseen ocean can be sensed, in this part of the city, by the aftertaste the air leaves in mouth and nose.

Annabelle and Jemmy slam the back doors as I shout, "Lock them." They run half a block to read the menu on the outside of a small Chinese restaurant. Faded red plastic letters on the building front say "Chu Hunan." With the restaurant so nearby, Ruthie might have eaten there frequently enough to become known to them. Not likely, but I will try talking to the owners.

I walk up the steps of the apartment building where Ruthie used to live, dragging my gimpy leg which has loosened up only a tad. Ruthie's place, apartment 303, now rents to C. Doyle. That person probably won't know anything about her. I look for the nearest neighbors. Not that nearest neighbors necessarily know the most. I'm looking for an alert tenant, the one committed to learning about the neighbors no matter what the obstacle.

The manager lives in apartment 100. I'd rather not tangle with the manager if I don't have to. I decide to start with the first and second floors. I press buttons until I get a resident to sound the buzz which unlocks the front door. I go inside and find that the tenant hasn't lived here long enough to have known Ruthie. I walk carefully down the front stairs to find Honor. I see Honor down the street, giving the kids directions.

I press some more buttons and Mrs. Charnoff in 206 asks my name. I introduce myself over the intercom and then the outside glass door shrills to signal the door unlocking again. I hurry to push inside before the noise ends. I know Honor may be irritated if she comes back and doesn't find me. I'll have to hurry down after I speak to 206, assuming I can hurry on my bad knee. I get inside a tiny elevator which quivers slowly to the second floor.

From the open doorway, a short square woman with long thick greying hair pulled back in a barrette, wearing scarves and several shawls, peers suspiciously at me. I find I am able to walk normally if I endure moderate but not hideous pain.

"A little cold today, isn't it, Mrs. Charnoff?" I offer a tried-and-true pleasantry. Her eyebrows lower.

"How do you know my name? Who sent you?" A heavy Slavic accent weights her English. Maybe she doesn't understand that I'm being pleasant.

"I got your name from the directory downstairs. I'm looking for a friend of mine who used to live in your building. She moved about six years ago. I was out of town for a while and during that time she moved and we lost touch. Were you a resident of the building back then?"

"Give me some identification. I saw police on television who said should any person be at your door, ask for identification." I get out a San Francisco State University identification card with my picture in color on the front. I took a criminology seminar at SFSU a few years ago. People tend to like the card. She examines the card then hands it back respectfully.

"Mrs. Charnoff, did you live in this apartment in 1982?"

"Yes, I did. Some people come and go. Some of us make this place our home." She arranges a shawl across her bosom. I notice thick gold jewelry around her neck.

"The name of my friend who lived here at that time is Ruth Gold. It's very important to me that I find her. Can you give me any information that might be of help?" Mrs. Charnoff stares at me as I try a responsible and concerned smile.

"All right. Yes, all right. Come in. Wait here and I will check my Christmas card lists." I sit down on an exquisite bench carved from a dark heavy wood which takes up most of the space in a hall that serves as an entry room. I glance into the main room of the apartment and see richly colored rugs and imposing furniture. Books and ornaments cover every horizontal space. I smell oil and perfume.

The apartment leads me to believe that whatever Mrs. Charnoff tells me I can rely upon. But I'm not expecting her to make any leaps of logic that might direct me to Ruthie's

43
▲

whereabouts. She appears to be reliable rather than creative. I mark off the minutes.

Mrs. Charnoff paces back through the living room shuffling papers and cards. "Yes, in apartment 303 was Ruth D. Gold. I now recall."

"Do you remember anything about her that might help me track her down?" I ask encouragingly.

"She was not one I knew well enough to find a new address for my Christmas card list the next year." Her thick eyelids don't seem to blink with ordinary frequency.

"Would you mind looking at your 1982 list and telling me which of the present tenants lived here that year?" She nods in reply and carefully refers to the list.

"The Mexican man and his wife in apartment 305. The man's wife was gone for some years. Now she is back. I don't know where she went, either.

"Mr. David Gray was here in apartment 301. Mrs. Helen Staples, apartment 104, she's elderly. She has a volunteer woman who drives her to the hospital every day except Sunday. And me, I was here in apartment 206, of course." She puts her glasses down on her chest in a gesture of finality.

"Thank you so much, Mrs. Charnoff. I'm so grateful for your help. I hope we meet again. I may be back to the building if I don't find the tenants in apartments 305 and 301 at home." Mrs. Charnoff clearly hasn't been so charmed by my company that she's hoping I'll drop by again. She stands impassively, holding the door open as I leave with a cheery wave.

I take the elevator back down. Honor sits on the front steps looking not too irritated. "Where are the kids?" I ask her.

"They're having some eggs at the place down the street. The restaurant owner is eating with them. She's an older woman who loves kids. What have you done so far?"

"I talked to one tenant who was able to tell me which other people lived here at the same time as Ruthie."

"Don't run off again without telling me where you're going. What are we going to do next? I may as well come with you," she says. "You could use me as a crutch if you need to."

"I'm going to try two more apartments. What will the kids do if they get back here before us?"

"They're going to wait by the car. They know not to separate or let anyone come near them," Honor replies, sounding more relaxed than usual about the children's safety. She makes both our children carry whistles at all times in case they need to call help.

I press 305, labeled "Juarez, Geronimo and Kathy." The buzzer sounds before I give a name over the intercom. I hold the door for Honor and walk with her to the elevator.

I have to knock for a while before the door to 305 is opened. A handsome young man with no shirt and a youngish woman, blond with smeared make-up, in a large T-shirt and no pants, stand at the door. They don't seem excited to see Honor and me but the woman says "Hi" in a friendly manner.

"Hi, I'm Eliza Pirex and this is Honor Sutton. We're looking for a woman, Ruth Gold, who lived here six years ago. Your neighbor in apartment 206, Mrs. Charnoff, tells me that you lived here at that time. Do you have any information that might help us find where she is today?"

They look at each other. I add, "A forwarding address she might have left with you when she moved, for example?"

"I think she was the one who brought her sister to a party here once," suggests the woman to the man. "Her sister was outgoing but your friend wasn't in the mood."

"She never told us she was going to move out of the building," the blond woman speaks to us now. The doorbell rings inside the apartment to signal that someone else wants to come up and see the pair. She walks over to press the button which releases the front door downstairs.

Kathy (I assume) comes back, slides one arm around Geronimo, hooks her fingers under his belt. I hear Annabelle and Jemmy shrieking and singing happily in the elevator. I turn around and they come pounding furiously down the hallway. They can move at the speed of lightning at times when I'd prefer they stayed out of the way.

"Here we are," they shout and come to a stop behind us. "We looked for you on the first floor and then came up here." This apartment building is comprised of fifteen apartments total, it's small enough that hiding from anyone would be difficult. The children stare at Geronimo and Kathy entwined.

I hand Geronimo my card. "If you two remember something that could help us find Ruth Gold, will you give me a call? I would make it worth your while if you helped me to locate her." Kathy reads the card slowly.

"I got an uncle who's a detective," she says, seeming to warm up to us. "Remember my Uncle Ron, Gero, who got real drunk at Sissy's baby's christening?"

"Oh, yeah," says Geronimo, also thawing, "Ron's a character." They both smile approvingly at the four of us, we turn to go down the hall, and we all part friends.

45
▲

"Why is he the lady's hero?" asks Jemmy when the door closes.

"It's a nickname for the man's real name, Geronimo. Like we call you Jemmy even though the name on your birth certificate is Jeremiah," Honor tells him in her schoolmarm tone of voice.

"You kids have to be completely silent while I knock on another door. Remember what I've told you to do when you're around while I work. Smile a lot but don't talk."

They both give me a practice smile. We troop to 301. I knock with a casual beat.

The door opens after a while. "David Gray?" I ask. The guy looks left over from the sixties. Not too far from forty, long hair and a beard, sweet face, Grateful Dead shirt.

"Yeah, I'm Dave. Just about to get in bed. What can I do for you?" I pause a second to enjoy the sensation of my family's warm breath at my heels.

"Sorry to bother you, Dave. I got your name from your neighbor, Mrs. Charnoff. I'm looking for someone who lived in the apartment next to yours in 1982. Ruth Gold. I'm trying to locate her. May we come in? We'll just be a minute." People don't tend to be as suspicious about your intentions when you're accompanied by two young children.

"You're looking for Ruthie?" he says, startled. "Sure, come right in. I work for the post office. I'm on nights right now. Didn't mean to be rude when I came to the door but I need to protect my sleep time during the day."

He ushers us into the living room. "Have a seat. Just shove some stuff aside and sit anywhere," Dave says, a genial host. The living room has a college student appearance even though Dave has lived here for many years as an employed adult. His books rest on boards lying across big sand-colored bricks. A paisley print bedspread covers the sofa.

"Ruthie Gold? I'd love to know where she is. We were good friends but Ruthie had heavy problems. She left real suddenly without telling me. But I got a card from her after she left."

"Really? Do you have the card?" I ask. This sounds good. Honor stands reading the titles of Dave Gray's books. Annabelle and Jemmy sit politely focusing their attention on Dave.

"No, but it wouldn't help you that much. Either of you guys want a glass of wine? I don't have milk or soda or anything for the kids but they can have some water out of a crazy straw." Dave nods his head toward the kitchen.

"No, thanks, they're okay." The children know I get to speak for them when we're out working. Honor shakes her head "no" to the wine.

46
▲

"Do you remember where the card was mailed from?"

"Yeah. It came from L.A. Ruthie came from L.A., so that made sense. I thought maybe she was staying with her mom and dad. Except her dad was pretty much a drag and she didn't really get along with her mom that well either.

"She had a brother in Los Angeles, too," Dave continues. "But I don't think the brother had a place where Ruthie could stay. Her brother was weird. Her family situation was always kind of sad, except for Jane, who lived near here, in Santa Cruz. Jane was a dancer. She was real cute."

"So there was no return address on the card?"

"No. I would've written to her if there was. We were incredibly close friends." Dave gets up, meanders to the kitchenette, and comes back with a chilled brown bottle of Budweiser. He sits down on the floor with his knees crossed and puts the beer on an orange crate with a tea tray on top, which serves him as a coffee table.

"Do you recall anything about the postcard's content? Anything at all?" I question. I notice Jemmy fingering little objects on the battered end table beside the sofa arm but Dave probably doesn't mind.

"Sure, I remember the postcard. I had a joke with Ruthie about her being Marilyn Monroe. You know, we would watch the movies and afterwards we'd laugh about the tragedy queen thing.

"The postcard had Marilyn Monroe on it. Ruthie said she was staying with all sorts of different people so she didn't have an address. She was depressed, I remember that. She got depressed a lot. She said she was looking for work that didn't involve music. She was tired of music. She said she'd write me when she got settled but I never heard from her again." Dave looks depressed himself but he takes a long swallow of beer and continues.

"I've thought about Ruthie for years. If she's just licked the depression, I bet she's doing something great. I always figured she'd end up married to someone important. Maybe get rich or famous herself but more likely just lie back and have some guy who's nuts over her keep her in style." Dave smiles wistfully.

Jemmy picks up a small bowl made from what looks like a seed pod and drops the bowl back on the table to see if it will bounce. It doesn't bounce much. I need to move the interview along before the whole family gets restive and makes trouble for Dave.

47
▲

Dave seems to be growing more dazed. He focuses on Annabelle suddenly and says to her, "My little girl is just about your age. I only see her once a month or so, nowadays." He turns to me. "My daughter, Lisa, just loved Ruthie. Ruthie always said she wasn't good with kids. But Lisa would have done anything for Ruthie."

"Is there any chance Lisa might have a clue where Ruthie lives today? Or would she have told you if she were in touch with Ruthie?" I try to steer him back onto the track.

"She would have told me. But, hey, I just thought of something. My ex-wife took Lisa to see Ruthie's psychiatrist. The guy is real famous for helping kids who have learning problems that are caused by trouble at home. I always wanted to meet the guy but what with my hours and, you know, the problem of fatigue that we night postal workers tend to have, I never did meet him. Anyway, if anyone might have kept tabs on Ruthie it would be this guy. He was insane about her. And I do mean insane."

"Do you remember the psychiatrist's name by any chance?"

"Hell, yes, I had to make checks out to him until my wife took Lisa out of therapy. Besides, I see his name in the paper every so often. And he's on TV talk shows but, of course, I don't believe in TV, never owned one. Stuart Lilienthal was his name. Ruthie used to call him Stu, sometimes she'd call him Lilly." Dave's expression suggests that he might be losing his concentration. He seems druggy even though he's had just one beer. I rush my next question.

"What did you mean when you said he was insane about her? You sounded as though you thought the relationship went beyond psychiatrist and client," I fish. I already know there's a story.

"Beyond is not the word for it. At first, I thought it was strange that a psychiatrist would date his patient. But I guess it happens. It was Ruthie who had to break it off when they weren't getting along."

"Not getting along?"

"They fought about Ruthie seeing other guys," Dave responds. "Dr. Lilienthal was married. He put Ruthie through all sorts of changes so his wife wouldn't notice anything was going on. But he wanted Ruthie to ask him for permission to sneeze. He got really weird when they broke up. It was like he cracked up even though she was supposed to be the patient."

"Cracked up?" I handsignal Honor and the kids to maintain their decorum a while longer.

"He wrote notes, for one thing," answers Dave. "Ruthie started getting notes all over the place. At home, at work, in her car. They all said the same thing, 'Forgot to put the cat out.' She didn't know what the notes meant but she thought they were from Lilienthal."

Dave begins to look unsettled at the memory. "Lilienthal had a thing about cats. He hated cats being locked up." Dave squirms in his seat on the floor.

"Did Ruthie ever find out for sure whether or not Lilienthal sent the notes?" I ask.

"She asked Lilienthal straight out. He played it like he didn't know what she was talking about. He acted like Ruthie was hallucinating or something. He always treated her like a mental basket case. Ruthie got jittery. She didn't want to get help from the police or anybody because she figured they'd think she was crazy."

"Lilienthal isn't exactly one of those humanistic practitioners of modern mental health care, is he?" I say, to voice solidarity with Dave's unspoken sentiment. He looks unable to cope with my wordiness.

Honor and Annabelle have gotten interested in Dave's story. We three lean toward Dave. I hear Jemmy mutter, "Forgot to put the cat out," as he unravels something made of rainbow colored yarn.

"When Ruthie's nerves got real bad, I gave her dope to smoke. Ruthie didn't ordinarily do any drugs. She was afraid she might get extra depressed.

"Anyway, we smoked some that afternoon and then I asked Ruthie out for a date, that one time. I think it was a date. I went ahead and decided for myself that it was a date." The corners of Dave's mouth turn up.

"We went to an Italian place over in North Beach. Ruthie had an anxiety attack during dinner so we didn't finish the pasta. I took her home. I have to admit I asked her, 'Please, Ruthie, let me come over just this once.' I was over at her place all the time so she knew what I meant." Dave catches himself, colors then pales, and looks into his Budweiser bottle.

"I can't believe I was so insensitive. But, God, Ruthie." Dave's recital has made him dreamy. His eyes reflect Ruthie, a sad gauzy presence dilating the irises.

"Ruthie said she needed to be alone. Her head hurt and her stomach was jumpy. So she went into her apartment and closed the door. She told me that when she got inside she left the apartment lights out. She didn't want them on because of her headache. Through her window, you catch some light from the Szechuan Princess on the street behind the building. Enough light to see by if you know where you're going. When Ruthie turned to go into the kitchen there was a horrible scream: 'FORGOT TO PUT THE CAT OUT.'"

We all jump and Dave grins briefly.

"Someone jumped on Ruthie's back. Someone medium heavy was riding her piggyback. He grabbed the bottom of her throat with his claws jamming into her neck. And he made purring noises and wheezes through his nose. I felt sick when Ruthie described it.

"She tried to shake him off. But she fell and he fell on top. They wrestled some. Then Ruthie got her hands on a big flashlight and hit him with it. She got away and ran to my apartment. By the time we got back to her place, he was gone.

"We called the police. I mean, I don't like messing with them, I'm downright allergic to them, but this was getting pretty heavy. They looked for evidence but never found anything that indicted Lilienthal.

"Then, this was a real drag, the police found the plastic baggie I had given Ruthie lying under a stool and arrested her for possession. Nothing came of the arrest. They decided to act like they thought the intruder had dropped the dope. But the police didn't have energy for her complaint about Lilienthal, or whoever it was, after the find. I made sure I never had anything to do with the S.F.P.D. again.

"This one guy Ruthie met that night, Detective Cologne, said he'd keep his eye on Lilienthal. He really liked Ruthie. I think he asked her out after the whole thing. She probably went."

Dave continues, "My ex-wife stopped Lisa's therapy with Lilienthal after that. We worried that Lisa would be traumatized about ending therapy with him but, actually, she didn't miss him." We all sit quietly for a moment.

"I heard that someone was murdered in Ruthie's apartment. Did that have anything to do with Dr. Lilienthal?" I interrupt the quiet.

"I don't think Lilienthal knew Claudia, the girl who got killed. Claudia lived in Santa Cruz where Ruthie worked part time. The police think Claudia's boyfriend killed her. Claudia was murdered the last night Ruthie lived in this building. Ruthie never got a chance to tell me much about it. I wasn't home when it happened. Neither was Ruthie." Dave sounds regretful.

"The landlord told me that the police were pissed that Ruthie skipped," Dave adds. "But they figured she didn't have anything to do with Claudia getting hit over the head. They concentrated on finding Claudia's boyfriend. But the boy-friend skipped too, disappeared. I'll bet Ruthie decided her apartment had bad vibrations after everything. So she needed to split from this place."

Dave's eyes slide closed and then slowly open again. Jemmy comes to my side and nuzzles his way under my arm. He's past the point of being able to endure any further adult conversation.

"Dave," I say in a livelier tone, "we won't keep you any more. You've been a big help. I'll let you know when we locate Ruthie. Thanks again for your time. By the way, would you mind a call from me if I need to ask you any further questions?"

"No sweat. Just call during the morning. It feels good to talk about Ruthie. I haven't gotten to talk to anyone who knows about Ruthie for a long time. Lisa was pretty hurt that Ruthie didn't say goodbye. I don't like to bring Ruthie up in front of her." Dave staggers to his feet.

"Nice to have met you. Have a good sleep," says Honor, who can always be relied upon for the social amenities, unless she considers the person with whom we're socializing to be meaningless. We cross the living room and I hold the door so everyone can exit. Dave follows us.

"By the way," he says, rubbing his temples as though he has a sympathetic headache after chronicling Ruthie's head-aches. "The postcard from Ruthie had a color picture. Marilyn was lying dead with the phone off the hook and pill bottles scattered around, the Kennedy brothers were making for the door. A sick joke card. The picture worried me some. So when you find Ruthie, tell her to get in touch. I want to know she's okay."

For some reason, my knee feels rejuvenated after the visit to Dave Gray. But I'm not sure how I would fare on the stairs so we head toward the miserable excuse for an elevator. Honor and the kids beat me there. They have pressed the button by the time I arrive and we hear the wires creaking below us. Jemmy turns to me thoughtfully. "Did Ruthie take good care of her cat?"

A couple of points that I hadn't considered leap to mind in relation to the question. "Now, there's food for thought, Junior Birdman," I tell him.

5

"**F**ancy pants." The words leap out of my phone receiver with a crack.

Doris Shipley's expletive sums up her current opinion of her ex-friend, Brenda, whom she hired me to investigate at the end of their friendship's honeymoon phase. But Doris' heart isn't really in revenge on Brenda. The latest material about Brenda, with which I just supplied Doris, didn't interest her as much as before when the smallest detail used to excite her.

I sense something different in the air. I sit, professionally upright, in my office steno chair. I am talking to Doris on my old-fashioned square black telephone, the receiver comfortably heavy in my hand. I sigh, but not into the mouthpiece.

"Doris, I'd like to repeat that Brenda seems like a nice woman to me. If you two are not going to be friends, why don't you forget her? There's no way, that I can see, for me to help you recover the money she extorted from you. Maybe she met you at a low point in her life. Maybe she needs a chance to pick up the pieces." I speak within the framework of Doris' reality, ignoring the issue of whether hers or Brenda's story about the money might be true. Doris doesn't interrupt me to quarrel so I plunge ahead.

"In all honesty, I feel that allowing you to continue paying for my services isn't really fair." I dig my heels into the linoleum to roll the steno chair toward my desk so I can grab my mug and sip cold coffee with non-dairy creamer. I wonder if Precious made this coffee today or yesterday afternoon. It doesn't measure up to her recent standards.

"You're right, Mrs. Pirex, you are," Doris agrees too quickly. "I've been checking references on you. They all have good things to say. They say you give your clients their money's worth." I have a slight twinge over the idea that my good name should be bandied in terms of thrift and economy rather than inspiration. I shrug it off. Most people do worse than give fair market value.

"So," continues Doris, "although I think I will take your advice and drop the Brenda Coller matter, I have more work for you." I stifle another sigh. "Will this mean I have to pay a new retainer?" Doris' tone becomes sharper. "I mean, in a way, I am *still* retaining you, if you get what I mean."

"We can discuss fees in a minute, Doris. After you tell me what's up." I keep my voice even.

"I told you about my friend, Andy? A wonderful boy. He lives with his father and that man has caused Andy more heartache than any nice young boy should have to cope with. Andy has been a big help to me since Brenda turned out to be no better than a common thief. I really appreciate his help. But I do have a lot riding on him."

Doris' voice becomes hard. "I can't go trusting my money blindly, the way I did with Brenda. I want you to do some checking on Andy."

"Doris," I try to cut her off but she pretends not to hear me.

"I need to know how much money Andy has and what his record in school was like and if he has any friends other than me. He says he doesn't. And do you think you could find out about his mother, who doesn't live with the family? He won't tell me anything about her."

"Doris," I repeat her name, after taking a deep breath, "I like to encourage my clients to become comfortable using investigative services. In your case, though, I think we're going too far." I talk fast so Doris can't cut in.

"Don't you think that when you've maintained your friendship with Andy longer, he'll be glad to tell you all these things himself?" I make a bid to Doris' almost nonexistent common sense. "Maybe you should hold off placing money in his hands until that time. That way you won't incur charges for services you don't need."

"I do need your services," Doris speaks eagerly. "I'll pay you a bonus. Or I'll help you out in exchange. I could straighten your office or do some light detection out of my home."

School records can be acquired quickly, I begin thinking, and I can get a fix on the kid's associates within a few hours. I fold in my hand and say, "Okay, Doris. But stay away from my office. Just give me any basic information you have on Andy and I'll see what I can do." I make a few notes and hang up before Doris can push me into hiding under Andy's bed, which would be God knows how unpleasant an experience.

Speaking with Doris doesn't leave me with the feeling that I've gotten my day off to a productive start. I return a few more business calls, put some notes into the office diary until I feel more pulled together. The desk calendar's notation reads "Eileen Goldeen 11 a.m." in ink, green, to indicate an appointment. The quote on the quote-for-the-day calendar, Wednesday, April 28, reads: "If truth were self-evident, eloquence would not be necessary—Cicero."

I muse over Monday's attack on my handbag. Who cares whether or not Eileen Goldeen finds her friend from college? The only party who could possibly be concerned, and who knew that Eileen was hiring me that day, is Rich Goldeen, the husband who Eileen presents as a respectable suburban businessman. Rich does not appear a likely candidate to have hired an Oakland thug to threaten me and steal from my purse.

I know Oakland thugs myself, friends and neighbors. But it's harder to make your way into those circles when you lead a neatly pressed life in the suburbs. Unless your life has dirty underwear. I resolve to make some calls about Rich Goldeen. Maybe I should let Honor scrape up some dirt.

I go across the courtyard to let Precious know my plans for the day. As I enter the office, I find Mike Woolley standing with one foot propped on a teak coffee table. I hope he doesn't cause it to collapse before we get new furniture. Two old telephones with their dismembered wires dangling occupy the seat of the luxury model armchair. We're putting in a sleek new phone system for the front office.

"Eliza, I've been meaning to catch up with you," Mike says, standing up. "How are you doing?" Both my office-mates who practice psychotherapy ask me how I'm feeling before they speak, no matter what the urgency of the business.

"I'm great, Mike, how are you?"

"Can't complain. Maybe I've been working a few too many hours, I should do something to nourish myself like work on my house or go for a walk down at Jack London Square, but I really can't complain," he replies in one breath.

55
▲

"Good, good. What's up?" I let him know I'm ready for whatever he actually wants to say. Mike begins to pace in the way I assume he does when speaking with clients.

"I've gotten some disturbing calls about you in the last week." Mike wears a young urban professional tie, burgundy, underneath a lamb's wool sweater. He pushes at the tie as though it needs adjusting. "I kept some brief notes in case you could use the information." I have Precious give Mike's and Lucas' names, among others, to prospective clients who want references.

"Sure. I like to know who's checking up on me." I flash my teeth at Mike. He doesn't smile back. He gets stiff with me sometimes because he isn't comfortable with my profession and perhaps for a darker reason.

"Do you know a Doris Shipman?" he asks. I expected this one.

"Shipley. Yes. I'd love to get rid of her. I hope you didn't knock yourself out telling her how good I am."

"I didn't. I thought she was unusual. She wanted personal information about you. I told her that I only give a business reference. She even seemed to want information about me. I didn't like it."

"She's strange but harmless, Mike."

"She used a lot of detective terminology."

"With some people, we lose their esteem once they figure out the solution to an Agatha Christie mystery before Hercule Poirot reveals it to the suspects. They think they're qualified as professional investigators," I say, with an eye to Mike's edification. "I'll handle Doris, Mike. I'll try referring her for therapy if I get the opportunity. You want her?" Mike grimaces.

"Who else called?" I ask him.

"Mr. Richard Goldeen. He sounded straightforward at first, then he started asking strange questions."

"What questions?"

"Like whether you'd be willing to bend the law for a client. How many hours per week you work to earn how much. Whether you travel often and to where," Mike reads.

"I'm working for his wife," I tell Mike. "Mr. Goldeen isn't enthusiastic about my services."

"There was a casual call from a woman who had seen your ad. And one from someone who wouldn't give his name, asking about how you take care of your cat."

"What cat?" I ask.

"I don't know. The guy sounded very concerned about some cat. Watch out, Eliza. Maybe you *should* start making more referrals to me." Mike pats my shoulder companionably. He doesn't need clients, he maintains a long waiting list.

"I do meet the twisted and the sad in my line of work but they don't want to make internal changes. They want enough action to distract them from whatever's going on inside," I tell him. I pick up and bite into a piece of the banana bread stuffed with chocolate chips which lies artistically arranged on a teal blue plate with white irises around the rim. "Your wife baking again, Mike?"

"Yes. Isn't she great?" He looks down at the banana bread with a sour expression that contradicts his words.

"She's great. Give her my love," I say. I wish I could send more of a message to Rochelle Goffstein Woolley, but I can't via Mike.

I hope the spate of calls for references dies down before Mike gets irritated. The cat call will require some thought. I write a short note for Precious with phone numbers where I can be reached. She always has things in order whether she's present or not.

Though the drive to Orinda should take me about 20 minutes and I'm going the opposite direction from most of the morning traffic through the Caldecott Tunnel, I have allowed 35 minutes for the trip. I keep the headlights on even when I leave the tunnel behind. Orinda's air in the morning looks cleaner than the Oakland fog but not clear, a sheer mist decorates this bastion of preferential treatment. The range of hills dividing the messy, sprawling city from the ranch-style holds of the wealthy creates a separate meteorology.

Knowing only Eileen Goldeen's address, 1 Grouse Court, wouldn't have helped me get to her house. The Goldeen's address must be too new to appear on my map. Her directions take me through the town of Orinda and up into hills solid with old oaks.

I see discreet mailboxes by the roadside as I maneuver up the hills. Eventually, I find the right mailbox and start up a winding and poorly paved road. The road ends in a circular driveway at the front of a long white one-story house.

The door opens at my knock and a fat red-haired woman faces me. She wears an uneven lime green skirt and matching short-sleeved blouse, an outfit that means to be a uniform. We eye each other, two strangers meeting in a foreign locale.

Since she hasn't spoken, I ask to see Eileen. The woman replies, "I guess she'll be expecting you," in a voice laced with unwarranted sarcasm. She hasn't asked who I am, but I nod. I have to step lively to keep up with her. She seems oblivious to whether I'm following behind her or not.

We reach a light, spacious living room with two glass walls. One frames large old oaks and one, an expanse of redwood deck. Southwest Indian art decorates the walls and sits on furniture. Someone with good taste put this room together, probably not Eileen or Rich. Eileen more likely exhibits good taste in where she shops for a consultant than in art.

I keep my eyes on a turquoise clock as quartz minutes click by. I become restless, wander to the bookcase. The Goldeens kept a lot of textbooks from college.

I browse through an encyclopedia set called *Treasury of the Familiar* and read the Bill of Rights. One shelf holds children's books with bookplates reading "This Book Belongs To Eileen Mandlebaum" in a childish hand. I haven't seen books with cardboard covers like *The Bobsey Twins* and *Trixi Belden* since I read them on days when I stayed home sick from elementary school.

Finally I come upon two books that I have in my bookcase as well. I am only too familiar with the one by Newell Sutton. Honor's father runs a medium-sized company, Sutton Farm Machines, which has plants throughout the country. Newell was able, in spite of his responsibilities, to squeeze backpack trips through the mountains of the world into his busy schedule during Honor's childhood. Newell claimed that glacier lakes and granite cliffs were the only balm to heal the wounds left by life in the tractor trade and the only glue to bond his family. The heartier the haul, the heartier Newell Sutton felt.

Mr. Sutton was inspired, the year Honor turned ten, to share his reservoir of hilarious, pithy, and enlightening adventures in the wild with the very world he earlier took to the mountains to escape. When Honor reached the difficult age of thirteen, Newell published *Our Family Took to the Woods*, a book which was to bring fame and aggravation to her teenage years. Many people of the right vintage remember intimate details about Honor's childhood. The book flourished, an international bestseller, on the stands for years.

I open the book. Newell's bold slanted writing inside the front cover reads, "To my good friend, Rich: Glad you've come out of the woods." I'm sorry to see that Rich Goldeen invaded Honor's past through this book. She would hate it. Honor once dropped a full pitcher of iced tea when someone unexpectedly brought up an episode from the book in which her father involved Honor and her now-dead mother in a frightful game. Having read the book twice, word for word, I know all the details.

I can't imagine what might be the connection between Rich and Newell. Next to *Our Family* on the book shelf sits *Thinking About Drinking* by Christopher Sutton. The Sutton children, Christopher, Honor, and twins Linden and Lucy, scorned Newell Sutton for embarrassing the family in print. Unfortunately, Honor's older brother, weakened by a bout with California wines, gave way as an adult and published memoirs glorifying his indulgences and his salvation and return to sobriety.

Christopher hasn't autographed this book. But why does Rich have a second book by another Sutton? Since I don't want to admit to Eileen that I investigated her bookshelves, I'll have to get Honor to work on clarifying what her father's relationship to Rich might be.

I hear footsteps and slide the Suttons' books back into place. I turn and face Eileen. Eileen has had time to make herself presentable but she hasn't taken advantage of the opportunity.

"I just couldn't wake up today." Eileen runs her fingers through her hair, which I now recognize as a habitual mannerism that doesn't help her appearance. She wears casual light-weight lavender pants. Her grape-colored shirt, tucked in at the waist, sports funny ruffled shoulders designed to keep the outfit from looking too stark. She looks like she's wearing yesterday's make-up. The look doesn't flatter her as much as the dressiness she affected several days ago when she visited my office. Although Eileen is probably close to me in age, I'm not very familiar with her type, a disadvantage in assessing her needs.

"Let's get out of here," Eileen says, for some reason disdaining the elegant living room.

She leads me to a huge well-equipped kitchen. A diet soda sits on the white formica counter. Casablanca fans turn slowly even though the heat's on in the house, neither seem appropriate for April weather. The brass fittings on every appliance, from the dishwasher to the espresso maker, gleam, a testimony, I suppose, to the diligence of the lime green red-headed worker. She appears, walks past Eileen without a word, and enters an adjoining utility room, closing the door behind her.

"Would you rather meet here or out by the pool?" Eileen asks. She looks inclined to stay in the kitchen but I've never had a client offer to meet with me by the pool before.

"Let's sit outside," I say coolly.

"Would you care for some orange juice? It's fresh squeezed." I'm pleased with the offer.

"Thank you, I would," I respond. Eileen pours a generous quantity of orange juice into a chilled glass. She pours herself a mug of coffee from a pot warming in the coffee maker. I would have taken coffee too but Eileen doesn't offer.

We go out shiny sliding glass doors and reconvene in a backyard built into a hill. Dried oak leaves from up the hill float in the pool. Steamy tendrils rise from the water, proving that the Goldeens heat the pool year round.

Eileen lowers herself into a metal pool chair and pulls the chair forward so that her knees are well under the glass table top. You learn to sit that way in grade school. A lot of people revert to it when they have to answer questions.

"Rich entertains business associates here but I don't come out much myself." Eileen looks around wonderingly as if her surroundings are completely unfamiliar. "Rich probably thinks I do sit outside. But when I'm home I like to be on my bed. I have a television and a desk right in my room. I've thought about putting one of those half-size refrigerators in my bedroom. I mean, it's nobody's business but my own, is it?" Picturing Eileen opening the refrigerator in her bedroom to get out some low-fat yogurt depresses me but I don't say anything.

"My friend's faces look like old potatoes from the sun," Eileen says, as though I had challenged her habitual absence at the poolside. She peers at me as if seeing me sitting here beside her own house makes her notice that I am a person, separate from her and Ruthie. "You've got beautiful color and I bet you don't even try." I find the compliment odd because Eileen hasn't looked at me until this minute.

"Thanks," I reply. I assume that when Eileen relaxes, I'm not going to hear as much errata.

"Mrs. Pirex?" Eileen once again looks off to the right of me but she's zeroing in more.

"Call me Eliza."

"Eliza, my husband doesn't want me to waste any more time looking for Ruthie. He says if I have to find her, he has a big firm of private investigators he would engage. I wouldn't have to be involved."

Her eyes finally focus on me steadily. "I want to do it myself. I can afford you. And you'll tell *me* what you're doing. So I want to keep you." Eileen looks for my reaction.

"I'm working for you until you tell me otherwise," I assure her. She nods.

I move us on to business. "I know you've worried about the circumstances around Ruthie's leaving. But we have no reason to believe that Ruthie didn't just decide to leave San Francisco on an impulse. She was probably upset by her friend's death and felt like getting away. That means my job involves dogging after any information on Ruthie that you haven't acted on so far."

"So you'll find her soon," Eileen says, looking away fatigued for a minute and then refocusing on me.

"It's hard to disappear in our time. Even when you really try. And I don't *think* Ruthie's trying. You lost her, that's all."

"Where are you going to look for her next?" Eileen asks. A keen expression livens her appearance at last.

"Eileen, before we get down to details, I want to ask you something. Is there anyone other than you and your husband who knows about this investigation? Anyone who would like to curtail my search for Ruthie?"

"I don't think so. I've told some of my girlfriends that I'm hiring someone to look for my friend. But nobody's very interested. Why do you ask?" The woman in uniform swaggers up to us and wordlessly pours me some more juice, Eileen more coffee. I wait until she walks away.

"A thug type with a gun came up behind me on the sidewalk in Oakland and told me to stay away from Ruthie. Not from you, but from Ruthie. Don't get upset, I'm okay. Do you have any ideas?" Eileen stares at me wide-eyed.

"None of my friends would even believe that I could be mixed up in something with a gun. This is scary," says Eileen, not helpful.

I decide to risk the question, "Does this incident strike you as anything that your husband could be a party to?" Eileen seems to consider the question without surprise.

"Rich? No. He shouts a lot when people he works with do something he doesn't like. His dad shouts too. And he talks big when he's had a couple scotches. But he went to Crest High School, you know."

"Oh?"

"The Crest guys are never really bad. If they become criminals, they do white-collar crimes and pay fines for it. I went to high school in San Jose with guys who turned out bad." She considers further.

"Can I tell Rich about the guy with the gun?" she asks. "This is funny. Not funny, ha ha. Strange."

61
▲

"Any information I give you about the case is yours to use at your discretion," I tell her.

"Rich is in construction," Eileen comes up with spontaneously. "So maybe he does consort with criminals. He doesn't tell me much about his work because it upsets his stomach." Eileen looks further enlivened at the thought of Rich having a shadowy life in the construction underplace. She seems to have no inclination to defend her husband's good character.

"I'm just checking every angle. I'm sure your husband wasn't involved in accosting me. I hope that when I locate Ruthie, he'll be pleased with your decision to hire me."

"It's not that he doesn't like you. I'm sure he would like you a lot if he got to know you. Rich mentioned he thinks you're attractive."

Unfortunately for our budding relationship, Eileen opens her mouth to continue, "He said it must help to be good-looking because you could always act as bait and get men to spill their guts to you. Of course, I said I bet that you could do everything the same way as a man except maybe hand-to-hand combat." Great, I think, hearing this would build the self-esteem of women investigators everywhere.

"I'm equipped to handle any situation that comes up." I make my voice hard. "Your husband should be confident of that. He checked my references thoroughly." I try not to sound annoyed.

"Yes," Eileen says, looking off in the distance again. I'm pleased to see that she looks uncomfortable about Rich checking up on me.

I'm ready to forage for background on Ruthie. "Who does your landscaping? It's lovely sitting here," I say to start the transition.

"I don't know. Rich has somebody new. I like the little pond that drains into the pool. Don't you? That's where the water is processed or whatever gets done to it." Eileen looks around as though bewildered again to find herself outside the house.

"Eileen, can we go over some facts that might help me locate Ruthie?"

"I guess we haven't done that yet." She folds her hands on the table, even more reminiscent of the obedient child at school.

"The neighbors at Ruthie's last known address in San Francisco didn't yield much information," I tell her. "Except that one of the residents heard from Ruthie after the time she left San Francisco. She sent him a postcard from Los Angeles.

It didn't have an address or any references to her plans that might tell us where she is today. At least we know where she went after she disappeared from here."

"So now I know that she was all right after she left San Francisco," breathes Eileen.

"Sounds like it," I reply, remembering that the postcard pictured Marilyn dead. I drop the subject of Dave Gray's information.

I move forward and say, "I want Ruthie's parents' old address in Studio City for my information sheet. I haven't located them by name check, either Morris or Maddy Gold, so I need to work with the address next. I can also use any information you have about the dance company in Santa Cruz where Ruthie played the piano. You mentioned you know where Ruthie's brother Jonathan used to live?"

"He and his friends were in a political group," Eileen responds. "I'm not sure whether the group was left-wing or right-wing. They were always trying to buy guns. I don't know what they were going to do with the guns. Or whether they ever bought any guns, actually." Eileen may be about to wander, her eyes have that lavender glaze, so I take up the conversation.

"I'll check Jonathan out," I declare. "Now what about Santa Barbara? You and Ruthie went to school there for two years. Any names or addresses of people who might be in contact with her now?"

"We had a friend who I think is still in Santa Barbara. Antonia. She married a teacher in the math department. Ruthie had taken a math class from him and they started dating. When she didn't want to see him any more, Ruthie introduced him to Antonia and he and Antonia ended up getting married.

"Antonia's husband grew up in Santa Barbara. He lived with his parents. I'll bet you anything they still live near his folks." Eileen's disproportionate features contract with remembered pain.

"Ruthie got along with Antonia better than I did. Toni might not be that glad to hear from me. Whenever I said a word around her, Antonia would say she had a hard time following me. Ruthie always said she wanted Toni and me to communicate better. So we could all be friends. But communicating never really worked. No matter how I put it, she couldn't follow me." Eileen winds down again, still looking pained.

▲

"What was her name before and after the marriage?" I ask.

"She was Antonia Noyes. She married Geoff Lowe and changed her name to Antonia Noyes-Lowe. I remember the hyphen. I saw the match books from the wedding although I wasn't invited." Eileen's voice trails away and lilac-purple mist collects in her eyes.

Eileen must have taken some drug other than caffeine. The doctor could be prescribing something for Eileen's nerves. A foreign substance would explain Eileen's tendency to ramble and her failure to make significant eye contact.

"I'll call her," I say. "I don't even have to mention your name."

"Wait," says Eileen, pulling herself to a more upright sitting position and taking a sip of her stagnant coffee. "I woke up in the middle of the night last night and swore I wouldn't forget to tell you something interesting I remembered."

"What's that, Eileen?" I ask.

"Ruthie mentioned several times that Ottie Dresner is her cousin. Do you know him?"

"I don't. Who is he?"

"He was a hippie artist during the sixties who became very successful. He painted all sorts of famous people who were his friends. Wild paintings with stuff stuck to them. The paintings hang in famous galleries in southern California and even in New York City.

"I couldn't find anything at the library about what happened to him," Eileen says, sounding disappointed in the service rendered by her local public library. "I think he fizzled out. Maybe from drinking. But he should be easy to find in southern California. Because he was famous. I know they keep track of all the people who have been famous, someplace in southern California. They do retrospectives on them for *Entertainment Tonight*. The TV show."

"Do you think he might have maintained contact with Ruthie's family?" I ask.

"He lived with them when he was a boy. Which he didn't enjoy because Ruthie's father was a maniac who made the kids brush their teeth and wash their hair constantly. Morris, Ruthie's dad, thought the kids had dangerous germs in their mouths and hair." The reference to hair causes Eileen to further rumple her own hairdo with her fingers.

"Ruthie was Ottie's favorite cousin. Ruthie didn't mention him in the year before she disappeared, though. You don't think he's disappeared too, do you?" Eileen's thick brows knit.

64
▲

"If you can't find him right off the bat, please don't put yourself out. Rich wouldn't want me paying to find a bad painter I don't even know. Maybe you could write to *Entertainment Tonight* and see if he's in their files."

"I'll take it under advisement." I maintain a serious facial expression. "I'll do a superficial search for Ottie Dresner. Will you fill out an information sheet on him?"

"Yes," Eileen snatches the sheet. "Isn't it amazing how much comes back when you get on the right track? I was dreaming about Ruthie last night and when I woke up Ottie's name just popped into my head."

We catalogue the people I will contact trying to reach Ruthie: the Jazzmatazz Dance Company in Santa Cruz; neighbors at Ruthie's parents former address; Ruthie's brother; her sister, Jane, if Jane can be found; Ruthie's friend, Antonia, in Santa Barbara; and Dr. Stuart Lilienthal. "There's one person you shouldn't trifle with—" begins Eileen, breaking off abruptly. I have to guess the person with whom I shouldn't trifle.

"Oh my God. It's Rich. Home from work at this time of day." She calls, "Hi, honey," and waves, looking nervous. She rises halfway out of her seat when he nears and reaches toward him. He ignores her and comes to my side offering me his hand to shake. I shake his hand firmly.

"I thought I'd drop by to get in on the powwow." Rich speaks with a large businessman's-special grin across his face. He strides toward the pool, speaking to me over his shoulder.

"When my wife started using all those tracking skills she learned in the girl scouts to find her bosom buddy from college, her girlfriend didn't show up. I assume you haven't solved the case of the missing college chum yet either, Mrs. Pirex," he says smugly. "I'd like a brief run-down on where we stand."

Before I can respond, he booms from across the table, "My wife invested a great deal of time trying to find her friend. Of course, my wife would be the first to admit that her time is not worth its weight in jelly beans." He continues speaking with a not-very-disguised sneer in his voice. "This woman spends a whole day 'organizing the house' and when I get home, I can't find so much as a single pair of shoes in better order than it was when I left. We must own 50 pairs of shoes between us and they're all thrown on the closet floors underneath the clothes no matter how many hours my wife spends 'organizing.'" For a minute his face falls and he looks like a boy whose mom hasn't been taking good care of him.

"But, sorry," his face resumes it's usual patina of derision, "I'm digressing as badly as Eileen. Someday they'll find us both out combing the streets for pals we knew in college and talking gibberish. Marriage is like that, I guess. You're married, aren't you?"

"I have a family, two kids, but I'm not married, no."

"So, it's Ms. Pirex, I'll bet."

"Just call me Eliza, Rich."

"Sure, great. Now let's hear where we're going with Eileen's problem."

I glance at Eileen. Her face has taken on a grey pinched look since Rich arrived. I adopt a brisk mein. "Rich, Eileen and I have outlined the direction of the case more thoroughly than I want to repeat right now."

"To date," I tell him, "I have invested three working hours. The bulk of the hours have been spent making certain that no occupant of Ruth Gold's last known residence could simply tell us her current whereabouts.

"Eileen," I say to Rich, "did an excellent job following up the initial leads she had in her possession. I'll be eliminating the last of the preliminary checkpoints. I'm sure you don't want me to go into my techniques in any greater detail here and now."

Techniques like asking questions and making phone calls, I think to myself. Rich and Eileen both stare at me.

"Well, I'd like to hear some follow-up pretty soon," says Rich with less force. Then he picks up momentum again. "I look for results. I'm known for cutting through the crap and asking for results, results, and more results. What's the goal? What are the results? Those two questions make me the manager I am."

Now Eileen and I stare at Rich. Rich marches over, picks up my orange juice, which I assume he thinks is Eileen's, and swills the whole glass. The maid appears, simpering, and says deferentially, "More orange juice, Mr. Goldeen?" She certainly didn't simper for me and Eileen. I try to catch her eye just to figure out if she knows Rich pre-empted my juice. I can't tell. Eileen takes a sip from her empty coffee cup.

"You know, Rich," I bring up now, "you once went on a double-date with someone close to me. Honor Sutton." I am trying to keep the upper hand with Rich. Maybe he'll reveal why he has the Sutton books in his living room.

He blanches visibly. "She was a little rich for my blood. Pretty stuck on her good looks when she was a kid, let me tell you." He's mistaken. I know Honor intimately and I can vouch for the fact that she has an apathy about being extremely beautiful. But I pay attention to Rich's comment. I like to know when I can't rely upon a person's perceptions or integrity.

"Yes. She's beautiful," I reply. I look carefully at Rich to see whether he knows about Honor's and my relationship. He doesn't.

"Was she your date?" asks Eileen, trying to grasp the significance of the conversation.

"No," chuckles Rich. "I was with a cheerleader type from my school. I'm afraid Miss Sutton may have expected me to call her later, though. And I'm afraid I never got around to it." He glances sideways at his wife as he speaks. I know, because his story about the date doesn't match Honor's, that Rich Goldeen is distorting his personal history for appearance's sake.

I say nothing and Rich eventually clears his throat and says, "I just hope there were no hard feelings."

"I doubt it," I tell him sweetly. "I mentioned I'd taken a case for your wife and Honor recalled that she'd met you. She didn't seem downhearted by the recollection."

Rich obviously wants to drop the whole thing. He parades over to the pool, lifts the thermometer out of the water by its chain, and examines it carefully. Eileen turns to me and says uncertainly, "I'm so glad Rich has decided to lend us his support. I'll have an easier time staying in touch with you if Rich gets excited about finding Ruthie." She gazes at Rich, who stays busy patrolling the pool.

"I can handle Rich," I tell her. Suddenly she looks like she's trying not to giggle.

"You know when Rich and I were first married, I used to call him my teddy bear. I know he's not really the type, but we hadn't known each other that long. It seems so ridiculous now." Eileen takes out a pill box, selects a pill and washes it down with some of Rich's juice. She must take them so routinely that she doesn't stop to consider who might notice.

"And then one time Rich was trying to tell Ruthie how she had savoir faire. Actually, I don't think Rich much liked Ruthie's savoir faire. He used to complain that she was pushy and snotty." Eileen starts to make burbling noises.

"Ruthie used to call him my savage bear ever after. Because he kept repeating 'savoir faire' with a phony French accent. And I called him 'teddy bear.' You know, I still think of him that way in my mind. A savage teddy bear. With no savoir faire." Eileen starts snorting through her nose with mirth.

Rich trots back, alert to our interaction. "I see you ladies aren't too concerned about the absence of clues leading to Ruthie Gold." I notice that Rich has a difficult time saying the name, his jaw locks, giving Ruthie Gold a sibilant sound when his tongue hits the back of his teeth.

"We have plenty of clues leading to Ruthie's whereabouts, Rich. I have every expectation that I won't have to put a tremendous number of hours into the case before I can give you a current address."

The maid walks past me and Eileen. She says to Rich, "The lady has a phone call. Should I put her in your office or put her in the kitchen?"

"I guess economy detectives don't have phones in their cars," says Rich to Eileen, a belittling smile pasted on his face.

"Richard," says Eileen, "don't be ridiculous. No reasonable person has a phone in their car except you."

"Mrs. MacWilliams will show you to my office," says Rich in a suddenly affable voice, "so that you can have some privacy." I hurry to follow Mrs. MacWilliams. She wears what seem to be white bedroom slippers with no backs.

We pass through the sliding glass doors and cross the gleaming kitchen. We turn down a wide hallway with skylights. No picture, or anything, hangs on the wall except a family tree with Rich's and Eileen's ancestors written in the blanks with felt-tip pen. Both sides feature a lot of empty blanks but Rich's side has the most holes.

Mrs. MacWilliams points to the phone on Rich's desk without speaking and leaves, closing the door behind her. I pick up the phone and at first hear dead air. Then I hear a click and Precious' voice comes across the line saying, "Eliza Pirex, are you on the line?"

"I'm here, Precious. Sorry, I think they just switched the call to this phone." Precious doesn't like any screwing around when she's transacting business by phone.

"Eliza, we got a problem. Your client, Doris Shipley, has herself parked in here. I said 'move' and she didn't move. That's bad. You know there's hardly anybody who doesn't jump when I say so. You're going to have to come and force her out somehow." I notice Precious restraining the level of her voice for propriety's sake.

"What's she doing there, Precious?"

"She says she needs to check on the operation. Now I ask you, what does that mean? She's been listening to phone calls and looking at all the statues on my desk. She writes notes in a pad and when I try to get a look at what she's got down on the paper, she hides the pad in her purse.

"She's been asking people whether they know you. She's more of a pain in the butt than any of the doctor's clients with mental problems. Do you know what she's up to?" I'm startled by how wound up Doris has gotten the normally imperious Precious.

"She's a fruitcake, Precious. But she is a legitimate client of mine right now. I'll come and deal with her. You keep trying to get rid of her in the meantime, though."

"I can't go getting tough on a lady with a walker. It doesn't look good. I've got one of Sarah's people sitting here in a fancy jacket, looking on. What's the matter with your lady's legs? She's not that old."

"She broke her ankle. I'm sorry, Precious. I guess I could try talking to her for a minute. I don't know how far it will get me. I don't have much luck with her on the phone."

"You try being tough, Eliza Pirex. I'm going to sit here and give her my evil stare," growls Precious.

I talk to Doris as though I just happened to call her up to chat. After a decent interval, I gingerly mention that we have a peculiar office etiquette. I tell her that my office partners demand that clients spend only a very transitory time in the front office. I make it clear that the same thing applies to law practice and psychotherapy clients. Doris bad-mouths Precious but promises she'll leave the office.

I get out my wallet calendar and schedule a stop back by the office after I leave here, to check on the situation. The door opens and Rich stands in the doorway. I leap to my feet. Rich has carpeted his office in a fiery red which seems incongruous with the rest of the house. But when Rich enters the room, the shade of carpet makes sense considering the effect Rich probably wants to achieve. The color highlights Rich's attempts to aggrandize himself. I like the silliness of this royal room.

"I want a private moment with you before you go," Rich announces. The office windows probably overlook the back yard where Eileen still sits but heavy drapes are drawn. The room's light comes from a big bronze desk lamp. "What can I do for you, Rich?" It's irrational but I dislike Rich standing between me and the door. Rich moves toward the desk and stops to prop his foot on the brace of a heavy chair with a red velour seat.

"I know I've come on strong with you. I want my wife to get her money's worth. But I like the way you've handled yourself so far, Eliza. I like your style. I hate to see a professional waste her time." I know he picked up the use of the word 'professional' from me when I was shooting the breeze with him. He's parroting the word to win me over.

"Thanks, Rich," I reply.

"I've checked references on you to make sure that we would get a certain quality of service. And you checked out fine. At this point, I have enough confidence in you to let you handle some problems we've come across at my company." Rich smiles paternally. He's too young for that kind of smile, not that I enjoy that smile ever.

"This will probably mean," he winks meaningfully, "bigger money than you usually see come over your desk. And I think you might find that you attract a different kind of clientele once you've gotten a chance to do some valid work."

"I only do valid work," I say coldly. "As you should know from my references. At the present, I'm not able to accept new clients."

"I'm talking a job that'll mean you get all the sad sacks off your books. We'll talk price. Early next week if you want to." Rich advances toward me until he stands uncomfortably close. I smell my orange juice on his breath and a strange plastic smell about him as though he has been exposed to something toxic. I stand my ground.

"Rich, I am determined to wrap up each of my cases. And after that, I have a waiting list. There's no point to any further discussion." Rich smiles a younger, unfortunately oily, smile and leans forward just enough that I have to bend back to avoid becoming overly intimate with him. He clearly means to push me.

The office door opens with a swoosh and Eileen barrels in. Rich takes a step back. Eileen moves like someone who doesn't know whether she's invited but wants in anyway. I'm sorry that she's had to make an undignified entrance, so I turn my attention to her with respect.

"Eileen, I'm leaving now. I want to thank you for setting up the case so well. I'll report back to you next week." I try to make my way around Rich.

Rich's voice takes on a tone that's now aggressive instead of smarmy. "My wife and I will want to meet with you in person, Ms. Pirex. I believe I have a free slot next Tuesday morning. Can we make an eleven o'clock appointment? At your office?" Eileen looks at the red pile under her feet.

"Okay," I shrug my shoulders. I turn to Eileen. "If there's any problem with the appointment time, get in touch with me."

"We'll see you then," Eileen says with no trace of her former hilarity.

Eileen marches forward and seizes her husband's arm. They walk together, the host and hostess bidding adieu to an unfortunate guest. I follow them out to the front entry, pausing only to scan the genealogical chart briefly. I see Goldeens, Goldsteins, Deans, and Mandlebaums. Eileen used to be a Mandlebaum, as I knew from her bookplates.

"By the way," says Rich. "I knew you'd be contacting the people whose names my wife gave you. I called someone you might have had a problem getting through to, so you won't have to bother." Eileen looks perplexed.

"Stuart Lilienthal," announces Rich. "The man has quite a reputation. He's a prominent guy. He doesn't go taking calls from any economy crank, no offense intended, who pulls his name out of a hat. He said to let you know he hasn't heard a word from Ruthie Gold in many years and never had any idea where she went."

"You called Dr. Lilienthal?" hisses Eileen to Rich. Rich suppresses her with a tight smile.

"Good day, Ms. Pirex." Rich opens the door and waves me out, pulling Eileen inside.

Once over the threshold, I smell old acorns and peat moss and I smell jasmine although I don't see any. I make a break for my car. Suddenly the front door of the house opens and Eileen shouts, "Eliza." I turn around noticing that their cluttered doorway boasts a mezzuzah, a family coat of arms, and an electronic eye.

"Yes," I answer. The savage bear suddenly frames Eileen, Rich walks up behind her.

"He doesn't mean to be a nuisance. He's really very sensitive." She jerks her thumb at Rich, behind her, to indicate she refers to him. He lowers his face modestly. I wonder if he asked Eileen to apologize for him.

"I'm sure he is. He married you, didn't he?" I yell back charitably. I find it important in my work not to forget that two people are always married for a discernible reason, good or bad. I will never disparage Rich in front of Eileen even when she gives me openings.

I wonder how the scene at the office goes. I don't know because my car doesn't have a phone.

Honor would never have seen the mail on a weekday, not being one to go down to the box on her own initiative. But because it's Saturday, we sit at the kitchen table with the thin spring sun lighting the tablecloth's amelia pattern under our coffee cups. An astro-bright blue circular lies among today's mail.

Honor works at constructing the Aztec city, Tenochtitlan, by gluing sugar cubes together. She refers frequently to Annabelle's elaborate diagram which calls for the cubes serving as roof tops and window ledges to protrude one-quarter inch from the surface of an outside wall. I read our mail.

The picture on the flyer features an androgynous person exercising by lifting all the astrological signs above his/her head. The blue sheet invites us to a publication party and book signing. Large block lettering reads, "The Heavenly Bodies Guide to Astrology and Fitness." It came addressed to both of us. I pass it to Honor.

"Shit," screams Honor. She stares down at the piece of mail in horror. I point out that she told me just the other day that she doesn't want the children repeating "shit" or "Jesus Christ" at school and therefore wasn't going to use those phrases anymore. She glares at me nastily and rightly so.

"Look at this, Eliza. They've published. Linden and Lucy have published some book. Their book sounds like invasive nonsense, just like my father's. I wish I were an orphan. I practically am an orphan. From now on, I'm devoting myself entirely to you and the children. I have no other family." Honor tosses the blue paper back at me.

73
▲

Honor's brother, Linden, does astrological readings and classes. His twin, Lucy, teaches aerobics and fitness. They own a store together in Berkeley, called Heavenly Bodies. At work, they both wear leotards with the solar system in silver against a black backdrop and the words "Heavenly Bodies" running vertically in red letters that look from head-on like the silhouette of a sexy but genderless human being. I think of Lucy and Linden as the human embodiment of heavenly bodies, a light and twinkling constellation.

"It *is* irritating that no one in your family except you can quell the urge to tell everyone else in the world what to do," I say, to acknowledge Honor's despair. "But you must have known that Lucy and Linden had the tendency. You've lived with your family imprinting before. Just ignore this new book." As a matter of fact, I'm surprised that Honor hasn't broken down and dashed off a guide to finding meaningful work or a mother's primer of some kind. My girl obviously has more restraint than the rest of the Suttons.

"Linden and Lucy were the last meaningful tie to my childhood," moans Honor histrionically. "Just the other day, I took the children to their store for a soy milk smoothie and bran muffins. I've started feeling at home there. Lucy has stopped trying to make me and the kids exercise or unblock our chakras, she lets us sit at the juice bar and print up pictures on the computer."

A look of further horror widens Honor's eyes. "Eliza, what if they've put Annabelle and Jemmy in their book? I'll have to enroll the children in a boarding school under an assumed name. When I was a child, I always wanted my father to send me to Switzerland so I could live out from under the shadow of his nonfiction."

"Maybe the book won't upset you, Honor, when you read it. Lucy and Lin haven't written *Our Family Took to the Gym*. The book's probably technical. Give the twins a break."

"I'd like to break both their index fingers," mutters Honor. I'm glad I have no urge to chronicle my adventures in the detective business. Honor's eyes flick dangerously. I'm glad they're not aimed at me.

I scan the flyer more closely. "The party that Linden and Lucy are hosting is at Heavenly Bodies tonight. Why wouldn't they have let us know sooner? This event must have taken a lot of planning."

"I'll tell you why they didn't invite us sooner," Honor retorts darkly. "They didn't want to give me a chance to get at them before I see them make their debut as writers. They think I won't make an ugly scene in public, at their party. Of course, they don't understand that I consider our bonds of affection severed. All bets are off now," she menaces.

"Come on, you know when you get there tonight you're going to forgive them. They're family. And not as difficult as most of your family, either." Honor pries up a misproportioned village hut without a reply and walks over to flip it viciously into the garbage can.

She crosses the kitchen out to the living room, and I hear her yell up the stairs, "Annabelle Siegel, I'm going to destroy Tenochtitlan if you're not downstairs in fifteen minutes. I'm tired of being duped into doing your homework, Ms. A plus." The kids hide from her when she uses this kind of language. I'm glad Annabelle has fifteen minutes grace.

Honor whips back into the kitchen and slams into the chair in front of the twins' circular. "Eliza, I'll bet those two slimy little rats have signs up in their store advertising their publication date. But I didn't see any. I'll bet they scurried around taking the signs down when they saw my car pull up the other day. I can see it all." I believe her scenario. The Suttons all visualize each other's ridiculous behavior vividly and accurately.

"You are going to go tonight, aren't you?" I ask.

"Of course. Do you think I'd miss the opportunity to make them host me, an aggrieved party? All their well-wishers will see that not everyone is thrilled about their 'literary triumph.' You can wear your new rose-colored silk blouse. I'll wear cream linen," she directs.

"We're going disguised as girlfriends from the Wednesday Afternoon Tea and Garden Club?" I ask, picturing our attire.

"Don't trifle with me on this, Eliza. It's my ordeal and I need to confront it as best I can."

"Honor, I'm working tonight. I'm due at the college."

"Call in sick. Even janitors get sick. They're probably sick more often than other people. Who knows what kind of contamination lands in classroom wastebaskets? Eliza, you'll have to call in sick. And I'm getting you heavy rubber gloves for Monday."

"I'll call and get out of working tonight if you'll drop the idea of the gloves," I counter.

"Eliza, I have enough to worry about without wondering what you're picking up through your pores. Can't you humor me?"

"I am humoring you, Honor, believe me. You've been ranting ever since we got the party invitation."

"I'm going to pull myself together." Honor squares her shoulders, the high-minded heroine shrugging off pain and mortification. "I'll build a stable for the Aztecs. Annabelle has plastic llamas that need shelter."

I put down the bill from our newspaper carrier which I've been reading. "I think I'll invite Rochelle Woolley to go with us," I put forward casually.

"To the public spectacle tonight? Why would she want to come? I don't know what kind of shape I'm going to be in." Honor, fortunately, doesn't seem to perceive any implications.

"Lucy and Linden enjoyed Rochelle at our New Year's Eve," I remind her. "You liked talking to her too. Remember?"

"I guess I don't care. I'll invite Nancy," Honor volleys. I look at her to gauge her motivation. Nancy, our bohemian neighbor, admires Honor to distraction. I don't enjoy her.

"Nancy would probably be a comfort to you," I acquiesce. I have to go along with Nancy to get Rochelle.

Rochelle Goffstein and I met through a background check I did four years ago for a firm of attorneys. Honor and I were fighting a lot, about my work. Then I met Rochelle. She provided a nourishing diversion from the diet of provocation that Honor was dishing up.

Rochelle's unspectacular but good-humored face caught my fancy immediately upon meeting her. The pleasant creamy-brown freckles across her face, back, and hands touched me. I liked the distinctive melding points of her bones, I liked her politics. She was working as a paralegal and planned to go to law school. I only slept with her twice before I happened to introduce her to my building-mate, Mike, and heard three weeks later that she and Mike had married.

I have never felt that questions about what became of Rochelle's earlier plans to pursue a legal career would be tactful. Rochelle did not go to law school, she hasn't had children, and she and Mike have been in couples therapy for two years. Still and all, Mike usually speaks about her respectfully and fondly. She appears at office parties with a basically happy nature reflected in the set of her mouth.

Honor never found out about my two trysts with Rochelle. She embarked upon a campaign to re-establish the loving quality of our daily life together and make peace with my occupation. She succeeded, because I have never really doubted that I want a life with her. I didn't acknowledge Rochelle's existence for several years.

Lately, however, I've felt as though Rochelle might be baking especially for me. She doesn't always bake my favorites, sour cream cake or apple turnovers. But I sense some nuance boxed with the baked goods that Mike brings to the office. Her pastry stimulates fond memories.

Honor fetches the broom from the pantry. She begins cutting bristles off the broom's head with a steak knife. The strands will serve as accessories in the Aztecs' stable. Her long, perfect hands handle the knife with endearing competence.

"You know, Eliza?" Honor sounds composed now. "I think I'll greet the twins as though I'm pleased about their book. Don't you think it would flummox them if they never got any criticism from me at all?"

She smiles a conniving smile. "They're probably all braced for a lot of screaming. I just won't give it to them. My mother would be able to rest more peacefully if she knew I'd suddenly become gracious. I think I can bring it off if I wear my linen suit and have a glass of wine with dinner. The wine should have a sedative effect."

"I think gracious would be nice," I agree. "I'll try to be gracious too. And Jem and Annabelle are naturally gracious."

"Good. That's settled," Honor pronounces. Annabelle still lurks in hiding upstairs. Honor begins unraveling a potholder for the Aztecs to use as weaving material.

After Honor leaves to do errands, I spend the day discussing the Aztecs with Annabelle and ferrying Jemmy to soccer. Jem ranks second youngest and second most unskilled on the Ferocious Feet, but he's very disciplined. I love to watch him out on the field exhibiting potential, his lips grimly set. No one else on the bleachers knows I'm backing a champion.

In the afternoon, I check in at the office. Honor's latest marketing ventures for Eliza Pirex Investigations have been paying off. I look at a small file of potential clients from which to choose. I am in a position to make some referrals to other investigation firms which would then owe me a favor in return, but I put the possibilities for the future away, pending the conclusion of Eileen Goldeen's business.

I wonder where Ruthie is. I don't plan to make much money off her. She's a nuisance, actually. But I'm going to make sure she's settled.

Rich Goldeen's wishes aside, I've put in a call to Dr. Stuart Lilienthal. I check the answering service. He hasn't left a message in return. His call may put to rest some of the nagging suspicions I inherited from Eileen.

I expect the doctor to be slick. And what else? I'll be talking to the man who allegedly terrorized Ruthie. Who murdered a cat. Who overcharged a postal worker (I checked back with Dave Gray for a few follow-up details and was stunned by the fee Lilienthal charged for young Lisa's therapy). I'm going to try again on Monday to get through to him.

After dinner, with the children in their rooms putting on their assigned clothes, I ask Honor, "Did Ruthie forget to put the cat out? Was she the protagonist or was she the victim?"

"I don't know," says Honor. Honor has been sworn to confidentiality and has heard the latest details of the case. "I picture your Ruthie as a seductive type. Everyone wants her. Have you noticed? To know her was to want her. Eliza, don't wear those pants. We'll look like we're color-coordinated."

"You're right. About Ruthie, I mean," I say, changing to grey slacks. "I hadn't focused on that. I keep wondering why Eileen is paying me to find her. But that's it, that's the reason. Ruthie inspired desire. Eileen desires her, so does Dave Gray, and Lilienthal, even the police officer who met her the night she was attacked in her apartment."

"And now you, you want her too," Honor says, holding up pearls to evaluate them with her outfit. "You don't even know her but here you are talking about her at a time when we have other things to worry about. Like family treachery." The Suttons are going to regret publishing their latest tract before another hour has passed. I can tell.

Honor hangs the pearls back in her jewelry box and tries on a gold chain set with small garnets at inch-long intervals. She picks up our previous discussion and remarks, "Rich Goldeen doesn't admit he was drawn to her. But we know he lies about that kind of thing. Maybe Ruthie left town to get away from him."

"I can't conceive of Rich having enough impact on anyone to drive them out of town," I reply. I have achieved an elegant and sophisticated appearance, I see in the mirror. I sit down on the bed.

"Which necklace?" Honor turns and asks.

"How about your chain and locket?" I suggest. "I thought you want us to look prim." I need to prove I'm taking the event seriously.

"You're right." She approves my input with her smile.

The doorbell rings and I hear Jemmy yell, "I'll get it." I give Honor a squeeze to let her know that I, her eternally unpublished lover, stand behind her. She runs her fingertips down my face and neck, a soft loving gesture that never fails to give me a tingle. We go arm in arm out to the living room.

Our neighbor, Nancy, stands admiring Jemmy's egg-carton art. His eager voice rattles nonstop, explicating the technique used to create each special effect. I don't like the way Nancy's praise rings untrue. I love all Jemmy's creative output.

"Honor, you look lovely," gushes Nancy. "I'm really happy that I'm going to spend the evening with your whole family. I know you hate their exhibiting themselves this way, in a book. But it's so colorful when you're not directly involved. Isn't this pretty exciting, Eliza?"

"I consider myself directly involved," I tell her.

"Eliza, you're so serious. Honor, I brought you some flowers from my garden for you to give the twins. Give them these and they'll at least think you're trying." Honor takes the bouquet and gazes into it.

"No flowers," she says coldly. "I don't think you understand, Nancy. We're not bringing anything. Annabelle, put these in water and leave them in the kitchen."

"I'm sorry, Honor. The flowers are in your honor then," Nancy says. Honor doesn't like honor quips and ignores her.

"Eliza," Honor speaks officiously to me, "why don't you have a snack? I don't want you to look like you're enjoying the food. Jem, Annabelle, have an after-dinner bite. I made frozen strawberry puree yesterday. Nancy, you don't have to have any. Nobody knows you." Jemmy and Annabelle sidle closer to me hoping for protection from Honor's onslaught.

"Honor," I say patiently, consciously recalling how much I love her, "I promise I won't enjoy anything about this evening. We're off to a great start. I'm not enjoying myself so far." She drops the snack idea and glares at me to indicate that we're not supposed to differ in front of Nancy.

"Let's move out, everybody," Honor commands. "I want to arrive before the party gets running smoothly. And leave early. Annabelle, Jemmy, you guys look great."

Honor has decked the children out in stylishly conservative attire. Annabelle wears a moss-green print dress and leaf pattern tights. She's sacrificing for her mother. I know those tights don't stay up around her waist. She'll have to go into the bathroom and hitch them up throughout the evening. Jemmy has on designer jeans, crisp cotton shirt, and vest. They don't look like clothes that have seen any good times.

"Everything will turn out," I tell Honor. She melts against me for a moment. Nancy always seems very aware of when Honor and I touch. I smooth Honor's hair but don't kiss her.

We head up past the Claremont Hotel in the van to pick up Rochelle, who I am thankful to see. Rochelle wears a belted blue dress and flat-heeled shoes. Her undistinguished reddish-brown hair has been artfully arranged at the nape of her neck. She says hello to Honor and after one look, doesn't push for any further conversation. I don't ask Rochelle how she arranged with Mike for me to take her away on Saturday night. I had a feeling that Rochelle would work things out and she did.

Honor drives silently into central Berkeley. The kids murmur to themselves. Nancy tells Rochelle lively stories featuring the Sutton family which she has learned second-hand from Honor. I'll bet this will give Honor pause the next time she starts to entertain Nancy with Newell Sutton anecdotes.

We see the beam of a search light, the kind that attracts people to a store's grand opening, before we even get close to Heavenly Bodies. When we turn onto Center Street we see that the beacon comes from Lucy and Linden's fete.

People and lights flood the sidewalk up and down the block in front of Heavenly Bodies. Red and silver balloons and colored cloth streamers decorate the storefront. I'll bet Newell Sutton has picked up the bill for the whole occasion. The event looks too lavish to have been afforded by the store owners.

Honor parks in front of a driveway. I refrain from saying anything. She has probably planned a certain entrance. She doesn't want to risk disarray by walking any distance. I can get the car from the police on Monday between 11:00 and 1:30 if they tow it. I have some breathing space between morning and afternoon appointments. Honor careens out of the car.

The rest of us struggle with seat belts and attempt to follow. I check the door locks and then run flat out to catch up with Honor. "Eliza Pirex, you better stay with me," she snaps. I point out that I'm doing my best.

Honor leads us through the milling throng at a brisk pace. The crowd seems to be composed more of the fitness contingent than the astrology clan. Most people on the sidewalk wear middle-of-the-road Berkeley dress rather than exotic and mystical garb. When Honor hits the door of Heavenly Bodies, she slows to a regal stride. Just inside the door stands Newell Sutton, shaking hands like he's in the receiving line at a wedding.

"Father," begins Honor, and narrowly misses shaking his hand by putting hers in her pockets. He looks up to see who withholds their hand and sees her. "Two more lambs into the fold," she finishes, meaning Linden and Lucy. I'm not sure Newell understands the allusion to livestock but he gives her a fatherly smile.

"I assumed you wouldn't come," replies Newell. "Lucy and Lin said that if they sprang an invitation on you at the last minute, you'd come on impulse. And they were right. *They* were right. Think of that. I used to think that I was the one who could predict your every move." He turns to me. "We used to be *that* close."

"Here I am," Honor states formally. "I've brought Eliza, and the children, and some friends."

"We're holding up the line, let's talk later," says Newell.

"Daddy, I'll bet no one asked you to create a line. Everyone probably wonders why you're standing here obstructing traffic." A small crowd gathers to watch Honor and her father, puzzled over why Honor appears to be sniping at him. Newell must have been pulling off his own gracious act pretty well. The crowd, of course, mostly doesn't have any background on Newell. I do, so I let her scream at him if she likes because he deserves it. Not that I'm not fond of him.

Honor decides not to spar with her father and flounces past him signaling to our group to follow. I pass Newell Sutton and he holds out his hand to shake mine. He remarks to me, "She's a real beauty, isn't she?"

"Yes sir, she is," I reply. We often have this exchange, during which we confirm the one fact upon which we mutually agree. I introduce Rochelle and Nancy. Jemmy and Annabelle hug their grandfather, wrapping their arms around his broad belly which hides discreetly under a well-tailored button-up cardigan sweater and jacket. He pats them stiffly on their shoulders.

Once inside, Honor walks away muttering, "I'm going to take care of Linden and Lucy." She has obviously forgotten that I was ordered to stay by her side and has dismissed her intention to be gracious.

I set the children up with various blue-veined cheeses, healthy whole-grain crackers, and cookies, before Honor can prevent them from enjoying the refreshments. I introduce Nancy to Lucy's boyfriend, Ed something, a fiftyish doctor. Nancy begins regaling him with stories of Suttons. He looks fascinated. Lucy may be in for some embarrassing explanations.

Near the exercise floor some low-key jazz plays and the group in the area dances, medium-slow. I ask Rochelle if she'd

81
▲

like to dance and she replies, "How nice." We make our way to an inconspicuous corner and sway to the music. I don't hold her next to me. We could be two people who just happen to be dancing near each other.

"How does Honor usually get along with her family?" asks Rochelle.

"About like this," I tell her. Rochelle nods.

"What's Mike doing tonight?" I give her an opening to tell me something about her marriage.

"He went to a basketball game with friends," she answers. She moves closer. I put a light arm around her and take one hand. I lead. She's an amiable and competent partner.

Women tend to be more monogamous than men. So in a relationship between two women, the odds that it's monogamous are good. I don't know why I stray against the odds every so often in a while. Probably because I'm a detective and we detectives have a yen for romance and adventure as the literature bears witness.

Rochelle seemed worth the risk. And she was. I wonder how the rest of the interlude would have been, if she hadn't met Mike.

I stop musing and attend to Rochelle until I realize that I hear a voice repeating, "Excuse me" and "Pardon me." The Suttons all say "Pardon me." The words always sound foreign. No Pirex was raised to use so meaninglessly polite a phrase. I turn around and face Honor's brother, Linden.

Linden might more easily be Honor's twin than Lucy's. His beauty rivals hers unless he goes overboard and makes himself appear outlandish. Sometimes he wears an entire costume embroidered with mystical symbols, like a walking needlepoint. He also wears Lucy's discards which don't reach his wrists and ankles. Today, he wears well-tailored sports clothes.

"Linden, this is Rochelle Woolley. You two met at our house on New Year's Eve. She's married to Mike, who shares the office with me." Linden, making no comment on having hunted me down dancing with someone other than his sister, nods to her. Rochelle says something cordial.

"Eliza," Linden says, "we're having trouble with Honor. We thought she'd get caught up in the party mood. But she's furious." He looks over the dancers' heads anxiously. I strain to hear across the store. A noise with a familiar resonance does seems to overlay the party din. "This way," he gasps. Rochelle and I follow him through the trendy assemblage.

82
▲

The crowd around Honor keeps a cautious distance. Honor stands in the center of the only bare floor space in the store. She seems to be screaming at Lucy who shrinks on the other side of a long table laden with copies of *The Heavenly Bodies Guide to Astrology and Fitness*, artistically stacked in hexagonal piles.

"I will not accept this. I will particularly not accept this dedication. You'll have to repair the fourth page of every damn copy," I hear Honor rampage as I move toward her.

"Do you think she tried the diet in the book?" whispers a woman near me to her male companion. "Maybe her electrolytes are out of balance."

"I want you to check with Dr. Yamaguchi before you do the diet," the man cautions seriously.

"Could you go take care of Annabelle and Jemmy?" I ask Rochelle. "I don't want them to wander over here and see Honor carrying on."

"Sure," she says and turns to walk, tactfully, away from Honor's direction.

I take a breath and go to Honor, slipping my arm around her waist. She stops waving the book she holds in her right hand and relaxes a little.

"Eliza, look what they've done." She flips open the book, turns to the fourth page, and stabs her finger at three lines of text.

> "To our well-loved sister, Honor,
> who is both spiritual and fit
> in a special way."

"Where do they get off?" Honor's voice rises again. "Do I scrawl my relatives' names all over? Never. I'm the only one in the family who's even remotely civilized." She looks down at the inscription and steams up again.

Lucy cringes. Lucy sports a pretty version of the Sutton good looks, more sprightly than resplendent. She looks insignificant next to Honor right now.

"In a *special* way," Honor shrieks. "They make it sound as though I'm probably crass and flabby. They sound like they're trying to apologize to the world for having a sister who's not spiritual or fit in any *normal* way. Don't you see that, Eliza?"

"I probably wouldn't have read that meaning into it," I suggest.

Honor ignores me and wheels to confront Lucy. "You feel morally and athletically superior to me. Admit it, Lu. Get out from behind your mildewy books and face me."

83
▲

"Just a minute, Honor," Lucy calls back weakly. I would recommend that Lucy stay put, signing books. Discretion is the better part of valor in this case.

"Honor," I say, without flinching. I have decided to pull out the big guns, the ultimate threat, in order to get Honor to behave. "The children are going to be embarrassed by you. I know you've been humiliated by your family tonight but the kids will be upset if you keep it up." Honor looks around for them, finally guilty over this aspect of her behavior.

I use another ploy for good measure. "You know, I haven't been supervising them. I'll bet they're loading up on refreshments. I noticed sugar and whole-milk dairy products on the hors d'oeuvre table." It works. Honor's expression changes to one of extreme distraction.

"Where did you see them last?" she asks, now wholly the concerned mother. Honor's mothering makes up in intensity what it lacks in consistency.

"Over by the juice bar," I say without mentioning that I already sent Rochelle after them. Honor puts the twins' book down, bent on rescuing her pups from mediocre nutrients and potential allergens. I signal Lucy that I have the situation under control and struggle along at Honor's side.

Honor lays into the children for guzzling refreshments (I feel bad, since I encouraged them to partake). Soon she recovers at least as much equanimity as she possessed before she saw the book's dedication. I propose to Honor that we mingle, mingling will provide a new chance to make a good impression. Rochelle, exhibiting more genuine graciousness than anyone else this evening, volunteers to help Annabelle and Jemmy use the exercise equipment.

Honor and I begin mingling. Honor behaves, chatting with the twins' clientele and hugging those of their friends with whom she is acquainted. I pick the right moment and advocate an apology to Lucy for the ruckus at the book-signing table. I point out that Lucy will still be Honor's sister long after the book goes out of print.

"Honor wants to make up," I tell Lucy, to expedite the reconciliation. Lucy has been talking to an olive-complexioned woman wearing a leotard with the logo of a rival aerobics center and a soft full skirt.

"We meant to win you over with that dedication, Honor." Lucy addresses Honor in a deferential tone that identifies which sister is the older sibling, which the younger.

"You shouldn't have sprung the book and that dedication on me both in one day," Honor blasts, slipping slightly out of control. She collects herself, giving me a look. "But if that dedication was a heartfelt gesture, I'm sorry I got so upset."

"I'm sorry, too, Honor." They actually smile at each other. Honor pats Lucy's arm. Lucy remembers the woman with whom she'd been talking and pulls her forward.

"I'd like you to meet my sister, Honor Sutton," Lucy does introductions. "Honor's a commercial artist. And this is Eliza Pirex. Honor, Eliza, this is Claudia Hollings." The woman inclines her head our way, not focusing her attention.

I freeze.

Something doesn't fall into place immediately. Then it does. I've heard the name before, and recently.

"Did you once dance with the Jazzmatazz Dance Company in Santa Cruz?" I ask her.

"Yes, I did, a long time ago. But I didn't appear with them prominently. Did you see me dance and remember all this time?"

"No, someone mentioned you to me. I heard that you had a lot of promise." Did I hear that? Claudia smiles, vivid and confident.

"I got excellent mentions at the time. I guess a lot of dancers have initial promise. I had personal problems, though. I was never able to perform to capacity. When I think back, I could kick myself for not going all the way." She preens.

"I guess we do the best we can," she continues with hollow-sounding sentimentality. This woman looks too hard for sentiment. "Linden recently made me see that the flow of our lives has a course that isn't necessarily within our control." She gazes at me with a mocking, clever expression as she finishes the discourse.

Linden, our now-published spiritual adviser, obviously hands out a variation on the maxim "Go with the flow." Claudia may be camouflaging herself with his cliché.

"Who mentioned me to you?" Claudia asks, with audacious casualness. Honor has just grasped the significance of the woman's name and looks at me waiting to see what comes up. Claudia adds languidly, "I can't imagine who might remember my career with Jazzmatazz."

"I talked to a Mr. David Gray in San Francisco."

"I don't think I know him," says Claudia, looking genuinely blank.

"Funny thing," I tell her. "He stepped out of his apartment one day six years ago and, while he was gone, you were bludgeoned and killed in the apartment next door. Murdered." Claudia loses her composure only for a second. Then she pulls herself to full height and looks at me closer.

"God," she says. "I haven't thought about that for years."

"Dave isn't the only one under the impression that you were brutally killed. But I guess it may have slipped your mind. Just out of curiosity, can you tell me what happened?"

"It didn't slip my mind," she replies with frost on her voice. "There are events in my past which I have chosen to put behind me. I'm ashamed of things I did back then." Either she doesn't want to tell me the story, or she's stalling for time to put a story together. She pushes her soft fine curls behind her ears and assumes fifth position. I notice her excellent muscle tone, no rag doll, this one.

"How did you meet Dave Gray?" she asks, challenging me now. Lucy and Honor are riveted on every word. I can't create a fiction to trick the story out of Claudia without the risk of the Sutton sisters inadvertently tipping my hand.

"I'm a detective," I tell her. "I'm working on behalf of Ruth Gold." Every muscle in her face becomes rigid.

"I knew Ruthie," she chokes through clenched teeth. "But I haven't kept up with her."

"Well, you've been dead, you know," I point out. "She might be surprised to hear from you." I pause for a response. Would Ruthie be surprised? What did she know about Claudia's 'murder'?

"How is Ruthie? I missed her terribly after I left the company," Claudia now sounds matter-of-fact.

I consider how much I should reveal. I can't claim to be in touch with Ruthie. I have to proceed under the assumption that Claudia might know more about Ruthie's present state than I do. Maybe Ruthie knew the murder was a hoax and was in touch with Claudia after the time of Claudia's 'death.' I try to recall how much I heard about the alleged murder. Did Dave Gray mention paramedics, the neighbors who gawked at the body, the body's chalk outline on the floor, or an obituary in the newspaper, any of the things which constitute evidence of death in a city apartment? I can't remember anything concrete. I need to check my notes. I want copies of any police reports filed from Ruthie's old apartment as soon as I can finagle them from the S.F.P.D.

"I was hired to try and locate Ruthie," I tell Claudia after my deliberation.

"Eliza's a super detective," inserts Lucy loyally, "and much cheaper than most." I give Lucy a look intended to quell the endorsement, which she does. Claudia doesn't volunteer any more information.

"Did Ruthie know that you weren't really hit with a blunt object and killed?" I try the direct approach. Claudia gives me the impression that she's inching away although she isn't actually moving.

"No. I'm afraid she didn't." Claudia falls silent again.

"Did you ever think about letting her know?" I continue. Claudia's eyes scan the room, trying to arrange an exit.

"I couldn't," says Claudia, no warmer. "She'd left town by the time the joke was up." I have something to seize onto now.

"What do you mean by 'the joke was up'?" I ask before she can get away.

Claudia draws out the words reluctantly. "It was my boyfriend's idea of fun. I just agreed to go along with him."

"You agreed to let your friend, Ruthie, think for the rest of her life that you'd been murdered in her apartment," I spell out for her, "as a joke?"

"I said, it was my boyfriend's idea of a gag. He said he and his friend had a score to settle with Ruthie. It was only going to be for a while. But Ruthie left town without telling anyone. She certainly didn't tell me." I have become exasperated with the sullen Claudia.

"It probably didn't occur to her to give you a buzz at the police mortuary," I suggest. "Isn't that where she thought you would be?"

Claudia's look takes on a more hostile cast. "It was a childish joke. I admit that. You'll have to excuse me. I'm on my way to another engagement."

"Just a couple more questions," I ask, trying to sound respectful when, in fact, I'm frantic to discover why she stands here in the flesh. I wish I'd worked harder to ingratiate myself so she wouldn't be as eager to escape me now.

"Eliza's very dogged," Lucy jokes. "You may as well give up and tell her what she wants to know. Be nice to her, Eliza, Claudia's one of our hottest competitors. She teaches aerobics at South Street Spa and Gym. She's a partner in the place." Claudia glares at Lucy. I assume Claudia would rather that Lucy didn't tell me anything.

"Where is Jane Gold, Ruthie's sister?" I throw out.

"I have no idea. Jane left about a few days before Ruthie. She had become anorexic while she was dancing with the company. She went to stay with her parents in Los Angeles to recover."

"You didn't keep in touch with her at all? I heard that you and Jane were good friends." Lucy looks lost in this past history. Honor seems to follow.

"We had a very final falling out. I never heard a word from her again." I haven't checked social security records, etc., but I would be willing to bet that I will find no records on Jane after that year. Four Golds appear to have disappeared from the earth at the same time. By now, I'm irritated.

"What was your boyfriend's name?" I want Claudia to feel barraged by questions.

"Kurt," she says shortly.

"Kurt what?"

"We had a short, lousy relationship and a bad break-up. I barely remember his last name." The two onlookers and I try skeptical silence. Lucy studies Claudia, obviously ready to re-evaluate her opinion of her fellow businesswoman for the worse. Claudia rotates her shoulders. Fitness instructors know these kinds of tricky techniques to relax.

"I'm sure Eliza can track down the guy's last name in a snap, if you can't remember it," says steadfast Lucy.

"Brewster," Claudia says finally, through still-gritted teeth.

"So. Why in the world would your friend Kurt Brewster want to play this murder joke on Ruthie? How did he per-suade you to go along with it?" I ask. Honor leans forward aggressively.

"I think it was mainly his buddy's idea," Claudia says as though she has been dredging her memory. "They were always getting in trouble together."

"What was the buddy's name?" I ask, trying not to sound sharp.

"He was just a drinking buddy. He didn't spend much time at our apartment. Ruthie knew him." I am shocked to hear her volunteer a piece of relevant information. "He got pissed at Ruthie," she volunteers further.

"See if you can remember his name," I press. "Was it a common name? Like John or Bill?"

"I don't exactly remember." She realizes right away that 'exactly' was a bad word to use. We know she knows. She pretends to have an inspiration and grudgingly tells me, "Kurt called him Stu, but Ruthie called him Lilly." Honor and I glance at each other meaningfully. I catch a satisfied glimmer on Claudia's lips. I wonder what's the source of the satisfaction.

I need to snatch clearer answers from Claudia before she gets away. Could Claudia be constructing a story on the spot? Or did she actually get involved in the murder setup as a joke, a joke constructed by Kurt the boyfriend and Dr. Stuart

Lilienthal? What happened between Ruthie and Claudia to culminate in Claudia selling Ruthie out?

"You gave up your place in the dance company at the same time as you got involved in the 'joke' on Ruthie?" I continue with the least threatening question that I can think of.

"I injured a tendon the year before. It was nothing major but it affected my work. I had to face the fact that I might never make it as a professional. I let myself drift before looking for a new direction. Eventually, I realized that I wanted to help people get fit and live longer. That's what I've done ever since."

You didn't do much for Ruthie's fitness, if I have the story correct, I think to myself. I say, "Can we get together some time? At your convenience, of course. I might be able to set your mind to rest about Ruthie, when I've completed my investigation and located her."

Claudia doesn't look like she's expecting me to dance Ruthie through the door tomorrow. She doesn't deign to reply. I continue, "In the meantime, maybe if you would give me more information about Ruthie at the time you knew her last, your material would fill in the picture. I'd be happy to compensate you for your time."

"I don't need to know whether you find Ruthie. She and I wouldn't have anything in common at this point. I'd rather not discuss the past any further. I'm a different person." She sashays away, as though on point, saying to Lucy as she goes, "I'm so excited about your book. Thanks so much for putting us in the appendix."

Claudia heads into the crowd, passing us on my side. Her gaze rests on me and although she's technically smiling, I feel menaced. Ruthie had odd taste in friends.

"I've always thought Claudia seemed cold," says Lucy. "She's a terrific instructor, though. Her classes have waiting lists a mile long." Lucy seems to consider her rift with Honor repaired. She links arms with her older sister and smiles ingenuously.

"You and Eliza have to meet our fortune teller, Myra. Myra's her middle name actually but her first name, Georgette, doesn't sound right for a working psychic reader," recommends Lucy. Honor and I have no intention of looking up the fortune teller. We check on Nancy. Nancy seems to have transferred her admiration for Honor to the dashing Linden. She ogles him and repeats rapturously his every sententious remark. Honor doesn't waste time needling Linden.

She's probably relying upon Lucy to convey her threats and disillusionment to him.

Newell Sutton searches us out to introduce a lady friend who accompanied him here. We stand with party guests occasionally streaming between us. Newell's friend, Genevieve, looks about 55 and her body doesn't have the lean and taut look to which the crowd in general aspires, a pleasant change. I enjoy the soft, fleshy handshake before we're separated again.

"Newell," I call on impulse, "Jemmy confessed that he told you about one of my clients. I think you know her husband, Rich Goldeen. Are you friends with him? Or were you?"

"Never heard of him," Newell says without missing a beat. "Have a nice evening, girls. I'll see you soon." He and his date disappear in a flash.

Honor and I sight her brother, Christopher, and hustle to avoid him. Christopher, infatuated with his drug-free state and recent business coups, might be the straw that breaks Honor's back. I ask Honor if we can try some refreshments after all. I promise not to eat appreciatively. On our way, we pass a woman in bangles and scarves sitting at a card table draped with a bedspread, or cloth, of mystical design.

"You must be Honor," she cries when she sees us. She sends an athletic-looking couple, who've been sitting in front of her, on their way with a standard fortuneteller line. "You look just like your brother," she tells Honor. "Linden tells me that you're a sensitive. Although your inner resources may be out of use."

"I give my resources plenty of exercise," answers Honor smartly. No inner voice, I see, tells Myra that trifling with Honor tonight won't accomplish anything good.

"Let me lay out the cards for you," she wheedles. When she moves her head, cumbersome plastic earrings click and thud against each other and against her collarbone.

"No thanks," Honor quashes her.

"Then for you," she persists, pointing at me.

"Well," I hesitate.

"Don't," says Honor. Myra smiles at me and the cards start snapping into place.

Suddenly, Myra's face contorts, the stock reaction of a circus fortuneteller in a B movie. "Death. Near you, very near you."

"Jesus Christ. I asked you not to do this number," Honor yells at her. "I'm not in the mood. Eliza, tell her to stop."

"The cards hold a warning for you," Myra says in a subdued voice.

"I've had enough for one fun-filled evening, Eliza. I want to go home, immediately. I need a bath." Honor seizes my hand.

"Nice to meet you," I say to Myra as I'm dragged away. Myra looks up, her black eyes very open.

She raises her left hand and shakes her rings. She's wearing a lot of rings and they must be loose, they make a clanking noise. I see a card on the table with a man hanging by the neck on a chain. I'm sure the card can't mean good news.

"God damn it, Eliza, let's leave," Honor pulls me off-balance in her haste.

Honor elbows her way into the crowd. Still staggering a few steps later, I look up into the face of someone with spectacular muscles and a far-from-scholarly face. I hope that he has materialized here on his way to somewhere else but no such luck. He flexes one over-developed bicep and addresses me in a low harsh voice, another B movie bit player.

"Don't come near South Street Gym or you won't leave in good shape. Don't call, don't give us another thought." He grabs my arm. I twist his arm back. I may not pay dues at a gym or keep my muscles perfectly defined but I am tough enough to make sure I'm not manhandled, ever.

"I'll go where I like," I say.

"Eliza, I thought we agreed, no more lollygagging with the party guests," Honor comes back to collect me. She often talks like Mary Poppins when she's mad. She doesn't give the muscle from South Street a second look, which is good because I don't want her anywhere near him.

I send him a parting arch of an eyebrow which I hope conveys defiance and strength although I'm not sure how much one eyebrow can articulate. First thing tomorrow, I am going to pursue records on Claudia Hollings. But why look for trouble? I'm going to send Dennis to South Street Gym instead of going myself. If Claudia thinks she can persuade me to ignore her resurrection, she misjudges me.

We collect our party. I have no energy left for enjoying Rochelle. Honor winces every time Nancy's high-pitched voice shrills across the van. Annabelle sits behind Honor and massages her mother's neck muscles with strong twelve-year-old fingers. Jemmy falls asleep beside me. His little-boy breathing becomes deep and even, a soothing sensation.

When everyone has been deposited in their proper places and made comfortable, Honor and I go into our bedroom which has a balcony overhanging the back garden. All the bulbs that Honor laid in the flower beds two years ago have started to enjoy their most perfect period of growth. I see them in black and white below and smell them in our room. I expect to go straight to sleep, but Honor doesn't turn down the comforter. She comes toward me with her arms open.

She moves against me, her hips circling in a warm pressure I know becomes sex. I carefully touch the deerskin-brown down on her subtle beige skin. I undo the grey and black silk-covered buttons at her throat. Goosebumps light her skin and she shivers next to my fingers.

The phone rings.

"Jesus Christ. You get it," murmurs Honor. She detaches slowly and lets me move. I try to clear my head enough to get the phone. I make my way to the bedside table and pick up the receiver.

"Eliza Pirex, please," a strained official voice comes out of the receiver.

"Speaking."

"This is James Arteuga, with security over here at Kains College. I've been trying to reach you this evening." He has a lot of responsibility at the school after hours. He's the person to whom I called in sick this morning. As far as he knows, I'm a Busy Bee Building Maintenance employee. He doesn't sound like he's calling to complain about me shirking my wastebaskets. He normally treats me considerately, however, and I notice that tonight he doesn't even say, "How are you."

"How are you this evening, James? What can I do for you?"

"Roy Garber, the administrator on call, gave me your name. He said to call you right away. Then he told me that you've been on duty here to keep an eye on my men." James sounds increasingly sober. Does he resent having had a woman private investigator secreted among "his men"? I wonder.

"Yes, I have, James. I think it's okay to let you know that I haven't encountered any problems with your men." I don't know what to say further since I don't understand the purpose of his call and don't know exactly how much I am at liberty to say. Honor lies on the bed in a camisole and underpants doing a good job being distracting.

"There sure are problems now, Eliza. We got another black girl roughed up over here."

"I beg your pardon?" slips out of me.

"Leakey found her in the D Building dumpster with hardly anything on. Roy Garber came and he's holding

Dwayne Blount up at the Main Office until you get here. I know you and Dwayne have been friendly. Roy Garber let Dwayne know who you really are and Dwayne wanted you to come right over."

I consider the news. The news sounds bad. "Do you know any more than what you've told me?" I ask finally.

"Not much. I wouldn't have thought Dwayne would do something like this. He's too hot to trot, you know that. I believe he would try hitting on the college girls, maybe too hard, to get a date. But he's basically a decent guy. He works with the Scouts and all. If he doesn't like black people he never let on to me. They said you're here to look for someone who doesn't like the black girls."

"I've been looking for improper conduct of any kind. But as I said, I haven't seen anything going on that shouldn't be."

"Are you going to come over and, uh, check out what happened with this girl?"

"Have the police been called?"

"Mr. Garber said to wait on you. He thinks the girl will keep." I certainly hope Garber's right. His background is in Business Administration, I doubt he has much expertise in emergency medicine.

I glance at Honor stretched in elegant contours across the bed. "Yes, all right. I'm on my way." Honor raises her head, surprised.

I hang up and begin to shed my party clothes. I fill Honor in on the development at the college. She's upset, not having looked for this particular job to bring physical violence into our lives. But since the violence has already settled itself upon someone else's head, she agrees without a fight to let me go survey the trouble.

"I'll miss you. Thanks for being my faithful protector this evening. I'm crazy about you," she says. She wraps herself around me in a goodbye embrace.

The phone rings. "I'll get it," Honor sighs. I begin getting out work clothes, pants, boots, and a heavy sweater.

I'm rooting around for thick socks when I hear Honor suck her breath in with a low sound in her throat. She drops the receiver noisily into the cradle. "Great," she says.

"What was that?" I ask her.

"Someone left a message and hung up. I didn't get his name."

"What message?" I demand.

"Forgot to put the cat out," she repeats unhappily. We don't have a cat.

93
▲

Former Christian missionaries founded Kains College. The school moved from Santa Maria, further down the coast, to its present site in Oakland, well over one hundred years ago. I've read their catalogue. They bill themselves as an elite women's college with a striking assembly of California architecture, including famous examples of Mansard Roof and Victorian design. Scholars stroll through exotic formal gardens, in a lush park-like setting defined by a meandering stream. The place glows like a well-kept and matchless rose surrounded by acres of common plants with tangled weeds among them. I went to a different kind of college.

My drive takes me through quiet Oakland communities which inherited the college as a neighbor. Inside small stucco houses, residents lie drowsing uneasily on their mattresses, preparing for tomorrow's commerce and quandaries. Their children slumber in colorful cartoon bedsheets. These children probably won't grow up to become students at Kains College. The college's neighbors don't attend the school in as great a number as they seek employment there, becoming clerks and laborers. They reap subsistence wages, if not a classical education, right in their own back yard.

I try to keep my mind, as I drive, on the pleasures of Honor. I can't, though. The insinuation of violence subsumes sex. So I let myself wonder whether I will be able to continue the job I was hired to do at Kains College.

Unlikely, I decide. I can't operate from the inside now that the guys with whom I've been working know who I am. I don't want to hire other operatives who would report to me, too time-consuming to be profitable. I'll need to refer the job to another agency and get out altogether.

The college administration might not even trust my guidance on a referral if they blame me for the incident tonight. As an independent contractor, I have every right to skip one day's surveillance. Unfortunately, the boom fell while I was out playing hooky.

When I pull into the near-empty parking lot at the college, I see James Arteuga standing at the far side of the Service Staff area. Mercury lamps cut through thickening fog. I jump out and lock the door of my car. When I turn around, James has moved behind the car and it takes me a few nervous seconds to focus my eyes on him again. I can't afford to be jumpy when I work. I switch into operating mode, a state in which I detach myself from tension and sensations.

James clutches his Oakland A's mesh baseball cap. I have never before seen the cap off his head. He has twisted his hat into serpentine form. I wonder if he owns a set of similar hats or just the one. I saunter toward him and clap him on the shoulder, trying to be comforting. He doesn't seem able to initiate speech.

"You okay, James?" I ask.

"What am I going to do, Eliza?" he asks in a heavy voice, now that I have made the first effort to communicate. "A young lady got hurt after hours, when I'm responsible for safety on campus. And I've never had one of my men in trouble like this before." James, a black man in his fifties, supervises Dwayne and Lee, white men in their twenties. Dwayne and Lee are buddies with each other. I've never known how much James likes the rambunctious Dwayne and arrogant Lee but, at this moment, James appears genuinely concerned for Dwayne.

"James, it sounds like a girl has been attacked by some unknown assailant. The right thing to do is call the police," I point out to him.

"Before we do, will you take a look at her? Maybe she really is okay. Once we call the regular police, Dwayne is in a real big mess. I know it. The police aren't going to turn loose a poor slob like Dwayne. Dwayne was born for trouble. The police will see trouble the minute they set eyes on him and keep him shut up tighter than a cashbox after hours, whether he did anything or not." There's a fuzzy line, in America, between cover-up and friendship. I don't take time to survey that line with James right now.

"What made Garber decide that the girl doesn't need medical attention?" I ask. "What's her name?"

"She won't tell us her name. She doesn't want us to call her mother." James shakes his head. "She doesn't want a doctor even though she doesn't look right as far as I can see." James reshapes his hat as he speaks and puts it on.

"Didn't one of you check her carefully?" I put to him.

"She won't let any of us in the dumpster with her," James replies with no trace of defensiveness.

"She's still in the dumpster?" I feel sickened by the image of a young woman thrown into a dumpster like a piece of trash. I assumed that they had, at the least, extricated her from the scene of the crime. "Let's get moving, James. Do you know anything about the girl, or about what might have happened to her tonight?"

James' eyes rove the empty paths ahead. "I don't think Dwayne did it. That means maybe the real perpetrator is still around. We need to look out. I guess that's your kind of job. You being a detective. Me and my men have no practice with injury. We get disorderlies."

"I'm keeping an eye out," I guarantee. I do have experience with crime victims, more even than I bargained for when I became a private investigator. But I don't take time to discuss my résumé a short radius from an injured young person whose assault demands reprisal.

James looks down at his gun and seems surprised to find it at his side. Gentle James doesn't strike me as the type of security guard eager to exercise his firearm. Dwayne and Lee, on the other hand, have regaled me with stories of the spectacular style in which they might "take someone out," should the occasion ever arise. I give brief thanks that I have James at my side and Dwayne out of the way, rather than vice versa.

"Some girls from the dorms say they saw Dwayne following the girl," says James, "maybe scuffling with her over by Henry K. Roe Hall. I called Roy Garber, he was on the list as on-call administrator, and when Roy got here he felt like he should keep Dwayne locked up in the main office while we waited for you to get here.

"The college girls think Dwayne caused the problems. None of them has gospel proof it was Dwayne though. They also say they might know the injured girl. If the girl in the dumpster is who they think she is, she's a quiet girl and one of the witnesses has a class with her but doesn't remember her name." I think I follow. Circumstances and concern for

Dwayne have rendered James both more garrulous and less lucid than usual.

"You and I will reserve judgement on Dwayne," I say.

"Right," James says hopefully. He seems to have made, without faltering, the leap from interacting with me as a non-tenured janitor to relying upon my facility to bail his man out of a bind. His pleasant face sags with concern. The moist baseball hat droops down over one ear.

I decide to applaud James' character to the administration in my exit report. He has been respectful and professional in his dealings with me. I recall small niceties James has done for co-workers who don't garner much attention from anybody else. James and I walk around the side of B Building and through the boxwood hedges in the back. James uses one of his passkeys to let us in the front door of D Building.

"Lee, we're up front," he yells down a corridor. His voice gets swallowed by the stairwell instead of bouncing back. The building, as usual, gives off that stale, sour smell that the nocturnal absence of students brings to the attention of the senses. College students don't leave much gum under the tables but something they do produce is a grubby aura in their wake. I realize that I've developed an expertise in the area of college cleaning, one which will probably lie fallow after tonight.

Frances Leakey, who likes to be called Lee, shouts, "I've got the exit door propped open with a sponge. Come on back here." Lee doesn't get to carry a full set of keys. I, too, in my janitress persona, was issued only keys for inside locks. James carries external and internal door keys. James locks up the buildings when they have been patroled and cleaned.

"I told Lee to sit watch over the dumpster," James explains. He looks apprehensively down the corridor. He takes off his hat, wrings it, and puts it back on. We tread the passage cautiously. The floor's gleam and slipperiness prove someone else's industry earlier this evening. We pass the washroom with its double sinks scoured and mops stored on their hooks, but never again by me.

When we get to the corridor's end, James stops. "I should go back and check on Dwayne. He's bound to be nervous sitting in the office with Mr. Garber, not knowing if we're going to call the police on him. You have Lee help you all you need." The offer of Lee's help doesn't inspire jubilation in me but I sense that James finds seeing the girl in the dumpster upsetting. "I'll unlock any outside doors you might want to go through if you join us later in the Main Office," James promises in parting.

I slip outside, replacing the hardened sponge in the door. Lee brightens when he sees me. "James take off? He trusts me with her," Lee says. I assume 'her' pertains to the injured woman.

"Anything you can tell me before I talk to her?" I ask.

"I'm the one that found her. I saw the dumpster lid open so I shined my flashlight down from the platform on the other side. I saw a body. She looked dead but I knew it could be that she had so much fun at one of those dorm parties she came out here and passed out." Lee doesn't leave me time to take offense before he continues his narrative.

"I went down the ramp, climbed up top the bin, and looked in." Lee modulates his voice to avoid revealing his growing excitement. "Could be she's a real pretty girl. If she were dressed up she might look real good. Like the girl on the billboard for rum I always look at on High Street in front of Lucky's. Except her clothes are torn and her head is messed up. It came to mind right then that maybe she hadn't passed out from liquor, maybe she hurt herself." Lee speeds up so I can't stop him. I look through the dark for the easiest route into the dumpster.

"I could have gone in and touched her right away. I have nothing against touching the blacks. I bump shoulders with James all the time. But I remembered—never touch the injured. You don't know when their back might be broke. Of course, this one turned out to have hurt her head not her spine, so it didn't matter, but James said it was good how I kept my head and remembered the procedure for the injured."

Lee comes on duty at 11:00, so I have shared an hour of every evening shift with him. After a while, Lee began to fascinate me. He faces his narrow existence with total self-absorption instead of anger, or sadness. I found myself looking forward to hearing whether his dispirited wife, with her high blood pressure and colon condition, "put out" for Lee over the weekend. But I'm not enjoying him now. This man neglected to call paramedics to help a woman with head injuries. He placed concern for his possibly guilty buddy over her life.

We stand in the lighted circle projected by a caged industrial wattage bulb which overhangs the service door. The territory beyond the bulb's province looks threatening. I am tired, I let myself get distracted for a second thinking about the numbers of Lees, thoughtless, prejudiced, and sanctioned to carry a gun, running around a city populated by people of many colors and diverse ways of being. I take comfort in the thought that, as a private investigator, I meet a higher percentage of Lees than I would in another line of work and might have developed a distorted perspective.

"She was talking fine by the time I got back here with James." Lee has been droning on as I have been concluding how to approach the injured woman.

"Stick around in case I need you to help me get her out," I say. I am determined to compensate for the lousy treatment this woman has received thus far. "And Lee, be ready to call for help after I see what shape she's in."

I don't have easy access to the sturdy wheeled ladder we bring up to the bin when we want to get rid of rubbish. It's been moved to Building A which had its big cleaning earlier tonight. So I have decided to chin up on the dumpster's sheer wall. After pulling myself aloft, I sit balanced on one knee with one leg hanging into the rectangular dark cavity.

I look across at the dumpster's heavy, hinged lid lying thrown back against the platform on the other side. I notice a smear that could be mud, could be hair and blood. But the smear might mean that the woman was carried here and thrown into the dumpster, hitting the lid and then falling inside. Or fell in accidently? Not possible. If it's blood I see, she could be hurt worse than I have been led to believe.

I peer into the gloom. The few threads of light that emanate from the back door bulb illuminate, dully, a body with womanly contours. Subtle silver-grey glimmers highlight her form as though the police have outlined the position of her body with their white chalk. She sits atop refuse composed mostly of paper. The garbage accumulated here comes from classroom and lavatory wastebaskets.

Still hanging onto the side, I glance back at Lee. He eyes me, jealous because I get to look close up at a lady pretty as a billboard and he must remain standing below just like on High Street. I've learned to shut off so I don't have to experience the impact of proximity to a victim. The impact I would have felt presses on my temples. Lee, for some reason, salutes me, touching fingers to his forehead.

I boost over the rim, hang by two hands along the inside wall, and then drop into spongy, damp paper. I fight for balance as though I'm trying to make a turn while walking through snow. Finally, I face the girl. The thin wall of iron that separates me and Lee separates us entirely. Some journeys happen inside small containers.

She pulls her knees close to her body and wraps her arms around them. She doesn't make a sound. Her thin white dress, patterned with pictures of summer fruit, would have torn easily. She appears scared but I can't see where she's been hurt. Her eyes look alert. When James told me that they had a "roughed-up" black girl, his language conjured the image of an ordinary college girl in need of iodine.

She doesn't have technically perfect looks, but she possesses an enticing quality which expands the blood vessels in my fingertips and forehead. I hate the idea of putting her charms under the jurisdiction of the Oakland Police.

"Please tell me your name," I say quietly. When she doesn't reply, I add, "I'm here to make sure you're all right."

"I'm fine. I can walk now. Leave me alone." She speaks with a keen but sultry voice.

"I have to know your name," I tell her. "I'm working with Campus Security. If you've been injured, we're responsible for you. Did someone hurt you?"

I jump out of my skin when the young woman screams and keeps screaming until she expels a satisfied breath, a last puff of tension. I can hear muffled echoes of yelling from outside the dumpster. "We're all right, Lee," I shout. "Lee, we're fine."

The girl cups her face in her hands, looking more relaxed, and gazes at me. She's muddy. She could have been over at Critten Gardens which were watered tonight. I stare back at her, looking for a hunch on how to handle her. I stop expecting her to respond but eventually one side of her shining mouth curls.

"You all think you can push at me. You all think you're the masters of the human mind. I hate it. Pretend you lost me, leave me alone," she confronts me with passion. With her riveting appearance and eloquent speaking voice, she could go into the theater or sell real estate in San Francisco.

I view the girl with greater attention. The security force didn't exhibit brilliant powers of observation. My eye, honed by years of child-rearing, picks up something they did not—this girl doesn't look old enough to be a college student. She looks about fourteen or fifteen. Her breasts haven't really bloomed and the dimples on her knees lie in a light layer of baby fat that will have burned off in a few years. Her skin radiates a dewy quality that disappears around the age of graduation from high school.

"I'm not going to tell you what to do," I say to her in the placating tone I use when my children have gotten worked up. Now that I realize I'm dealing with a kid, I will communicate with her in a slightly different fashion. "I need to figure out what I can do for you."

"Nothing," she cries. "I want nothing. Except I can't get out of here without a ladder. I need a ladder but don't want to get out until everyone has gone. I can get home by myself." She seems pretty in control, I'm not going to try to examine her condition further, which would distress her.

I notice for the first time a jarring element in the environment. A new pink canvas backpack with a suede bottom lies tossed in the back left corner. If the janitorial staff made such a find in the school, they would have taken the object to the lost and found closet in A Building. They would never have dumped the thing with the trash.

"Is this yours?" I ask, having already deduced that it must be. She doesn't reply. A fine-boned hand with nails carefully painted shell-pink with silver glitter goes to her mouth. She chews at the paint on one finger. I notice that the girl has lost one of her flashy shoes. The set of toenails I can see matches her fingernails.

I pick up the canvas backpack and examine the outside for clues about the owner. Nothing. The top flap has been tied down neatly, the front pocket zipped.

I unzip the front pocket first. I watch the girl with one eye. If she objects, I will desist from invading her property. She doesn't demur. I find a pair of underpants and a plastic toothbrush holder with two tampax inside. I have to dig with my fingernails at the knot securing the top. I pull out a black purse containing a plastic wallet with pictures encased in the plastic holder, a lipstick, eyeliner, a small Kleenex packet, emery boards, and keys which look like car keys. Is she older than I think? She'd have to be sixteen to drive. I find no driver's license or identification. At the bottom of the knapsack, I locate a notebook and two paperback books, one large, one standard size.

I turn to the first page of the wide-ruled notebook. The right-hand page has been covered in twirls and doodles interspersed with small line drawings of women's faces, faces with caricature features and elaborate hairstyles. On the left-hand side, the notebook manufacturer put a box with spaces for the owner to write name, address, classes and classroom numbers. The box stares blankly back at me. The girl stares blankly too.

102
▲

I open the large book which could be a high school French language text book. A name written in the lined paper glued inside has been scratched out messily with ball-point pen. I flip through the book, put it down beside me and fish for the other one. The second book appears to be stuck to the canvas. The sticky paperback cover pulls away easily in my hand.

The book's cover says *Sweet Valley High: Too Much In Love*. The illustration pictures a sappy-looking white teenage boy and girl. I open the book. Written inside the cover in careful, curving script, I read, "Tara Timmin." The handwriting fits. I'm here with Tara Timmin.

"You must be Tara. Tara, can't I call someone to come and get you?" I smile, a not too overbearing smile. Her face doesn't even twitch in return.

"I am my own person. You don't even know my name," her voice drips sarcasm and hostility. After eighteen, the majority in our culture lose the ability to make other people feel foolish and wrong the way teenagers can. I remember when I had the talent. Honor retains a remnant to this day. Tara's power hasn't even peaked and it's already impressive.

"Tara." I almost call her "honey" as I would an injured child. I swallow the endearment. "I admire your independence but I have to take matters into my own hands. Since you seem basically okay, I'm going to leave you here. Lee will be right outside. If you do decide you want out, call for him. You want to change your mind and come with me?"

"Leave me alone," she says. For such an attractive girl, she sounds mean.

I knock on the wall of the dumpster. "Coming out," I yell to Lee. I look back one last time at Tara. She emits a mild unearthly glow. Enchanting women possess this evanescence in good times or bad times, I'm happy to see.

I drop neatly onto the asphalt outside the dumpster. "I'm going to make a few phone calls," I tell Lee. "I think that I can contact her family." Lee gawks at me, mouth open. He still feels accustomed to being one up on me, security over maintenance.

"How do you know who she is?" he asks.

"Tricks of the trade," I reply lightly. He salutes again.

I decide to use the secretary's phone in the Philosophy Department. We've spent time in that office during work nights because they have a good new General Electric coffee maker. When I get there, I phone to tell the main office where I am.

If Lee were here watching, I would sacrifice some of the mystique generated by my newly revealed detective status: I have to engage in a clumsy hunt through the shelves and drawers around the secretary's desk to find an Oakland phone book. I miss the book at first because of the blue plastic jacket with advertisements for local businesses printed in white letters, obscuring the familiar cover. The Department Secretary keeps an open mayonnaise jar full of cellophane-wrapped butterscotch candy. I eat one, now that I'm here as myself rather than as a contract maintenance company employee.

I look down the columns of 'T' names. The page lists a fair number of Timmons, but the girl's cursive spelled her name out clearly. I'm sure I have the correct spelling. I move my eyes back up the columns and locate three Timmins and one Timmin, Earl Timmin, 463 Muto Boulevard.

I try Earl Timmin's number. A woman's voice says, "Hello, who is this?" She sounds like she's been sleeping heavily.

"Is this Tara Timmin's residence?" I don't want to explain myself to someone drugged with sleep. I hope for a short answer.

"Tara? Vonda's girl? What would she be doing here? Who are you?"

"I'm looking for the parents of Tara Timmin," I tell her, speaking slow and loud. "I'm with security at Kains College. Are you a relative?"

"Earl, he's my husband, his brother used to be married to Vonda, Tara's mother. Kenneth, Tara's daddy, hasn't been around for about ten years, though. What do you want with Tara? What's that girl got herself into now? Worrying her mother with every boy in town calling her up night and day. And now you. What do you want with us?" Her voice gets sharper with each sentence.

"It's college business, ma'am. Can you give me a number where I might reach Vonda Timmin?"

"She's Vonda Everett now."

"It's important that I reach her tonight. Can you give me a telephone number?" She finally lets exhaustion take precedence over her natural caution and coughs up the number. I tell her to call Kains College Security tomorrow for further explanation if she wishes. Maybe she won't have any memory of my call by then. I dial the number she gave me.

"Vonda Everett?" I respond to a terse hello.

"Yes. Who is this? Is this about Tara?"

104
▲

"My name is Eliza Pirex. I think I might have Tara here with me at Kains College."

"What's she doing there? She went out with her step-daddy and didn't come home yet. I've been sitting here on the sofa for hours, ready to scream." Vonda sounds close to screaming right now.

"What's happened to my little girl?" she cries out.

"The girl we have here has minor injuries, cuts and scrapes, but nothing more as far as I can tell." The mother breathes rapidly as though I've punched her in the chest. "Let's make sure this is your daughter," I say. "Can you describe Tara for me? Age, height, weight, distinguishing features?"

"Who are you?" Vonda asks in lieu of a reply.

"I'm with security at Kains College. I need a description of Tara to know whether or not we're talking about your daughter." The phone goes silent long enough for Vonda to take a cleansing breath.

She makes a derisive noise into the receiver. "You couldn't get her name out of her?" Her tone changes, she panics again. "She can talk, can't she?"

"Yes, I spoke with her. She was a little uncooperative. Can you please tell me what your daughter looks like?"

"She's prettier than girls her age. She makes a good impression and everyone remembers her. She's a good girl. She tells me everything. We're real tight."

"How old is Tara?"

"She turned fourteen this last February. But some take her for older," the woman's voice trails off nervously. I have to keep digging at her.

"Height?" I ask. It's the question with which people feel the most comfortable, the least personal.

"Five foot seven. She's tall for a Fay, that's my family name. She's just the right weight. She has straightish hair, naturally straightish." She pauses. "What else do you want to know?"

"Can you describe anything Tara was carrying when you saw her last?"

"She had her black purse with her. And she had her knapsack. A pink knapsack she carries odds and ends in and her books."

"Was Tara wearing nail polish on her fingers and toes? Do you know, by any chance?" This mom sounds like the kind who would know what nail polish her daughter has on. Vonda has become too agitated not to answer.

"She was wearing 'Coral Sands,' and it has silver in it. I buy her polish. What are you getting at? Why do you want to know about her polish? She was wearing white heels with pointy toes. What about them? Where are her shoes? Why have you been looking at her feet? Her stepfather should have brought her home safe. Give me my daughter." I wince at the pitch of her voice.

"Can you meet me at the Main Administration Office on the Kains College campus? We'll go together to pick up your daughter." I give Vonda Everett directions to get to the college. She tells me she'll be coming by cab so she doesn't need my useless directions because the cab driver will know the best route. She hangs up on me.

I haven't handled this call one whit better than the Oakland Police would have. Probably not as smoothly. I left the woman hysterical with anxiety. Maybe the girl will have gotten out of the dumpster before her mother gets here. I would much rather she didn't have to see her child sitting in damp paper towels.

I walk over to join James Arteuga in the office where he guards the suspect Dwayne. Administrator-on-call Roy Garber has been in the men's room for some time. Dwayne tells us that Roy Garber's secretary calls him "old pea bladder." Dwayne doesn't look chagrined by tonight's events, he must be unsquelchable.

I stand beside the central faculty bulletin board and skim the posted notices. The staff 'Welcome Summer' barbecue will be held in Joaquin Miller Park, Sunday, June 5th (attendees must contribute $8.00 per person by May 27). Graduate assistant Bradley Evigan gave a free Saturday evening lecture on "Pre-Menstrual Syndrome and Resultant Auditory Distortion in the Therapy Setting." Some faculty wag scribbled on the flyer, "Last chance to pitch eggs at Brad Evigan, master of the human mind." A stern warning threatens a fine for staff members whose automobile burglar alarms sound off and interfere with classroom instruction. I get bored and offer to help James with paperwork.

James and I wade through 'Accident Report,' checking 'result: injury,' and proceed to detail the discovery of Tara Timmin. We move on to 'Security Incident—After College Hours.' We check 12 a.m.-6 a.m., at which point the door to the Dean's Office opens. A tall, tense-looking professorial man, wearing a sand-colored jacket over a sweater and corduroy pants, pads toward us on those thin-soled shoes that academic men wear when they're not wearing running shoes.

"Evening, Mr. Garber," chorus James and Dwayne.

"Hi," I say without much enthusiasm. I don't expect him to be pleased to see me this evening, with a black girl whom I should have protected cooling her heels in the D Building dumpster.

"Will someone be coming to collect the," Roy Garber pauses, searching for a reference, "the alleged victim?" He seems to have missed the fact that the victim does not allege anything, she just wants to get away from us.

"I've contacted her mother," I tell him. He looks relieved.

"Thank you, Ms. Pirex." Garber gets out a notecard. "Which man is this, James," he asks, "Blount or Leakey?" I doubt Roy Garber's shift has ever coincided with Dwayne's. The administrators pop in and out of their offices between 10:00 a.m. and 4:00 p.m.

"This one here is Dwayne Blount," says James, twisting his A's cap in his hands again.

"I don't have anything to do with this," Dwayne speaks up. "I didn't even talk to anybody all night." Dwayne sounds less perturbed than James.

Lack of sleep has made Roy peevish and he barks, "That's for Ms. Pirex to determine. This is what we're paying her a substantial dollar amount per hour for." James sends me and Dwayne a condoling look.

"I will, sir," I assure him.

"Hopefully, we'll be able to head off any implication that the College is responsible or that there are racial overtones to this incident. I think a public revelation that we hired you, Ms. Pirex, in order to prevent an occurrence of this kind before the fact, will show that we are in no way accountable." Roy sounds pedantic even late at night.

We all jump, as if guilty, at the volcanic entrance of a well-dressed woman with a fierce look on her face. "You must be Vonda Everett," I say. "I'm Eliza Pirex and these are college employees, James, Dwayne, and Roy." For varying reasons, no one looks happy with my introductions.

"Take me to my girl before I call the police," replies Vonda. She doesn't strike me as a mincer of words.

"Go right along," urges Roy. "I'll take care of things on this end." I feel obliged to him because of missing this evening's work, so I tacitly agree to take on the raging Vonda, the hard job.

Vonda erupts into movement, toward the door. I follow in her wake. Outside in the corridor she demands to know, "Which way?" instead of waiting to follow me. I jerk one thumb to the right. We don't halt until we face the dumpster.

"Tara Timmin," yells Vonda, "It's your Mama. Get out of that trash heap right this second or I'm going to turn your social life into garbage for the next two years. This lady says you're not hurt bad."

"How am I going to get myself out of here, Mama?" Tara calls meekly.

Vonda turns to Lee, boiling, and says, "Are you going to help her out or not?" Her tone implies that Lee's conduct has been anything but gentlemanly.

Lee's eyes gleam at the chance to make physical contact with the glimmering girl. He turns to me. "How do I get her out? I can't get around to the other side, I don't have the keys. Shall I go get the ladder?"

Before I can reply, Vonda does. "Tara has gymnastics every week. If you give her a boost up the wall on the inside, she can climb over and out."

"Mrs. Everett, your daughter has been injured," I tell her.

Vonda bangs on the dumpster. "Tara? Are you hurt bad enough you can't get out if this man gives you a boost?"

"I can do it, Mama," Tara calls back, "but I don't want any man in here with me and I don't want that white lady. Come and get me, Mama."

"Ma'am, I can't let you try to get inside the bin," Lee seems alarmed at the thought. Vonda looks well put-together, like she never got undressed this evening. She wears a flowing lightweight raincoat over a nicely cut brown dress with a turtleneck. Her legs are shod in heels and stockings.

"Hasn't she been in there long enough?" Vonda says to Lee. "I'm coming, baby." Vonda kicks off her shoes and with complete disregard for the stockings, starts to scale the side of the dumpster. Lee and I, respectful of a powerful natural force, remain transfixed, watching her.

"Eliza?" Lee bows his head. "Eliza, I want to thank you for not saying anything to Roy. About me and Dwayne. I guess by now you understand we didn't mean anything by it. Dwayne would get bored, you know how he is. And I would think, 'What the hell, I'll just go along with him.' Dwayne being so lively to be with and all. I know you appreciate that." I don't realize until midway into the speech that Lee is confessing to the incidents I was originally hired to put a stop to.

"I don't know if Dwayne ever mentioned the whole story to you," Lee says without raising his eyes from the asphalt. He stands at the very perimeter of the floodlight and the gloom shrinks his physical presence. "We didn't think about how most of the girls who got our goofy messages in their mail-boxes, and the ones we made noises at, were black girls. Dwayne just picked out the ones he thought could take it.

"We didn't do it as often as they said either. The whole story got bigger when those students started calling for the college to find out who was behind it. We know what happened and what didn't, you see."

Lee lifts his face enough to give me a shy smile. "Once you got here, Dwayne wasn't bored any more. You being a real good conversationalist. So it never came up again." I decide to consider this later.

"I want to make sure that it never happens again." I toss out an all-purpose phrase I employ when the children have screwed up but I don't know yet what to do about it.

"It certainly won't, ma'am. If you could just manage to forgive Dwayne. He figures you think well of him now that you know him. You never turned us in, after all, and now we know that you could have. Can you get him out of this thing tonight? He doesn't have anything to do with it." The two of them not only believe I'm sharper than I really am, they attribute to me a fine sense of justice and rightness. I can't help but be touched, even under the circumstances.

"I'll see," I tell him. This phrase never satisfies my children but adults tend to forget it's not very meaningful.

"We'll never forget you," Lee mutters, uncomfortable with gratitude.

"Don't," I warn. I drop the case of Dwayne and Lee from my mind. Several clues lead me to believe that they might be small potatoes and I haven't yet located the rotten egg.

"Level with me, Lee," I ask, hurried by the eminent appearance of Tara and her mother. Scratching, dull, thudding sounds reverberate from the dumpster. The top of Tara's head appears and disappears. Given Vonda's strength, I don't offer to intervene yet. "Lee, how many times did you play games with the college girls?"

Lee says in an undertone, "Five, then hell broke loose." I've read convincing accounts of eight episodes, five silly, and three serious.

"Did either of you ever jump a girl from behind, force her down, hit her, tear at her clothes?" I question, stepping forward to look into his eyes, my face grave and threatening.

"God no," Lee cries. "They made that part up. Neither Dwayne nor I was here two of the times the girls say that stuff happened. I can prove it."

109

▲

Neither Dwayne nor Lee possesses keys for the outside door locks. Whoever threw Tara in the dumpster did it by coming through the building on the other side, I saw the fresh mud left where she hit the lid as she fell. Tara's backpack tumbles over the wall and lands on the ground. Tara soon alights outside the dumpster in front of me. Vonda descends beside her.

Lee cranes his neck for a close look at her. Tara, lit by the door's light, still makes a will-o'-the-wisp impression like she did in the dumpster, one of the silver apples of the moon come here in a girlish guise. "Get back, Lee, while I question them," I order. Lee slinks away to sit on an upturned bucket in the dark.

"Tara, how are you feeling?" I inquire.

"How's she supposed to feel?" Vonda says with scorn. "She's been protected from this kind of evilness all her life. She's a decent girl who's always in bed before 10:30."

What would a decent high school girl be doing at Kains College late at night? The obvious answer comes to me. I haven't completely lost my remembrance of those younger years.

"Tara, were you here tonight with someone you know?" I ask her. "Was the person who hurt you someone you had arranged to meet?" I attempt to sound as stern as Vonda.

"I can't remember how I got here," Tara tells me with defiance. Vonda's eyes narrow. Vonda knows something and that something will be useful, she's not a woman who soft-pedals.

"I was told you've been out with some college boy older than you. I was told it by that lying husband of mine, Eugene Everett, so I said to him, 'Not my Tara, we don't have secrets. I can look into that child's very soul and besides she hangs up if it isn't her girlfriends or family.'" Vonda pulsates with anger.

"I'm sorry, Mama." Tears begin to pour down Tara Timmin's face, transforming her from an alluring maiden to a miserable teenager.

"What did he do to you? Tell your Mama, or I'll make you wish the trashman hauled you away before I got to you," says Vonda. I decide to let her proceed with the interrogation.

"At first he was fine. He talked so nice tonight, everyone thought so. He didn't want anyone to know I was with him, because I look too young. So I met him when he was done with his talk," Tara hiccups.

"After we went walking in the dark he started acting spooky, Mama, saying nasty things. I tried to run away. Then

110
▲

he went crazy. He came after me and pushed me down. He hit me. I thought he was going to kill me or worse. I must have passed out. When I woke up, I was in the garbage. I wanted to be alone but all these people who work with him," Tara gestures at me and Lee, "they kept coming at me." Vonda turns to look at me and I fear what comes after that look.

"Not one person called the police to help my girl? What's going on here? Do you people have something to do with this? Do you?" Vonda has determined the heart of our negligence. The first person to find Tara should have called the police.

I think about Dwayne Blount. I have to presume Dwayne to be innocent. I'm not going to set Vonda Everett on him. Dwayne's no match for her under the best of circumstances.

I feel hard-pressed for a response to Vonda. Miraculously, a phrase floats up from my consciousness, "master of the human mind." I've heard it twice tonight, too much of a coincidence, once from Tara, and again on a publicity notice.

"Did you come here to meet Bradley Evigan, Tara? Did you come to meet the professor, graduate assistant rather, who gave a speech tonight in Lister Hall?" Tara's face incriminates the master of the human mind, teenage girls don't tend to be master of their own expressions.

"Bradley. What kind of a name is that for a black man?" screams Vonda, able to make every leap of logic except the one that lands her across an interracial barrier. Tara cringes.

"Did this professor beat you up?" Vonda gets back on the track again. I wait to hear Tara's answer, not 100 percent positive what it will be. Tara could have come to meet someone other than Bradley Evigan. But there wouldn't have been many men around tonight except for Mr. Evigan, present here to give his lecture. Nothing about Tara Timmin suggests that she might have come for a tryst with a college girl. Of course, a male faculty member might have come to hear Bradley speak and the college has a few men enrolled. Are there men who nurture enough interest in Pre-Menstrual Syndrome to give up a Saturday night to hear about it?

Tara stands on her one foot with a shoe. Her round thick-lashed eyes take quick glances at her mother. I want to badger Tara but Vonda will get better results. I keep in mind that Tara has been victimized and deserves gentle treatment. Vonda reaches out and pulls her daughter close to her. She puts her face next to Tara's.

"Who hurt you? No more messing with us, answer quick now," Vonda commands.

"It was Brad," the name issues forth with a sob. "I've seen

111
▲

him two times for pizza and he was nice. He was working with the head counselor at my school. She's a nice counselor except she talks too personal. I was working in the counseling office for an extracurricular activity."

"Did he try to take advantage of you tonight?" Vonda howls.

"I don't know," weeps Tara. "Everything was nice until I said could he please call me by my right name and he said that I kept bugging him. I told him I wouldn't ever want to bug him but I did have a name. He started shaking me and I got real scared and cried. He threw me on the ground. I don't know what happened, Mama." Vonda and I don't either. We turn to look at each other, allies for the first time in our confusion.

"Were you at the lecture that Bradley Evigan gave tonight?" I ask. Tara looks too done-in to have much hostile energy to vent on me.

"I caught the end of his talk. Everyone clapped. He met me after, out at a special bench that goes all the way around a tree. We went for a Coke but we had to come back so I could pick up my stepdaddy's car." The fact that Tara saw her assailant giving his lecture tonight confirms his identity. No chance remains that someone else introduced himself to Tara as Bradley Evigan.

"You've been driving again. That damn Eugene Everett. I told him not to let you have the car until you're sixteen years old. It's the law. You're going to give up a lot of TV for this, Tara Timmin."

"All right, Mama." Tara doesn't have any fight left.

"Mrs. Everett, I'm going to put this matter into the hands of the police. I'm sure they'll be contacting you tomorrow. Or if you feel anxious to file a police report, call them tonight." Tara's head hangs low. Vonda squeezes her tighter in what has become a loving clinch.

"We don't want to make a big deal. My Tara made a mistake, a bad mistake, taking up with this professor. He's a white man, isn't he? It's best forgotten. I'll take care of her now." I've unearthed another cover-up in progress.

"I'll try to keep Tara out of this but I won't be able to completely. We need to make sure that what happened to Tara tonight doesn't happen to any other girls. Am I right?"

"Leave us alone," Tara begs, back to her earlier refrain.

"I'll do my best for you," I tell her. I feel like I've been on quite a trip with this young woman tonight, a voyage in a metal boat buoyed by darkness.

"Lee," I call, "take these two to Roy Garber in the Main Office and tell him to pay their cab fare home." Lee jumps up with covetous alacrity. He doesn't understand that Vonda would never let him say word one to her daughter.

"We don't need a cab," says Vonda, withering Lee's eagerness. "I'll drive Tara home in my husband's car. Do you have the keys, daughter?" I happen to know that she does have the keys.

"Goodbye, Tara. Use what you got to get what you want, kid." Tara and Vonda look startled by my unsolicited parting advice.

I visit the Philosophy Department again to check the staff roster. Bradley Evigan, a member of the Psychology Department, lives in Berkeley. Figures. He's been visiting here to pick up a graduate degree and assault women, then he goes home to the safety of a different turf. I call the Berkeley Police.

Before I leave, I go by the Main Office to let Roy Garber know that we don't need to hold Dwayne as a suspect any longer. "About time," says Dwayne cheerfully. "My shift isn't over but I'm going to get a beer. Want to come help me celebrate, Eliza?" Roy Garber looks to see whether I will consort with Dwayne. I am insulted in spite of my training in dealing with insult.

"I have work left to do. Goodnight, Dwayne. Things are under control. Roy, I'll report in to you tomorrow. Why don't you go home and get some sleep?"

I drive through Oakland, past my neighborhood off to the East of the freeway, and on into Berkeley. I go up University Avenue and turn left onto Shattuck. When I turn into Bradley Evigan's neighborhood, off Cedar, I can't see much. Big brown shingle houses sit well back from the street, behind unkempt front yards.

I don't see the police in the vicinity of Bradley Evigan's house. Have they come and gone? I park a few houses down the street and get out of my car. The police probably haven't shown. I could go back to a phone booth on Shattuck and call them.

My footsteps seem magnified by the dead-of-night's silence, until screams issue from one moderately respectable Berkeley home, Bradley Evigan's. I put one hand on my gun and run to the door. A tall woman in jeans and a vest, more mature than a college-age student, opens the door and stands in front of me with a weary attitude. "Sorry about the racket," she says. "We'll keep it down now."

113
▲

"I'm looking for Bradley Evigan, master of the human mind," I say. I let myself be coy, cute, like paperback detectives. I don't like this guy. I hate what he did to Tara Timmin. I'm fuming. I can afford to mouth off all I want.

"Brad?" the woman repeats. If Bradley were a wholesome person she would wonder why I am here on her doorstep playing with his name and title at three in the morning.

"I'm with Kains College Security. I want to ask Brad a few questions." I take my hand off my gun to fish out my Kains College Security badge which I have carried in my shoulder bag since I began the job.

"I'm Donna, Brad's fiancée. He had a speaking engagement tonight and he's extremely tired. Can you come back tomorrow morning after eleven?" Is the woman a fool? Does she think that when people come after you in the hours before dawn, they'll go away if you ask them politely? No, she knows the story. She's under stress and functioning on automatic pilot.

"I heard you two fighting just now. I want to make sure you're going to be okay. Where is he, Donna?" I ask. Her eyes move over toward the living room instead of to the closed door on the right. I take the path that her eyes indicate.

We go through the dining room, around a scarred table covered with computer equipment and piles of books, and push open a swinging door in the kitchen. Bradley Evigan sits in the kitchen at a table littered with newspaper and more books. He drinks from a tall glass filled with dark amber fluid. My nose can't identify what kind, only that I smell heavy-duty alcohol.

"I'm here to talk to you about Tara Timmin." Bradley Evigan's mouth and nose display a tic but he doesn't reply. Brad doesn't look like a lady-killer. A small skinny man whose long gleaming blond hair constitutes his best feature, Brad looks to be the type who would have had a hard time getting a date in high school. His type becomes more desireable to women when they achieve graduate school status or make some money.

"Who is this Tara? Is she the Kains Anthropology instructor who collated your field work with you the other night?" Donna asks him. She has that well-bred manner which crimps the emotional impact of her speech even under duress.

"Tara Timmin is a child. This child told me that your fiancé attacked and injured her this evening."

"I don't want to hear that name again," yells Bradley Evigan hoarsely. Names have a lot of power for maniacal people. Brad goes from inertia to rapid movement.

A cat sails through the air in my direction. Bradley Evigan has hurled a blue ceramic kitty whose irritable face, which I focus upon as it flies, gives rise to a fantasy that the cat suffers from pre-menstrual syndrome, Brad's area of expertise. I duck and pull my gun. I almost shoot the cat. The piece of porcelain misses me and shatters against the kitchen wall.

"That cat was a gift," wails Donna. She may have ignored Bradley's criminal tendencies but she isn't going to stay quiet for rudeness and destruction of knickknacks.

"Put your hands behind your head," I say. "Don't move." Brad doesn't have the boldness to go against a gun. I hope I am right in the assessment I have made of Bradley Evigan— chicken shit, a man who keeps his juices flowing by physically assaulting vulnerable women.

Before I have to keep my sights trained on Bradley Evigan for a prolonged period, I hear voices from the front of the house. Two Berkeley Police officers troop to the kitchen and eventually accept my story. Brad manifests no mastery of the human mind whatsoever in conversation with the police. His lawyer will be unhappy when he reads the police report.

In detective work, intimate relationships with people and places often end abruptly. When I turn Brad over to the authorities, I wave goodbye to rapscallions Dwayne and Lee, James, Kains College, that rare rose Tara Timmins, and janitorial work. I didn't enjoy janitorial work much.

They lead Brad away in cuffs, a sight I enjoy. Although he taught as a graduate assistant in a field which demands excellent communication skills, Brad doesn't have anything to say to me or his fiancée on his way out the door.

Donna walks out onto her front porch and turns to me. She has something to say, so she talks to me.

"I'm glad they're going to lock him up. I hope they watch him carefully. He's been getting more edgy and bitter all the time." She chokes back tears.

"Maybe he'll get help," I say, glad I don't have to offer to help him.

"The next girl," Donna's voice trembles badly, "he could have killed the next girl."

"**B**ull's-eye. I turn 42 and it's good luck time. My luck changed the day after my birthday." Dennis sits beside me, the afternoon after Tara Timmin's ill-adventure at Kains College, in a curved corner booth eating an omelet with avocados and salsa. Red and green eggs. "After five and a half rotten years," he adds, still musing over his life.

"Who would have thought it?" I reply fondly. "This year, your lucky 42nd, didn't have an auspicious start. Your birthday party wasn't great. Remember? Patty got drunk and told everyone about the exercises that the sex therapist had you two try before your marriage broke up." Dennis and his ex-wife, Patty, have remained friends.

"Oh God," Dennis moans, "that's right. I think I blacked out right after Patty started in. Remember Avilla Appliances sent over some cases of champagne and I drank about half of it? The last thing I remember is Honor telling me how alcohol can be toxic. She told me some story about her friend's husband who drank a whole bottle of B & B and died."

"She's a comfort," I say. "So. What's gone right for you since the party?" I cut a bite of doughy waffle with whipped cream, syrup, and nuts on top. At the mention of Honor, I check the clock to make sure I'm not due at home yet. The diner's clock, a donation from the bottlers of Miller Lite Beer, says that it's only 2:15.

We're eating at Trudi's Pancake House because it's near Kains College. Trudi's food seems more intense today, on Sunday, than during the week. Trudi mainly attracts employees of the potato chip factory a block away, a few college girls, and people too old or infirm to walk any place else. And Dennis, who likes the food.

"I have Sharon working on the Rhodes case. You remember, the guy who has set himself up all over the state. Sharon has her foot on his butt and he has no idea yet." Dennis chews down toast so damp with the oil they paint on with a brush that it hangs limp in his hand. He tosses down some coffee white with artificial creamer. A pleased smile sits right beneath his lips, changing the normal line of his mouth.

He's sleeping with her, I realize with a jolt. Dennis, with his neatly ordered code of etiquette. A code to which I adhered for years in order to maintain Dennis' respect, before he started giving me unconditional respect. Getting involved with a fellow investigator is definitely unacceptable for reasons of security and propriety. I wonder how the sex is.

"How are you and Sharon getting along?" I ask casually. Dennis blushes blood red.

"Good enough. Of course, she's not as clever or as cool as you are. She might not have quite as much muscle as I need. But she's a good partner."

Has she offered to introduce you to her mother? I wonder but don't say.

"Sharon's tired of hearing me tell Eliza Pirex stories. The other day she said, 'Lizzie probably would have had this figured out and written up in the twinkling of an eye but you'll have to bear with me.' I figure you'd be happy with the way I've talked you up." Dennis grins at me. He's working to be engaging. He wants to make sure that he can sleep with Sharon and keep me close, too.

"I like the sound of this," I acknowledge. "What stories have you been telling her? I'd like to know so I can share them with people at parties or put them on my résumé. And where did she get the 'Lizzie'?"

"She likes nicknames. But don't hold it against her. You haven't even met her yet."

"What nicknames does she call you, Den?" I ask. His blush has been receding but it spreads again.

"Don't start, Lizzie," he says. I drop this line of questioning as unproductive.

"I want to meet her," I say, with as much warmth as possible considering I'm in the process of adjusting to the new scheme of things. "After all," I tell him, "Sharon and I have you and our careers with Lighthouse Investigations in common. We've scaled the pinnacles and we've seen the seamy side of life. Well, maybe Sharon hasn't yet but I could let her know what she's getting into." Dennis smiles into his beige coffee. He doesn't have to be excessively concerned about my loyalty, he knows he has it.

"I'll bring Sharon over next week. Am I going to run around doing your Ruthie odds and ends?" Dennis picks up his last cottage fries in his fingers and eats them.

"Ruthie may turn up when I do my phone calling session tomorrow morning," I tell him optimistically. "But she's been elusive so far. I see a parallel between what happened last night and what could have happened to Ruthie. Don't you?" I've recounted last night's episode, a story of trash and academia, to Dennis. "I've made a guess about Ruthie, based on that equation. If my guess is right, I won't find her by phoning around." Dennis looks like he doesn't believe in or care about any parallel I might see.

"So you want to reserve a couple blocks of my time in advance," Dennis says, beckoning for a coffee refill. "Do you know what day?"

"I meet with the Goldeens on Thursday morning. I'd like to have something to tell them other than 'Forgot to put the cat out' stories. Can I have you on Tuesday so I can talk to you on Wednesday before I see the Goldeens?"

"Sure. I'll leave Sharon at the office monitoring Rhodes. I'll go out and devote myself to helping Eileen Goldeen update her address book," he smiles.

"Eileen's paying for it, Den. And I myself want to find Ruthie at this point. I don't want Ruthie nagging at the back of my mind forever. I'm going to straighten up Eileen's little longings and memories before I take on any other business."

"I'm with you. You want Ruthie, you got Ruthie. Which of the players are you going to send me after?"

"The psychiatrist, Lilienthal. He knows who I am. He knows I'm looking for Ruthie. The call I got at home last night, assuming it was from him, makes me feel that maybe I shouldn't confront him in person."

"He must not know Honor's reputation, if he dared call your house," Dennis jokes. Dennis admires Honor's ferocity where her family is concerned. Dennis might even be jealous. He's had to fend for himself a long time now while I have enjoyed sustenance from Honor.

I rub my eyes. "I might also send you after a woman I met last night at a party. She used to be a friend of Ruthie's. I was told that she was murdered in Ruthie's apartment just before Ruthie disappeared. But there she stood in the flesh." Dennis raises his eyebrows. "She got jumpy when I mentioned

Ruthie's name. All very curious. I'll fill you in if I put you onto her."

Dennis and I have both scraped our crockery clean. At Trudi's they don't pick up your plate until you leave the table. Some customers like to lick the stains off with a finger or use their dish as an ashtray.

"So," I say and my voice sounds tired to me, "I have to ask. What's my standing at Kains College?" I requested that Dennis go by the college this morning, excusing his presence by offering his services to the administration. I want to find out whether they hold me responsible for the incident last night. I'll go by later when the people I know are on duty.

"The name Eliza Pirex is not necessarily mud at Kains College, maybe not even dirt. They're happy that their problem is resolved. That's what they hired you for, after all. They're going to publicize the fact that they paid out good money and got the situation dealt with. Tomorrow there'll be newspaper coverage on the arrest of Brad Evigan"

I tell him, "They don't know that their security guards, Dwayne and Lee, actually did play mild practical jokes on four or five different college students. I'm not going to tell anyone except you. I intend to keep an eye on the guys to make sure that they honor the promise they made, that they will tow the line forever."

"Forever leaves plenty of time to backslide," Dennis comments.

I feel tired thinking about checking up on Dwayne and Lee indefinitely. I don't know why I'm doing it, I could have gotten them fired, except that I ended up liking the creeps in some weird way. Charity isn't free, you have to work for the luxury of being charitable.

"How do they feel about the girl getting injured during a time I was supposed to have been on duty?" I question.

"You're not going to like it," says Dennis. "They're happy you weren't on the spot last night. The administration official, Garber, thinks that you could have been the one in the trash heap if you had been hanging around the college, alone and defenseless with their thug-teacher, Evigan, on the loose. I guess Garber hasn't gotten to witness your tremendous physical prowess and lightning reflexes, the way I have."

"I'd rather they held it against me that I was off screwing around when they needed me," I snap at him, "than that they think I'm as defenseless as a fourteen-year-old child."

"I know. But you've come out of this pretty well. They're going to tell the world that you're sharp and that you brought

120
▲

in the bad boy, Brad Evigan, and got him sent up on charges. You may as well not waste your time convincing the stuffed shirt, Garber, how tough you are. People who really want tough wouldn't hire you or me." A nice touch, lumping himself with me.

"Okay," I give it up. "I'm not going to go over to the college flashing my gun and imitating James Cagney the way I did when I was younger. I have less investment in my dignity the last couple years, anyway.

"Are they upset that I had to turn in a graduate student who has been teaching at the school? I'm sure they would have been happier if some random unknown party had been implicated." I need to know all the ramifications.

"I think they're happier that a graduate student, just passing through on his way to a degree, turned out to be the culprit. They definitely didn't want anyone from their own security force incriminated. They're supposed to have screened those employees, evaluated them on a regular basis, and all that."

"Of course, they have to come up with some explanation for why they didn't notice that Bradley Evigan had become the servant of his baser impulses," I point out.

"Kains College will make it sound like they barely heard of the jerk. They'll put a piece in the school paper naming the school he got his B.A. from and make it sound like he got screwed-up there. They'll say that he was able to conceal the fact that he had a troubled personal life because he was trained in psychology. I've seen how these embarrassing liaisons, like the one between Brad Evigan and Kains College, get packaged. Kains will come out smelling like a rose."

"I hope Bradley Evigan has a bad time during the trial and I hope people keep leaning on him to make sure he doesn't feel comfortable for the rest of his life," I say.

"You're tired, Muscles. By tomorrow you'll have gathered your good energy again. You'll collect your balance due from the college, all in one check, and proceed to unlock the mystery of the missing Ruthie."

"With your assistance, if you can tear yourself away from Sharon." I wish I hadn't mentioned her. Tiredness has relaxed my boundaries. Sharon intruded on me, by sleeping with Dennis, but I'm officially happy for him. I've got to watch myself. I notice his hair looks shinier now that he's having sex with someone he cares about.

"Sharon's one of us, Eliza. Give her a chance." When Dennis talks about 'us' he's pulling out the big guns. 'Us' is Dennis' naive vision that everyone he cares about constitutes a group. In fact, a lot of us don't like each other but we hope that Dennis doesn't find out.

Dennis tries twinkling at me, hopeful he has convinced me to be friends with Sharon. "Let's order Trudi's sundaes," he winks. "She'll be so happy with the total we've racked up on the bill, we'll have made her week." Trudi's employs two huge older women, Jean and Marion. Dennis calls them both Trudi, which they like. "Something sweet will cut the grease," Dennis adds.

"The lunch I just ate had whipped cream and nuts, Dennis," I point out. Dennis looks crestfallen. But he signals for the check. He's looking paunchy today, actually, and doesn't need the ice cream. Paunchy doesn't build the public's confidence in a P.I.

I'll bet Sharon cooks for him to inveigle her way into his affections. Dennis has always been suckered by offerings of heavy food. And I'll bet Sharon eats light. I don't envision her as the type that runs to fat.

Dennis puts his arm around me tightly on our way out to the car. I am going to appreciate Sharon, even in my thoughts, for Dennis. I hug him tight and thank him for running interference at Kains College. Dennis reminds me that his Tuesday is mine if I need him. I feel myself surrendering some of my stake in Dennis to Sharon. Maybe I'll love her.

I drive home carefully. Fatigue has impaired my coordination. I turn left on Tahoe and feel cheered when I see that my parking place behind Honor's van has been left clear.

I park and get out. I see trash wherever I go. Litterers, probably kids dressed in stiff black suits on their way back from the church on College Avenue this morning, have dropped wrappers from banana and cherry push-ups in front of our house. Someone threw a Kentucky Fried Chicken box from their car onto the sidewalk just beyond our yard. I pick up the garbage and walk around to our cans which stand under the stairs behind the house.

I jump when I hear the back door unlock. The screen door flies open and then bangs shut with a thump. I hear Honor trot out onto the deck yelling, "Eliza? Eliza? Hurry up, we've had an emergency. Something's happened to the children."

"What's happened?" I bound up the back stairs with my heart pounding wildly.

"Shhh. I have them in the kitchen drinking peppermint tea," says Honor. "I don't want to talk about it in front of them and upset them more than they already are."

"Honor, what happened?" I shriek.

"Your Doctor Lilienthal got them," Honor states, looking distraught.

"My God. What did he do to them? Did he threaten them or touch them?"

"It's just as bad, Eliza. He did child therapy on them." Honor leans into my arms for comfort.

"What do you mean, Honor?" My panic hasn't subsided yet.

"The children said that a man in nice clothes came up to them outside Toys for Girls and Boys. Annabelle walked Jemmy over there so he could buy a new set of felt-tip markers. The guy said that he was your therapist and that he needed information about our family in order to be able to help you. I don't know why Annabelle fell for it. She said he seemed to know a lot about you and that he seemed a lot like the way her friend Rachel describes her mother's therapist."

"Doesn't Annabelle think she would know if I were seeing a therapist? She and I make out all the checks for household bills together. She would never forget an account." Honor's presentation of the crisis has made me crazy. Now I'm off on a tangent.

"Dr. Lilienthal is a sick man, Eliza. He must be the one who called here last night. Today he did unsolicited family counseling on our children. He asked them a lot of questions about us, and told the children to 'go with their feelings.' I'm sure it's illegal for him to invade the privacy of our children's feelings and to coerce information about our lives. He bought them ice cream and chocolate chip cookies at Dreyers, so Jemmy forgot to suspect a thing. Annabelle got nervous, finally, and told him that they had to go home or she was going to call me."

"Then he left his trademark," Honor continues into my ear. "He told Annabelle to tell you that you forgot to put the cat out. Annabelle told him that we don't have a cat. He said, 'That's what you think.' Then he started laughing. Annabelle and Jemmy started running.

"Eliza, it's time for you to go into financial management. Your client has seriously frightened our children." Honor's steely eyes fill with tears and one breaks loose and rolls down her cheek. I reach for her but she backs up the stairs.

"Lilienthal isn't a client, Honor. It was Ruthie who attracted him, not me. He seems to have energy left over from his time with Ruthie and that energy has spilled over onto us. He needs to be defused. I'll take better care of you and the children from now on. I promise."

"I can see that you're not going to stop this lunacy," Honor says flatly. "What are you going to do, Eliza? A sicko has his eye on us and our children. If you're not going to call the police or use your wiles to outsmart him, I'm going to call my father." Honor and her father might not seem like the best of friends but he would have a small militia here in a moment if Honor asked him to. I picture our quiet sunny house patrolled by henchmen hired by Newell Sutton.

We both jump when the screen door hinges screech. "Momma, Eliza, Jem and I are waiting for you. Jemmy's nervous now that I've explained that the man who's after us was like a mad scientist. I'm sorry I exaggerated. He's a bad doctor more than a mad scientist, isn't he, Eliza? Maybe you should explain the situation to Jemmy." Annabelle peers down at us, her forehead wrinkled with anxiety.

"I'll take care of this by tomorrow," I whisper to Honor. "Don't call your dad."

I walk through the back laundry room and into the kitchen with Honor muttering under her breath at my side. Jemmy sits on a high stool at the counter, his tea mug near his hand.

Jemmy possesses a sturdy psyche. Both Honor and I credit ourselves for instilling him with this good equilibrium, although I think I have a more compelling case. Right now, I would guess, Jemmy's puzzling out where Lilienthal's behavior fits into his concepts of adult conduct.

"Mom," says Jemmy, looking me in the eye, "a man with a gold necklace and a gold chain hanging from his belt asked me and Annabelle questions. He wanted to know if you keep a gun in the house. And he wanted to know if guns upset us or give us bad dreams. I don't think he liked us. He kept saying, 'you can tell me,' after everything we said, like there was something we hadn't told him. He said that he was your doctor." Jemmy pauses, waiting for me to contradict this or not. "Momma was almost crying when we told her about the questions he asked."

"He was wearing a pocket watch on a chain, Jem," Annabelle interjects loftily.

"I wasn't upset by the questions themselves, Jemmy. I was upset that the doctor interfered with you at all," inserts Honor. She becomes more severe. "I'm particularly upset that both of you talked to a stranger and let him buy you treats. What do you think 'Never take candy from a stranger' means? You two just flunked, you forgot the most basic rule we've tried to teach you."

124
▲

Annabelle looks mortified. Jemmy, also discomfited, says, "But he said he's your doctor. He knew all about you and told us he wanted to help you."

"He's not my doctor, Jemmy. I've never met him. He's involved with a case I'm working on. I don't think that he's a balanced person. His regular job, though, is to talk to kids about their problems. So it probably came naturally to talk to you guys in a personal way." Jemmy nods.

"If you ever see him again," I add, "run. And call me or Momma right away." Jemmy nods, his tangled brown hair falling onto his forehead. I experience a gleam of the anger that Honor experiences often, anger at someone who has threatened my somewhat innocent children.

Jemmy looks at me thoughtfully. "If the doctor isn't balanced, why do people let him talk to their children?"

I try to think of an answer. "He has good credentials and he's well-known. It probably sounds to parents like Dr. Lilienthal should be a good person to help their children. They probably don't spend enough time with him to notice what he's really like. The important thing is for you and Annabelle to remember that I am a very good detective and I can fix this situation. So you don't have to worry about the doctor, he'll be out of our way soon."

Annabelle asks, "Is he legally liable for lying to children, Eliza? Momma thinks he might be."

"People are only liable for their lies under a few circumstances. If they have lied to extort money or to cover up something criminal during a trial, for example. But," I add as I see Honor open her mouth to interrupt with some inspirational words about Truth, "I do believe that you get back in life what you put in. Lilienthal has plenty to contend with, because he does things like run around accosting children."

"Is Dr. Lilienthal looking for Ruthie too? Like you are?" asks Jemmy. I wonder how well the children remember Dave Gray's story about Ruthie's ordeal with Lilienthal. I wish they hadn't been exposed to this case at all.

"I think he might be looking for Ruthie. Or maybe he knows what happened to her and doesn't want me to find out." The phone rings. Honor answers and then hands it to me, looking irritated.

"Eliza Pirex?" Doris Shipley's voice comes across the line resonant with the accusatory tone I've heard all too often. "I need to see you tomorrow. I have urgent business and it has to be in person." Doris' voice makes me feel one notch more exhausted than I was before I picked up the receiver.

125

▲

"Doris, how did you get my home number?" I rarely give this phone number to clients. I have Precious or the answering service call here and then I call the client back.

"I have this number in my book. So your office must have given it to me," Doris replies coyly. I make a mental note to find out where she got the number. Precious would not have handed it over without my consent. I agree to see Doris at my office tomorrow at 12:30 p.m. The timing works because she'll have to leave when I go to lunch.

I make playful conversation with the children, hoping to dissipate any anxiety they have left over from the meeting with Lilienthal. I'm so successful Jemmy decides that all and all he had a good time with the doctor. Annabelle remembers that Lilienthal had scratches on his hands. I try to retain details that might be useful if I decide to go all out after Lilienthal.

Later, we take the children and two of their friends to Tilden Park. Honor and the kids practice with a softball while I sleep in the grass near a picnic table. The outdoor light jumbles my sleep. I see Stuart Lilienthal, Tara Timmin, and Ruthie, running about, doing their daily business in the underplace. Or maybe the figures I see are all shadows of myself, going about the business of docketing the rest of them for inclusion in my files. Maybe I can bill somebody for this delirious bustle.

launch words into the unknown. "Hello, Mrs. Neidlebaum, I'm calling because I need to locate former neighbors of yours, Morris and Maddy Gold. I have important business with them." Silence. "Nothing unpleasant," I say reassuringly. More silence.

"What house were they in?" crackles the voice on the other end of the line, finally.

"1067 Poinsettia Court."

"1067 is the Carrs now. I don't know who came before them. You need to try the Hammersteins. They've been in their place 43 years, since these houses were built." I look down at the photocopy of the reverse directory to check whether I have a number for the Hammersteins or whether I've already called them and gotten no results. There they are, 1092 Poinsettia. I haven't called them yet.

"Thanks, Mrs. Neidlebaum. Sorry to disturb you."

"Nothing disturbs me, young woman. I was so disturbed for the first 50 years of my life that nothing has bothered me since." It's amazing how people have tidbits of themselves to spare, even when they've been phoned out of the blue.

I slide my chair over to the filing cabinet, using my feet to locomote, so that I can fetch my coffee. The office looks tidy and tranquil with bars of Monday morning sun sneaking through the blinds. No clients, with their opportunities in jeopardy, have intruded yet.

The coffee tastes like Mocha Java. Precious has been wooing everyone in the building today with a daily newspaper on each office doorstep, good coffee, and pastries from some bakery that makes delicious dough. She knows that we're probably in the process of selecting the anniversary gift with which we will present her at the big party her family's giving. We realize that something lavish would be appropriate, and deserved, but these touches do make us all feel even warmer toward her than usual.

"Hello, Mrs. Hammerstein? I was given your name by your neighbor, Mrs. Neidlebaum. She thought that you might be able to help me locate some former neighbors of yours, Maddy and Morris Gold. They used to live at 1067 Poinsettia where the Carrs live now."

"I don't like Esther Neidlebaum giving out my personal number to strangers. And I'm going to tell her so directly. What do you want with Maddy and Morris?" This voice sounds irascible. The neighborhood crank.

"I have important business with them. Nothing unpleasant. Oh, and Mrs. Neidlebaum didn't give me your number. I got it from a reverse telephone directory. They have them at the public library."

"Are you a credit agency? You've got the wrong Golds. Maddy always paid. Monthly. So no interest would go onto the bill. Unless she's changed these last six years. But those things don't change." This woman speaks the truth. People's way of dealing with money doesn't change, I've found in most cases. I've already verified that the major credit card companies don't have a record on Morris or Maddy.

"I'm a private investigator, Mrs. Hammerstein. I have good news for the Gold's daughter, Ruth. I'm trying to locate her."

"What kind of good news?" she counters. I hardly ever run across garrulous, unsuspicious acquaintances of people I am tracking, like TV detectives do all the time. I'm going to have to find an angle to warm Mrs. Hammerstein up.

"An old friend of Ruth's wants to find her. Her friend feels that it would be to Ruth's advantage if they got together." Is it true, I wonder? In fact, I have the feeling Eileen's interest rises from her own hunger. Eileen has never expressed consideration for how Ruthie might be affected by a reunion. After all, Ruthie could have found Eileen any time she wanted to.

"Oh, baloney. Ruthie never had friends who would want to do anything for her once they were done with her. That girl just couldn't keep a boyfriend and I'd bet my bottom dollar she hasn't married to this day." The woman has assumed I meant "friend" as a euphemism for an old lover.

"When was the last time that you saw Ruth?" I ask.

"I haven't seen hide nor hair of the Golds these last six

years. They didn't tell me where they were going. And if that's the way they want to be to someone who was always a good neighbor and baked bread and cinnamon buns for them, then I don't know what. Of course, Morris was always vulgar. It's his nature. But I thought better of Maddy."

"You haven't heard anything about them since they left?"

"Nothing. I didn't even see the movers come for their things." Mrs. Hammerstein still sounds put out about missing the event.

"They hadn't talked about moving anywhere? They hadn't mentioned inheriting a house in Wisconsin or relocating to be near a sick parent in Omaha, Nebraska?"

"I didn't even know they'd been left a house and I certainly didn't know they had folks in the Midwest," she replies, interested in spite of herself.

"Sorry, I was speaking theoretically to see if anything jogged your memory." It works sometimes.

"You've got quite an imagination, haven't you? But I don't need my memory sparked. After they went, the realtor lady wouldn't tell me and Nate anything. So we sat down and thought, where could Morris and Maddy have gone so suddenly? You live on a street with people and watch them raise three children and you think you know them.

"But you know what? You're lucky if you know your own husband and kids. You probably don't. Barbara Glass found out after her husband died that he had another wife in a mobile home near Irvine and two other grown kids. I wish I could hire myself a detective. I'd make sure that I knew all about somebody so that I could count on it."

"I wish I could help you out," I tell her. "I work in the San Francisco Bay Area but if I were near you I'd be happy to do a background check on anyone you felt uneasy about, for a moderate fee." I'm sorry that Mrs. Hammerstein feels so powerless in the face of human duplicity and human thoughtlessness.

"That's very nice, that you want to ease my mind. Maybe there's a nice lady detective somewhere in my neighborhood. I could find out why my best friend Lucille Davidson went off me after her daughter got married. I'd like to know." Mrs. Hammerstein probably does know the reason on some level but this isn't the time to bring it out of her.

"Mrs. Hammerstein, can you think of anyone else I might speak to about where to find Ruth?" The line goes silent for a short time.

"Maddy and Morris socialized with the group at Congregation Beth Shalom. They went on the bus tours to keep up the Jewish graves in the Gold Country and they went to all the potlucks. I stopped seeing that group a long time ago, they're all more outgoing than me. So I never did call and see if they knew where the Golds went."

She falters slightly, then continues. "You could try calling Marcia Finkle at the temple. She's been the president of B'nai Brith for many years. You don't need to tell her I'm the one who told you to call. I wouldn't want to give her the satisfaction. Just say 'a neighbor.'"

I thank Mrs. Hammerstein several times for the information. She wants to keep me on the line. "You haven't said what you want with Ruth," she says, avoiding my maneuvers to dislodge her. "I have to tell you that Ruthie is not easy to get along with, for all that she is a sweet thing. When she was a girl she would cry at the drop of a hat. Her daddy would say, 'Ruthie, I'm going to take you out for ice cream this afternoon.' Next thing you know you'd look over at the girl and her face would be a mess from crying. In high school, she was always upset over someone. Her mother always said that Ruthie's life got more difficult every year." Mrs. Hammerstein plunges ahead to prevent me from getting off the phone. She likes me now.

"Jane was the easy one. Nicer looking than Ruthie, too. Jane was the one I'd expect someone to hire a detective over. Although she was hard of heart."

"But you haven't heard anything about Jane either, since they left?" I find a moment to interrupt.

"Janie went away before them but Maddy never talked about where. You know, Mrs. . . . ?"

"Eliza Pirex."

"Eliza, you could bill me a small, a reasonable fee, like you said, and postage, if you would let me know what happened to Maddy and Morris. Our children grew up together, even though they never got along because their ages weren't right for playing together. I probably won't ever find a detective in the neighborhood. Would you mind?"

"What's your given name?" I ask.

"Rita." The reverse directory doesn't list a wife's first name.

"I'll make a note to send you any information that would be valuable to you, if it's all right with my client. Thanks again for your help." I hang up quickly, make some notes, and cross-reference them with a key indicating that I need to send the Golds' address and any explanation for their departure to Rita Hammerstein. I phone information and ask for the number of Temple Beth Shalom.

The secretary at the Temple tells me that Marcia Finkle won't be in until later in the week and can't be detracted from her good works in the meantime. I insinuate that I might join the group, donate support and services. I let slip that I make reproductions of antique dolls, which I don't. Doll-making skill seduces many people of a certain ilk. The secretary, Jean, gives me Marcia's home phone number and I reach Marcia there.

"Mrs. Finkle, I was given your name by a former neighbor of Maddy Gold. She reminded me that Mrs. Gold was an active member of your B'nai Brith chapter. My parents were close friends of the family when we were younger. My parents died about fifteen years ago and I've been living with an aunt in New York City." I take a breath.

"I lost touch with the Golds but I'd like to look up their daughter, Ruth, who used to be my good friend as a child. They don't live at their old address and the neighbors don't know where they went. Can you help me locate Mr. and Mrs. Gold or Ruthie?" I allow a plaintive quality to creep into my voice. I'm assuming this woman will be more likely to help a pathetic orphan than aid a missing person investigation.

"What's your name, dear?"

"Susan Abrams."

"Were Ben and Rose Abrams your father and mother?"

"No, my parents were Kay and Ed." When I fictionalize, I like to make sure that the quality of the names I invent meld with my story. Marcia waits, considering.

"I didn't know Kay and Ed. Were your parents part of our congregation?"

"My parents were agnostics," I say bravely, sadly. "They didn't participate in activities connected with the Temple." My religious grandma and my mother would be horrified to hear these words come out of my mouth, but they work.

"I'm not prejudiced," says Marcia primly, sadly. "And this doesn't mean that you can't become a member of the Congregation if you make Los Angeles your home. It's funny that Maddy never confided in me about your mother. I used to be Maddy's greatest confidante."

"It was hard for Maddy that Mother didn't share in such an important part of her life. Their values were so similar in most other ways."

"I'm sure," says Marcia, all understanding.

"I wonder if you could tell me where I might get in touch with Ruthie or any of the Golds?" I can hear Marcia considering whether to tell me anything. I don't know yet whether she's bought the genteel hard-luck story that I've given her.

"I wish I could help you," she says, a civic-minded concern conveyed in her words.

"Thank you. It would mean a lot to me," I prod.

"But I can't."

"You can't?"

"I don't know what happened to the Golds. Maddy was treasurer of the chapter, never missed a meeting. Then, one day, the phone was disconnected and the house was being shown with no furnishings. The mailings we sent started coming back about a year after they left. They weren't being forwarded any more.

"I've never lost a member so completely except, of course, when they've passed away. But our deceased members all reside at Heimowitz Mausoleum on Bogata Avenue and the Golds aren't there."

What a waste, I think. She could have gotten the address out of the post office during that period of time they forwarded the mail. At least, this confirms that the Golds weren't murdered en masse six years ago and buried secretly on the grounds of the Heimowitz Mausoleum or washed to sea.

"Is there anything you know about the Golds that would help me find them? Relatives in another part of the country? A business venture they mentioned that involved relocation?"

"I racked my brains for years about where Maddy might have gone. I missed her even though she was different. She had a way of being involved in everyone's quibbles," Marcia's voice trails off. She doesn't want to elaborate on Maddy's character.

"You couldn't think of any clue?"

"I put notices in the newsletter of every congregation in the Los Angeles and Orange County area. Beth Shalom put up a reward. We offered pecan pies for any information leading to Maddy. We had a student rabbi at the time, Samuel Shem, and he thought there might be something fishy about their disappearance. If the Golds were anywhere in southern California, I would know."

"I did think I saw that boy one time over in Venice," she says reluctantly. "The son, Jonathan, who they disowned when he joined a group that wanted to overthrow the government. You must have known Jonathan. Morris told Maddy that she was not allowed to phone Jonathan ever again. It broke her heart. But Maddy never went against Morris." Venice sounds like a logical place to find the brother who lives with a pseudo-political group.

"Can you think of how to locate Jonathan?"

"His group was called the World Views. His mother called them the Whirvies. He might still be with them. But you can't just look up 'Whirvies' in the phone book. I'm sure they're in hiding from the government."

"Do you know the name of anyone else in the group?"

"I don't know any members of underground terrorist organizations, Susan. If Jonathan Gold is a member, I don't know him. You may have them right out in the open in New York City but this is Los Angeles." I don't comment. I don't know New York or Los Angeles that well.

I say goodbye. Marcia advises Susan that the humiliation of being raised in the cold should not cheat her out of the richness of religious life. In fact, Marcia wants Susan to know that any time she reports to Temple Beth Shalom, the entire congregation will attempt to compensate for her childhood's spiritual paucity. If Marcia puts me together with the innuendo I left at the Temple, that I might produce antique dolls for fund-raisers and Sunday School projects, she's going to regret that she didn't nail me down.

I hang up. I get up and walk to the window. Through the slats of the venetian blinds I can see a client of Lucas' walking furiously across the courtyard, crying. Back at my desk, I call Los Angeles area information and ask if they have a number for Jonathan Gold. They don't. I wander over to my small reference area. I check a carefully indexed book on organizations that includes underground groups. No World Views. I call my contact with a local political/hippie group of the amorphous variety, he doesn't know any World Views.

In frustration, I dial L.A. information and ask if they have anything listed under World Views. No. I ask for Whirvies. A recording comes on in a few seconds telling me what the number is.

I dial the Whirvies and a man on the other end of the line says, "Hello, World Views." I assume I am speaking to a flake who gets excited at the idea of buying crates of very-used weapons for overthrowing the nearest authority figure to be found. I expect his name to be either "Rainbow Child" or "Snakes," depending on the philosophical leaning of the organization and whether they model themselves after hippies or bikers. I intend to approach him delicately since he'll probably think I'm with the FBI or the County Health

Department. I won't ask that he identify himself over the phone.

"Hi. My name's Eliza. I'm calling from out of town. I need to get in touch with Jonathan Gold. It concerns his younger sister, Ruthie." I hold the receiver away from my ear in case he hangs up abruptly.

"This is Brent. I'd like to put Jonathan on for you but he's not available, sorry." His tone has a collegiate ring. I wonder if Marcia Finkle got mixed up and Jonathan actually lives at the Whirvie fraternity house.

"Can you tell me how I might get in touch with Jonathan?" I let my voice graduate to a more upper crust tone.

"No one can get in touch with Jonathan. Our group became religious in nature seven years ago. My brother, Jonathan, chose to take vows of silence. He hasn't spoken often in many years and may never speak again." I'm irritated even though I have no right to be.

"Might Jonathan have stayed in touch with his family in spite of the vows?" I ask.

"Jonathan forswore his secular family many years ago. He has been secluded from everyone but the enlightened, and petitioners for the light, for seven years. We protect him, and the others in our order who have transcended, at a safe house where they live on pure thought and air." If it's been seven years, the transcendents must have required a few peanut butter sandwiches too, I think but don't say.

"What religion are you?" I ask as politely as possible considering that the question sounds rude.

"We don't believe in organized religion. We were a political group dedicated to establishing our vision of a better world, but we discovered spiritual values during a retreat at Big Sur seven years ago. We take from the best and most enlightened thinking in every religion, except the Mormons. We've established that the Mormons might be wrong." What a hard way to live, I think, believing almost everything. Jonathan may be floundering so badly that he can't even remember the family from which he originally came.

"If I came to your house, would I be able to see Jonathan? Perhaps petition for a little enlightenment? I'd make sure that I don't intrude on his spiritual state."

"I'm sure you're very sensitive. But we have to protect our less worldly brothers and sisters from the crassness of dealings with those who have not been spiritually awakened. Sometimes we need to protect them from their own past." The guy's tone remains calm, down-to-earth, very grad student, but menacing at the same time. Brent must be more into the gun-runner side of the business than the monastical.

"Your address is in the phone book, right? If I dropped by to explain why I'd like to spend a few minutes in Jonathan's presence, would I have a chance?"

"You couldn't go unescorted to the house where Jonathan resides. It's a more graceful place than this. We're in Venice. But if you do come here on a weekday, you may speak to Jennifer Whiten, Jonathan's protectress." The fabricated religion makes approaching the group both easier and harder.

"Thanks, Brent, that's great."

"I didn't mean to make a promise that won't be kept. No one from the outside has ever asked for Jonathan, so I don't know how the request will be handled. Jennifer Whiten doesn't let much diversion, even food and talk, stimulate the brothers' and sisters' senses and draw them from the plane to which they've been elevated."

"I'll keep in mind that I might have to sacrifice for the greater spiritual good," I tell him.

I tell Brent that I hope to see him soon. He suggests again that I don't. After I hang up, I enter a few notes on the last couple phone conversations. Somehow, the air's sweetness which I savored earlier seems gone. I feel a prickling at the back of my neck and look up quickly.

Doris Shipley sits on my padded chair with wooden arms that end in claws. The chair sits right inside the door. She grips a crutch with a cloth wrapped around the elbow rest. I don't like it at all. Doris got in the door and seated herself without my noticing.

"Doris, I didn't hear you come in." I speak more sharply than I mean to.

"I want to see the file on Andy. I want to see what you're doing for me," she says in a cold harsh tone. I get out the file while I try to figure out what's going on with Doris. Her eyes widen greedily when she sees the file with her code on an Avery label at the top. She hoists herself out of the chair. She's wearing a light blue and white checked pants suit with legs so short that I can see a lot of her white nylon socks above the scuffed white shoes. She shuffles toward me with one hand outstretched.

"Doris, I don't hand case files over to clients. I'm happy to share material verbally or prepare a written report." She curls the outstretched hand into a fist and steps forward to brace herself against the side of my desk.

"You think I don't know what's in that file? A bunch of nothing. You don't care if Andy's one of those mass murderers, I mean serial killers, who's going to tie me up and rape me and bury me down in the cellar." I try to interrupt but Doris can't wind down.

"I know everything you do. I know you spend your time looking for Ruthie and wasting time with that movie star woman and her kids. And I won't tell you how I know. If Andy bludgeoned me to death and left the body in my living room, it would be days before my private investigator would find me. Big help you'd be then. I'm going to hold you accountable."

"Doris," I falter under the barrage of displaced anger and then resolve that I will be calm and sensible. "Doris, I feel that I've explored Andy's background and present circumstances enough to assure myself that he is probably just what he seems. I talked to a couple guys he went to school with. I checked on his father. Andy's a weak but fairly nice guy, end of case.

"That doesn't mean it's my personal judgment that he's the best choice of companion for you. But you picked him out. I feel that it's a waste of time to accumulate more worthless data about his life."

"Worthless to you. I may take that boy into my home and make him family. The only one you're interested in is that trashy Ruthie. How much are you getting paid to drop me? You have all kinds of plans for Ruthie, but name one thing you've uncovered about Andy that was worth knowing. One thing."

I notice that Doris wears an outlandish necklace with a huge blue costume jewel which thuds back and forth just above her spotted white cleavage like the pendulum of a garish reproduction clock. I want to get rid of Doris. The world has been cruel to her but I feel like I've done my share of trying to offset other people's deficiencies.

How does she know about Ruthie? When did she get a look at Honor? I've never had this grave a security problem.

My resolve breaks down. "I've uncovered that Andy is a manipulative little twirp," I tell her. "Maybe that makes him more dangerous than some people, but not much. You asked me to tell you what I got from the background search and that's the bottom line. I hoped you'd figure it out yourself. You don't need a P.I., Doris. You need to find a couple of wholesome people, other than me, to spend time with. I'm not going to bill you for this piece of advice, either, it's my gift to you."

I know she must care about me in a weird way but a disarming smile doesn't melt her a drop. She's wheezing in her chest and she braces herself on my desk with both hands.

"I'm after you," she spits. "You can't give all your time to Ruthie. Not without giving me what I deserve. I paid my deposit first. Just remember that I'm going to get you." I'm shocked by the malice in her voice.

I have a certain feeling for Doris because I know so much about her life and because she has so much energy for me. But her demeanor right now strikes me as way off. She has made herself privy to information about cases I'm working on. Information that isn't available anywhere but in my files which are coded and ingeniously filed. And she's seen Honor.

"Doris, what exactly do you want from me? Let's talk about it."

"I've just decided I don't want anything from you," she scoffs. I recoil. "I'm a better detective than you'll ever be." She gropes for her crutch and fumbles until she has her weight supported by it. I try to meet her eyes. For one moment she looks my way. I catch a longing expression, and then she extinguishes it. She stumps away from my desk.

When she reaches the door, she grasps the handle and inclines back toward me. "You're not so cheap, either. I've paid a lot for what I got from you. Considering what it took out of me. I would never recommend you to anyone on a low budget. And I am going to get you," she raises her head regally, still resting her weight on the knob, "no matter what the price to myself." She throws her weight back to open the door and flings herself outside.

I knew this woman had strong feelings generated during my work for her, but I hadn't realized how crazy she has become. I open my top middle drawer and fish for a peppermint candy. Peppermint always restores my good nature.

I have one last call to make. I dial the Santa Barbara number of Antonia Noyes-Lowe, who never understood a word that Eileen said. "Geoff Lowe," a man answers her phone. I ask for Antonia.

"My wife is on an extended visit to her mother in Seattle. Can I help you?" I explain that I'm looking for Ruthie.

"Ruthie Gold? I knew her in my wife's college days. Antonia hasn't mentioned her for years." I'm learning to not expect much from anyone connected to this case. I'm not surprised to encounter another dead end.

"Would your wife be likely to tell you if she had heard from Ruthie in the past six years?"

"Toni and I tell each other everything. Ruthie and I were friends, too. She was a character. I liked her music." He sounds clear in conscience and willing to converse.

"How long will your wife be away?" I ask, to check whether there's anything odd about the situation.

"She's having a difficult pregnancy. She's going to stay with her mom until she's back on her feet." Geoff Lowe sounds forlorn. I tell him I may try to get in touch again later.

I haven't collected my messages all morning. I lock the front door as I leave my office. Not that the locked door has made my office inviolate. Doris seems to enter at will. Relations between me and Doris seem to be severed, so I may have a hard time finding out how.

I stare across the courtyard, trying to see if Sarah, Mike, or Lucas might be available. Collegiate solace would be welcome after being screamed at. Everyone's office suggests that they're occupied with business.

I open the door to the front office and smell some kind of savory pastry. Something that must have meat and onions inside, a new offering from Precious. Precious refuses to hear about annoyances encountered in the detective trade but she does a good job providing solace of another kind. She salutes me jauntily when I walk in, and signals that she has messages for me. I bypass the refreshment tray and make my way to her.

"Hi there," she says, good-humored today, "how's the number one attraction in the West Grand area doing today?" Precious wears a dark green and brown Western shirt with gold metallic threads shot through the fabric. Sculptured gold earrings swing enticingly when she moves her head. She has even integrated her hands into the look, a heavy coat of gold on each nail. She looks hot.

"Me and Berger's Low-Cost Furniture Corner are tiptop today," I reply to her opening banter. I check my mail slot and find nothing interesting.

"My friend, you haven't been getting enough sleep," says Precious after a closer look. "You still got your basic good looks but there are black circles under your eyes." She comes out from around her desk and pinches my face on either side. Now she tweeks at the curls around my face until she's satisfied with their placement.

Precious likes to flirt with me. It's her way to tell me she enjoys my friendship in spite of the phone messages I get. She treats the others in the building more seriously, because their professions seem more serious to her, but I get the roguish charm.

"If you've finished my touchup, could I have my messages?" I ask in as dignified a manner as possible. Precious snickers at me on general principle.

"You've been running around stirring up hornets' nests these last few days, haven't you, girl?" she accuses.

"What do you mean?" I've had enough harassment for one day.

"What kind of messages are these?" She gets out a small sheaf of pink 'while you were out' slips. She thumbs through and discards three or four. She retains one in each hand. "Woman calls and says, 'Ruthie doesn't need you. Stay away from Ruthie if you know what's good for you.' I mean, I ask you. I got this kind of message from my enemies in grade school."

Precious holds aloft the paper in her left hand. "Man calls. No name again. Says you know who he is. Wants to leave a message. So the message is, 'Forgot to put the cat out.' I go to tell him we don't allow animals around the building on account of Sarah's allergies but he's hung up."

She looks me in the eye. "Now you know I'm good on the phone with all your drips and drabs but you're scraping the bottom of the barrel lately. I'm happy to do for you. But too much more nonsense and you're going to be on the answering machine during office hours."

"Okay, okay," I say, taking up the remaining messages. "What can I do?"

"You could think twice before you leap." I should have known that Precious would have an answer. "This Ruthie associates with the wrong kind of person. Maybe you *should* stay away from Ruthie. Did you think about that?" She marches back to her desk and sits down in the optimally efficient posture for an office worker which she learned from an article in *Working Woman* magazine.

I can't, I think, she's my work. I can't stay away from Ruthie. If she's alive, I want to talk to her. If she's dead, I want to know. To know and to straighten out the hoary speculations of the people she left behind. It's all on Eileen Goldeen's tab as long as I don't invest anything of myself. And I never do.

head for Santa Cruz, where Ruthie played piano for the Jazzmatazz Dance Company to practice by, and Claudia Hollings and Jane Gold last moved in rhythm. I start down Interstate 880, enjoying the drive this first Monday in May. The route doesn't become scenic until I reach the woods leading to the pass. From the road leading in, the coastline looks clear of morning fog.

My directions lead me past quaint seaside cottages and U.C.S.C. student dwellings. I arrive at the correct address but I don't see a big sign advertising the organization for which I'm looking. When I walk up to the weathered three-story building, I find a discreet plate: Jazzmatazz Dance Company. Founded 1938.

Honor doesn't dance, doesn't like to be seen flailing and squirming, as she puts it. She hasn't given me the opportunity to trip the light fantastic much either, since I met her. So I decided not to infiltrate Jazzmatazz as a prospective performer. I made a mid-morning appointment with the director, telling him that I might be a benefactor. But when I see him I will admit that I'm a P.I., that I want information on Jane, Claudia, and Ruthie.

The receptionist has left the front desk unattended. I cross the lobby toward double doors that lead to what must be a large room. I stick my head in. I'm shocked by a familiar face among the dancers milling near the doors. At least, I think I'm familiar with the face, I only got a glimpse when we met before. He looks up, startles, then panics.

I'm positive when I see him from behind, running, that he's the guy who mugged me. I had more time to familiarize myself with his back side than his face. I take a few leaps toward him. He glances back, sees me coming his way, speeds up. I pound across the springy wooden practice floor, one hand touching my gun in its holster against my side. Not that I'm going to snipe at a jazz dancer, with his buddies standing around gawking. His running makes no noise, but each foot-fall of mine makes the floor thunder and jiggle. I should probably consider taking dance lessons some time. I thunder onwards.

"Halt," yells someone from the group of dancers which has quickly moved to one side. I ignore the Jazzmatazz corps-de-ballet. My quarry and I seem to be heading for a narrow doorway. The mugger disappears. A handsome young man wearing leg warmers and a red sweatshirt with black figures doing karate on the front. He's going to look funny on the street if he makes it outside.

I get to the open door on the far side of the room well after the nimble mugger has bolted through and disappeared. I find another door in front of me. The door feels durably constructed and it's locked with a heavy-duty deadbolt. To my right stands the shore of a sea of clothes, drapes, and furs, hung on racks. The mugger could have fought his way through the swells but I don't see any motion. To my left rises a narrow stairway with a metal guardrail.

I choose the stairs and run up until I hit a grey metal door on a narrow landing. The door opens onto a corridor laid with yellow industrial linoleum. Framed photographs, awards, and messy bulletin boards clutter the walls on both sides. I pound down the linoleum heading for a door at the far end that might lead to stairs that go down to the street.

As I pass an open office door, a flash of red and black catches my eye. I make a fast U-turn and come to a standstill outside the door. I hear a deep, pompous voice say, "Law-rence, you've just disrupted a rehearsal involving 62 people. Mrs. Trent phoned from below. Now I catch you fleeing past the administrative offices. This whole floor is off-limits to artists, as you well know, except at the express invitation of administrative staff."

"I freaked out when I saw someone I thought I knew. It will never happen again, sir. I can't apologize enough." The mugger's voice doesn't sound like an Oakland thug. The voice sounds very middle-class and, at the moment, obsequious. I notice that the dancer isn't even breathing hard from the run, which I am. And I keep fit.

I tuck in my shirt to create a look of authority. Then I step around the threshold. A tall, dark-haired man, too heavy to be a dancer, and my mugger, both look up.

"I have important business with Lawrence," I say, "and I think he'll want it to stay private." Lawrence turns, quick with nerves, to the older man, clearly trying to find a way to stay in the man's good graces.

"You're looking at Tasio Megia," Lawrence speaks to me theatrically, "one of the founders of Jazzmatazz. His mother, of whom you may have heard, is the co-founder. She's the ma, he's the tazz, and we all provide the jazz." Lawrence manages to sound as though he has been called upon to introduce two party guests who don't know each other.

He turns to Tasio and says smoothly, "This is my sister, Danielle's, friend. She's been plenty angry at Danielle and me lately, so I panicked when I saw her. I just couldn't take it." His presentation of the mythical situation sounds convincing. I'm impressed enough that I'll go along with the friend-of-his-sister story in front of the big guy.

"Susan Abrams," I say, and hold out my hand to Tasio. He looks adverse to shaking with me but conditioning gets the better of him. He mutters, "Anastasio Megia. Charmed," insincerely.

"Lawrence," he reprimands the fawning dancer. Lawrence smiles adoringly at him. "I want a fuller explanation for your behavior. In my office, tomorrow, 8:30 a.m. I'm going to require some assurance that your behavior won't disturb Jazzmatazz again." Lawrence lucked out when I found him. If I weren't here, Tasio would be on his case right now, I can tell. Tasio isn't sure who I am and whether he should behave politely in front of me for appearance's sake. He signals Lawrence to leave and nods goodbye to me.

"See you tomorrow morning, sir. I promise you this will never happen again." Lawrence is good at sincere. In the corridor, we turn to stand facing each other.

"Don't try to get away, Lawrence. I could always go back and talk to your father figure in there," I threaten.

"What do you want from me?" he sounds aggrieved, as though I'm hounding him unnecessarily.

"I want to sit down and reminisce about the first time we met. Where would you suggest? I'm not leaving your side until we talk." Lawrence looks anxiously down the corridor. Someone at the far end comes out to use the copying machine.

"Let's walk over to the Odd Man Out Deli. I'll buy you a cup of coffee and we'll get this misunderstanding straightened out. I think you'll enjoy the atmosphere." He pulls off that trick again. He sounds as though he had been meaning to invite me out on a coffee date any time. He spoils the tone a little when he adds, "I don't want to be seen with you when the troupe gets out for break in twenty minutes."

I stick with him while he goes to his locker. He pulls on a beautiful pair of fawn-colored breeches and a crisp white shirt. I make him stand beside me while I call from a phone booth and cancel Eliza Pirex's appointment with Tasio Megia. I have no hope of enlisting the director's assistance after galloping behind one of his dancers, center stage.

When we're both seated over cups of coffee, Lawrence alternately smiles at me with entreaty in his eyes and swivels to check the depression era-style clock on the back wall. He uses lots of sugar in his coffee.

"Lawrence, why did you mug me and threaten me? We're going to sit here until I find out." I don't feel like wasting my more sophisticated interviewing technique on Lawrence.

"I was paid to," Lawrence says self-righteously. "I'm not a criminal. This is embarrassing. I'm getting acting jobs and I'm respected in the company. You could talk to people who would vouch for me." His tone has gotten less suave.

"The fact is, you did something criminal, Lawrence. I'm your victim." I want him to stay tense. "So who paid you?"

"A lady. She never told me her name and she paid me in cash."

"Most employers pay hired thugs in cash," I point out to him. "How did she pick you out to do the dirty work, if you don't know her?"

"I found a note in my box at the company. The note asked me to meet the lady at a bar in the Mission, in San Francisco, to talk about a job. A lot of people know I do odd jobs for cash. I have two sisters at home. I help pay their way because I want them to finish school. For real. Usually, I do gigs at parties, sometimes I do tree trimming."

"How did she get your name?"

"She said she'd heard my name around Jazzmatazz. I don't know who she talked to. She wasn't the type to have friends with the company."

"What happened when you got to the bar?"

"She knew who I was when I walked in. But that wasn't so strange. Everyone else in the bar was mucho sleazy. Then she told me what the job would be. It didn't sound bad the way she put it. She said she had a good reason. No rough stuff, she said. She knew I wasn't good for that.

"She said it would be like delivering a message," he recalls. "She wanted me to go through your office looking for stuff labeled with certain names. But I told her that I wasn't going to get caught breaking and entering for any amount of money."

"Why did you steal the tape? How did she know that I had the tape with me?"

"Oh, the tape. She said I had to get something for her to prove that I did the job. Like your wallet or something. But I didn't want to be stealing your wallet, so I grabbed the envelope. When she got the tape she gave me some extra cash and told me I did an excellent job. I guess it was a lucky break for me. I hope I didn't inconvenience you," the courteous lad apologizes. I sigh.

"What did the lady look like?"

"Crazy glasses with diamonds all around. They went way up into two points on the sides. Like antiques. But you could tell this old lady wasn't wearing them to look punk. She was serious."

"How old did she look?"

"I don't know. I'm not too good with the ages of older people. Maybe she was 40 or 50. I guess she could have been 60. I don't know if her hair was grey. She was wearing this old lady kind of scarf that tucked into her coat."

"What was her coloring?"

"She was a white lady. But I could hardly see anything between the glasses and the scarf. She also wore lipstick and little round red circles of rouge on her cheeks."

"What kind of clothes did she wear?" I'm getting frustrated.

"An old lady kind of coat. I think it was pink or orange. She kept her coat on. And awful shoes. She wasn't my style, to say the least. It almost hurts to try and picture those shoes." Lawrence, the dandy, shudders.

"How much money did she pay you, Lawrence?"

He hesitates. "$100 deposit. $200 after. If I'd thought about it, I wouldn't have risked it for that kind of money." I'm beginning to think Lawrence speaks the truth. He would have made up a story in which he came off looking more glamorous if he were fabricating.

"How did you receive payment and when did you give the woman the tape?"

"We met at the same bar last Monday evening. She doesn't like you. She loved hearing everything about the job. She had the money for me in an envelope."

"Lawrence, when she handed you the money, what did her hands look like?" He searches his memory. I'm not going to give him the satisfaction of knowing that he has better recall than most people I've interviewed.

"She wore gloves. Maybe white gloves." Figures.

Lawrence remembers, "She said I better not talk to anyone about the job or she would make trouble for me at Jazzmatazz. She didn't scare me much. But I haven't said a word to anyone until now."

I talk to Lawrence about his life and career to see if I can get a sense of whether he's being honest with me. I think he is. With, perhaps, some omissions to enhance the dignity of his role. Nobody tells you everything. But if there were other significant points of interest, Lawrence probably would have enjoyed parading them for me. He's had to keep this story quiet for a week now.

I conclude our interview with some threats of my own. I design my threats to have more impact than those of his former employer, the old lady. I let him know that if he learns any more about the woman who hired him, I better hear about it, because I *will* make serious trouble for him with the Tazz in Jazzmatazz.

"Sorry about pushing you down on the stairs," he says, in a last effort to win me. "I overacted and I apologize." He pulls some shiny lip gloss out of his pants pocket and rubs the gel on his lips with a finger. It makes a smart effect. I wish I had some.

As we leave the deli, I see the dancers start to straggle out of the building, heading across the street. I take off my jacket, hoping they won't recognize me as the person they last saw chasing Lawrence across the practice floor. A few of them glance curiously but most don't notice me. I don't have any interest in speaking to the young dancers. Lawrence joins a group headed back to the deli, I enter the building again, walking purposefully.

The receptionist, at her desk in a small area under a cupola, looks faded and mean around the mouth. She smokes and types and answers the phone all at once. Her desk has a plastic statuette of a koala bear dangling from a tree limb with the inscription, "Hang in there 'til the weekend."

"Excuse me," I interrupt her after she hangs up the phone.

"Are you here to look at the typewriter?" Her voice sounds nicer than I had expected from her physical aspect.

146
▲

"No, sorry. I'm a private investigator hired by Cushman, Instill and Schraeder to track down a missing heir in the settlement of a large estate. I may be grasping at straws but the party in question had a minor job here about six years ago. There's a substantial amount of money floating around so we're following every lead we have. How long have you been at Jazzmatazz?" This story sounds more intriguing than the case of the missing college friend.

"I was a temp here until three years ago. I took over the full-time position from Lucille Dempsey when she retired. I wish I could help you." She looks like she really does wish she could help me. She must be bored with the phones and the 3″ X 5″ cards.

"Do you have employment records of some kind on the premises?"

"Yes. All the personnel information is kept in Ella Halliburton's office. She's Mr. Megia's secretary. He's the company director. We need his okay to release information to the public. Who are you looking for? I know everybody who's come out of here and become anybody."

"I don't think my party became anybody, Mrs. . . . ?"

"Trent," she chirps. I turn to get away before I become more involved with her. She blows off her disappointment in a next cigarette. "They don't have to be famous for dance," she makes one last try to engage me, "we display the picture of anybody who's anybody." I wave as I make for a small elevator.

I need to avoid any further contact with Tasio Megia. I need to find a person, other than him, who knows the characters and events in Jazzmatazz history. First, I want a look at the personnel files.

The elevator doors open onto the end of the office corridor farthest from Tasio's office. I stride up the hall trying to look guiltless in case Tasio steps out from his office into the hall, but inconspicuous at the same time so no one else will be interested in what I'm doing here. I'm betting that the secretary has her office next to Tasio. I'm hoping I'll find her office on this side of his.

I pass an open door. Inside, a short woman wearing a spangled skin-tight bodysuit and a tiara waters a plant on top of a wooden closet. She glances up and then looks back down at the plant, disinterested. I arrive at the office next to the director's, walk in, and swear under my breath. A young man in his early thirties wearing a pale blue shirt and suspenders occupies the room. He has the earnest look of my co-workers when I did bookkeeping.

"May I help you?" he asks politely.

"I'm Lucille Dempsey's niece," I tell him. "She sent me to check on a detail concerning her retirement." I cleverly employ the information that Mrs. Trent just gave me about the retired receptionist. I hope she's not dead or a frequent visitor.

The suspendered young man smiles helpfully. "You want Ella Halliburton. One office to your right, across the hall. She has all the records. And say hello to Mrs. Dempsey for me. Tell her the place hasn't hummed since she left." I gather that her replacement, Mrs. Trent, downstairs, doesn't have a hummer of a reputation.

"I sure will," I say, annoyed with my luck. The secretary's office sits directly across the hall from Tasio's. There's nothing for it but to brazen my way. I pace across the hall without looking back. I don't hear anything from the direction of Tasio's office.

The secretary's door stands ajar so I slip in. The office lies empty but not dark, the fluorescent lights have been left on. The records are at my disposal. I never have any qualms about reading anything. A piece of information set to paper, anything set to paper, becomes the private investigator's domain.

I flip through a file drawer that seems to have current concerns such as ticket sales, bookings, scheduling for staff. Another drawer holds reference material such as job specifications, union memorandums. A third they keep filled with building operations and equipment warranties and manuals. I open a large built-in cupboard and find office supplies on top and bank and payroll records below. I move to a side closet and hit pay-dirt. Personnel files in legal size folders and on 3″ X 5″ cards.

I flip through the working files in front. I pick out Lawrence Taylor's card. Then I hear footsteps at the door. I stick the card into the drawer as fast as I can. They would have a difficult time ascertaining at whose card I have been looking. I try grinning fecklessly at Tasio and a lovely older woman standing in the doorway.

"Young lady, what are you doing looking at files in my secretary's office?" Tasio sounds truculent, accustomed to having people under his control. I quickly recall the story that Lawrence gave him earlier to explain my presence.

"Sir, I wanted to leave a note with your secretary apologizing to you for my part in the disruption this morning. I waited but your secretary didn't return so I decided to look for a blank sheet of note paper." I slow down to study my story's effectiveness. So-so.

"I'm a friend of Lawrence Taylor's sister, my name's Susan Abrams," I say deferentially to the woman I assume to be Ella Halliburton. She bows her head slightly in acknowledgement. She wears a rich blue dress, the kind you have to dry-clean if you sweat at all. She looks too cultured to be overly protective of her files.

Tasio gives me the fish eye. "May I see some identification?"

"I came up without my purse. I'm sorry. If you would like, I'll go down to the car and bring my driver's license back." I don't carry I.D. when I do this kind of work. Except for the photocopy of my license inside my shoe.

"I'm going to call our security officer, Mr. White. You sit here until he comes up." He turns to Ella Halliburton and says solicitously, as he starts dialing Security, "I hope you won't feel intruded upon if I retain this young person in your office until Alvin White comes up. I just want to make sure there's nothing going on that could compromise us."

Tasio motions me to sit down. I do. I try to move sylphlike since these two are accustomed to being around dancers.

"Alvin White has been with the company since it was founded," says Tasio. "You'll have to be truthful with him. He's heard young people's stories for two generations and he knows to the word what parts of a story are true." Good, I think, it sounds like he's the person I hoped to find.

"I'm happy to speak with him," I say. I am sincere.

"Call for you, sir, from downstairs." A dashing young man with a fashionable short beard and mustache sticks his head through the door and addresses Tasio.

"Would you take a message, please, Stephen?"

"It's the senior Mrs. Megia, sir. She says she needs to speak to you immediately."

"Can you handle this for a moment?" he asks Ella Halliburton.

"Certainly," she says. Of course. She's the type of woman who accommodates everybody.

I could bolt when Tasio leaves but I'd be humiliated doing anything so rude in front of this woman. And Alvin White could be useful. Tasio exits with a last disapproving look at me, sitting with my legs crossed, trying to look civilized.

"How long have you been with Mr. Megia?" I ask Ella although I already know the answer. She obviously hasn't interacted often with people to whom she doesn't owe regard.

She hesitates as though it occurs to her for a second that she doesn't have to respond, but habit prevails. She clears her throat.

"I've been a patron of Jazzmatazz for many years and I consider myself a friend of the Megia family. My husband died suddenly last year. I found myself at loose ends so I agreed to act as Mr. Megia's administrative assistant." She adds with a trace of humor, "Secretary." I smile at her. I ask her to identify the dance productions in the photographs displayed on her desk. She speaks amusingly about each of them.

We both stand up when Alvin White enters. He's a thin, white-haired black man, pontifical in his movements. He and Ella Halliburton give each other a dignified nod. He motions us to sit back down.

"This is Susan Abrams, a friend to one of our young dancers," Ella does a formal introduction. "We've been having a nice talk just now. You'll want to speak to her and straighten things out for Mr. Megia. He's on the phone in his office. I'd better go see if he needs help with Mrs. Megia Senior." She gives me a last courtly smile and leaves. She looks like she doesn't want to be around if any embarrassing questions about my conduct get asked.

Mr. White settles himself on a short sofa bench by the door. "What's going on?" he asks impassively. "You must be the one who made a scene in the practice hall earlier. A couple of kids described someone who looks like you. And now I hear you may have been tampering with some of our files." A lot of career security guards I find to be gullible and out of it, this man isn't.

"My girlfriend's brother dances with the company," I say without my heart in it. "It's a long story but when he saw me here he panicked and ran. I went after him. Reflex, you know. I wanted to leave Mr. Megia a note apologizing for the disturbance but no one was here in the office so I had to hunt for a piece of paper. That's when Mr. Megia and Mrs. Halliburton walked in."

My story, authored by Lawrence Taylor, sounds stupid in the face of Alvin White's solemn bearing. "I guess it may look suspicious," I conclude on a weak note. I don't want to trip myself by saying more. He's going to try silence. It's an effective device. Alvin White sits gazing at me with one long scarred hand on each knee.

Finally, I win out. "What do you want here?" he asks.

"I'm ready to leave any time, never to return," I say lightly. A confrontational approach might get this guy's back up. Now that I've met with him, I'm willing to give up on getting information out of him, if he'll let me go without a fight.

White sits gauging me while the silence builds. I'm not going to win in the long run, the old man can probably wait indefinitely. I may as well try to win his confidence and see if I can get something useful out of him. I try looking like I have cracked under his scrutiny, to flatter him.

"Actually, I'm a P.I.," I pour out to him. "I need some information about a couple of people formerly associated with Jazzmatazz." Alvin White shifts quickly when I bend over to retrieve my license from my shoe. He sits back again when I hand him the card.

"Ms. Pirex, I wonder why you didn't feel that you could inquire directly about the information that you need. I have a policy of openness in all things. Tell me who you seek. I'll reveal anything to you that is within my power." The words roll slowly out of him in a rich bass.

I'll bet this guy sits down in their basement and reads religious tracts. His voice sounds like a preacher's and his diction smacks of the Bible. If I find out that Lawrence Taylor has misled me, I can direct the wrath of Alvin White onto him.

"Would you say that you're familiar with most people who have come and gone from here?" I ask him. He sanctifies my request with a further silence which grates on me.

"I remember those that have a significance for me," he says in his preacher's cadence. "Most folk have a significance for me. Some don't make a mark." He stops and folds his hands in his lap. "Give me the names," he says, suddenly down to business.

"Claudia Hollings and Jane Gold. They were here about six years ago." I haven't found any reason not to let the names loose here. I have to hope that no one connected to Jazzmatazz has any secret stake in the murky aspects of my case, excepting the old lady who hired Lawrence, whoever she might be. Alvin White looks heavenward and shuts his eyes. I try not to fidget in my seat while he scans his memory.

Finally he looks at me. "I have only the slightest recollection of either of those souls," he says. "Two friends, one, lively and quick, the other, timid. I couldn't say which was which."

This seems significant. Jane was not a rising star in this company, as Eileen believed. She and her friend, Claudia, passed through without leaving a big impression. I'm going to cross-check Alvin White but I don't think he has any reason to deceive me.

"I've met Claudia Hollings and she seems feisty. It must be Jane Gold who struck you as shỳ." I study him to see if this information provokes any further recollection. He looks profoundly impassive.

"I think more likely the other way around but perhaps I err. And now, I assure you, I've shared with you all that surfaces in my memory."

"You don't remember Ruth Gold, by any chance? She played piano here part time around the same point that Jane, who was her sister, danced with the company."

"Ruthie? I remember her. A remarkable woman. I spoke with her many times about what path her life should take. You wouldn't have found any written record of Ruthie here, we don't retain files on temporary practice pianists."

"What path do you think Ruthie's life took? Do you know where she might be now?" Alvin White goes inside himself and slowly returns.

"I think she went to Limbo," he states. I'm getting used to being thrown into the company of cranks, I don't even miss a beat.

"What do you mean? Can you explain? Do you have any addresses for her?" I press.

"I can't explain. I've told you all I know. I haven't seen her for many years." Alvin White looks troubled and tired now.

"I'm sorry that I didn't come to you initially to talk," I say, feeling benign toward him now that he looks old.

"I'm going to inform Mr. Megia that you meant no harm." His words flow as though he means to convey something of great importance. "Our professions are related. I would like you to consider my example."

"You toil not and neither do you spin," I reply. He stares at me and then smiles for the first time, a smile slow to surface.

"Exactly."

"I'll consider," I tell him. I consider every example.

Alvin White takes me downstairs, assuming that I'm going to straighten up and fly right. Once downstairs, I wait a minute to make sure that he doesn't follow me. Good-looking young people in practice clothes or jeans mill around the lobby.

I head toward the front doors on a hunch. A fortunate hunch. Alvin White's head appears at a side door. He looks reassured that I'm on my way out and shuts the door behind him.

I cut quickly across the lobby to the practice room. My glissando up to the administrative corridor takes only two

152
▲

minutes. The old testament tone to Alvin White's dismissal leaves me with a sense of foreboding. In my profession, one incurs a sense of foreboding often and ignores it always.

When I hear voices down the corridor, I duck into someone's empty office. The office's occupant has left cut-up newspaper in piles everywhere. I can't breath or I'll scatter newspaper clippings.

"She's completely out of control, Ella. Worse than she was during the episode on Easter morning. If you and I can't subdue her, we'll have to call the doctor." It's Tasio's voice. He and Ella are approaching the office in which I stand.

"Your mother usually responds to me, Tasio. I'll try again to calm her down." Ella uses a voice to answer Tasio which would soothe any small child or agitated adult. All the Megias probably take her like a tranquilizer.

Their voices die away. I give them a minute and then emerge. I jog down the empty corridor to Ella Halliburton's office. She's left her door open.

I retrieve Lawrence Taylor's card again just for kicks. He shows a spotty previous employment history, a mediocre school career in the San Mateo Unified School District, and a surprisingly diverse list of dance and acting credits since he joined the company. Some work he's done for the company has stars beside the notation which, I gather, means he got some special commendation.

Lawrence has been successful with Jazzmatazz. He's probably not from the underplace. He's probably what he said, a struggling artist who risked taking an odd odd-job because he was hard-up for the money.

It turns out to be harder to decipher the indexing on the older personnel files. They don't seem to be in chronological or alphabetical order. The order may have something to do with the company member's longevity or their prominence. I hurry my search. A second encounter with Tasio, Ella, and especially Alvin White would try my soul.

Eventually, I find a drawer of cards with the right dates entered on people's histories. I indulge in a relieved whistle of air through my lips when I find a card headed, "Hollings, Claudia." She gives no address except for an apartment she shared with Jane Gold in Santa Cruz. The card states that her education took place in various countries. Her father, a career Navy officer, died several years before Claudia came to Jazzmatazz.

Nearest relative, Claudia listed as Kurt Brewster: the nasty boyfriend who invented the murder scam and showed no remorse for Ruthie, if I have the story correct. At the bottom of the card I read, "Terminated," and a date six years ago. She could have been dismissed or left of her own accord, I can't tell. Not much useful information, considering her entire life to the age of 24 is supposedly capsulized on this card.

I refile the card. For some reason, the card marked "Gold, Jane" appears in a different batch of cards, at the beginning of the next file drawer. I experience a rush of eagerness and yank the card out without marking the place. My first glance gives me a jolt. Written at the bottom in neat red ink is "Deceased," a date, and a note.

According to Jazzmatazz' records, Claudia Hollings left and a month later Jane Gold died. Jane's death was reported to Jazzmatazz by—Claudia. And Ruthie vanished. All this, apparently, without anyone at Jazzmatazz getting excited. Alvin White didn't even particularly remember. Who choreographed this peculiar dance?

11

hit the gas to get home from Santa Cruz in good time. Honor is working this afternoon. A client wants her to create the art work for an elaborate antique auction catalogue. I'm assigned to pick up Jemmy and then Annabelle. There's an hour difference in the times the two of them get out of school so the pick-up takes a good chunk out of the afternoon.

Annabelle, Jemmy, and I are going to get T-shirts made for ourselves this afternoon. Jemmy plans to "Save the Dogs," which ties in with a personal campaign he initiated after observing the burden of unkindness borne by Oakland dogs. Annabelle needs one that reads, "Incorrigibles," with a picture of a teenage girl in tight clothes. Hers will match those of the girls in her club. The children think mine should say, "The Eyes Have It," but I'm the one who has to wear it and I haven't decided. My kids will make for a lot better company than the not-so-jazzy folks I've seen this morning.

I want to stop by my office before I pick up Jemmy. I feel like I'm on Ruthie's trail now even though the country that the path leads through isn't on the map. A lot of the pursuit has taken place on yellow scratch paper as I compose my notes detailing the weird, meaningless threats against me and the interviews that end up nowhere.

I check in with Precious and pick up a few routine messages. I haven't received any off-kilter phone calls yet today. I remind Precious that she can call Lucas, Mike, Sarah, or even 911, if Doris Shipley shows up again to torment her. I'm thankful that Doris hasn't been in contact this morning. I stroll into the courtyard, heading for my office.

On the way, Lucas Jang has me take a photograph of him and an apprehensive client standing on the uneven bricks with their arms around each other. Lucas practices innovative techniques in therapy. Our dejected gardener chops at the strips of lawn on the sides of the courtyard with an edger.

I approach my door with the sun on my back, open it, and leave the commonplace scene in the courtyard behind me. I feel assailed by a sense that something menacing waits in my office. I step inside.

The man stretched out languidly in my desk chair, feet casually crossed at the ankles, is attractive in the most conventional sense. Every feature could have been painted by number from a paint-your-own-handsome-man kit. His skin has the radiance that Honor and people in the media maintain. He wears a brown-grey suit, elegantly cut, a dazzling white dress shirt and a green and grey silk tie. He smiles and the lines of his mouth lengthen prettily.

"I killed her," he says in a TV broadcaster's voice. I debate whether I should remain where I am, or open the door so that I can yell for Lucas if I need him.

"Dr. Lilienthal, I presume?"

"I killed her. She died of unrequited love for me." He starts chuckling and then bursts out laughing.

"You mean Ruthie?" I ask.

"I can tell you don't believe me. I knew you'd be the skeptical type. And practical. I knew that you'd be skeptical and practical. And affordable, I hear. Skeptical, practical, and affordable. And I can tell at a glance that you have many more virtuous qualities, my dear. It's my business to put this kind of profile together using my intuition. But I'm not here to praise Eliza, I've come to save her from spinning her wheels."

"Dr. Lilienthal, I find your manner peculiar. I have reason to believe you *are* peculiar. I don't think that we have anything useful to say to each other."

"You're interested enough to send your seedy friend to spy on me. He didn't uncover my secrets, though. Not even my shallowest secret. His mission failed." Lilienthal raises both arms and locks his fingers behind his neck. A poolside posture.

He continues easily, "I'm a psychiatrist, you see. I can read a human psyche in the smallest retraction of a big toe. You might read my article on non-verbal communication in *Psychology Today*. It could only help in your endeavors. I simplified my body of thought for a popular audience. I codified my insights and laid them out in numerical order. You

156
▲

wouldn't have to try to comprehend the depth of meaning behind them, just memorize and retrieve them from your memory using the handy key. Last year. November issue." He maintains a satisfied smile as he unlocks his fingers and leans forward in his chair toward me.

"She pined for me and then declined into a final lethargy and death. I'm highly desirable. And unattainable. Desirable, unattainable, and extravagant."

"Dr. Lilienthal, I don't feel like listening to your ravings. I have two guys out in the courtyard who would help me get rid of you. Why embarrass yourself?" I feel exasperated by the man rather than afraid of him. He strikes me as a self-indulgent kind of maniac.

"You're right, absolutely right. I won't waste your time, I'll confess to you now. She turned her back to me. So I jumped her and sank my claws into the nape of that white, white neck. I clawed her carotid artery open and mauled her to death. She never petted me enough, never, so she got scratched." He leers at me across my desk.

I could have gotten a position, on the tenure track, teaching public speaking at Laney Community College. When crazies, the likes of Doris Shipley and Stuart Lilienthal, started in at me, I could have called campus security and had them taken away. In my business, I can't get away from them. They're like the building materials I need to construct a case. Even when they could be a hazard to me, even when they annoy me, I have to work with them.

"Dr. Lilienthal, do you have any actual information about Ruthie's departure from San Francisco? Otherwise, you *are* wasting my time and you'll have to excuse me, I have work to do."

"Was she able to depart? Or did she come back to die here? Did she die here? That's your dilemma, Eliza Pirex, Economy Sleuth, since you won't take my word for it. You know what I'm going to do? I'm going to take this case. I'm going to oversee. I'm going to make sure no old graves get violated and no catnaps get interrupted. I don't want you turning up any skeletons or little cat bones that should stay in their urns."

"That sounds like a threat, Dr. Lilienthal. I want you to know that I won't put up with you badgering me or irritating the woman who works in my office. Don't call my home, or threaten my children, ever again. If you persist, I'm going to find a way to put a lid on you. No matter how well-connected you are, it shouldn't be that hard to bring you down because

157
▲

you're crazy." I've never had to trade threats with anyone in such a nice suit.

"You're bullying me," he says playfully. "Threats roll right off me, though. My coat has a top layer that's not water soluble so I can go out stalking in the rain and then lick the beads of insult off." He rises gracefully and slinks to the door.

"Dr. Lilienthal? I don't know what your story is and I don't care. You seem able to maintain a psychiatric practice and a good reputation even though you're completely nuts. That's impressive." I face him squarely. He doesn't blink.

"I have been hired to get a current address for Ruthie Gold. I want the business and I have my reputation to maintain. If you decide to give me information that might be helpful, I'll be finished sooner and you won't be troubled by me. If there's an item I might uncover in this investigation which would compromise you, I'll ignore it if I can. I'm not out to make you more uncomfortable than you already are. I care only about getting results for my client. Think about it." He listens to me with his head cocked to the side.

"In one of my former lives I was involved with Ruthie Gold." His purring tone sounds forced, as though he'd love to spit at me. "I don't want old feathers ruffled. I'm done with that life and you're trying to rub my nose in it." He bares his teeth and licks them.

"I've become friends with Rich Goldeen in the last week." The mouser puts an emphasis on the word 'friends' in an intimidating way. "Rich was always impressed with my credentials and now we're friends. I'm going to lie down on your face and smother you while you're sleeping. Soon." He leaves the door open behind him. Does he think I'm going to cower at the name Rich Goldeen?

Then he pads back in, nudging the door open wider. He says, pleasant as a therapist, "You know, I feel that I can really talk to you. Just like talking to Ruthie." Then he's gone before I can compose an appropriate rejoinder.

Precious spoke truly when she pointed out that Ruthie tended to excite off-center people, she was dangerous in that way. Ruthie could have met an even uglier fate than I've been supposing. I think about the notation on Jane's card at Jazzmatazz, "Deceased." Did someone get killed in the course of Ruthie's decline and departure or didn't they?

Why hasn't Dennis' contact at the S.F.P.D. come through? I know the guy, Detective Fleet Hansen. I've met him at Dennis' parties. I call Dennis and get the policeman's office number and permission to ask why the guy hasn't come up with copies of reports for me.

"I'm on top of things." Fleet's high-pitched nasal voice doesn't instill confidence. "Ask Dennis to vouch for me. I owe Dennis a hell of a lot and I always put out for him."

"Okay, good. So where are the police reports on any occurrences at 1200 Leonid Avenue, apartment 303, spring of 1982?"

"There are a couple reports but a big gun in the department has been sitting on them for years." Fleet responds defensively.

"What do you mean? Who's got them?"

"Detective Sergeant Philip Cologne seems to have an ongoing interest in your cases."

"What might his interest be?"

"I don't know. He was on the scene for one of the incidents. I know he has nothing to hide. He keeps his nose cleaner than anybody in the department." Fleet sounds breathier and huffier after each question I force on him. He must be a real prince to work with.

"No one can even see the reports? Or use the computer to find out what's in them?" I ask, irritated.

"I didn't say that. I've seen them. I just haven't been able to get ahold of them long enough to copy them."

"You know what's in them?" I yelp.

"Oh, yeah. I skimmed them," he replies.

"Can you give me a brief run-down?" I request with what I consider remarkable restraint.

"Hang on, I'll dig out my notepad." He drops the phone noisily and I hear tremendous shufflings. He scrapes the receiver across the desk and returns.

"I guess I never made any notes." Fleet's voice now reminds me of an unseen bug's intermittant whine precluding the desperately desired respite of sleep.

"What do you remember?" I break in before I have to listen to him further explain his lack of enterprise.

"I'll try. I have a trained memory, after all. I'll give you the facts as I remember them."

"Okay," I interrupt, "what are the facts?"

"First, officers were called because the apartment's occupant, whatsername, claimed to have been assaulted. After the officers investigated, they busted the woman—"

"Ruth Gold," I put in.

"They busted her for possession of marijuana. Just your routine kind of happening in the City By The Bay. I can't tell you what came of the whole thing. I'd guess nothing came of it, except that Cologne still retains the files and except that someone got killed in the same apartment a short time after." This is the order in which he remembers the facts? Possession of marijuana before murder? At least I don't have to put up with Fleet and his trying little ways on a regular basis.

"Can you tell me about the time someone got killed?" I ask.

"The woman, Ruth, called to report a homicide. She identified the victim on the spot and again a while later at the morgue. The victim was Ruth's sister. Too bad."

"Her sister?" I ask, to make certain.

"I remember the victim's first name. Jane. Same name as my brother's girlfriend, a mouthy bitch. My brother's Jane, I mean, not the dead girl."

I try a few more questions but there doesn't seem to be any point in enduring Fleet longer, he's tapped out for now. He promises to get me the actual reports, by hook or by crook, at whatever risk to his good name, soon.

So what went on? Dave Gray thinks Claudia Hollings is dead. Ruthie told Eileen that Claudia Hollings had been murdered. But later Ruthie positively identified the body in her apartment as her sister's. Claudia says no one got killed, it was a joke. Jazzmatazz and the S.F.P.D. recorded the death of Jane Gold. Stuart Lilienthal says Ruthie died, he killed her. Or maybe she left, came back, and died. I have no idea how much of this convoluted story pertains to Ruthie. The moonshine and reflections off a cat's eye I can disregard.

An uneasy prescience, rising out of my worries about Ruthie, leaves me anxious to get the children from school as soon as possible and have them under my care. I don't think I'm going to be late but I hope Jemmy remembers he should go to his playgroup if he doesn't see my car right away. I don't want him hanging around the schoolyard unsupervised, with Lilienthal, Doris Shipley, Brad Evigan types, and God knows what other loonies, cruising the area.

This constitutes a landmark in my work history, I have never been the target of so many people with bad characters until this recent run. I decide not to take the time to pick up a slice of pizza even though I'm starving. I head out toward Jemmy's school and then on to get Annabelle.

The three of us sit comfortably around a white metal table under an umbrella after having our shirts made. I'm letting Annabelle and Jemmy share a cappuccino. They have promised not to tell Honor, no matter what tricks she uses. My shirt reads, "Looking for Ruthie." Annabelle and I like it. Jemmy is afraid that I'll forget and wear it while working undercover. He doesn't want bad guys to be able to spot me. I promise that I would never be so sloppy.

"You know," Annabelle begins thoughtfully. She looks content, coffee makes her happier than anything. "I don't see why, if this Dr. Lilienthal keeps picking on us, that you can't charge him for the time you're spending taking his calls and listening to him. Tina's dad is a divorce lawyer and he bills even when his client's kids call and tell him how their dad is taking the cast-iron cooking pots out of the kitchen and putting them in his car while their mom is at the store. Or when a grandma calls him to ask if he could save the marriage." I have schooled Annabelle to be fiscally conservative, although she's not a stingy person. I find her to be an enjoyable financial consultant.

"You're probably right, Annabelle, thanks."

"I think Dr. Lilienthal is a chicken," states Jemmy.

"What do you mean, Jem?"

"I don't think that he was the one who killed Ruthie's cat. I think he's afraid of everything. I think he'd be afraid of a cat's dead body. He was trembly when he was talking to us." Jemmy fishes some ice out of his water glass and cracks it between his teeth.

"You're hardly ever wrong about this kind of thing, Jemmy. Maybe I should relax about Dr. Lilienthal and concentrate on following up other angles." I still can't remember the irksome aphorism that Dennis likes to cite, but I think it would fit into this conversation.

"Don't relax too much," says Annabelle, worried. Jemmy wiggles in agreement. Then he sits up straight, struck with a pressing thought.

"Mom, you're supposed to work at my class' booth at the School Faire this Saturday, remember? They told us to remind our parents."

"I know, I know. What's your Momma signed up for?" There isn't any shade at their School Faire, you stand on an endless expanse of asphalt surrounded by swarms of hot little bodies bent on a good time.

"Momma made the flyer for the silent auction and the rummage sale," says Annabelle. "She says being at the Faire is too much stimulation for her." I can never figure out how Honor gets out of this stuff and I don't.

"Can I have your leftover?" begs Annabelle, peering into my glass. "It's cold already."

We go home and lie in the backyard until Honor gets home. Once home, Honor tells me she's going to a meeting this evening to discuss doing meaningful work to aid Latin America. She's gotten Annabelle and Jemmy a gig helping the childcare worker with the younger children. I warn her not to sign up for anything that involves living further south than Hayward until our children are older. She assures me she knows that our children are too young to be of use constructing building foundations in Nicaragua. I decide I'll go back to the office and get some letters into the mail.

Honor makes pasta and mixes it with pesto sauce, thick with basil grown in our garden, which she keeps bottled in the refrigerator. Honor usually directs our conversation at the table so that the children get maximum social development, but tonight she's in too much of a hurry. We eat hunched over the counter in a row. I miss her daily dinner theater and wish she hadn't skipped it tonight.

I hug Annabelle and Jemmy and give them a special kiss because I don't know if I'll see them before they go to bed. Honor kisses an "o" and an "R" on my new shirt and then kisses me goodbye. I wish I were staying home alone with her but she seems dead set on doing good for the world and the children would never leave us by ourselves anyway.

I park across from my office building. The front office has been locked and the alarm set. Mike and Lucas aren't working tonight. Sarah's lights glow behind her shades so she won't have activated the central alarm system yet. I enter my office and look around contentedly. The artificial light creates a cozy glow and improves the general appearance of the office decor. I am relieved to find that Dr. Lilienthal didn't leave any evil aura around my desk. I sink into my chair and coast on its wheels over to my big table.

I check the phone answering machine. Honor has already recorded a message telling me to bring home throat lozenges for Jemmy. His throat started tickling after I left and they don't have time to stop at a store before the meeting.

Next, I hear a communication from Lawrence Taylor. He wants to offer me his services. He wants to fight on the side of right. No matter what I need done, it will be between the two of us. Lawrence is a go-getter.

I begin some correspondence on a case I'm toying with taking, something tedious but more lucrative than most of my jobs, which would require using operatives reporting to me.

162
▲

I'm ambivalent about whether I want the work, so I write reluctantly, slowly. At the sound of a few taps on my door, I spring to my feet, hoping for a more interesting proposition than the one on which I'm working.

Rochelle Goffstein Woolley stands, very straight, in my doorway. She holds a grey handbag and she's wearing an interesting, maybe stylish, hat. She doesn't immediately offer an explanation for her presence. I invite her in, asking her if she'd like a seat. I offer her a stale pastry. She smiles engagingly across my desk.

I usually have a fizzy, pleased reaction to the mention of Rochelle's name. Tonight, with her sitting in my client chair, in person, I feel nervous. She looks comfortable.

"Is Mike working this evening?" He'd have to be working in the dark but I need some opening repartee.

"Mike left this afternoon for a conference in Washington, D.C. He'll be back Saturday."

"Did you think about going?" I ask. "Washington is even more fascinating than you'd expect. There's the political climate. Even the guided bus tours are interesting. It's easy to find your way around. The streets are laid out by numbers and letters and then by states on the diagonal. I had a job with the State Department. Years ago." I hear myself degenerating into nervous chatter and I know why. "I won't bore you with my whole resumé," I say, to cut myself off.

"I'm really interested, Eliza," says Rochelle, leaning forward. Her head tilts so that I can see one earring, a mosaic of amber and deep blue.

"Yeah," I flounder. "What brings you here tonight?" I'm hoping that she's stopped by to pick up something for Mike from his office.

"I saw your lights and came in hoping I'd get a chance to talk with you," she says, leaning still closer toward me.

"How nice," I reply, unsure whether the implications of this visit are nice. Then I make myself add, "Anything special?" She nods.

"In the last year, I've felt confused. Mike and I are working on our relationship. I want us to make it work. We're good for each other, Eliza."

"I'm happy for you, Rochelle." I ignore her first comment in case she wants to skip it. Some kind of good feeling between them made her choose Mike in the first place and then stay with him. I don't need her to share that part of her life with me. She didn't even call to break our last date, the week she got married. An explanation would have been in order years

"I know you wish me the best, Eliza. I won't talk about Mike anymore. He has nothing to do with it." She sits back, waiting for me to make the next move.

"With what?" I'm forced to ask although I already know.

"The reason I'm confused. You see, I've been attracted to a couple of different people in the last year. They're women. I haven't told any of them. I don't know how to handle it." I find myself targeting my eyes on her earring.

"Have you considered seeing a therapist?" I say, softly, so she won't feel like I'm brushing her problem away.

"My husband's a therapist, remember? I don't know how I would find someone to see me without possibly embarrassing him. Or me." I don't know whether this is a weak excuse or a valid concern. The therapy community probably is confined. When I mentioned earlier this week that Lilienthal was obliquely connected to my current case, Mike and Lucas told me that I should do anything I could to help the guy out. They gave him rave reviews. I haven't brought his name up to them again.

"That's too bad," I say.

"Eliza, how did you know that you were going to relate to women?"

Because of our history, this talk isn't the shock it might have been if Rochelle were nothing more to me than the happily married wife of a colleague. But I don't want to be having it anyway. I don't want Mike to find out that I counseled his wife on this issue. I don't want to be quoted espousing some line that gave his wife the impetus to abandon their relationship.

"Rochelle, there are support groups for women who are dealing with this issue. I think you would get a lot of insight from talking with other women in the same situation. And they would keep your confidence. Everyone in the group has the same motivation for being discreet." I fumble for paper so that I can find a telephone number, write a prescription, and dispense with this conversation.

"You don't want to talk about this with me, do you?" she asks, in the lambs wool tone we've both adopted for this talk.

"Well," I begin, "you know I care about you. But I don't feel like the person who should—" She interrupts me.

"Let's go get dinner. My treat. I'll take you to Ciardi's. It's new. It's got interesting food that uses a lot of fresh vegetables and it has a nice atmosphere." She smiles invitingly and the earring twinkles.

"I've already eaten. A lot of noodles."

"Then come watch me eat and I'll buy you a very good mixed drink. I had one there week before last. It was delicious, like an adult milkshake." She holds out an open hand so that I can see those sweet bony joints sculpted by the light of my desk lamp.

"I guess I could," I say, caution to the wind. Honor and the kids probably won't get home until ten.

After I watch Rochelle eat two artichokes stuffed with crab and spicy sausage, followed by a salad of green leaf lettuce and endive, we go to the Goffstein-Woolley house so that I can see the huge stained glass door that Rochelle has almost finished constructing after taking an adult education class. The door's design incorporates Berkeley buildings and local plants and animals in a pattern close enough to geometry that the piece suggests traditional windows.

I call the door a "brilliant piece of Californiana." The core of my being has been warmed by two drinks with generous portions of rum, sugar, and fruit, served in high round glasses. I feel very articulate.

When Rochelle takes her clothes off and drops them over the moss-green and lavender rug that came all the way from China to rest on the floor of her guest bedroom, I feel warmer. I lie back on a handmade quilt with my jacket on still, stalling for time while I figure out how I could have let this happen.

"I think about you every day," says Rochelle. "I go to sleep a lot of nights with my hand underneath me between my legs and the pressure reminds me of you." I remember that Rochelle was an interesting conversationalist when I was with her before. She moves forward and takes off my shoes, then pulls off my socks and rubs my feet with her thumbs.

Always with Honor, I feel privileged to be sexual with so beautiful a person. The multitudes who would envy my place in bed with her seem sometimes to be looking over my shoulder. I have invented my own kind of quality control to make sure I'm giving her as much pleasure as she could command from anyone else. Rochelle looks attractive but durable and ordinary as I study her now. When she lies down beside me, pulls loose my shirt, and slides her hands underneath, I touch her without hesitancy. The rest comes easy.

After, we lie on top of quilted pinwheel stars, more of Rochelle's lovely handiwork, and she says, "I hope I haven't inconvenienced you."

Rochelle invites me to her kitchen. She takes out two dessert dishes filled with apricot mousse from the refrigerator. She serves them with mugs of espresso made in a stainless steel espresso maker with a galloping horse crest on the top.

"I had forgotten that you're a very passionate person," I tell her. "It's so painless to be with you. You supply most of the energy and I just enjoy the ride."

"Mike thinks just the opposite," she says. "He's always cheerleading me when we're lovers. Bringing up encouraging signs of improvement in my technique at just the wrong moment. Disturbing me with his fantasies that are supposed to be arousing. Or just saying once too often that he understands me and he hopes I know that he'll always be patient. He makes me feel like a piece of leftover meat loaf." I don't know what to say.

The phone rings. I look at the round kitchen clock over the stove. The clock is hard to read because white roosters circle dizzyingly its navy blue face. 2:10 a.m.

"It's for you," Rochelle holds up the phone. Now she looks anxious and apologetic. No one knows I'm here. My stomach feels lousy, as I walk across the white linoleum, from the drinks earlier and the dessert I've just eaten.

"What are you doing there at this time of night?" It's Honor, her voice kills the warmth that has been making me so liquid.

"Eating apricot mousse," I say, before I realize what a decadent-sounding food it is, so sticky and heavy.

Honor hangs up on the other end.

The sun won't be up for a few hours. Our house stands with a black eye turned to the street. Inside the front door, an empty ringing and muffled shiftings down at the foundation greet me, deserted house sounds. Honor has taken the children and left. I stumble miserably through cold rooms and into the kitchen.

Honor stuck a note under our 5″ portable TV on the kitchen table:

I'm at my father's, thinking. You can have the children on weekends. They'll be at the house Friday, 6 p.m.   Honor

Used to notes from Honor with lots of xxx and ooo, kisses and hugs, I gape in despair at the stark notepaper in my hand. The paper bears Honor's professional logo at the top. I run my finger across the row of Victorian houses with a sun above them on one side, and a configuration of moon and stars at the other end. I put the tea kettle on to boil and take my assigned seat at the right side of the table. I've screwed up.

The peppermint tea I'm steeping was cultivated, gathered, and dried by Honor. The aroma embodies some of her finer qualities and stops my nose from running. I start to pretend that I am Honor critiquing Eliza's actions today. I get maudlin. Finally I shake the mood.

We're crazy about each other. I'm going to salvage our happy life together. Honor isn't naturally forgiving but I'll argue for one more exception. I'll give up looking at other women, except in the line of business. Honor has said she'd do anything for me. Many times.

I walk slowly upstairs to our bedroom. Honor made the bed before she left. I pace back down the hall and look into the children's rooms. She made their beds too. Each fluffy comforter hangs smoothly over neatly tucked sheets. I dread getting into sheets so recently emptied of Honor. I lie down on the small sofa in front of the fireplace in our room.

After a few wretched, sweaty hours' sleep, I come to and look over at the nightstand for the time but Honor took her clock radio. I close my eyes again and try to think about my agenda for this morning.

The doorbell chimes repeatedly at short intervals a few minutes later. I force myself up and put on Honor's fleecy pink bathrobe which she left hanging on a hook inside the door, shuffle down the stairs, and look out the peephole in the door. Through the cylinder, I see the distorted visage of Nancy, from next door, who considers herself a close enough friend of Honor's to come over this early. Nancy wears a petulant look on her face.

I open the door wearily. Nancy flounces in. She has dressed for the day in pointy Peter Pan boots and an immense sweater with a silver belt cinching the bulk in at her waist. Her hair has been styled into poodle curls on the top of her head and limp straight feathers down the back of her neck. With the ease of familiarity, she sweeps through my living room headed for the kitchen.

Nancy says, over her shoulder, "Honor's driving the kids to school today?"

I remember that I left Honor's note on the kitchen table last night and trot rapidly, overtaking Nancy, to the kitchen. I snatch the note and slip it under the toaster. Nancy follows me, looking puzzled and disapproving because of my sudden sprint. She looks for some coffee in the coffee maker and seems further put out when she finds the pot cold and empty.

"Honor and the kids went to visit her father for a few days," I tell her, responding to the obvious curiosity on her face. She looks skeptical.

"Really? We talked about going to the Nature Company this morning, just yesterday."

"She got the urge on the spur of the moment, Nancy." Nancy runs her eyes up and down the woolly bathrobe, not my usual style.

"I want to tell her that I'm having dinner with her brother, Linden," says Nancy with an odd smile. "He called last night. Of course, it's not a date really. I mentioned investing in a videotape project that Heavenly Bodies might sponsor. So we're going to talk it over. Honor would be excited." I wonder why Honor would be excited. I'll ask her, when we reconcile.

"I'll let her know when I talk to her," I say. I hope Linden Sutton doesn't hear from his father about Honor and me and tell Nancy. I have to see Nancy every day on my way in and out of the house. She's the last person with whom I want to discuss this mess.

My mind strays to business. With Honor gone, how will I investigate the possible connection between Newell Sutton and Rich Goldeen? I dismiss the question. The three untenanted beds upstairs with their perfect hospital corners distress me more. I swallow, feeling awful. Maybe I'm getting Jemmy's tickly throat.

"I didn't come over to see Honor anyway," Nancy suspends my brown study. "I was hoping I'd catch you before you left for the office." She looks at me with more attention than usual.

"Me?" I say, not wanting to encourage her. I look into the coffee canister and find a good supply of some potent smelly beans. I load some into the coffee grinder. Nancy looks more relaxed now that she sees the amenities, to which she's accustomed, on their way. I get two frozen bagels out of the freezer and put them in the toaster oven.

"Yes, you. Some guy in a fancy suit came to the door and asked me if I'd lost a cat. I told him no, Pavarotti was sleeping out on the back porch. So he says, 'Sorry, my mistake.' He was smiling in a strange way. I can't describe it. I think I've seen the guy before, driving real slow around the neighborhood. Is he dangerous? Honor wouldn't say, if she knew, because she doesn't talk about your cases. I have a right to know since he came to my door." I get out butter and herbed cream cheese while I consider.

"I don't think you need to worry about him, Nancy. He's crazy. But I don't think he'd cause you trouble for no reason. Call me if you see him again."

"Okay. Honor says you're cautious. And if Honor says you're cautious you must be very cautious." I sigh. I hadn't known that Honor knew that I try to be circumspect, for a P.I. Nancy and I sit glumly chewing, and sipping at the too-thick coffee.

"Nancy?" I say, after I have thought about her newsbrief.

"What?" She startles as though I have jarred a daydream.

"Why don't you keep your cat indoors for a while. I've heard about some accidents involving cats lately. I wouldn't want anything to happen to Pavarotti." Nancy opens her mouth to question me, looks over at the not-forthcoming look on my face, and purses her lips together.

I get to the office with an hour and a half to prepare for my meeting with Eileen Goldeen and Rich. I start by finishing a letter that I left on my desk last night. I'm disturbed that I left paperwork exposed, considering the uninvited visitors to my office lately. Next, I outline every item pertinent to the search for Ruthie, in the order that I want to present them. I block out a map of the avenues that I might explore if Ruthie remains hidden.

I'm interrupted by a knock. Someone waits politely for me to respond. I yell "come in" and Lucas Jang enters, seating himself on the arm of my client chair.

"Working late last night?" he says, to make conversation.

"Yeah, why?"

"Sarah said Honor called her last night to ask where you were. Honor was trying to track you down for one of your kids."

"We got in touch," I reply.

"Nothing serious going on with your children, I hope," Lucas responds. These therapists take everything seriously unless you convince them otherwise.

"Jemmy developed an urgent need for throat lozenges."

"You seem out of sorts this morning, Eliza. I won't intrude on you very long. You remember that Precious' anniversary party will be held a week from next Saturday? You weren't around for the discussion, but Sarah, Mike, and I thought maybe we should give her a painting or wall hanging for the master bedroom in her new house. Her family will be giving her a bed and mattress set. We've talked to her mother, she says that the room is brown and orange. Don't you agree that we will want to give something especially nice?" I nod. "We discussed yesterday whether you might be willing to choose the painting."

"Why me? Look around this office. *Architectural Digest* has never requested an interview and a layout featuring this place, believe me."

"We assumed that Honor would assist you in acquiring the perfect piece at a reasonable price since she has that good friend who owns the Versailles Storage Store."

"Oh, Honor. I can ask her. She's busy but she'd probably be willing to do it for Precious. Otherwise, why not you? You have excellent taste, your office is the showpiece around here."

"I'll look into the purchase if I need to, let me know." I press the bridge of my nose where I feel like I'm about to spike a headache. Lucas leaps to his feet and circles the desk. He stands behind me and begins massaging my neck and shoulders with his thumbs. The headache recedes. Having therapists at hand can occasionally be helpful.

"Lucas? You know what Dr. Stuart Lilienthal looks like, right? Can you do me a favor? If you see him around here, keep an eye on him. I don't want him in my office. If you should get a chance to talk to him, I'd appreciate written notes of your impressions about his state of mind." Lucas' fingers keep working.

"I assume the reason has to do with privileged information between detective and client?"

"For now. I'll fill you in when I've cleared up the case that I'm working on," I tell him.

"It's good seeing you, Eliza. Let me know if you can come up with the gift for Precious." Lucas leaves whistling. Lucas appreciates the amusement with which my business provides everyone in the building. I'm glad I made someone happy this morning.

I check my desk clock and see that Eileen and Rich are ten minutes late. I'm not surprised to find Eileen tardy but Rich strikes me as the punctual or early type. I debate calling their house to make sure that they've left, when there's a crash as Rich blows through the door, throwing his weight against it before he has completely turned the handle.

Rich wheels around and grabs Eileen by the arm to yank her through the door as well. She misses a step and lurches after him. Eileen hasn't dressed for this occasion. She looks almost disheveled and the knees of her hose have dirt marks.

Rich stands in front of my desk with his chin thrust up far enough for me to see the cords running up and down his throat. "I told my wife we didn't need to take up your valuable time by coming in and meeting with you but she insisted, so here we are. But you're not going to change my mind." He sends Eileen a challenging look. I smile, trying to lend some power to her, my actual employer in this matter.

"Mr. Goldeen, Rich, if you'll recall, you set up this meeting so that I can relate to you what progress we've made in locating Ruthie. I'm prepared to do that."

"Never mind. We've had new information. We're here to settle our account with you. I consider the case closed." Eileen won't meet my eyes now, she looks downward and twists her wedding band.

"What's going on?" I inquire of Eileen but Rich sits down, crosses his legs, and replies after clearing his throat.

"I've been in contact with Dr. Stuart Lilienthal since we met last. Dr. Lilienthal tells me that in checking his files, he

171
▲

finds that he did have some correspondence with Ruthie after she left San Francisco. It slipped his mind until now."

I give Rich no encouragement but he continues. "Ruthie let him know that she would be staying with her parents in Los Angeles while she worked toward a graduate degree in music. There's no mystery about it. Eileen can track down the Golds' current address herself and get in touch with Ruthie sometime." Rich has gone limp and shaky. He sends Eileen a look designed to insure her silence. She doesn't raise her head.

"If you worked fast instead of cheap you'd have been able to tell us this yourself," Rich adds without authentic vehemence. His usual stuffing seems to be missing. He grimaces and grasps his stomach under his coat. Then he takes out a roll of large white pills and chews one. Eileen's flaccid posture indicates that she took her pills before leaving home.

"Rich, my investigations don't lead me to believe that your information is correct." I turn to Eileen.

Neither of them stop me when I begin to outline the unusual circumstances under which the entire Gold family, except brother Jonathan, disappeared. I discuss the odds of a whole family vanishing at the same point in time. I verify that there have been no credit records, DMV information, tax returns filed, no clues about their existence since that time. Then I touch upon the subjective, I recapitulate the despondent quality of Ruthie's last postcard to Dave. And a last telling point, that not one but several people seem to have an interest in preventing me from learning the fate of Ruthie.

To emphasize my next point, I slow my speech. "I have firsthand evidence that Dr. Stuart Lilienthal is a disturbed person. He could be directly involved in Ruthie's disappearance. He has attempted to harass me into dropping this case. I discount any statements from Dr. Lilienthal which are intended to prevent me from pursuing Ruthie." Rich stares unresponsively. I decide to be direct. "Dr. Lilienthal is a wacko," I tell them. "I'm positive."

Rich rallies and blusters, "Dr. Lilienthal has a nationwide reputation. He's famous. I'm going to start wearing the same line of shoes as he does. The man's got taste."

Eileen says, without spirit, "We've always known that Dr. Lilienthal was the one who jumped Ruthie, Rich. Eliza's right. He's mentally unbalanced."

"Lilienthal and Ruthie had a falling out," Rich begins an attempt to argue his case. "Who knows now which of them lied about what happened during the breakup? Ruthie was not a stable girl. She's more likely to be the one who lied than

Stuart Lilienthal. He probably didn't jump her. After all, Ruthie had stories about when she was a teenager that would make you wonder. She was always melodramatic."

"Ruthie never lied," says Eileen categorically.

"Ruthie was a wreck," says Rich.

"Ruthie should have turned up by now," I reiterate.

"I don't think you get it," says Rich. "You're fired. We want your final statement. We want the case closed. When we need a detective we'll give you a call."

I walk around and sit on the front of the desk, in front of Eileen and Rich. Then I turn away from Rich.

"You hired me. Do you want me off the case?" I ask Eileen. Because her dyed leather purse is lavender, it looks as though her downcast eyes reflect upon its surface.

"I'm footing the bill around here. We're done with this," Rich barks roughly. Eileen looks up and sends me a lift of the eyebrows imploring, "Don't push him." I decide it doesn't make sense to provoke a potentially savage bear with digestive problems and no savoir faire.

Rich speaks snidely. "It wouldn't be your style to donate your services. I doubt you're going to volunteer to hunt for my wife's screwed-up friend who's probably giving piccolo lessons at a nursery school in L.A."

His watchful face tells me that he desperately wants assurance that I will drop Ruthie. Would I donate my services, I ask myself? I make sure my billing hits a certain mark each month even if I have to compromise my integrity slightly.

Eileen turns to look at Rich. "You're meeting Dab Clevenger. I'll drop you off." Rich looks taken aback. The undone feeling of our business turns Rich's feet to lead as well as mine. None of us moves right away.

"I do have a business engagement," Rich says after an interval. "Send me a bill and I'll put a check in the mail." His normally insolent but open face takes on a more devious cast.

"If you decide to think about my offer to do some real investigative work for my firm," he says, "I'll talk to you about it." The guy has absolutely no finesse. Eileen still doesn't raise her eyes from her lap. Maybe she's looking at the brown stains on her knees. I raise one hand and Rich jumps like I'm going to hit him. I wave goodbye.

"Let's go," Rich says. He takes Eileen by the forearm and leads her to the door. She doesn't look back.

I wonder what, besides chemicals, sapped the vim out of Eileen and most of the punch from Rich. I'll find out later from Eileen, although it might be hard to get in touch with her, sequestered in Rich's detention facility on Grouse Court. Most of my clients, in their busy Oakland apartments, are easily accessible by public transportation and visible from the street when the shades are up.

I look at my checklist after they leave. I cross off the items that just transpired. Eileen didn't call me off Ruthie so I intend to proceed as though the talk with Rich never happened. I move on to my next chore. I pick up the phone and call Dwayne Blount, not yet on duty for the night at Kains College.

"Did Lee mention to you that I'm not expecting to hear about any more incidents like the ones that happened before I was hired to work at the college?" Dwayne deserves to squirm more than I've made him squirm.

"Yes, ma'am, you won't ever hear anything. Lee and I, we're real good workers now. And he says you'll be checking up on us all the time. I hope this call doesn't mean that you might go changing your mind and get us in trouble with the college?" I feel that he deserves the discomfort, even panic, in his voice because of his former unscrupulous behavior toward women college students. I wait long enough to let him have a good long squirm.

"If you behave like two gentlemen and two productive employees, I won't say a word. If either of you screw up, the college administration will hear everything I know." I don't believe in sentences with no hope of pardon except for people who have turned into monsters instead of human beings like, perhaps, Bradley Evigan.

Dwayne tells me that he and the other guards plan to visit the courtroom tomorrow when Brad Evigan gets arraigned. They want me to join their party for the outing. I picture Brad, in professorial garb, looking earnest and intelligent, as he hears the charges read against him. I tell Dwayne that I'm touched by the invitation, glad they still consider me one of the guys, but I won't be able to make it. I might have to testify at some point during the trial. That would be enough time spent in the presence of Bradley Evigan.

"You know what Lee read in the local paper?" says Dwayne, now ready to prattle away at me. "That girl, Tara, her mom says she wants to go to a convent and be a nun when she grows up. Can you believe it? What a waste." There's no way I could have changed Dwayne Blount very much, what did I expect? I end our discourse with a last mild threat or two, feeling like I've fulfilled the last of my obligations to Kains College.

174
▲

I am about to begin work on item five of my checklist when the phone rings.

"Eliza?" Eileen's voice carries her characteristic stamp which was missing this morning. "I've dropped Rich off and I'm at a phone booth down the hill from the Claremont Hotel."

"How are you doing, Eileen?"

"Not very well. I wonder if you could meet me someplace. Someplace where no one Rich knows would go. It can't be Jack London Square or that kind of place."

"How about the Berkeley Public Library? Or do Rich's friends tend to be readers?" I have things to check in old newspapers and I want to get some back issues of *Psychology Today*. Precious throws all but the last few month's magazines away.

"That would be great," agrees Eileen. We establish a meeting place in the periodical section.

I call home to see if Honor has come back. Honor loves her routines, loves spending a whole day doing repetitive chores in her own orderly house. Even if she hasn't forgiven me, she needs me—to avoid disrupting the habits of eight years. I let the phone ring until the answering machine clicks on and I hear my own voice telling me no one is home.

Eileen sits among a crowd of propped newspapers. She manages to blend into the atmosphere of the library, golden with old wood, grimy from years of traffic. She leaps up when she sees me. A few readers lower their papers to make sure our meeting isn't news.

"Let's go out where we can talk," I tell her. "We can get some frozen yogurt for lunch."

We buy huge yellow cardboard cups filled with Mandarin orange and deep-Dutch chocolate yogurt, and we both order cashews sprinkled on top. We walk back in the direction we came and sit down on the wide concrete ledge surrounding a planter box in front of a bank. Students eating tremendous cheese and pepperoni-covered pizza slices off sheets of waxed paper create a savory steam in the air.

"First of all, the most important point to clear up," Eileen speaks with an erratic moment of authority she lacked this morning, "involves Rich." I wait for some grand pronouncement. "You may have noticed that Rich and I have different approaches to this case." This silly statement reassures me that Eileen has been restored to herself. I'm happy to see it.

"Rich has no approach. He wants the case closed," I remind her.

"He doesn't deserve to say a word and I'll tell you why. You're on the case. You were never off it, but I had to let Rich think so. I hate to keep things from him but he's not being fair. I'd love to tell Ruthie everything that's been going on. She'd be very upset for me."

The lavender eyes grow cold as amethysts. "While we were fighting about finding Ruthie, I found out that Rich had been unfaithful. He was unfaithful to me with Ruthie's sister, Jane. My friend's sister. I couldn't stand Jane. She looked down her nose at me. I was always bumping into things when Jane was around. He was unfaithful to me with someone I didn't even like." The amethysts secrete tears. She bends her face into the frozen yogurt.

"Eliza?" she continues quietly, so that the surrounding students can't eavesdrop. "You know what else he as much as admitted? Rich was after Ruthie. All the time he talked about what a walking disaster she was and how scrawny, he wanted to sleep with her.

"Rich had been drinking a lot when we discussed this. Alcohol irritates the lining of his stomach, so he doesn't usually drink. He got pretty crude. When I started yelling at him about Ruthie, you know what he said? He said, 'So what, you wanted her too and never got her.'

"I asked Rich if he was saying I was homosexual. He said he didn't mean that, he was just talking." Eileen stops and checks my reaction in a way that makes me sure someone has told her the basics about my life.

"I'm sure he was talking about the way you valued her friendship," I say, so that she won't feel awkward.

"Finding out about Rich made me think. Strange things always did happen around Ruthie. Rich being with Ruthie's sister is a strange thing. Rich has never gone out on me any other time."

I don't comment. Since we're speaking of strange, I tell Eileen the rest of the peculiarities that have come to light.

"Is Jane dead?" I ask her. "The police seem satisfied that the body in the apartment was Ruthie's sister and the dance company records list Jane as deceased."

"I don't know," says Eileen, not looking radically upset by the idea that Jane died soon after sleeping with her husband. "Ruthie seemed to be in her right mind when she told me about her girlfriend, Claudia, getting murdered. Wouldn't she have been a lot more upset if it were her sister? Of course, she *was* upset, I just assumed she was upset about Claudia dying in her apartment. She left so soon after that, I don't know any

176
▲

more. Wait. I do know that Jane left her job at the dance company a short time before Ruthie went away. But it's not like someone killed Jane for leaving Jazzmatazz, is it?"

"Did you know Jane Gold well?" I ask.

"Not in the biblical sense," returns Eileen unexpectedly and breaks out in high-pitched laughter. "She'd been in school back east before she moved to Santa Cruz. And she and I realized right away that we didn't get along. She'd be gliding around like a swan while I was crashing into furniture. A swan is a very mean bird, you know. Jane and I had a miserable relationship."

Eileen's tone becomes angry again. "Rich says he ran into her by accident the time the thing between them happened. He says it only happened once."

I nod wordlessly.

"If you had already found out his secret about Jane, why did Rich want me to drop the case this morning?"

"Unhappy memories?" suggests Eileen.

"Eileen, did you know Claudia Hollings well? Have you thought of any reason why she would have been involved in calling the murder a joke?" I don't expect much more from Eileen, not a woman with hidden depths, than I have gotten already.

"I didn't know her. Ruthie always made it sound like Claudia was nice but not very exciting. Ruthie said she never dated because she was a nebbish. Rich met her once. He might remember her. He likes the quiet type. He always says that if I go before him, his next wife is going to be the strong silent type. He has some other qualities he's looking for, too." She pauses.

I idly consider how marketable a commodity the savage bear would be in the remarriage market. Between the Orinda house, the company that Dad owns, and the veneer of respectability, probably very saleable. I refocus my thoughts. I'm not going to be able to cull any more forgotten material from Eileen. She has turned into a dead end, like every avenue in this case.

Before we part, Eileen insists on detailing her personal finances. "I'm going to put all the money we need to find Ruthie in my Money Market checking account in Walnut Creek. Rich doesn't know about the account. I use it to buy him presents or to buy presents for people Rich doesn't like. Don't worry about money. I'll pay for everything." She beams at me.

"Thanks, Eileen. If nothing comes up between now and then, I'm going to leave for L.A. on Sunday evening. We know Ruthie probably went through there after she left San Francisco. I've called L.A. but I couldn't locate Ruthie or her parents by phone.

"I'm going to try to see Ruthie's brother, interview people at the temple Mrs. Gold belonged to, maybe get in touch with the artist, Ottie Dresner, who was raised with Ruthie," I tick off the list. "Maybe I can find some leads on Jane, find out who might have wanted to see her dead and why."

"I'll send you a check before the trip. You can bill me for any extra expenses or apply any remainder to my account." I've never had a client so eager to pay.

Eileen's face grows hopeful. "Do you think I could help if I came with you? I know the family well enough to introduce myself."

"I think I'll be able to move faster and more economically by myself. Thanks, Eileen. I'll keep in touch, so we will be working together. How can I get through to you without talking to Rich? Or are you going to clear this with him?"

"Let's keep this between you and me. I'd rather let Rich know when I've already found Ruthie. This way, he'll tell Dr. Lilienthal, for now, that you're not looking for Ruthie any more." She fishes in her purse and finds a filthy cloth handkerchief. She delicately wipes yogurt from the corners of her lips.

Eileen details her weekly schedule, indicating safe time slots to call her, iffy time periods when Rich might stop home to make himself a sandwich on his way to sites, and off-limit times. She explains which phone numbers attach to what telephones. I take careful notes.

Eileen can't recall how to get back to her car even though she is able to tell me the address where she parked, which she has faithfully memorized. I walk her one block, then we turn right at a drab, scantily stocked hardware store which has been a landmark for years. Eileen doesn't remember walking past the store before. Finally, to her relief, we get to the side street where her car waits.

We arrange a time for us to get in touch on Friday. Eileen digs for her keys, first methodically and then frantically. I wait to see if she'll need a ride from me, wondering how she will explain the location of the car to Rich if she doesn't find her keys. Maybe he's used to hearing flaky stories from Eileen and won't worry about it.

Eileen begins thumping her coat pockets. She reaches inside her coat and plucks her key ring out, crowing happily. She opens the door and gets in. She rolls down the window, smiling. I lean over to say goodbye.

"Something's wrong in there. Get out." I open the door and drag Eileen out by the arm. The smell inside the car reminds me of cases I've worked in the past. I pull the back door lock and open the door. A red and white shoe store bag lies on the back seat.

"Is this yours?" I ask Eileen, pointing to the bag. She looks bewildered. She must have a pretty dead nose.

"I don't know. I don't remember." A dog dish, wadded waxed paper, a pair of boots curling at the toe, and other garbage litters the floor of the back seat.

"Have you left any perishable food in here recently?"

"Maybe I lost a corned beef brisket last week. But I think I never bought it. We had canned chili on rye bread instead. The chili gave Rich stomach cramps, so I remember." Eileen peers further into the car as she speaks.

I reach in and pick up the plastic bag. The bag has a recognizable heft to it. I look inside. A distinctive-looking cat, with a stylish earth-tone coat matted with moisture, rests inside. The cat's head lolls sickeningly to one side. The smell suggests that the cat died some time ago.

I wish I didn't have to reach in the bag and take out the letter attached to the cat. Especially because I already know how it reads. Eileen inches forward and looks into the bag.

"Dutchess," says Eileen. She bursts into tears and slumps against the car. "I've breathed in that fur while I sleep, for nine years," she sobs. "I'm losing everything." I put my arm around her. I pull out the note and read, "Forgot to put the cat out." I feel a surge of vexation.

My irritation centers around the beleaguered, emaciated figure of Ruthie. Ruthie, you loser. Couldn't you have picked one normal easy-going associate to make this case easier for me? Even Eileen, either druggy or agitated, always a cross between garrulous and touching, feels like a burdensome legacy.

"He can't hurt me anymore," says Eileen after she exhales deeply. I assume she means Dr. Lilienthal who I implicated most heavily in our earlier talk, unless she thinks Rich killed her cat, or killed two cats. "I only had one more kitty to lose." She achieves a certain pathetic dignity. I decide not to let her hold onto this comforting thought.

179
▲

"Dr. Lilenthal may be instigating a campaign to make sure that you drop the case. If so, I'm sure that he'll try to get to you again. Probably through Rich. It's just as well that you're going to let Rich think you've dropped the case." She agrees with a raw smile.

"God. It's going to be awful when I fight with Rich, now that Dutchess is gone." Accustomed as I am to Eileen's leaps in logic, I don't bother to answer.

I consider the possibilities. Eileen left the car locked. Was the bag with the cat there all day? Did Rich put the cat in the car? How much of this case could Eileen have rigged herself? To keep things going. I look at her closely. She looks ravaged over the death of her cat. She herself seems to have leapt to the conclusion that Lilienthal got to Dutchess.

"Eileen, I want you to keep your eyes open. Call me if anything else happens that makes you at all nervous. I don't know how physically dangerous Lilienthal is. But until this all unravels, let's be cautious." Terrorized, grief-stricken, and slightly exhilarated, Eileen bobs her head in agreement.

"Give me the bag," I tell her stiffly, "I'll do something with the cat." Eileen picks up the bag and holds it against her chest.

"Dutchess will have a final resting place next to three of her children, where she will be near Rich's mom's golden retriever, Dairy Cream, who was a friend to her. Rings isn't in the plot of course. Ruthie let some city sanitation workers take him away in a trash can liner before she talked to me. I didn't get a chance to make burial arrangements for him." Eileen looks at her watch.

"I've got to pick up our new window blinds before I get Rich. I'm going to put Dutchess in the trunk. I can put the shades in the back seat. I think it wouldn't be bad if Rich thought that Dutchess died of natural causes."

Eileen's eyes go out of focus. "I'll let him think Dutchess got loose yesterday when Bill Gersh had some immigrant people, who don't speak any English, spray all the foliage they happened to think might be blackberries with terrible poison. I said to Rich, we may as well have been sent to Viet Nam and showered with Agent Orange. Rich said there's no comparison between the U.S. Military and Bill Gersh. He's always standing up for Bill." Eileen still clutches the plastic bag emotionally. "I wouldn't mind if Rich thought Bill killed Dutchess."

"I'll let you handle this the way you think best," I concur. Eileen heaves Dutchess into the trunk and covers her with a beach towel decorated with electric guitars. Once diverted from the scam implicating her despised neighbor, she gets in the car. I promise her I will clean up the whole shebang, soon. Her car bucks before moving into the street.

Dennis and I meet later at the Cavalier's Corner, a Mexican bar near his house. We sit down at Dennis' favorite table, under a Coors Beer sign illuminating the Rocky Mountains. Dennis, a true friend, doesn't ask any invasive questions like 'How are you?' before we establish emotional contact. So I don't have to talk about Honor and my absent children. Two guys in cowboy outfits with turquoise-studded belt buckles get up from the bar and move to the table next to us. One looks much smaller than the other.

"The first three years went okay but the last sixteen have been hell," says the small cowboy.

"Me—it's been hell since the first night. Except for the vacation, when we went to the Smith Valley." They both stare morosely into their mugs.

"I've had enough of this kind of dialogue for one lifetime," says Dennis. "I have to move tables." I like this kind of conversation. But I get up and follow Dennis to a damp little table against the far wall. Someone left a basket of tortilla chips on the table. Dennis salts them and starts eating.

A big shiny man with a dish towel tucked in the front of his pants comes out from behind the bar bringing Dennis a warm-looking margarita and me a thin cup of coffee. Dennis looks edgy. I ask him to report in.

"I spent about five hours running around after your Ruthie," Dennis informs me. "I hope it was worth the time. I'm having a bad week." Dennis lifts his glass, wipes underneath with a paper napkin, and takes a gulp. "I'm involved in an estate case with everyone bickering and crying."

I open my mouth to defend Ruthie's significance. To talk about how the search for her has triggered shifting along some old faultline. I decide not to bother.

He opens a spiral notepad. "I talked to Claudia, aerobics instructor with nice muscle delineation. She turned mean the second I asked about her past. Asked me right away if I was with you. She knew I couldn't be a coincidence." I shrug.

"She tells me she lost track of Ruthie, sister Jane, and the boyfriend, Kurt Brewster, years ago. Then she suggested that she'll file charges if she sees either of our faces again."

"I tried talking to one of her employees, a guy name of Steve, who works out with their heftiest customers. He wasn't very verbal but he let slip that he doesn't know diddly shit about Claudia Hollings before she came to South Street Spa and Gym."

"Did you verify that she's a partner in the gym?" I ask.

"Yes, but the names of other partners are screened by legal stuff. You'll have to dig for them." He frowns.

"In spite of how Claudia looks in a South Street Spa and Gym T-shirt," says Dennis, "I didn't like her. She's a smart-ass. I'd hate to push her more if I don't have to." Dennis doesn't enjoy pushing anyone. I don't point this out.

"Thanks," I tell him. "So, what else do I get from my five hours?" I continue.

"Stuart Lilienthal. I got together with my police contact in the city. Lilienthal's had charges of harassment and assault brought against him and dropped. He's had three malpractice suits lodged and then dropped and hushed up. So he hasn't covered his tracks all that well." Dennis looks disgusted.

"His reputation among his fellow shrinks is good, though," Dennis adds. "They think he's competent and he's a media pet."

"Did you talk to him?"

"I tried. He didn't want to let me at him. So I cornered him. He acted like a nice, sympathetic guy. Until I asked him if he's been friends with Kurt Brewster. Then he started howling.

"Lilienthal said Brewster was a 'lapdog.' Said 'dogs have only one life' and that was Brewster's 'downfall.' I asked him to come off it, give some straight answers and I'd leave him alone. He called me a rooster, threatened to 'chew my feathers loose and bite my drumsticks.'

"What's the story?" Dennis asks, his upper lip recoiling. "Does this guy think he is a cat or is he a cat-killer? You told me that he murdered Ruthie's cat when he was involved with her."

"He seems to go either way," I reply. "Today he assassinated my client's cat. The last time I saw him, he was meowing."

"I think I prefer the worms I work with more than these crazies you dig up. All a matter of taste."

"It's Ruthie who attracted the crazies," I argue. I suppress the remembrance of Doris Shipley, my devotee. We're interrupted by someone calling Dennis' name. Dennis hunches down in his chair. I crane my neck to see across the bar.

A woman about my age, wearing a sensible suit and nice jewelry, hones in on Dennis. This must be Sharon. I check the look on her face. I decide Dennis may have dumped her before I even got a formal introduction. Sure enough, she ignores me and takes a seat at our tiny table.

"Dennis, I can't leave things this way. You've got to stop pushing me. I need time to figure out what I want." I sit enthralled. I've seen Dennis run light-years to avoid relationships. Hearing him accused of wanting more, instead of less, fascinates me. I try to sit inconspicuously so that Dennis won't remember to get rid of me.

Dennis stares at Sharon with a besotted and miserable look on his face. She continues when he doesn't respond, "I haven't been out of my marriage long enough to give you what you want, Dennis. I feel hounded. The scene this morning scared me. We have to step back from this."

I study Dennis, trying to figure out how I could have missed so vital a change in him. Or maybe there's been no change. He must have always had the potential to fall for someone this way. I missed it because he put so much energy into withholding himself.

Dennis is almost too far gone to be humiliated that I'm witnessing this scene. But he rouses slightly and turns pleading eyes upon me. Sharon notices his attention has been diverted.

"Hi," she says and sends me a tight unhappy, smile. "You must be Eliza." I nod acknowledgement.

"Eliza," begs Dennis, "could you get a newspaper or something and give me a minute with Sharon?" I have no choice but to reluctantly get up and go.

"Come get me in McCaswell Park," I tell him. On impulse, I lean over and kiss his hair. Sharon can make what she wants of our intimacy.

I see an abandoned newspaper on a chair as I leave. The two cowboy hats signal me to go ahead and take it. Dennis knows I'm addicted to the *Chronicle*. Getting a chance to read the gossipy stories on the inside pages is a good way to get over being excused from a juicy scene.

I walk three blocks to the park and find a seat on a big rock imbedded with a plaque. So it happens that I make my way to "Bay Area Report," page 19, column three of today's *Chronicle*. The caption reads, "Teenager Shoots Oakland Woman." I don't focus immediately on the first words. But I certainly become involved fast:

> Oakland youth, Andrew Beeson, has been charged with the shooting death of wealthy Oakland resident, Doris Shipley. Shipley, 53, was discovered yesterday morning by nearby residents. Neighbors observed no signs of struggle. Beeson has allegedly

admitted to a spending spree using the victim's credit cards prior to the shooting. Beeson will be arraigned tomorrow on charges of first degree murder and fraud.

Shit.

I've had this experience with the *Chronicle* before. If you have any special interest in their story, you always find misinformation. Andy, for example, is 23 but looks young. And he lives with his family in Emeryville. So much for "Oakland Teenager." Doris, wealthy Oakland resident, does reside in Oakland but exists one step from being a bag lady.

How could Doris have died without a struggle? I don't believe it. She's a dirty fighter if I ever met one. I wonder if I'm trembling because this particular wretched person, a thorn in my side, has died. Or just because someone I know has died, period.

I would have sworn by my background check on Andy. He must have gone over the edge recently. Or there's more to the story. Doris, lying with her toes pointed up, waiting to be buried in polyester, dark red rouge, and fake pearls, is going to harangue me when she gets to the other side. I'm not on firm ground when I answer her. I hope there's a heaven and I hope Doris gets a cozy situation there, so she doesn't have the motivation to hang around in spirit form and plague me everlastingly.

I hike back to the bar. Dennis and Sharon sit with faces bent close together. "Dennis," I yell, without going too close to their table. "I'll talk to you later." I wave to keep him from getting up.

Dennis' eyes, puckered with tension, meet mine briefly. "Sorry about this," he calls. I leave with a smile that I hope conveys small solace, the best I can do.

I need to get to my office and check my files on Doris Shipley. Her death doesn't make sense. My notes on Andy might give me a clue.

I pull up near the office and leave my car parked by a green curb. I've let myself get perturbed. Sam Spade and Miss Marple never got jumpy like this. But they never faced such a messy, embarrassing sequence of cases.

I slouch through the courtyard, alienating Sarah Frybarger by muttering, "Talk to you later," before she has finished telling me about a decorator's warehouse which might yield a new color scheme and ambiance for our reception area.

The red light on the answering machine glows in the gloom of my office. Precious must be on a break. I raise a shade and then grab the phone receiver. Eileen's voice babbles into the tape.

"Eileen, it's me," I yell. "Hold on while I turn off the machine. I just got in." I try to sound like a fully functional professional. I don't want to risk losing Eileen's confidence during my current state of discouragement. And the poor woman has just become bereaved over her cat.

"Eliza, I can't believe it. I was just telling your machine. I got home a while ago. I was still very upset. So I went out to the back pantry. I thought I would wash out Dutchess' food and water dishes with her name on them, and take them up to my bedroom. You would have fainted over what happened next. Well, maybe you wouldn't have fainted. I'm sure your nerves are very good. But I felt woozy."

"What happened, Eileen?"

"Sorry, I told the machine already so I forget you don't know."

"Know what?"

"It's Dutchess. She came through the cat door asking for her chopped veal supper."

"What?" I'm surprised for a minute.

"She's fine. The cat in the car was someone else. It's so improbable. Dutchess' coat is a very unusual shade for an Egyptian Mau. She has some feathery flecks of black that aren't standard for a purebred. Dutchess has traces of rings on her tail like Ruthie's kitten had."

"Eileen, will you go out and check the cat we put in the trunk? I'm curious to know how closely they match."

"I'll check. I already left the body at Furry Memories, our family pet cemetery. I'll call and tell them I want to visit the body one more time before they prepare it for its urn."

"You're going to go ahead and pay for the cat's, uh, funeral?" I ask out of curiosity.

"Yes, I am. I have a special feeling for that cat, even though I never knew her in life."

"That's good of you." I commence my speculations about the cat.

Someone shatters the silence, slamming their weight against the door lock. I swing around, startled. Two people in my acquaintance abuse a door this way, Rich is one of them but it can't be him.

"Hang on, Eileen." I put the phone on hold. I run forward to get the door before my lock gets damaged. I turn the handle. Someone on the other side applies counterpressure. I win and draw the door open.

Standing in the doorway, I face Doris Shipley.

"Some day, you're going to damage the door frame," I say, motioning her in. I feel like I have tachycardia for a minute.

I pick up the phone and get out the words, "Eileen, we'll get this figured out. I'll talk to you later."

"Rumors of my death have been greatly exaggerated," Doris says smugly. I can't blame her. How many people actually get to employ that line?

I feel a sudden surge of optimism. If Dutchess and Doris can return unheralded, maybe Honor will be next.

" **I** want my money back," Doris hisses. I fumble among my poorly kept secrets and pull forth her file.

"You did hear that I'd passed over, didn't you? That's why you look so awful?" I assure Doris that I suffered the news of her demise and the blow caused me to look as if I haven't slept for days.

I skim my notes and then look up from her file. "Doris, what happened?"

"Andy is no good. That's what. And you said he seemed just fine."

"He doesn't seem to have hurt *you*." In shock, I prick at her, risking her ire.

Doris breaks down instead of carping. A few skimpy tears fall. She gets out a tiny lace handkerchief.

"Andy had a fight with a lady he's been visiting and he shot her. He's been using *my* money to buy things for her. She had my credit cards in her purse when she died, that's why the police thought it was me Andy killed. He's known her since before we met but he never mentioned her to me. I'm positive he must have slept with her. And she's an older woman, much older than Andy. The thought of Andy with a whore, an old whore, breaks the last of my spirit." Her eyes have dried.

"Is that how you feel about her? Or was she in the business?"

"Both," says Doris, her righteous indignation flares. "The police knew about her. Unlike my detective who never knew that Andy was seeing her."

I do rapid calculations. How much do I owe Doris? I think about the balance of payments received from her and the services rendered. I don't owe her a thing. But the obnoxious-ness that makes me, and everyone else, back away from her, also binds me to her in some absurd way.

"Look, Doris, you haven't come close to paying for the hours I've invested in your case. But I'm going to figure out what happened. After that, we're done with each other. Deal?" It's crazy trying to make a deal with Doris but I may as well try.

"I suppose that's the least you can do," Doris accepts.

"I'll check with the police but I don't expect them to tell me much," I tell her.

"They wouldn't answer a single one of my questions," agrees Doris. "They weren't the least bit interested in me once they found out I wasn't dead."

"Andy's probably being held at North County Jail. I'll try to talk to him there. Do you know anyone I can talk to who knows the woman that Andy shot?"

"I might have known you would want me to do your work for you." Any gladness I felt over her rejuvenation dries up. I give her a hard glare. "I'll tell you what I know," she says begrudgingly.

"The dead lady's name was Lou Denny. The police told me that her mother, Nella Denny, lives in Oakland." Doris' ran-corous eyes shine through slits, further verifying that her life's energy has not been smothered.

"I'll talk to her mother. I'm donating my services to you, Doris. Now sit down, I want to show you exactly how many hours of investigative work you've received for the money you paid." I enjoy a few moments of peace for the first time today, as I lead Doris down the neat columns.

Doris leaves without a note of applause for my tidy books and adroit elucidation of her charges and receipts. She says only, "My hypertension has flared out of control. If you don't give me some explanation for Andy's actions soon, I might really die and you'll be to blame." She totters across my floor and collects her walker outside the door. I open the venetian blinds.

A call to North County Jail seems pressing. I get a friendly Deputy in Charge of Classification, and ask whether I can see Andy. I'm told that his P.D. has asked that he not be inter-viewed for a week, pending pre-trial arraignment. Doris' hypertension doesn't carry much weight with them. I write off the idea of talking to Andy.

My phone buzzes.

"I've got a fat envelope for you. I signed. The rules are same as always, pick it up in 24 hours or I get to read what's inside to see if it's anything interesting." Precious doesn't make cross-courtyard deliveries.

Back in my office, I take out bootlegged S.F.P.D. reports sent by Fleet Hansen. He has photocopied all the material starting from the night someone died in Ruthie's San Francisco apartment through the investigation that followed.

A Caucasian female, approximately 25 years of age, no identifying marks or scars, slight build with a high percentage of dense muscular tissue, died from a blow to the head by a carpenter's plane. The wood plane lay near the body at the scene of the crime wiped clean of fingerprints.

Police got a positive identification of the dead woman from her sister, Ruth Gold, and friend, Claudia Heller Hollings. Ruthie and Claudia stated for the record that in life the body belonged to Jane Gold. Police were told of no other next of kin. No other next of kin? Didn't Ruthie think her parents should know that their daughter had been killed? What had happened to the Golds by then?

San Francisco Police Detective Philip Cologne conducted the case then and since. I remember that both Eileen Goldeen and Dave Gray have alleged independently that Cologne dated Ruthie after he met her while investigating the incident when Ruthie was assaulted in her darkened apartment. His notes compliment Ruthie better than they document the investigation.

At the scene of Jane Gold's death, Ruthie Gold and Claudia Hollings pointed a finger to indict Claudia's boyfriend, Kurt Brewster. Claudia explained that she severed relations with him two months previously because he had exhibited violent tendencies. She told Cologne that Jane Gold spurned his advances repeatedly after that time and Brewster became obsessed with winning Jane's favor. Ultimately, Kurt Brewster's brutal nature asserted itself when, thwarted in his pursuit of Jane, he flew into a rage and bludgeoned her to death.

Ruthie wobbles throughout the transcript, taken the night Jane died. She first says she didn't know Kurt Brewster. Later, Ruthie states that she had met Kurt Brewster several times and found him fearful.

The police, technically, still regard Kurt Brewster as the prime suspect in this homicide. There is no statute of limitations for murder but, in fact, the police department doesn't care about a murder no one else cares about. Ruthie might have conceivably cared, but she disappeared.

The spoor has grown cold by now. Claudia's boyfriend, Kurt Brewster, disappeared into thin air, police turned up almost no leads on him. Another player evaporated like the ozone.

Cologne interviewed a few peripherally involved acquaintances of Jane Gold. Dave Gray managed to be unavailable enough times that Cologne wrote him off. Cologne noted that he had been told that Dave Gray knew Kurt Brewster only slightly, knew Claudia and Jane barely at all. Ruthie seems to have told Cologne that Dave Gray was no more than a bothersome neighbor to her. Probably true. Dave Gray struck me as someone who would form bonds of affection with little encouragement. Tasio Megia, Tasio's mother, and Stuart Lilienthal are immortalized in the transcripts. But Cologne missed some key questions.

Cologne didn't bother to cross-check Ruthie and Claudia's assertion that Jane had no near relatives except Ruthie. Cologne didn't put much effort into the case generally. He took Ruthie's word that Kurt Brewster, a nobody escaped to nowhere, murdered her sister. The focus of his attention was Ruthie. I surmise that he has held onto these files in case they should ever provide entree to Ruthie.

Cologne might even have done my work for me, hunted for Ruthie after she fled the murder, but he couldn't justify using department funds. Ruthie was not an indispensable witness. Cologne didn't violate any department regulation, that I can see, in the course of the investigation. Finally, I read the most colorful testimony.

"Jane Gold was a tramp," avows Mrs. Megia Senior, for the record.

Cologne asks for details.

"Her sister, Ruthie, was a tramp and they sprung from the same nest."

Cologne asks what the old woman knows about Jane or Ruthie Gold that would lead her to form this opinion.

"The proof lies in Ruthie Gold's relationship with my dear, trusted physician, Stuart Lilienthal. I have bad spells, I admit it. And I need my medication. I need it administered by hypodermic which Stuart always does personally when he is able to get down here from San Francisco. He specializes in children but he's an old friend of the family, so he sees to me. He's very busy. When Stuart can't get here, he has Dr. Melrose oversee my care."

I wish I could hear Cologne's reply. I think he rises to Ruthie's defense when he asks Mrs. Megia how reliable are her perceptions during these "bad spells."

"I'm never wrong about people," she answers, probably not sweetly.

Cologne asks for a second time what she knows about Jane or Ruthie Gold.

"Ruthie Gold was employed to play the piano at our dance company's rehearsals for some insignificant number of hours each week. One day, after I'd had an attack while interviewing managerial candidates in the Jazzmatazz executive offices, Stuart Lilienthal was called down from the city to attend me. Ruthie Gold accosted Stuart as he was leaving the building and manipulated him into a tryst with her.

"She lured him into an affair of the flesh. Stuart confided to me that during his relationship with Ruthie Gold, he began to experience minor emotional difficulties himself. Ruthie connived, she convinced him that she is a spectacularly afflicted soul and that he, Stuart, had to salvage her, a Herculean task indeed, Mr. Cologne.

"Meeting Ruthie Gold's emotional and sexual needs taxed the resources of even such a man as Stuart Lilienthal. After all, Stuart is fifteen years older than the girl, a devoted husband and father, but for this indiscretion, and very much in demand professionally."

Cologne tells Mrs. Megia that Ruthie has left San Francisco and that Stuart Lilienthal, when questioned, indicated that he no longer has a relationship with her and doesn't know where she went.

"Stuart will be all the better for putting that mistake well behind him."

Cologne asks how Ruthie Gold's past relationship with the doctor corresponds to the death of her sister.

"That should be obvious," the old lady says.

Cologne responds that it isn't obvious to him. I'm glad I don't have to hear his tone of voice now.

"Jane Gold was a bold, irritating hussy, like her sister. She had a gentleman friend, didn't she? I'm sure she goaded him into killing her."

Detective Cologne concludes the interview.

Friday night at 6:00 p.m., I hear a car pull up in front of the house. I bolt for the door. I'm determined to catch Honor. I fling open the door, my heart literally leaping at the rat-tat-tat of Annabelle and Jemmy's voices. I've been away from them before on business but I've never felt so cut off as I have in the last few days.

Love lends me clarity of vision. I'd almost forgotten what attractive, thoughtful-looking children they are. I run down to greet them. I stop in my tracks when I see the driver of the car.

Honor has sent the children with the Sutton grounds-keeper, Ramsey. I've spent time with Ramsey on occasions when I've needed to escape from Sutton family functions at their house. Ramsey keeps a coffee pot warm in his work shed, which fruit trees conveniently shield from Sutton eyes.

I wave. Ramsey gives me a friendly wave in return. He hits the gas and his Jeep Wagoneer takes off down the street at a fast clip. He doesn't want me pumping him for information about Honor.

Both children carry a neat piece of lightweight luggage. The suitcases look new. Honor has probably equipped them with all the accessories they need to be part of a joint custody arrangement. I suppose I could have it worse. Honor could take the children out of my life forever, but she won't. Her ethics might seem unintelligible to the average mind but I'm sure of her integrity.

"What did you do wrong?" shouts Jemmy when we've all untwined ourselves.

"Did your mom tell you I screwed up?" I ask.

"No. It just figures. What did you do?" he persists. I'm prepared for this.

"Your mom and I have agreements between us about how we're going to live our lives. And I broke one of the agreements. That's all I'm going to say for now no matter how many questions you guys ask." Annabelle steps back and levels her eyes on me.

"Would you like to go to the Moroccan restaurant tonight?" I poll them, to redirect the conversation. "You sit on pillows, remember?"

"Did you sleep with somebody else?" asks Annabelle coolly.

"Annabelle, Jesus, I've asked you guys not to pop off with these things on the street. Nancy's home and you know she hangs out her windows looking for dirt on everybody. And stop grinding your teeth, Annabelle, everything's going to be fine." If this lovely child winds up with caps on her teeth, it will be my fault.

"If you did sleep with someone else was it a woman or a man?" whispers Jemmy.

Honor and I planned to discuss sexual preference later. I glance at the house next door. Nancy has the stereo on and she's out of eyesight. "Get in the house and we'll talk," I say, sotto voce. I'm shaken. I've always assumed that our children are sweetly naive, almost old-fashioned, thanks to their wholesome upbringing.

"Who's talked to you about sleeping with other people and about going from women to men?" I ask them when we're safely in the kitchen.

"Jemmy still doesn't know much but since you and Momma don't like to talk about that kind of thing, we asked the librarian at the main library for books on human sexuality. Otherwise, Jemmy and I would sound like idiots when we talk with our friends," Annabelle declares.

"I honestly thought that we had covered all the basics," I tell them. "I guess we were too abstract.

"The situation we're in now has to do with trust," I submit. I hope the children can take some comfort from more not-very-useful abstractions, since they're all I have to offer. "I've lost your mother's trust, temporarily. I'm going to earn it back. Then we'll all be together again." Both children emit a depressed sigh.

The children feel their way through the house, reassuring themselves that home still exists in their absence. We decide we aren't up to digesting Moroccan food, so we go to the Good Earth. The children like the chewy dinner rolls and the jicama that comes in the salad.

We finish dessert and do puzzles on the paper placemats. I hold back words trapped in my throat. "Okay, junior investigators, I have one piece of work left to do today. I need to see a woman tonight. Your job will be to hang out and observe. If you guys pick up any clues about her by absorbing the atmosphere, that would be great."

"Who is she?" asks Jemmy. "Does she know the doctor who likes cats? I don't feel like seeing him again." Annabelle looks up from adding the items on the check.

"No connection," I guarantee them. "This woman's daughter was shot and killed. So we need to be quiet and respectful. I want to get some information about the man who shot her daughter." If Honor were here, she would be debating with herself whether this kind of experience, visiting the grief-stricken, counts as broadening or as potentially detrimental for children twelve and under. I don't want to give up time with the kids, so I'm taking them regardless.

"Was the woman's daughter older or younger than me?" asks Jemmy.

193
▲

Oh dear, I think. I'm glad Honor never let me tell them about Tara Timmin and the dumpster. Lou Denny's death won't affect them in the same way. Lou lived long enough to become another category of person to Annabelle and Jemmy, not someone with whom they would identify.

"She was a grown-up. A grown-up who was in a dangerous business."

"What kind of work did she do?" asks Annabelle.

"She did favors for strangers and then charged them money," I tell her. Annabelle gives me a hard look. What has this child been reading? I make a mental note to talk to her about being selective in her reading, especially when browsing through Newell Sutton's library.

Nella Denny, mother of Lou Denny, lately shot by Andy Beeson, gave me intricate directions to her home near Lake Merritt when I talked to her this morning. The fact that she has no obligation to speak to me doesn't seem to have occurred to her. This phenomena happens with people who have had a crime settled upon them. Because they have no control over whether they will or will not speak to police, hospital personnel, and miscellaneous other authorities, their personal boundaries blur. They forget they have the right to discriminate about who they give their time to. So media people, neighbors, and private investigators can invade them when they need seclusion most. For this reason, I'm not waiting until next week to hit on Nella Denny. By that time she might refuse me.

Annabelle navigates for me as I drive. We pull up in front of a nice-looking apartment building, a tasteful light grey with dark green awnings. I let Jemmy find the buzzer for apartment 2C and press. Someone upstairs releases the lock on the glass double doors and we enter the lobby. We take the elevator one floor up to the Denny apartment.

Mrs. Denny opens the door when she hears us approaching down the carpeted hallway. She steps out, a shapeless woman in a flowered dress and plastic sandals from which her feet overflow. A confused, unfocused expression, maybe a smile, forms on her face.

"Hello, hello, you must be Mrs. Pirex, and these are your sweet children," she gestures us inside. Annabelle and Jemmy start to giggle over being called sweet. I suppress them.

We step inside. The air smells like flowers and furniture polish. A tremendous wood veneer shelving system with cubbies for flower vases, statuettes, and ashtrays, supports a 25" television. In the next room, I see a very shiny dining room table and a massive china cabinet.

194
▲

"Yes, I'm Eliza Pirex, this is Annabelle, and Jeremiah. Thank you for letting me have this time. I know how hard this week must have been for you."

"It's been very hard. Thank you, thank you. It helps to talk about her. People don't want to mention her. I guess they think it would upset me. She gave me this beautiful apartment, you know." Mrs. Denny's mouth starts to tremble. She looks around helplessly for succor. Annabelle and Jemmy begin to look upset.

"You guys sit down." I tell them. "We'll be done talking in a minute."

"I just remembered that I have some toys," says Mrs. Denny, happy to please. "When we first got this place, Lou expected she would bring my grandchildren over to see me. But their father took them away. I don't even know where they are, to tell them about what's happened to their mother." She looks vacantly toward the back hallway as if the grandchildren might be having a birthday party in another room and she has only dreamed she's lost them. She fetches some stacking toys and a fold-away plastic house, toys for very young children. Annabelle and Jemmy politely play with them on the floor.

"Keep the noise down now, children. Most folks in this building go to bed early." I pantomime an apology to them. They have been totally silent.

I point to a vinyl sofa facing the television, out of the children's earshot. "Shall we sit down over here?" I ask.

"Why don't we. Can I get you something to drink? I think I have some soda pop, it's warm but I might have ice cubes. It wouldn't be any bother." She tenses with anxiety over whether I'll accept her offer.

"No, thanks. We just had dinner at a restaurant." I smile. She relaxes slightly.

"You were a friend of Lou's, you were saying?" She dredges in a pocket of her smock and pulls out a roll of candy. She sits down and begins sucking.

I listen while she tells me the history of her daughter. I don't even have to produce monosyllabic replies. The film keeps rolling. The father who abused her, a grade-school teacher who molested her, the group of teenage boys who should have been prosecuted for what they did to her.

After the accounts of jobs Lou might have had except for the employers who harassed her and the husbands who exploited her, and then the clients who hired and damaged her, I can't hear any more. This mother has not noted one milestone in the life she sketches that isn't sad and hard. Has she noticed?

"Lou must have gotten a lot of pleasure out of giving you this lovely apartment," I prompt.

"Lou and I didn't get along. I never knew why she did this. I was happy in my neighborhood down the freeway. I had all my friends and my house was so easy to keep nice. But she forced me out, almost, and put me here. She had her ways, she had ideas. I don't know what I'm going to do now, so far from my neighborhood where there are people who might remember me." Mrs. Denny looks at me as though I should suggest some solution. This isn't my case, I'm not a part of this.

But I can't restrain myself from trying to do-good before I go. "Are you Lou's beneficiary?" I ask her.

"Me and the kids. But the police told me she didn't have much in her account," Nella Denny says hopelessly.

"Women in your daughter's line of work don't usually trust their assets to one bank account under one name. The police will be checking. You need to get someone to look into things for you. You may end up well-off financially. Maybe you can move wherever you want." The thought of a hidden estate might inspire her to find someone to look out for her.

I can't put off the moment any longer. "What do you know about Andy Beeson?" I ask. Mrs. Denny's face lights up before she remembers, then falls, like a biscuit that rose, fell, and came out flat. Not for the first time, I curse Doris for exposing me to more pathos than I care to endure.

"He was like a son to Lou. When she brought him here that time, she told me I was a grandma again. The last time she called me, Lou said she was going to get him a special tutor so he could get into college. I just wish I understood."

I can't stand any more and I've learned as much as I want to know. The children don't need further exposure to her grief and helplessness, cloying as the air of her household. We say goodbye. I look back once and see her watching me go, as baffled by my departure as by my presence.

I may not feel like calling Doris to relieve her soaring blood pressure for a good long time. And why should I bother? Doris will probably live to be one hundred and five.

The children pump me for details when we get in the car. I give them a synopsis, passing over the more colorful details of Lou Denny's life. We find a place to park right next to the lake and set out for a walk on the well-lighted pathway, dodging the joggers.

As we walk, I try to present Doris Shipley at grade levels two and six. Annabelle and Jemmy are captivated by the seediness of it all. They try to extract some morals from the story.

"Doris should have looked into her own heart to see whether Brenda and Andy were true friends," says Jemmy with the gravity of a narrator on the afternoon superhero cartoons.

"I don't think Doris will ever choose her friends carefully. She just takes whatever friend she can get," Annabelle muses. In sixth grade, you grapple with the intricacies of friendship on a daily basis.

"That's probably true," I say, with real sadness.

"Doris didn't even know that Andy was a killer," Jemmy remarks.

"Nobody is a killer until they kill someone," I point out. "Doris didn't get to know Andy well enough to guess that he was someone with the potential to be irrationally violent. Even worse, Lou Denny didn't guess."

"Lou was the innocent victim," Annabelle says, like all children, wanting things to be black and white.

"Sometimes the roles really are cut and dry. Other times, the story gets more complicated." I can't leave my children with a distorted picture.

"What do you mean?" Annabelle and Jemmy chorus.

"Andy wasn't taught how to handle his conflicts without resorting to violence. He wasn't given the tools to build a civilized life. Lou Denny was trained to be a victim by a long line of perpetrators, starting with her own father. People have taken advantage of her ever since she was a child. No one ever taught her to take care of herself."

"I know how to take care of myself," Jemmy says.

"You do. We're a lucky family."

"Lou had bad luck," says Annabelle. "You could sort of tell by looking at her mother."

We spend Saturday at the Faire, milling among the throng of elementary school students and their overheated parents on the stretch of blacktop marked with hopscotch and basketball court lines. It's an annual affair and always just as hot as I fear. I earn $94 for the school, an amount which I gladly would have paid to be allowed to skip the event. All day, well-intentioned parents ask Annabelle, Jemmy, and me why Honor isn't participating in the merriment with us.

By the end of the afternoon, heavy with homemade international cuisine and bake sale goods, Jemmy and Annabelle ask to go back to the coolness and tranquility of their own rooms at home. We go home and spend the evening sitting in front of the television, a tired, melancholy group.

I let Jemmy and Annabelle watch the situation comedies and action shows that Honor usually forbids. In my guilty anxiety dreams during the night, Doris, Dr. Lilienthal, and others zoom about and crash into each other to the sounds of a laughtrack and organ music. Sometime during the night, Jemmy comes to sleep in my bed. I turn on my stomach and get some rest.

Sunday morning, we go to Oakland Chinatown and window-shop for the perfect brunch. We guzzle a stomach-churning selection of dim sum. The image of Honor silently rebukes us for giving no consideration to nutritional balance and ease of digestion.

I strain to show the children a non-stop good time. I'm vivacious and charming while we pick up shampoo and toothpaste and water the yard. All day, I watch single parents escorting formal children with whom they don't have the comfortable rapport acquired through daily contact. I watch them buy goodies and gesture promises of happy expeditions. I don't want to be one of them.

By evening, we all acknowledge that we have spent the weekend waiting to find out what will happen when Honor arrives Sunday at 6:00 p.m. We sit in the living room, officially reading, but in reality waiting to hear Honor's van pull up. Jemmy, posted by the front window, looks out at six and shouts with joy, "It's Momma. She came!"

Honor parks, glides up to the front door, and knocks with three sharp raps. When Jemmy opens the door, Annabelle runs to her and Honor folds them both into her arms.

"Are we going to stay?" asks Jemmy. His face shines with hope. I can barely stand it.

"Not tonight," says Honor firmly. "I'll explain to you two later. Run out to the car, my little slices of sweet potato pie. I missed you." Honor hands them their aerodynamically designed suitcases and ushers them out with a motherly smile.

She closes the door. The smile vanishes. I quail. Of everyone I know, Honor alone can produce such unexpected feints and punches that all my training will never give me any leverage over her or shield me.

"What are you going to do to me?" I ask, hesitantly.

"Why should I give you the satisfaction of knowing my plans, Eliza? You're the one who betrayed me. I sat home, hoping for throat lozenges."

"I'm sorry I forgot the throat lozenges," I reply. "I'm sorry about everything. Will you come back tonight so we can talk? I want to make things up to you."

"You don't get to see me at your convenience. And your apologies are not accepted," says Honor in an even tone. "You don't even get to know when or if you'll see me again."

"Honor, can't we be reasonable? For the children's sake, not for mine."

"I'll see to the children's health and happiness when I'm with them and I expect the same from you. But it's not going to be a joint effort."

"Honor, I want a chance to set things straight. Because of what we have together."

"I'm not sure what we have together," Honor says, eyes narrowed. She does know what we have together.

"Honor," I begin.

"You hurt me, Eliza. You let yourself be seduced by a pasty-faced straight woman." Honor can be clairvoyant, otherwise how would she know that I wasn't the seducer? I have a sick feeling that she can see the scene between me and Rochelle. She carries on as if she has picked up my thought.

"Rochelle reminds me of a human Hostess Twinkie. You didn't even dignify our relationship by sleeping with someone sexy. Never mind. I would be beyond your grasp right now if you'd made love to Eleanor Roosevelt. I don't want deceit and betrayal in my life." Her own magnificent coloring has been heightened by the heat of her speech.

"Honor, please."

"I'm going to figure out what will have more impact, to be cut off from me or to see me," she moves forward and says, low, "and not have my love." Standing this close to Honor would make an impact on anyone. The fine-grained texture of her becomes sharper; her clean, wholesome smell invites my touch.

I draw a ragged breath. My concerted energy goes into staying still. To be stationary while in crisis goes against my every native impulse.

Honor skims down the walk to her van. Our children reach for her. I feel old. I feel the flirtatious energy that has been a part of me since I was a child dissipate and die away. Let the male detectives worry over seductive dinner partners ripe for the picking.

I watch the car drive away.

14

Monday morning, the time of my retreat from the Bay Area, arrives after another sweaty night. I'm thankful to leave my bungled life behind and fly to Los Angeles. I book into a motel there that Honor and I have stayed in before, the City Star. I call Eileen from the motel before going out on my first foray.

"Maybe you'll talk to Ruthie today. I feel lucky. It's fun getting reports from far off," says Eileen, now giggly and anesthetized instead of bitter. That's why I've called her. In the event Ruthie never turns up, I want her to feel like she got her money's worth.

"Keep thinking positive," I recommend, "and I'll get back to you tonight or tomorrow. Or you can call me." Eileen writes down the motel's phone number. I hang up the phone and gaze for a moment at a painting of horses in desert moonlight which hangs above the bed. If Honor were here, she would probably try to wrench it off the wall and put it under the bed. Without her, I enjoy the clichéd peace of the orange and grey scene.

If I can communicate with Ruthie's brother, he may provide an easy and direct link to Ruthie. But my audience with Jonathan Gold couldn't be scheduled until tomorrow. I intend to spend today following up any leads left dangling in Los Angeles and, perhaps, speaking with Ruthie's cousin, Ottie Dresner.

I call the Golds' former neighbors to find out whether anything came to consciousness after I spoke to them. No go. I check with a friend of a friend at the Los Angeles Police

Department. Nothing. I try the Jewish Community Center and have them check their membership roles. The Golds were never members. Next I call art galleries.

I ask each gallery whether they carry work by Ottie Dresner. The salespeople to whom I speak imply that Ottie's work will probably be out of my range financially, unless I can prove that I'm big bucks. I parade a tone of largess in the next calls and eventually a manicured voice gives me the name of the gallery most involved with Ottie Dresner.

I dial the Ackers-Swinson Gallery and ask to speak to the manager. "Good morning, Mr. Moody, my name is Susan Abrams. I'm with *Entertainment Tonight*. I don't know whether you're familiar with our show?" Eileen would like this gambit.

"Yes, of course. I don't own a set myself but I keep abreast of what's going on in the media." I guess in Los Angeles no one gets excited by a supposed call from a nationally syndicated television program.

"We're doing a feature on what became of certain celebrity artists," I commence with the fraud. We discuss interesting angles to pursue in the program. Mr. Moody of Ackers-Swinson concludes by telling me that while I would have to pay a movie star's ransom for any Dresner piece at his gallery, there are bargains to be found elsewhere.

Ottie Dresner has flooded the market with his work during the last decade. Mr. Moody refers to the more recent pieces as "derivative" and "not exceptionally well-executed." Most respectable galleries, he tells me, do not handle his current output. They operate as though Dresner died years ago. Moody does have Ottie Dresner's current address. Eventually he gives it to me.

Dresner has no reason to agree to see me. I decide not to risk being rebuffed over the phone. I look for his address on my street map. Dresner's road isn't there. It's been that kind of case. I phone down to the motel lobby. Mr. Bryant, the motel owner, phones a wealthy friend. His friends know the road. I have a long drive ahead of me.

The drive up to Dresner's house gets my rental car dusty. Scraggly palms struggle for existence among bare rock and dry grass. Even this early in the year, Dresner lives with fire hazard, along with others of Los Angeles' rich. In Oakland, it's the poorest citizens who are at greatest risk for fire.

I expected that the house might be barred by gates but there aren't any. I drive directly up to a rambling building, not an artistic structure, an edifice in which California tract home architecture has been used in building a house large enough for a family of twenty-five. The front parking area could accommodate twenty cars but I see only one dilapidated white limousine.

I have to search to find a doorbell hidden under foliage to the right of the front doors. I stand ringing the bell for five minutes. The presence of only one car in front of the house might indicate that everyone in the household has gone out. But I have a feeling to the contrary. I travel around the right side of the house looking into windows.

I make my way through a small stand of bamboo and weeds growing close to the house at the back. When I emerge, I can see down into a huge covered patio area. Strange objets d'art decorate the sidings. An immense scummy-looking swimming pool lies beyond.

I climb down to the patio. Now that I'm closer to the pool, I notice a big blob floating on the water. The blob looks just the right shape to be the body of a large man. I move to the side of the pool. A big-bellied middle-aged man floats face-up in the green water. I may have just missed getting a chance to speak with Ottie Dresner. I know my duty lies in diving in and checking his pulse. I fight repugnance at getting that scum on my skin.

"It helps me think, floating out here. I pretend I'm a deck chair that fell into the sea off a sinking ship." The voice seems disembodied but I gather that the man in the pool just spoke to me. I had assumed that nobody, unless they were unconscious, or more likely, dead, would choose to put their body into such vile water.

"How do you do?" I call. "My name is Eliza Pirex. I'm looking for Ottie Dresner." A tremendous thrashing of water, and then the man begins to breast-stroke slowly in my direction. I back up as he hauls himself painfully onto the poolside. He holds out a pudgy, dripping hand.

"I can't believe this. They sent a real person this time. And very attractive too, in a proletarian kind of way. We'll start right after we have refreshment. I'm pleased to meet you. What did you tell me your name was?" He stands admiring me and dripping green.

"I'm Eliza. I'm afraid we have a misunderstanding. I came out here unannounced on the off chance I'd find you at home. I like to ask a few questions." Ottie keeps edging toward me so I keep backing away in order to avoid being splattered with the unhygienic water.

"You're not from the Glamour Girl Agency? I have a model ordered. I knew you were too healthy-looking to be true." His wide, sensual mouth quivers with disappointment.

"I'm sorry. I'd like to ask you a few questions about some relatives of yours." He brightens.

"Would you mind if I sketch you while we talk? It would put me in a better mood," his mouth tightens into a cunning line as he bargains. "The agency hasn't been filling my requests for girls lately. I could really use you." I consider. I can tell he's going to be an easy interview. He hasn't even asked why I'm here or what my interest is in his relatives.

"Sure. As long as I don't have to pose." I follow him to the patio and he disappears through an open door. I look through the door and observe a cluttered, filthy kitchen. Ottie seems to be mixing drinks for both of us, although I haven't been consulted about whether I want one.

He plods out and wordlessly hands me a smeared jar-like glass filled with about fifteen ounces of liquid. I take a sip automatically and shudder. The drink tastes warm and very alcoholic. A generous man with his spirits. I put the glass down in a planter which already houses a plastic cup with lipstick marks on the rim.

"Ottie, Mr. Dresner, I want to ask you a few questions about your relatives, the Golds. I want to locate Ruth Gold, or Maddy and Morris. When was the last time you were in contact with any of them?" Ottie gulps down his drink and puts the glass on the ground, under a chair.

"They're gone. I haven't seen any of them for six or seven years. They told me to forget them. Everybody else started to desert me years before. I never actually expected Maddy to dump me. She was like a mother to me when I was a kid. Not that Morris was the fatherly type. That guy was the jerk of the world."

"What do you mean 'they're gone'?" I ask Ottie, who seems to be wandering away again. He disappears through sticky sliding glass doors and reappears in a few seconds carrying a drawing pad and some wide black crayons. He sits down and crosses his hairy legs. I try to avoid looking at the obscene white belly which overflows his colorful shorts. A sick yellow cast overlays his skin. I shift in my aluminum chair in order to look more decorous. Ottie begins sketching without looking at me.

"They told me they had to skip town. That I'd probably never see them again. Maddy said they were in danger. And you know what Maddy told me the danger was? Typical

Maddy. She told me they were in danger of losing their mortal souls. We're an insane family, always had a lot of insanity in the family since way back."

"Where were they going? Do you have any idea?" I modulate my voice, as I often do, to avoid sounding like I'm pushing.

"They didn't give me a hint. Said I wouldn't be able to trace them, so I didn't try. Maddy was good to me. Gave me quite a few bucks. Said it was the money I'd have gotten off them anyway if they'd stayed around." Ottie stabs viciously at his pad now with the end of his crayon, rather than using strokes. Maybe he's become a disciple of the pointilist technique.

"You know," he continues, "I don't just miss them for money and somebody to eat with if I needed to. They were the kind of family who would always hang with you. They took family seriously. Everybody else got tired of me and my work. But Maddy would have stuck by me. She would have had my latest stuff right out in the middle of her living room." He sighs and burps softly.

"Did Ruthie go with them?"

"I'm sure she did. She was a basket case by then, skinny and strung out. She was always emotional, sensitive, like I am. Living with Ruthie and her father was never restful, let me tell you. Ruthie was worse right before they left. Hell, I'd like to know if Ruthie's still alive. I couldn't figure which one of us was going to flash out first."

I rotate in my chair, force myself to scan Ottie's countenance for signs of Ruthie. I can't see any resemblance between the failed sloppy cousin and the intense dark figure in the photograph that Eileen showed me.

"Did you have the impression that Ruthie was distraught over her sister's death?" I ask.

"What sister? There was just Ruthie, Janie, and Jon." Ottie sounds surprised.

"Jane. She was killed in San Francisco before Ruthie came back to Los Angeles."

"You're nuts. Janie hung around here after the rest of them left. She was the last to go. I tried to ask her where they went but she just laughed at me. Janie was a real cute girl but she got snobbish after she went into dancing."

Ottie considers for a minute and then adds, "Janie did tell me to consider her dead, if anyone should ask. Just like Maddy did. She was speaking metaphorically."

"The police reports aren't metaphorical. She's dead, Ottie. I know for a fact that Jane was killed before the time the Golds said goodbye to you."

205
▲

"Look, I'm not a total airhead. You think I wouldn't remember if my cousin were dead? Janie's fine. She can take care of herself better than the rest of them. Don't worry about her. Worry about how goddamn inefficient the San Fran police are." He sketches busily for a short while.

"You're not from my crowd. Who are you? Why are you after Maddy and Ruthie?" he asks with small interest. Ottie won't be the last person to accept my presence with few questions. I'm amazed every time it happens.

"I'm a private investigator. A friend of Ruthie's hired me to track her down. I haven't been able to do that. How could a Los Angeles family of five disappear? Except for Jonathan, of course. I'm going to meet with him later."

"Jon won't talk to you. He's been in seclusion with the fairy folk since before his parents left. He wouldn't say good-bye to his own mother. Hears no evil, sees no evil, sure doesn't speak any evil. He may as well be dead." Ottie's drawing pencil has slowed. He stares distractedly at his work.

"I have to admit I wondered why," Ottie mutters.

"What?" I vociferate so he'll stop doodling around and talk to me.

"We're a bright family. I used to be a lot sharper myself. Smart enough to arrange a disappearance. But what I wonder is why. They didn't trust me by then but I should have been able to add things up. I've never been able to." Ottie puts his drawing down. I strain to see. Protracted faces float in space with rain or salt all around them. The faces don't look like me, from this distance.

I don't feel like sitting here longer. "I need to be pushing off, Ottie. It's been great talking to you. Take my card. Call me collect if you think of anything that might help locate the Golds." I walk my card over and put it into his hand.

"Wait a minute! I could use you," says Ottie suddenly. He looks at me as a living human being for the first time. "You can find them for me too."

He looks away, as if ashamed, but continues. "I can't pay anything up front. I'm a little short right now. But I have money coming in. I'll pay you an extra commission when you find them.

"I'll send them a letter," he limns, "and they'll let me join them. My work has been off lately. A change of scenery and some moral support is just what I need."

"I'll see what I can do for you," I tell him. He catches me when I sneak another look at his sketch.

206
▲

"My better work has things stuck on it. But I just don't have the energy for more than two dimensions lately. If you were to go by the Ackers-Swinson Gallery, you can see some of my pieces on permanent display. Tell them you know me. Or tell them you knew me years ago. They'll think better of you if you're a past acquaintance," he laughs wheezily and ends with a bitter, "ha."

I raise my eyebrows sympathetically. Ottie gets up, picks up his empty glass and shuffles toward the kitchen. Not much man, not much artist, left beneath the yellowed varnish on his skin. "Nice to have met you," I call to his back. He waggles several famous fingers lethargically and disappears through the door. I'll cross-index my files and let him know why the Golds left.

I get into my flimsy rental car and point its nose downhill toward the city. I round a corner, hit the brakes, and pull over. The dust settles and I look at Los Angeles below me. I don't see a city, no buildings or greenery. I'm looking at a basin half-filled with orange-brown froth. I wonder how this sick scene at his feet affects Ottie Dresner's perspective. I decide that I don't want to be alone in the froth tonight. There are some people that I can call and invite out to dinner. I turn the key and head down.

I eat dinner with a couple of women I've seen only once since they relocated to L.A. three years ago. When I'm charging expenses to someone else's account, I feel more comfortable eating cheap. We have spicy Chinese food. The intimacy level isn't very high but the Mongolian Lamb tastes good.

We drive to the ocean after dinner. We look at tinsel town houses, see some beautiful places, and then get drinks in a place that hangs over the sea. Once you're inside L.A., you can't see the froth. We concur on how good the ocean breeze feels. When they drop me off at my rental car around 11:00 p.m., we swear that we'll get together again soon. They hope Honor will be with me next time.

When I get to the City Star, I stop to converse briefly with Mr. Bryant, who now wears squashy grey bedroom slippers. I let him know that I'm going to be in my room for the rest of the night. As I turn to leave the office, he says, "Your guest got here all right. She's waiting in your room like you told her." I try not to start.

"Thanks," I reply.

My thoughts race as I run up the stairs and down the corridor. Honor is furious at me, I don't think she would have followed me here. Maybe it's Ruthie. I'm on her home turf now.

207
▲

Someone told her I'm looking for her. Ridiculous. But maybe someone I talked to on the phone today has come forward to point me toward Ruthie. Who knows where I am? I left the phone number but I don't remember leaving the motel name.

I debate whether I should use caution when I enter the room. All the potentially harmful characters in this drama are tucked away in the San Francisco Bay Area. None of them knows I'm in L.A.

I use my key and throw open the door. Someone sits on the bed watching television with one small lamp shining. I look closer. "Eileen?" I say, confounded.

"Eliza! I thought maybe I should be here after all. On the spot. You've never seen Ruthie or her family and I have. So, surprise." Eileen laughs unsteadily. The woman has been at her pill bottles tonight.

"Eileen, I have only a few things left to check on here. Then I'm going to talk to Ruthie's brother. Jonathan will either tell me where his family went or he won't. An extra person around for the interview could throw him off. Technically, he's taken vows of silence. Remember?"

I look closer at Eileen's demeanor. She looks fermented but also depressed. "Why are you really here this time of night, Eileen?"

"It's only a short flight. I didn't get a call from you about whether you got to talk with Ruthie's cousin."

"I wasn't able to call during the times we set," I tell her. "I did see Ottie Dresner. The Golds didn't tell him where they were going. He didn't have much to say. He feels sure Ruthie went with her parents. He really seems to believe that Jane Gold is alive. I haven't put it all together yet. He cared about Maddy Gold. He'd like to know where she went. Ruthie was having a hard time when he last saw her. We already knew she wasn't in good shape. That's it."

"He wasn't the key," proclaims Eileen. "I didn't think he would be. You're the key, Eliza. You're beginning to remind me of Ruthie. Because you're my only tie with her, not because you're like her." Eileen puts on a suburban matron smile out of habit but it falls away soon.

"Eliza, I have some drinks for us. Would you like red wine or something canned?" I glance at the night table and see that Eileen has knocked off two canned Tom Collins in my absence.

"I don't think so, Eileen. I'm tired. I think I'm going to go to sleep soon. Where are you staying?" I take off my coat and sit down on the bed. Eileen smiles, mysterious now, a more urban smile than I've ever seen on her.

"I'm here now. That's all that matters." Eileen moves closer to me on the bed. Her skirt fabric makes a grating sound when it slides over the chintzy bedspread. I pull back to look at her.

"I've been with women. I bet you didn't guess. It was when I was in high school. Rich doesn't have any idea. I've always thought he might lose his mind if he found out. Of course, maybe he would, you know, get turned on by picturing it." Eileen wriggles closer, confidingly. I can't stop staring at her. I realize that she has turned down the thin, stiff bedspread. I registered the band of fuzzy blue blanket at the top of the bed when I came through the door. The blue band constitutes a bad omen for this conversation.

"Eileen, if you don't mind, can we talk about your past tomorrow? A lot of people have that kind of experience in high school. Right now I'm too tired to concentrate."

"I can tell you're tired. You put so much into your work." Eileen lifts the curls off the back of my neck and I feel her fingers stroke the hairs underneath which makes them stand on end. "Let me try and help you relax." I'm starting to sweat. Eileen takes a deep breath. I'm familiar with that breath, it prefaces one of her rambles.

"I was girlfriends once with a girl who helped repair washing machines after school. Beth. She was as big as any man. She always wore red and black plaid shirts, and boots with chains hanging on them. You're more aggressive than her even though you're littler." She leans against my shoulder. She smells like expensive perfume, more subtle than sweet.

The perfume doesn't fit. Eileen seems like the perpetual girl scout. The 'lurid' past she has just revealed doesn't mean anything, but the exotic perfume makes me curious. What do I do with her?

Eileen has paid for my allegiance. But if she were a man, I wouldn't have let her intrude on me this much. "You're even softer than you look," murmurs Eileen sincerely rather than passionately. What does she think? After bedding with a male bear, an ordinary woman must feel like silk. I decide I can't discriminate on the basis of sex.

"Eileen," I say, "I have certain limits in my relationships with clients. I think I'd better send you on your way so I can keep the boundaries clear. Where are you staying?" Eileen looks down at her lap, her habitual posture.

"I thought I'd bunk with you," she mumbles. I sigh involuntarily, more because the woman uses the phrase "bunk
with" than because she's out of line.

I look down at the floor. I notice that Eileen has elegant
ankles, chiseled, lengthening into delicate narrow feet. These
ankles could be alluring. Eileen shows them well, under
shimmery silk stockings. I'm getting distracted, I've got to cut
this out.

"No problem," I say. "We'll get you a room here. Where
does Rich think you are?"

"He thinks I'm staying in the city. San Francisco. I told
him that I'm taking a color workshop tomorrow. You know,
learn to do people's colors for them. So they can look good in
their clothes." Eileen sounds subdued. I don't understand the
story about colors.

"So Rich is taken care of," I say. I put a steely note into my
voice. "Eileen, don't you agree that it would be better if we
never bring this evening up again? Ruthie has unsettled you. I
think that's why you're here." She nods obediently.

Eileen puts both hands on her head and pushes from
either side. "I don't know what's gotten into me." She sounds
depressed now that I have set her straight. "I've been dwelling
on Dr. Lilienthal and cats, and Rich sleeping with Jane, and
our neighbor, Bill Gersh, being so unreasonable about his
spraying. It's all made me confused."

'Confused' rings a bell, it's the word that Rochelle used
before she took me back to her house. I stand up.

"You'll feel clearer tomorrow. You need a good night's
sleep." I pick up her suitcase and start to clear her out. But
there's one last thing I have to ask.

"Eileen, did you choose the perfume you're wearing?"

"No, actually. Rich gave it to me. But I don't think he
picked it out." She wrinkles her nose as though the fragrance
doesn't please her.

I get Eileen settled in a room on a different floor. I
straighten out my bedspread and throw away Eileen's plastic
cup and cans. I fall asleep immediately in a cloud of scent. I
dream that I'm stuck, with some kind of adhesive, onto an
Ottie Dresner painting.

I don't know how long I've been asleep when I jerk
upright in bed. Someone raps on the window pane beside the
door. I jump out of bed and run to push the curtain aside.

I open the door and say, exasperated, "Eileen, I want you
back in your room. I'm sleeping."

"Eliza Pirex, I hate it when you leave Oakland without me," snaps Honor waspishly. She brushes past me, fetches the luggage stand, snaps it open, and puts her case down.

"I don't know why you can't use the luggage stand instead of taking up all the space on top of the dresser, Eliza."

I am overcome with happiness. I snap on the overhead light. The glare highlights the light brown sheen of her hair and illuminates the vivid color in her face. Honor doesn't look any the worse for missing me.

"Are we going to reconcile?" I ask hopefully. I'm willing to appear piteous if need be.

"I'm just checking on you. I've been having those anxiety attacks where I can't concentrate on my drawing. You didn't even send me word where you'd be staying. I had to guess. I'm here for my own peace of mind." I don't say anything.

"All right," she bursts out, "I admit it, I miss you. I've been worrying about that alienated feeling you get when you travel alone. Don't gloat, either, or I'll leave and get a better room someplace, all by myself." Honor takes off her coat, then takes off her jewelry and puts it in a leather pouch which she uses when she travels.

Even if she's here to alleviate her tension, I don't care. I'll take what I can get.

She sits down on the bed. "You hurt me, Eliza," she says. "I was so mad, before, that I couldn't give you a chance to fix things." I miss her normal crisp diction right away.

We sit looking at the horses-at-night scene above the bed. Honor doesn't bother to criticize the decor, which only emphasizes the rift between us.

We both clear our throats. I wait for her to tell me how to fix things, but she doesn't. So I ask, "What's going on at your father's house? Are the kids upset about us?"

"They're fine. You know they always hope for the best. I'm having problems with my father and the rest."

"What's happening, honey?"

"Daddy's so happy that me and the children are at his house. He says he loves you, Eliza, and that you are the best person he could possibly imagine putting up with someone as spoiled as me. I don't mind that. But then he mentions that I've never really given myself a chance to relate to men, he still doesn't count the children's father, and later, he'll suggest that maybe this is a period of change in my life and I should use it for personal growth."

"Are you so surprised? Your dad can be sweet but he has the same problems most people do."

211
▲

"I know, but I thought I'd schooled him better than this. I haven't seen major instances of bigotry or tyranny for years." Honor paces across the carpet, looks into the mirror and shakes her hair back.

"There's one easy way to illustrate your preference in life," I tell her hopefully. "Come home. Let's present a solid front like we always do."

"Stop campaigning, Eliza. I haven't decided what to do about us yet."

"Is the rest of your family behaving?" I inquire.

"Lucy and Linden have bought an IBM computer with word processing software and graphics capabilities." She pauses as if trying to make herself consider rationally. "They say the machine will help them deal with their business correspondence. But I think they're writing something new." Honor sweeps her hair all the way off her face, turns my favorite grey-green eyes upon me.

"I may need you to find out what they're up to, Eliza. You being a detective might finally be of some benefit."

"You can have all the investigative work your heart desires, on the house."

Honor gets up and throws herself in the orange corner armchair. She eyes me again. "What led you to believe that Eileen Goldeen might be knocking on the door of your motel room in L.A.?" Honor never misses a point of interest. I take a deep breath.

"Eileen followed me down here. She's gotten overly involved with the case. And I think she might be disenchanted with her husband lately." Honor's steady green gaze unnerves me.

"She hasn't become enchanted with you, by any chance?" What the hell, I decide, I may as well overdo rather than underplay this opportunity.

"I would never have any involvement with Eileen, even if I didn't love you," I say, thankful that the evening's events went as they did, "even if I weren't going to be faithful to you from now on, forever." Honor shrugs and yawns. She's withholding a smile.

"Are you staying tomorrow, Honor? I have an appointment here and some drop-in visits. It would be good to have you." I plan to send Eileen back home first thing in the morning.

"I may as well," responds Honor, less enthusiastic than I might have hoped.

212
▲

"Honor, won't you bring the kids and come home? I'll find a way to make everything up to you. Really." This makes my second plea but I'm sleepy enough that I have no protective coating on my feelings.

"I can't think about it now, Eliza. I couldn't leave Daddy's house even if I wanted to. I'm locked in a struggle to establish myself with him as an independent adult." She could leave his house if she wanted, and continue to struggle.

I should be cool after the dampening conclusion of our talk but I beg her to lie down, I reach for her. And I take what I can get.

"You're softer than anyone," she says, later, on her way to sleep. Not in a position to be demanding, I take this to mean she still wants me.

15

ileen rises early in the morning, as I would have guessed. She knocks on my door at 7:15 a.m. We don't meet each other's eyes when I look out the door. If I mishandled the scene last night, Eileen and I may never look each other in the eyes again. I can't tell yet.

"I'm exhausted," she says, "from dreaming about colors last night. I dreamed about the colors I told Rich I was going to study at the workshop in San Francisco. I've dreamed in black and white all my life before last night. I need to get home to Rich. I made a mistake in coming here. I've made reservations on a plane that leaves at noon." She glances inside my room.

Eileen becomes dithery and red-faced at the sight of Honor lying with the covers over her head, trying to sleep through the intrusion. I step out into the corridor wearing my terry cloth robe and shut the door behind me. "A member of my family decided to join me," I say with as much aplomb as possible.

"How lovely," says Eileen, brave of her considering the circumstances. "Let's all go out for breakfast before I leave." I can push Honor only so far, so I tell Eileen that she'll have to wait until 8:30 to meet for breakfast. Eileen reluctantly agrees to find herself an early cup of coffee.

We gather to eat at a place that offers bran muffins, and omelets oozing Gruyère cheese and mushrooms. Like American tourists in a foreign country, we want the food we have around us in the Bay Area. Honor and Eileen don't take to each other.

215
▲

The three of us need to part ways. During the night, I constructed an agenda for Eileen. I am sending Eileen to the Gold's former neighborhood in the interest of keeping her busy. Viewing Ruthie's old home and trying to interview the neighbors should occupy Eileen until she flies home at noon.

I know them all by now. I am siccing Eileen on Mrs. Neidlebaum who probably won't open the door for her, Mrs. Hammerstein who might possibly call the police, and the Carrs because they had the bad luck to purchase their house from the Golds. Eileen invents an unusual line of questioning and I tell her to go ahead with it. I give her a notebook. She leaves, intent and happy. Honor breathes a sigh of relief and orders a last cup of tea.

"She's a steadfast person," I avow, thinking of Eileen's unswerving desire to find Ruthie and the way she paid for the funeral of a cat she didn't know.

"She wasn't in line when they handed out the conversational skills," replies Honor, displaying her superior streak. "What if you find Ruthie and she's ordinary, like her friend, Eileen? Or what if you find her and then Eileen wishes she could send Ruthie back to oblivion? You don't know whether you're wasting a good effort on something not-very-meaningful, do you?"

"I'm not going to find Ruthie," I confess for the first time. "I'm trying to find out what happened to her but I don't expect to bring her back to Eileen." Honor and I consider for a few minutes. "Of course, I could be wrong," I add. I like to hedge my bets.

Even should he be inclined to speak, I think Jonathan might be twice as spooked by two strangers. Honor points out that more than one reluctant interviewee has been inspired by her. But she agrees to let me speak with, or at, Jonathan Gold by myself. She volunteers to find souvenirs for the children while I talk to him.

We drive to Venice. Honor leaves me at a building with a prominent sign reading, "World Views." A logo composed of whirling circles appears on the sign and on the front door. When a collegiate-looking man in a pullover sweater and flannel pants opens the door, I ask for Brent. The young guy goes to fetch Brent without asking my name.

Brent turns out to be an attractive businessman type in his thirties with short, spiky blond hair. He does not invite me any farther into the building than the entry hall. The entryway might as well be the lobby of a small midwestern corporation. But the doors to every room within my range of vision are closed. Brent informs me that he will provide a personal escort to the house where Jonathan resides.

Brent chats glibly as we drive. I try to keep track of where we're going but we make so many turns I can't keep up with the unfamiliar street signs and landmarks. We come finally to a gate with no address and many tall pine trees shielding the upper reaches of the property.

Brent gets a remote control device out of the car's glove compartment. The gates swing open. Just beyond the gates, Brent pulls over to speak into a box mounted on a stand. He identifies himself with a number and lets the person on the other end know that he brings a previously cleared guest. I've been to drive-in restaurants where you would get hamburgers and fries after this.

"Why are they letting me see Jonathan?" I ask. I hadn't stopped to wonder until I saw the organization's setup.

"No one connected with Jonathan's past has asked to see him in six years. He's received no letters. Your appearance could be a test. Or a chance for growth. Jonathan will know once he is in your presence. He has a protectress, Jennifer Whiten, who will shepherd him through your visit."

Great, I think. I assume that Jennifer will be present to protect him from me.

We park under massive pines some distance from the building complex. The main building probably graced the property first. The outbuildings look like they were added later but designed to conform with the original. I would love to know where the Whirvies got the capital to invest in this property. Does their income derive from monies obtained by devotees selling cards and flowers? From the donations of their recruits?

Brent hands me over, into the custody of Jennifer Whiten. Jennifer wears robe-like clothing and a beatific expression on her face which makes me uneasy. I make conversation in a pleasant social vein while Jennifer leads me down a wide hallway. I follow her through a large auditorium, out the back, and into a garden where a man with a striking olive-complexioned face sits staring into space.

"That is Jonathan Gold," says Jennifer, giving great weight to the introduction.

Jonathan doesn't look up as we approach, perhaps meditating or communing with unseen visitors to his bench who got there before me. He makes an odd antithesis to someone in my profession. In my line of work, we value alertness above all.

The visit feels interminable. I listen to my own voice forge on through the stillness. I list for Jonathan all the dead ends I've encountered while searching for Ruthie. Jonathan gazes at me placidly. Jennifer nods, laughs if appropriate, even says, "How interesting," at one point.

When I run out of material and tire of speaking to the bland countenance of Jonathan Gold, I join him in his silence. I sit for some time and stare at him. The moments tick by. I study Ruthie's brother. Jonathan looks handsome, dark, and Jewish, but the vacant look in his eyes renders the face ordinary instead of attractive. I tire of his face.

"Do you have any information that I might find useful?" I question Jennifer Whiten.

"No. Jonathan's card has not been updated for over six years. Jonathan has moved on to a different spiritual plateau than you or me. He has no need to chase shadows from the past. His bonds have been cut. You see how unaffected he is by the slings you aim against him." She's right. The man looks unaffected by anything, practically comatose.

Jennifer rises. "Our time with you is over. I thank you. Jonathan's confidence in his own enlightenment will grow in the knowledge that nothing you represent is meaningful to him."

Gee, thanks, I think again. "I appreciate you giving up your valuable time," I say to Jennifer. She holds out a hand to shake, a surprisingly worldly gesture that demands physical contact. I put my hand in hers.

"You may find your way out the way you came in. Feel free to enjoy the house and grounds. Our select brothers and sisters are sequestered where you could not intrude upon them." Jennifer smiles prettily.

"Thanks," I repeat. I have nothing much left to say.

Jennifer turns and glides gracefully toward the western building. Jonathan rises and follows her. I get up and begin the tramp to find Brent.

"You there." I hear a rusty, deep voice. I whip around. Jonathan stands shielding his eyes with his hand.

"Is that you, Jonathan?" I ask quietly so I won't scare him.

"My family is gone. Dr. Stuart Lilienthal of San Francisco, an evil and spiritually bankrupt man, got rid of them. You must not direct his eye upon you. I want you to bury the memory of my sister and look for enlightenment in your own life. I wish you grace." The voice collapses on the word, "grace."

218
▲

Jonathan makes a hand gesture, not the sign of the cross. His face never moves. He wheels and glides away after Jennifer. My audience has ended. I hope Jonathan hasn't sunk to a less desirable plateau because of speaking to someone as unecclesiastical as me.

"Will Jonathan be in trouble with Jennifer, or anybody, for speaking to me?" I ask Brent when we're safely on our way back to Venice.

"Jonathan knows his way far better than you or me or Jennifer. No brother or sister at World Views would presume to question him," says Brent.

"What role do you have in the organization?" I ask out of curiosity. "P.R.? Marketing?"

"More like Security, *Susan*," his prep school voice evidences a new, threatening note. Our eyes meet and we understand each other.

I treat Honor to the best burrito we've ever had, stuffed with savory stewed pork. Dennis gave me the address and exact directions to the cramped kitchen at the back of a bar where they make them. Honor shows me two thick belts studded with turquoise that she's bought for the kids.

Honor and I enjoy being with each other, as if the new setting provides a respite from our troubles. I don't tell her about Jonathan warning me off the case, which would only spark a quarrel. We debate the premise that Jonathan wants Dr. Lilienthal to take the fall for his family's egress because Lilienthal is a psychiatrist and psychiatry is inimical to the Whirvies approach to living. Or does Jonathan have hard evidence? I guess that he could only have second-hand evidence, having been cloistered for years.

We go back to the motel where I make several phone calls. Then we leave for Temple Beth Shalom, figuring that a large number of people should be there around mid-afternoon. The Temple houses a community center which sponsors various activities. I am determined to avoid the strong-willed Marcia Finckle who might try to squeeze some antique-looking dolls out of me. Her type runs true-to-form in churches, synagogues, women's clubs, men's clubs, and PTAs throughout the United States. I feel sure I would know her by her voice.

We begin in the gift shop. Honor buys a mass-produced good luck piece for the kitchen of her father's house. We already have one, the Suttons appreciate good luck from any quarter. I try my Susan Abrams story on a woman with cropped black hair and a middle-Eastern style shirt behind the counter. She hasn't been a member of the congregation long enough to know the Golds.

We wander. We look in on a nursery school room filled with so much activity we can't see anyone who might have the leisure to speak. I try my story on a competent-looking woman sorting stacks of material in the book room.

We have the good fortune, at length, to mingle with a group of senior citizens just coming out of a meeting. The group consists of about twenty women and two men. I find various people who knew Maddy and Morris. All of them express regret over the suddenness of the Gold's departure. Honor and I jolly the group into talking to us for fifteen minutes.

Discouragement knots my shoulders. "Why don't you try Marcia Finckle?" suggests a beautifully attired woman. "She was such good friends with Maddy Gold. And so sorry to lose her. Marcia keeps track of everything. She'll be here to meet with Peggy Epstein, the rabbi's wife, very soon." It's time to go.

"You might talk to Hannah, too," she finishes. "Maddy used to cook meals for her when she was sick and take them over hot. Hannah?" she calls, "do you have a moment for these young ladies?"

I want to escape Marcia Finckle more than I want to talk to Hannah. I've seen enough of this group to decide they make for more dead ends. I take Honor by the arm and drag her away from a conversation about travel in Canada. I try to make her hurry but we are interrupted by a high, clear voice calling, "Girls, wait a minute."

A small woman with a sweet, round face darts down the hall toward us. She ignores me and angles her way directly in front of Honor.

"I've been hanging back, I never speak when there's no purpose. I don't indulge in idle gossip. But you have such a lovely face, child, I could tell you need to hear what I haven't told anybody these past six years." Honor beams splendidly into the little woman's eyes.

"I'm Hannah Appel. Maddy was as dear as a daughter to me. We had a special bond between us although I never went to her house. I couldn't bear to see her with Morris Gold, an unkind man if I've ever met one. Thank God, Morris rarely came to Temple."

"Did Maddy talk to you before she left?" I try to muscle my way into the conversation. Hannah Appel sends me a whithering look. I step back. She puts a hand on Honor's arm.

"You," she shakes Honor's arm. "You, Maddy would like to be in touch with," Hannah tells her. I resist rolling my eyes in disgust over what Honor gets away with.

"Maddy talked to me before she left. Oh, how she was crying. She told me to think of her as dead. And I did. I took her at her word. We sat shiva for her in my house and I mourned her like a flesh and blood daughter."

"Yes," murmurs Honor, in as fond a voice as Hannah's. Honor has always been a sucker for the sweetsy, motherly type. She has probably developed a genuine instant affection for this woman.

"She couldn't tell me exactly where they were going, out of fear of Morris. But I have my impressions from our talk. Maddy said she and Morris were going somewhere hot, like they were going to hell. She talked about hell. Jonathan was gone already to a foreign church. Janie had violated the rules of common human decency, Maddy said, and they let her go back north." Hannah shakes her head.

"And Ruthie," says Honor softly.

"Ruthie didn't go with her parents. Ruthie went north, also. Yes, north, I'm sure of it. Ruthie drove, while Maddy and Morris flew. I won't ask what business you have with these people who are dead to us here. But I know by your face that you would only do good for them."

Honor looks lovingly into Hannah Appel's face but also sends me, for a second, a smug look. "What exactly did Maddy say to create your impression of Ruthie's whereabouts?" I interject desperately.

"I formed the thought without remembering any details," replies Hannah, icy when answering me. "Perhaps it had something to do with Maddy's description of the kind of clothing that each person would require in the future." I tear Hannah and Honor apart only after they hug and hope to meet again. I, on the other hand, probably wouldn't have a shot in the world at getting Hannah to meet with me. A husband comes to claim Hannah. She's one of the ones with a man still living. Why didn't *he* cook the meals when Hannah was sick?

On our way out the door, I see a business-like face above a well-turned-out person. "Good afternoon, Mrs. Finckle," I say. I grab Honor and dash.

"Thanks for coming by," I hear behind me the temporarily perplexed voice of Marcia Finckle.

That night in bed at the City Star, I lie waiting for sleep. How much stock should I put in Jonathan's message about

Dr. Lilienthal? Where would Ruthie have gone that's north of here? Canada? Santa Monica? Santa Barbara? Back to San Francisco? I've had a supposition about what happened to Ruthie since the night I met Tara Timmin and now I'm becoming frustrated by not finding the spot where Ruthie cast away her mortal coil. Honor's breathing works, after a time, to soothe me gratefully into a state of dry, dreamless sleep.

Back home, I find a rental car parked in front of our house. The driver chose a luxury model rather than the small tinny box-style I always rent. I get out of my car and glance inside the car window. Warren Siegel, Annabelle and Jemmy's father, sits working on papers in the front seat.

I rap my knuckles on the passenger-side window. Warren rolls down the glass and says cheerfully, "Glad I caught you. I took a chance and waited here to see if you'd show up." Warren Siegel looks a lot like Jonathan Gold except that the lively, business-like gleam in Warren's eyes affects his appearance more than any other feature, while Jonathan's eyes look dead.

"Can I come in?" Warren asks, already gathering his papers and bounding out of the car.

"Sure," I reply needlessly. We walk up to the front door side by side. I see Nancy's head disappear quickly behind her living room drapes.

"I've been talking to Ramsey over at Newell Sutton's house. I hear you and Honor had a falling out," he says with honest sympathy.

"Yes. She took the kids to stay with her dad for a while."

"She *must* be upset. Newell makes her miserable," Warren says knowledgeably.

"She's pretty mad at me right now." I open the door and hold it for him.

"I can't believe you've put up with the scene all these years. You must have been steamrolled so often you should be flat by now." Warren has always admired me in this respect.

223
▲

"I get what I want from Honor, mostly," I tell him, as I have before.

"For my children's sake, I'm thankful you're hanging in there. You are, aren't you?"

"I think Honor and I will get back together. And I'd never desert Annabelle and Jem. Have you seen them?" I ask.

"We had dinner last night. Those kids. I wanted one cigarette after dinner. First, Jem started gagging and choking. A lady at the next table came over to do the Heimlich maneuver in case something was lodged in his throat. Then they both started lecturing. I felt like Annabelle was auditioning for Surgeon General. I wonder if those kids aren't getting more like their mother," Warren shakes his head.

"No more than usual," I reply.

"Well, it's okay with me if you want to inject more Eliza so they don't get too much Honor," he says and puts an arm around my shoulders.

Warren and I make ourselves coffee and thaw some frozen truffles which are nearing their expiration date. Honor probably bought them for a specific occasion which I have forgotten. Thirty minutes into the conversation, Warren snaps his fingers.

"I don't know why I didn't tell you right off. While I was waiting for you, some guy came around from the back of your house. Nice looking, in a good suit. I asked him what he was doing back there. He tells me he's stalking robins. Birds, I guess. I asked him what he meant. He said, 'I'm going to snap their necks and gnaw them.' Definitely crackers."

I tell Warren briefly about looking for Ruthie. "I like the more hard-boiled detective stuff, myself, but I do hope I'm in town long enough to find out what happened to poor old Ruthie," he laughs.

"How long are you here for?"

"My business should take four or five days to wrap up," he answers. "I have to get to Stockholm for a few days next week. I want to see the kids as much as I can while I'm here."

"Good."

"You know what? I have reservations at the Sheraton in San Francisco but I think I'd rather stay with you. It won't hurt you to have reinforcements on hand if Lilienthal tries to pull anything. We can have Annabelle and Jem over and I won't have to face the Suttons every time I see the kids. Unless I'd be imposing?"

I think about the proposition. Warren makes for pleasant company and I suspect that avoiding Honor and Newell motivates him more than the insulting idea that I can't take care of myself. So I install Warren in the guest room.

While I go about doing the chores Honor has taught me are required to house a guest, I turn the television on in my bedroom, which I have done a lot since she and the children left, for background noise. Suddenly, while hanging fresh towels in the bathroom, I hear an unpleasantly familiar voice.

The show I was listening to has gone off while I've been working and a talk show has started. The guest on today's show must be prominent San Francisco psychiatrist, Stuart Lilienthal. I run into the bedroom in time to find Lilienthal discoursing on love and trust. He looks terrific. I sit on my bed, glued to the screen, until Lilienthal gifts us with parting words of wisdom.

"Many parents feel that if they talk to their children, they are doing their job. But talking to your child is not going to work unless you *listen* to your child. Your child is communicating with you all the time, if not with words then with his or her actions. I can't encourage you enough to listen, listen, listen."

His paternal smile radiates across the studio. The music comes up. The audience claps and then roars a cheer. I wish I could get that kind of love and acclaim for mouthing platitudes.

Lilienthal looks saner than Jackie and Cal, the beloved TV hosts beside him. He used ordinary gestures and I didn't hear a hint of cat metaphor in the whole half-hour show. Is he conning me or them? I am in the time-honored position of seeing as crazy someone the world in general doesn't. The phone rings.

"Eliza?" Eileen's voice sounds teary and slurred. I hope I don't regret giving her my home phone number, but with the cat hocus pocus going on I felt I had to.

"Are you okay, Eileen?"

"No. Rich has left me. He's gone to stay at his folks' house for a while. I don't understand. I forgave him for what he did with Jane. I thought everything would be fine. But now he won't even tell me why he's left me. I think it has something to do with Ruthie."

"With Ruthie?"

"Rich is a tense person. I've told you about his nervous stomach and all that. But lately he's so jumpy he can't stand it when I talk. I even have to chew quietly. He blames me for deciding to find Ruthie in the first place. He talks about

225
▲

Ruthie and Jane in his sleep. Rich has always talked in his sleep for a few hours every night. But it's worse now."

"Maybe he's still feeling guilty about Jane, after all."

"No. Something must be going on. He got a phone call from Stuart Lilienthal. He went in his study to take it so I wouldn't hear."

"Dr. Lilienthal and Rich have talked again?" Eileen will never learn to present events in order of importance.

"Yes. Dr. Lilienthal sounds so normal when he calls and asks to talk to Rich. Considering how insane he is when he talks with you."

"Eileen, I'm coming over to your house. We'll talk. I'll be there in a half hour or so." With Rich absent, I can search for anything he might have secreted in his study which might clarify the nature of his relationship with Dr. Lilienthal.

I finish hanging the towels and tell Warren, who has begun reading the last three days' newspapers, to make himself at home. I think about calling the Sutton house before I leave. On the plane flight home from Los Angeles, Honor agreed, in a fit of generosity, to procure an anniversary present for Precious. I hope she will remember to get it today.

We're down to the wire because Precious' party will take place this Friday. I assume that by agreeing to pick out the present, Honor has implicitly agreed to accompany me. She wouldn't like the gossip that would ensue if she weren't with me. On the other hand, she won't enjoy the risk of seeing Rochelle Goffstein-Woolley if she does go. I start to plan what I myself will say if I run into Rochelle but nothing comes to mind.

I get the directions to Eileen's house out of the glove compartment before I get to the Caldecott Tunnel. When I pull up to her house twenty minutes later, I consider once again how much fancier Eileen lives than I do. The woman has a certain kind of gumption to have acquired this backdrop for her life and hung on to it.

The maid I met on my first visit opens the door when I ring. She looks meaner than ever and her general pessimism deepens when she sees me. I recall that she seemed very attached to Rich, she probably misses him. She sniffs disapprovingly when I ask for Eileen.

Eileen sits in her spotless kitchen. Her uncommon face looks puffy, the lavender eyes smudgier than usual. "I'll get you some coffee," she sniffles. She adds milk without my reminding her that I like it, so she's functioning on some level.

"Eliza, there's something wrong with Rich. I'm sorry for everything bad I've said about him." I push a box of tissues across the table to her and she takes one.

"What's wrong with Rich?"

"He took things when he went to his mom's. He took our family tree, the one that hangs in the hall. That's odd because most of the family on it is mine. His family doesn't really know where they came from, maybe Romania, but his grandmother died before anyone asked her. And, Eliza, he took my blue rabbit's foot that I've had since sixth grade. He's so normal usually. I mean, not quite normal because of his stomach problems and the fights he has at the company, but not strange like this. Do you understand what's the matter with him?"

"Maybe we can find an explanation. May I look at Rich's study? Rich would be upset, but he doesn't have to know. I want to establish what might be going on between Rich and Lilienthal that you and I don't know about." Eileen's eyes swell into round pools.

"I don't know. I suppose you can. But Mrs. MacWilliams will tell Rich. Wait until I send her out to the store." Eileen gets up, her face still befuddled by a gift from her family physician, and heads out into the living room calling for Mrs. MacWilliams. Eileen has to argue the maid out the door. I can hear the disagreement all the way across the house.

I root through Rich's study. I find that Rich keeps a large amount of boyish memorabilia for a man his age—high school trophies, balls, yearbooks. He appears to collect inscribed plastic shoehorns. The memoranda between Rich and his dad makes lively reading. Rich alternates groveling with aggression, neither of which gets him far in the power struggle. Eileen hovers in the doorway, wringing her hands and speculating what Rich would say if he walked in.

I don't find anything pertaining to Dr. Lilienthal other than Lilienthal's home and work phone numbers and addresses, recorded on a rolodex card file. My search may be fruitless because Rich also keeps information on computer disks at work. I'm tiring of Rich's paperwork when I come across something interesting.

A file labeled 'G, S, H & L Corp.' holds material indicating that Rich has been a partner in, of all enterprises, South Street Spa and Gym, ever since it was purchased by Claudia Hollings. The file bears a label on the cover slating it for removal from this cabinet when a batch of papers goes to

227
▲

Rich's office for computerization next Friday, so the information almost slipped through my fingers.

Eileen appears in the doorway, her face slack but tense. "Eileen," I ask, "what businesses does Rich have a partnership in, other than his father's?"

"Rich doesn't even have a partnership in Dad Goldeen's business. His father has been promising all these years but then they have another fight. Rich doesn't own any businesses. He thinks he's a good stock investor. All our money is in the stock market, it's sort of a game with him. I've said, 'Rich, everybody diversifies. Think about 1929.' Luckily, Rich doesn't work in a building tall enough to throw himself off. When they had that problem with the market last year, Rich took some extra atropine for his stomach and then he was fine." She sways. I don't tell her that Rich has diversified more than she thinks.

"Thanks, Eileen, I just wondered. I have a couple more things I'd like to look at. Can you go watch for Rich and Mrs. MacWilliams?"

I read through the history of Rich's financial transactions with South Street Spa and Gym. The gym hasn't made Rich any money, ever. From what I can tell, the only profit Rich might be making from the business has to do with the unusual way the finances get recorded. Claudia Hollings employs an innovative bookkeeper, the kind that helps with taxes and keeps secrets well.

The figures in Rich's file make slow reading over the next half hour until I reach the legal documents clipped at the back of the folder. I take a quick look at the partnership agreement and find something worth looking for.

Two other partners appear on the agreement, a person with a long foreign name and Stuart Lilienthal, M.D.

Where does the resurrected Claudia Hollings fit into this story? She may have threatened me and Dennis away from her but I'm going after her now.

"Eileen," I call. "I've gotten everything I need." Eileen appears, holding a sponge. I don't know why the woman has to clean when she employs full-time help.

"Have you figured out why Rich left?" Eileen asks helplessly. I shake my head.

"No, but I found a few interesting items. I'm going to talk to Rich. I'll ask him directly." I certainly am going to ask Rich some direct questions! "Eileen, I have other business tomorrow. But I'll get in touch with you Friday and let you know if anything has come up."

"What do you mean? What if I need you tomorrow?" Eileen gasps.

"Call my office," I tell her. "You can leave an urgent message 24 hours a day."

I have the misfortune to run into Mrs. MacWilliams on my way out the door. I hear her muttering under her breath, something about bringing trouble into the house. Not me, I want to say but I don't bother.

While driving to my office I deliberate over who I should confront first. Precious hands me a small sheaf of messages. "Have you picked out something fancy to wear to my party this Friday?" asks Precious with a satisfied grin, already playing the guest of honor. She wears a plum-colored sweater with flat silver circles in an arc across her chest, becoming and flashy. I send her a thumbs up and make my way out the back door into the courtyard.

Seated in my office, I check my messages. Dave Gray, postal worker and former neighbor of Ruthie in San Francisco, wants me to return his call. Doris Shipley wants a report about Andy's situation. I don't know how to convey what I know about the dark, beckoning quality of the murdered Lou Denny and about Andy's sliminess.

I am heartened by the next several messages. They will probably result in some offers of routine, income-producing work. I pounce on the last message. Honor left, "Sighted sub, sank same." She's gotten the gift for Precious. I have one less burdensome thought to bounce around in my mind.

My intercom sounds. "You have a visitor," Precious says. She sounds excited. The visitor has made his way across the courtyard in record time, I hear the doorknob rattle.

I take a deep breath when I see him. After all, when we met the time before last, he shoved me down. Lawrence, fastidiously dressed, looks even more comely away from Jazzmatazz. His appearance explains Precious' tone.

"Precious," I say into the intercom, "remember we're all gathering this Friday for your 25th wedding anniversary. It's not the time to consort with my business associates."

"You're so right, Eliza," Precious chortles into the phone.

"What can I do for you, Lawrence?" I ask, releasing the button that links me to Precious.

"I'm working part-time around here." I give him the once-over skeptically. I remember what his last job in the area was. I don't want to hear what mischief he's up to now.

"No, really," he says, a youth on the up and up, a solid citizen. "I'm teaching rhythmic movement to elementary school kids after school. Three days a week." I can't help rolling my eyes. "So I've been coming by to try and catch you in the office. I thought you might like to know about something that happened to me."

"Oh, yeah?" I don't feel like encouraging him to feel comfortable with me.

"You asked about the hands of the woman who hired me to threaten you. She wore gloves, remember? So I couldn't tell you anything."

"I remember." I remember every dead-end question that I've asked since I took this case.

"She called and said she wanted to meet with me again."

"Really? Why didn't you call me? I thought we had an understanding." I check his story, irritated.

"I tried coming by but you weren't here. I don't feel safe leaving messages." I don't ask why.

"Did you meet with her?"

"Yes. Same bar as before, not the kind of place I would have revisited on my own. The lady wore gloves again. She wanted me to steal some paper for her. I told her I didn't want to know about it, I've gone absolutely legitimate. I have." Lawrence cocks his head charmingly.

"So," I quash him, grouchy about his presence in my office. "I don't see what there is in this story to interest me."

"One thing. She dropped some change on the floor. She took one glove off automatically when she bent over to pick up the coins. She got it back on fast. But I managed to get a look and it was strange all right."

"What was strange?"

"Her hand was real young even though she's pretty old." He looks triumphant. "If she hadn't dropped the money, I was going to try spilling water on her gloves to see if she would take them off. You want to hire me for any detective jobs, you just call me at this number. You don't have to trust me, just tell me what you want and I'll take care of it."

"Thanks, Lawrence. I'll call if I need you. Keep dancing and all that." The debonair Lawrence tips his hat and exits.

I had at first suspected that Doris Shipley hired the mugger to warn me off looking for Ruthie. I assume Doris to be capable of almost anything. I knew she was keeping tabs on me and I figured the motive to be sibling rivalry. But Doris couldn't have gotten herself to Santa Cruz, Jazzmatazz is beyond Doris' sphere. And the hands check out wrong. The woman who hired Lawrence must be suspect B or C.

I pick up the phone, taking a few seconds to retrieve Lucy and Linden Sutton's work phone number from my memory. I get Lucy on the line. I'm relieved that she doesn't mention Honor. Maybe nobody has told her why Honor has been staying at her father's house. I ask Lucy for a large favor which she doesn't owe me.

Lucy, like all the Suttons, has no interest in what doesn't affect her. She asks me to explain the mechanics of how to bring about what I want. By the end of the conversation, Lucy has agreed to issue Rich Goldeen a personal invitation to attend a preview of Heavenly Bodies' new fitness program for executives at Heavenly Bodies, on Saturday morning at 11:00 a.m. She'll play to his ego by reiterating what an exclusive group will be present.

"A fitness program for executives," Lucy ruminates. "Can I use the idea if I want to, Eliza?" I give it to her.

I have to entreat her further. I explain that I want Claudia Hollings invited to a meeting, purportedly to discuss business of mutual interest with Linden and Lucy, Saturday at 11:15 a.m., at Heavenly Bodies. Lucy balks this time, not wanting to embarrass Heavenly Bodies in the aerobics community. I promise that I will make sure Claudia Hollings poses no threat to their reputation after the meeting. Lucy does owe me a couple of tiny favors. I mention a few minor matters I worked on for her, brought to a happy conclusion, and kept quiet. She'll never hear anything about this affair either, I tell her. She reluctantly acquiesces.

"Do I actually have to attend your meeting, Eliza? I teach a class at that time," she asks.

"No. I'd rather you were out of the way." I swear once again that I will handle everything without inconveniencing her.

Precious knocks and then opens the door. She carries a plate with croissants and butter and a pot of fresh coffee. Precious must not have been able to interpret Honor's message.

When she returns to her office, I pick up the phone and dial the number that Dave Gray left. I'm just about to hang up when I hear him mumble, "This is Dave." I'm afraid this may not be a time of day when Dave can think, he's probably working nights. I explain who I am.

"Good news," replies Dave. "Delilah and I are back together." Dave doesn't seem to remember that we don't know each other very well.

"At last," I say, trying to get into the spirit of the thing.

"Thanks," he says contentedly. I can picture him sitting in a near-prone position surrounded by artifacts from the 1960s, his incense bowl, his posters. "Oh, yeah," he recollects. "I called you because Kathy Juarez, my neighbor here at the apartment building, asked me to. She remembered you but she lost your card. She's real broken up. Her boyfriend, Geronimo, disappeared two days ago. The cops say he probably just went back to Mexico. But he's 100 percent reliable usually. He's illegal but he works steady over on Pier 61. Hey, you haven't found Ruthie, have you? I've been wondering."

"Not yet," I admit.

"Well, I'm sure you get results sometimes. I figured you'd probably be within Kathy's price range. Maybe you could look for the two missing people at the same time, Ruthie and Gero."

"I'm afraid it doesn't work that way, Dave. I can't really take on another case right now."

"Oh, well. Maybe I'll help Kathy. I've read some mysteries and I have a few friends who did some undercover-type work when they were in the service," Dave says, his good nature rising to the circumstances.

"Good luck to you, Dave. Start with the obvious. Has he had a paycheck forwarded to some place? That kind of thing."

"By the way," Dave continues cutting off my goodbye. "Remember we were talking about Dr. Lilienthal? My wife wants us to sue him. He, uh, took advantage of her. Our daughter, Lisa, is still screwed up. He did some crazy trips on both their heads. His bookkeeper also charged my wife for appointments she thought she had canceled.

"Anyway," Dave goes on, "here's what I wanted to tell you. Dr. Lilienthal told Delilah, my wife, that he has nine lives. Then he said he'd gotten away with murder, 'won a cat fight,' he called it. Do you think he could have been the one who killed Claudia Hollings?"

"I don't know yet. By the way, Claudia is alive and living as an aerobics instructor in Berkeley. It was Jane, Ruthie's sister, who was killed in the apartment that night."

"No, it wasn't," sputters Dave Gray. Dave and Ottie Dresner think hazily, but my job requires that I should be able to see through the haze. Dennis' favorite maxim has to do with this skill but I still don't remember it. I decide to issue Dave Gray an invitation to Heavenly Bodies on Saturday morning. He's flattered.

When I've finished my calls, I phone Honor and try to pin her down about Precious' party. She refuses to yield and tells me she'll come by herself if she comes, so she takes down

Precious' parents' address where the party will be held. She offers to deliver the gift the day of the party. Warren has asked her to let the children live at our house for the length of his stay, she tells me, and she has agreed. I hope that Warren knows he's doing childcare.

Now I have to face the most unpleasant task on my roster. I pull the file and get a pencil to copy Doris Shipley's address into my appointment book. I can't place the street on which she lives so I get out the Thomas Street Guide. I expected Doris to have an East Oakland address, a downtown address, or a room in a Telegraph Avenue motel. But Doris' tiny street winds through an exclusive area in Montclair. I never investigated her living situation. Doris has probably conned some wealthy person out of a bedroom for her poor bereft self at $75 a month.

As I travel up out of the flatlands and into the Montclair hills, I drive by a six-bedroom home with sculptured grounds that Newell Sutton wanted to buy for Honor and me. He argued that if we must live in Oakland, we should have adequate housing. When I pull up to Doris' address I feel burned. Doris has living quarters in a mansion. Not the setting I envisioned for her bleak and sparsely befriended life.

I have come unannounced on purpose. I don't want Doris to trump up some scene for me to witness, some scene from which I would be obliged to rescue her for free. I wonder if I should go to the front door. I see no alternative. A tailored housekeeper of about fifty years opens the door. I inquire after Doris.

"She is in residence, ma'am, whom may I say is calling?" I stare at her, my mind blank for a second, and then give my name. She ushers me into a large foyer and disappears. I walk over and peer around some heavy green drapes into a huge expanse of room with a massive redwood deck at the far end. I check the inventory, a huge gleaming grand piano with fresh flowers in a cut-glass vase, the statuary, exotic live birds in intricate cages.

The maid returns silently. "Mrs. Shipley will see you in her sitting room. I'll show you the way."

I find Doris sitting at a desk, a Georgian mahogany, nervously going through some pages of paper. Her face looks sheepish, a countenance I have not witnessed on her before. She almost smiles at me.

"Doris, your home isn't quite what I expected," I say, seating myself on an elegant beige and lavender sofa standing on delicate carved legs.

233
▲

"You never asked me how I live. You never investigated," replies Doris with a hint of her usual truculence.

"That's true. I wasn't hired to investigate you, and unlike some people, I rarely intrude upon other people's privacy without cause. You paid me to investigate Brenda Coller, which I did for you, as well as another investigation gratis." Doris narrows her eyes ready to counter my unpleasantness.

"When I hired you it was because I assumed you were sharp," Doris retorts. "I paid you to acquaint yourself with me and my concerns."

"The fee you paid, which wouldn't have covered the basic retainer for any other investigator, certainly didn't pay for enough of my time to make me want to spend extra time checking on your economic status. Which I'm sure you counted on. You're very good. I never questioned your masquerade." I have other questions I want to ask, for my own education.

"Why do you pretend to be what you're not? Why do they let you use the county hospital for medical care? You couldn't be on Medi-Cal, why would the state subsidize your health costs?"

"I pay my way at the County Hospital. And they appreciate seeing someone other than a medically indigent adult. I like the clientele there and I like the staff. That's where I met Brenda and Andy, you know. Not that those relationships worked out in the long run but they could have."

"Just the day before yesterday," continues Doris, brushing some imaginary lint off her polyester pants leg, "I had a terrible pain in my abdomen and was rushed to Emergency. Luckily the paramedics will not be billing me since I was in too much distress to authorize the ambulance service. While I was waiting for tests, I met a lovely couple, Pete and Eva. We spent the whole evening talking. We went out to dinner last night and although I could only take liquids, we were, I don't know how to describe it, sympatico."

To dig at her, I say, "Does this mean that you're going to suggest that I investigate Pete and what's-her-name?"

"Certainly not. I have no doubt, after this discussion, that you will try to extort some exorbitant fee from me in exchange for your shoddy work."

"Jesus, Doris," I begin, then I decide to write the whole thing off. I have no doubt that my discovery of Doris' financial status will finally keep her away. I've been trying to unload her for weeks and now I have.

"I've come by to explain what happened with Andy," I say in a professional voice. "You were going to die, if I recall, without this information from me." Doris relaxes when we cease discussing her finances.

"Oh, Andy. I hope I won't be called as a witness at his trial. I can't be bothered. I don't want to see his weasely face again," she says. She turns and pretends to spit.

"Doris, I'm going to tell you this so that you can learn something before next time. I know you don't want to hear this but I want you to take Andy and Brenda and apply them to the case of Pete and Eva."

"Pete and Eva are salt of the earth," begins Doris, icelike.

"Listen, Doris. Andy was salt of the earth too. Salt, the stuff that sucks moisture out of anything it touches. Andy ran into a siren, someone who had been abused all her life. Andy was the agent of her death. The violence in him lay dormant until then, so you couldn't see it."

"There was no danger of him killing *me*," replies Doris.

"You don't know that, Doris. Listen to me. Here's the crux of the matter as far as you're concerned."

"What?" Doris looks curious in spite of herself.

"Weak and empty people gravitate to you. And you don't provide enough satisfaction to rescue them or keep them." Because you're stingy, I think hostilely.

Doris' mouth screws into a critical sneer. "This is just like you. Cheap talk instead of facts."

"Pete and Eva are going to turn on you, Doris," I parry. "Listen to me and try to find new ways to occupy your life."

"I'm not going to stand here and let you sling mud at two beautiful souls who are kindred spirits to me. I'll show you to the door myself." She leaps up and marches out of the room. I follow her. Her ankle seems miraculously restored to working order. I feel relieved of a great load. I've done all I can for Doris. I've done all I'm going to for Doris.

Before I get to the door I ask, "Doris, where did you get your money?" Doris bridles and then gives me a priggish smile.

"I used to be an L.V.N. I subbed at rest homes around Oakland. I kept losing every permanent job through no fault of my own. Finally I got a two-week job at a nice place in Montclair. Norman Shipley fell in love with me at first sight." Doris smooths her poorly permed hair as though another Norman might be coming through the door.

"A week later we were married. He died tragically after a few months of happiness. He had a cerebral hemorrhage during lunch. Some people in his family never believed that

Norman and I knew true love. They tried different ways to break the will. But my lawyer beat them every time.

"My lawyer is the best, I located him through Oakland Legal Aid. If I was one speck less satisfied with you, I'd tell him to get my money back." Her complacent smile rankles me.

"Doris, I've just decided that I might stay on your case if I have the time. I wouldn't mind being around to see the Pete and Eva show." The humanitarian feeling that sent me here has been eaten up.

"Bitch," she sibilates.

"What you got from me today was a bargain," I tell her. "Only a counselor or therapist would bother to look at what's going wrong in your life. And they'd make sure you paid them an adequate hourly fee."

"Are you calling me crazy? Get out," Doris screams, and slams the door. I've ended two cases on this kind of note in the past. I feel a couple notches deflated but I don't dwell on it.

The next day's routine work for a small local business makes a pleasant distraction. Warren shoulders his responsibility and shuttles the children to school and to their activities. I do my bookkeeping in the evening, with great satisfaction. I'm bringing in a nice sum of money lately, from clients paying past-due bills.

I take the children with me to Precious' party on Friday evening, to give Warren a break. We arrive right on time but the party sounds like it's in full swing. Precious' parents stand side by side greeting people at the door. Luranda, Precious' mother, tells Annabelle and Jemmy, "Anything at all you want, you just tell me and I'll fix it for you. In this house, the only rule is be happy all the time." She wraps her arms around each of them in turn. The children look awed, having never before encountered such open-hearted hosts. Once inside, we find overflowing candy dishes, ice tubs with cans of soda pop and beer chilling. From out in back we can smell hot dogs and chicken on the grill. The crowd sways to pulsing music from tremendous-sized speakers.

"We've never been invited to this good a party before," Jemmy whispers in my ear.

We make our way to the back yard and queue for fat link sausages in hot dog buns. I turn around holding a sizzling hot dog. I bump into Rochelle with Mike at her side. "Eliza, I have so much to tell you," she yells over the music and voices. We move over to stand on the lawn.

"How have you been, Rochelle?" Annabelle and Jemmy have gone to eat with a hoard of other children at the redwood picnic tables.

"I told Mike everything," says Rochelle with pride. I notice that Mike glares at me unrelentingly.

"I'm sorry, Mike. My behavior was inexcusable. I want you to know how much I value your friendship and your partnership," I babble. Mike's face doesn't alter, so I stop.

Rochelle puts a hand on my shoulder. "No. No. There's no problem," she says. "After I realized I was ready to be honest with Mike, we really talked for the first time in several years. Now there are no hidden doubts and questions to keep us from being close. I feel freed. Our marriage is stronger than ever." I look at Mike's sour face. I love a happy ending.

"I love a happy ending," I say.

Rochelle sees someone across the yard who moved out of our office complex last year. I never liked the guy. He motions her and Mike to join him.

"We'll talk more in a while," she says. I'd rather not, I still haven't come up with anything to say to her and I think the condition might be permanent.

"Mike?" I say.

"Later," he brushes past me. I don't get a chance to tell him I've reformed, I'm going to be faithful to Honor and true to friends and business partners. And why should he give me the chance? Usually I like a party but this one is not for me.

I rove, trying to avoid people who don't like me. Precious and I connect and she invites me to look through her mother's photograph albums. I look carefully at page after page featuring Precious, a provocative, giggling girl posed in girl scout uniforms, bathing suits, frilly dresses with stiff slips underneath.

We come to a photograph of Charles when he was a wide-eyed immigrant from a small Texas town. Precious gazes through the cellophane covering him. "There was someone I was in love with more than him," she says. I don't say anything.

"T.F. Dockery. He was real dark with green eyes. He used to be able to imitate a harmonica so well that people would dance like he was really playing one. You would never be bored with a man like that, I know it. But he never got very interested in me no matter how much I danced. Then Charles came along and he was always desperately hot to be with me." We turn the page.

"Do you have a picture of T.F.?" I ask.

237
▲

"You don't keep pictures of people you never got to be with. It would make you feel foolish every time you looked."

"I suppose," I say, thinking of Eileen retaining the coffee-stained photograph of Ruthie squinting into the sun.

"I'm not going to say any more," Precious shrugs. "You have such a peculiar life your own self, Eliza, it seems okay to tell you anything. But I should stop now."

Lucas Jang taps us to come see the gift from our office group unveiled. The gift, standing on a table in the living room, looks big. Precious will be impressed by the size, Honor did well in that respect. Precious goes forward and pulls off the sheet draping the painting.

I try not to issue a dismayed noise. The painting incorporates many repetitions of the printed words, "the heart." Terrible weather, fogs and lightning, and weird twisted plants obscure the words. The message must be about love destroyed by the elements, or something worse. Honor has used Precious' gift to make a statement. I feel myself getting truly angry at Honor, one of the rare instances in the course of our relationship. The crowd views the painting silently. Charles, especially, looks speechless.

Precious speaks first. "The colors are just right for our bedroom." Oh no, I think, she feels she has to make the best of it. She's entitled to call me out.

Precious' face lights. "I'm no art critic but the meaning in this just jumps out at you, doesn't it?" I try to look comprehending in case anyone is looking at me.

"This painting is here to tell us how love triumphs no matter what goes against it. This painting tells the story of me and Charles. You shouldn't have done it," she opens her arms to us, "it must be worth a mint." The group from the office moves forward to embrace her. I go with them and share her warmth.

"By the way," Lucas recalls something when he notices he stands shoulder to shoulder with me, "you asked me to report to you if I saw Dr. Stuart Lilienthal at our building. Did you two get together?" Lucas doesn't understand that I see the prestigious doctor as a threat. He tells me that Lilienthal came to the building looking for me but I wasn't around. I wish I could tell him about my last meeting with Lilienthal in his tomcat mode.

I decide to get another hot dog. On my way back inside, I pass Sarah Frybarger talking to Jemmy and Annabelle. I take a bite and while I'm chewing, hear Sarah ask, "Why have you two been staying at your grandfather's house?" Sarah picks some white meat delicately from a chicken breast. I try to swallow fast enough to cut the children off but the food sticks in my throat.

"Our mom got mad at Eliza," discloses Jemmy sadly. Sarah looks embarrassed and soon wanders away murmuring how sorry she is to hear about our family problems. I decide to leave soon. Honor always arrives early. She must have decided not to come. Sarah will soon have relayed my situation to Lucas who will be overly sympathetic and Mike who will feel vindicated. Only Honor at my side might have salvaged the evening and my pride. Honor, another individual who doesn't much owe me a chance to redeem myself.

I look for Precious so I can say good night. She sits with a crowd of her father's friends, dressed in black suits and smoking pungent cigars, radiating around her. They laugh approvingly, responding to Precious' humor and swaying body. The music has gotten progressively louder. Everyone in the crowd seems to be dancing with their own self, involuntarily propelled by the volume of sound.

Precious rises and makes her way to me. "Earlier, I thought to myself, 'I could get a real big discount from Eliza and have her find out whatever happened to T.F. Dockery. Maybe look him up.'" I groan inwardly. Precious puts a light hand on my arm.

"But when I saw that beautiful painting, it was like magic. I just thank the Lord that Charles and I made it through these past twenty-five years with our hearts in one piece. I'm a happy woman." She squeezes me tightly for a moment.

Precious' parents delay us while they fill two brown lunch bags full of candy and party horns. They send me away with a stack of napkins with "Charles and Precious Harrold" and the date of their marriage and anniversary embossed in silver. Acting in place of Honor, I confiscate the bags of candy after we get in the car.

Lights blaze from our house when we pull up. We find Dennis sitting on the living room sofa watching a police show on television. Warren has set him up with a beer and a cereal bowl filled with pretzels. Annabelle and Jemmy run to throw their arms around him. Dennis looks concerned that his beer will spill.

Dennis' face falls in grim lines. I can't tell whether something in particular has gone wrong, because this has become one of Dennis' habitual expressions over the years. Unless a mood of exhilaration comes upon him and he grins wildly.

Possibly he looks droopier than usual today. I guess that Sharon could have broken off with him completely.

I walk over to press my cheek against Dennis'. Dennis shaves better and more often than any other man I've touched. "What's up?" I ask.

"I came by so you can give me a party," Dennis states. His eyes flick momentarily to check the source of gunfire on the TV show.

"Halloween, bar mitzvah, Tupperware? What's the theme?" The children wait eagerly for his reply, probably hoping the answer is birthday.

"Engagement," Dennis doesn't crack a smile. I sit down quickly. Sharon Clemens and Warren enter from the dining room.

"Congratulations," I say and go over to hug Sharon. I haven't been paying enough attention to Dennis lately, I realize. I don't know how this entanglement happened. Dennis didn't even try to talk this decision over with me. "Last time I looked you were trying to escape this guy," I say to Sharon by way of light banter.

"Dennis brought me around," says Sharon, smiling fondly at him. She sits down on the other side of Dennis and puts a possessive arm around his shoulders, a little too stiff an arm. I don't make any more conversation with her. I'll get the details from Dennis the first chance I get.

"It's a party," shouts Jemmy. I should thaw some more of those stale rubber truffles, I decide, and make espresso.

Warren follows me into the kitchen to put a party together. "I like Sharon," he says. "She's quite a sophisticated lady for a private investigator." Then he catches himself. "Oops, sorry. You, Eliza, are as polished as any of the international set I've been stuck with for the last few years. More. More polished." I wave his apologies away.

The phone rings. I yell that I've got it in the kitchen.

"This is Detective Philip Cologne with the San Francisco Police Department. You called my office during the last several weeks about an incident of assault six years ago which may have involved Dr. Stuart Lilienthal."

"Right," I answer.

"I want to enlist your assistance."

"What can I do for you?" I ask. Cologne's deep, somber voice impresses me as much more fitting for a defender of the public faith than Fleet Hansen's tedious whine.

"Dr. Lilienthal was reported missing two days ago by his personal secretary, Neil Cowper. We're trying not to let this go public but we're following up any leads we can, in conjunction with the Federal Bureau of Investigation." The authoritative voice hesitates. "You have a client interested in Lilienthal's possible implication in the assault. Would your client, or any other party involved, have any information relevant to Lilienthal's disappearance?"

"Not as far as I know. He was trespassing at my home two days ago, though," I tell the detective. I don't mind having my problems with Dr. Lilienthal unofficially on the record.

"What is Stuart Lilienthal's interest in you?" Detective Cologne sounds warmer, perhaps gratified that I informed him about seeing Lilienthal recently.

"I haven't quite figured that out yet," I am forced to tell the cop.

"If you have information pertinent to this man's disappearance, you have the obligation to surrender the information to our department." He does like formal language, but he has that great voice so I don't find him offensive.

"Why don't you meet with me next week? I'll pull the file and run everything by you," I offer. By next week, I plan to be off this case and free to give out information without restraint.

"I'd like to see you tomorrow. What time would be convenient? I'll meet you at your office in Oakland." I give in. With luck, I may be at liberty by tomorrow afternoon.

I carry finger food, thermal coffee pot, and mugs out to the living room on a huge tray. Warren will follow with the finishing touches. Sharon excuses herself to go to the bathroom and I grab my chance.

"Dennis, remember how irritated you were by Claudia Hollings?" I preface my request.

"Come on, Muscles, I'm celebrating the biggest break in my life and I know you're about to hit me up for a time-waster." He manages a confederate's smile mid-complaint.

"Dennis, there's a perfect time for you to make a quick visit to South Street Spa and Gym. Just a jiffy trip through the files. I'm looking for information on Claudia's ex-boyfriend who disappeared six years ago. Tomorrow at eleven, Claudia won't be there, and I'll bet her assistant goon will be subbing for her in her classes." Claudia will be safely out of the way at Heavenly Bodies.

"You'll be helping me wrap this thing up," I plead with him. "I want confirmation on what happened to Ruthie within the next few days. I could get tired of this soon."

"Will you walk me up the aisle if I do this for you?" Dennis asks. His smile has become less endearing and more malicious.

"I hate looking silly, Dennis. You can have my children for flower people, can't you leave me alone?" The children jump up and down yelling 'yay.' Dennis continues smiling devilishly.

"All right," I say. "You do something you think is meaningless for me and I'll make a monkey out of myself for you. It's a deal." We shake.

Warren comes in through the dining room balancing a folding metal table with milk, cheese, napkins, and silverware laid out. "Eliza," he calls, "that damn Lilienthal just crept past the pantry window. Can't you get him restrained?"

I push the drapes aside and look out at the dark street. A figure loiters on the sidewalk. A light fog has blown in. The figure looks too bulky to be Lilienthal, more like a bear than a cat. A car door slams and its motor starts. The marauder pulls away, disappearing into the terrible weather and the twisting plants.

"**W**aiting for Rich to come home has made me nauseous, nauseated I mean," Eileen's voice flutters. "Maybe I've caught his stomach problems.

"I don't know if I've told you," she says confidingly, "but I'm on medication for my nerves. Because of Rich fighting with his dad so much, and my not being able to have children. Now I've gotten too sick to take my pills, I can't keep anything down. I feel like I'm going crazy." Eileen sounds distraught, but sharper than usual.

"I think things will be cleared up when I see Rich later today," I tell her. "Calm down. Take it easy until I talk to you."

"I don't know what to do with myself. I'm writing to Ruthie. I know you'll find her soon." Eileen's voice does not express total confidence.

"I will," I say with conviction.

"When you see Rich . . ." says Eileen and then falters.

"Yes?"

"Don't force him to tell you anything if he looks like his stomach is giving him trouble." She loves him.

I call an L.A. number, the friend of a friend I talked to when I was there. You can call middle echelon police officers at home on Saturday because they are their work, they don't ever realize they're off duty. This time I ask the right questions about the name "Gold." He knows who to call and when he calls me back, he provides me with more ammunition for use in my hunt today than I had expected. And I owe him that much in return.

I hang up and regard my office, quiet in the Saturday sunshine. To help me think, I pull out my account books and record some information that I'll need for a quarterly tax payment. In a messy case like this, I sometimes question the cost effectiveness of my work. This morning, I may need to barter for the goods I need to find Ruthie. I don't know how much I'll lose in the exchange. If I lose Eileen, I lose my fee. If I can't afford Ruthie's location, I've lost status professionally, in my own eyes, and probably in other quarters.

I close my books and get into motion. The office complex looks deserted. Everyone else stayed later than me at the party last night and probably won't be working today.

I arrive at Heavenly Bodies and enter from the back. The twins make Linden's astrology clients use this door. Double-paned glass half-moons and stars are inset to give the door a celestial look. A warning sign, hanging from the door knob on a light chain, detracts from the effect: "Aerobics students, this is not your door, please use front entrance." I almost decide I should use the front entrance but I don't.

Linden Sutton sits deep in conference with a salesperson pitching herbal remedies. Linden considers various sizes and price ranges in cures for every modern ill. I stand still looking at him for a moment without his knowledge. Linden's face was stamped with the same mold as Honor's, he's the closest duplicate in the world. I listen to him sweetly quiz the peddler.

Honor's brother *is* sweet: he lacks his sister's character. Linden sees me and dismisses the woman and her bottles. She carefully packs them into cardboard boxes and stacks the boxes in a small black trunk.

"Linden, are you free for an hour?" I ask. "I need you to help me handle something."

"You want me to do a reading for you, Eliza? I never know whether you have faith in my skills or not," Linden says, looking into my eyes.

"I do, Linden. I've always respected your dedication. But right now, I need a butler." Linden looks confused.

"Will I need a suit?" he asks.

"No. I need you to take several people to the back weight room for me. They'll arrive at staggered intervals. You may have to hold onto my second and third visitors until I need them. You can offer to tell them about your work. One of the visitors will be interested in astrology, one would rather hear about financing the aerobics business." Linden looks unsure about his task so I give him more explicit instructions.

244
▲

I establish myself at a table against the back wall of the large room. I arrange a clipboard and pens in front of me. I pat my side to make sure my gun rests in place. The day I applied for a permit to carry a concealed weapon, I felt sick. Today, I pat the gun like an old friend, the way Eileen twists her wedding ring.

Eventually, Claudia Hollings enters through the far side of the room. I watch her stride across the expanse of golden floor in great long strides and onto the blue vinyl practice mat. She moves confidently, displaying an at-ease military bearing. Her dark brown hair bound behind her head, instead of softening her face, makes her look fit for any battle I might mount. Her face tightens when she sees me.

"You," she says spitefully. "Lucy told me I was meeting with her but I gather I'm here to see you. Lucy and I work in a small world. I can make sure people know she's been playing games with me."

"I want to discuss the murder that took place at Ruthie Gold's apartment six years ago," I tell her, making sure to sound as ominous as she.

"Why can't you let go of that? It was a bad joke but I was young at the time, I thought I made that clear. I'll tell you one more time: Drop it."

"The punch line wasn't funny. A dead body carried out in a bag. I've checked the police records and I've seen the files at Jazzmatazz. I've even spoken with your cousin Ottie in L.A. I've pieced together most of the story. That's why I need to meet with you, Jane. I'm looking for your older sister, as I believe you know, and none of my leads have fallen into place so far." I use a strong but neutral tone so I won't spook her.

"What are you talking about? I'm Claudia Hollings. Half the people in the Berkeley Hills have been to me for tone-up. I'll sue you for slander if you tell anyone this lie." Jane Gold remains cool under fire.

"I don't care what happened six years ago, Jane, what you did doesn't matter." I employ the line a parent uses to excuse the culprit child enough to induce a full confession. "I want to find out what happened to Ruthie. If you cooperate with me, I'll leave you alone."

Probably I won't leave her alone. She's a dangerous Gold. One day, she could get tired of worrying about whether Eileen and I will maintain our silence. If I let her walk away, she'd always be a threat to us. But I dangle the possibility that I'll let her go.

"I have no idea where Ruthie went." She flips the strap of her bag over her shoulder, making as if to leave. She has, deliberately or not, chosen a statement that either Claudia or Jane might reasonably utter under these circumstances.

"Look, Jane, it's no sweat to prove that you're not Claudia Hollings, even though you assumed that no one would ever notice the substitution. It's not like you went to South America and bought yourself a new face and had your fingerprints removed. Your convenient transformation wouldn't be hard to reverse." The supercilious look on Jane's face makes me feel churlish.

"Claudia didn't leave a mark in this part of the world, you banked on that. Your family, the Golds, got lost. But I could import any number of people to identify you, Jane. So your smartest move is to give me what I want and get me off your back."

I can see her scrambling in her mind to decide how much to say. The scramble turns her eyes mean, glittery, and tremorous. I wish I could see in her sister any of the charm that drew people to Ruthie.

I look across the room. Linden has failed in his commission. He has turned loose my next invitee too soon. The set-up can only be saved if I play my part well. I move around the table inconspicuously until I flank Jane Gold.

"Janie," yells the caller, Dave Gray. He breaks into an ungainly gait and heads across the floor.

"God, it's . . ." Jane pauses searching her memory for the name.

Dave stops abruptly in front of us, panting. "It's me, Dave," he says to Jane. He looks at her, mystified by the frozen look on her face. "Dave Gray," he adds. "Ruthie's old neighbor."

"Yes. Dave." Jane turns into a lead replica of an aerobics instructor, she no longer looks light on her feet.

"Jane, I invited Dave to illustrate how easy it will be to establish that you are Jane Gold and that it was Claudia Hollings who died in Ruthie's apartment. If you'd like to call an end to this reunion, just tell me where your sister went."

"Hey. I'd love to hang out with Janie and talk over old times," begins Dave happily. I step on his toe to shut him up. I needed the chance to prep him which Linden lost me.

"Forget old times," I tell her, "just tell me where Ruthie is." Jane remains fixated, pondering her course.

"Wow," gushes Dave, irrepressible in his 'hail fellow, well met' mode. "What have you been doing with yourself since Claudia died?"

"No one died," says Jane with increased spite. "Remember my old boyfriend, Kurt Brewster? His friend, Stuart Lilienthal, thought the whole thing up and talked Kurt into it." Dave looks vaguely troubled.

"Kurt and I once played a really far out card game for hours, I didn't think he was ever going to leave my apartment," Dave says slowly. "He seemed like a great guy until Ruthie told me he probably killed Claudia. But Kurt was Claudia's boyfriend, not yours. Wasn't he?" Dave asks Jane cautiously, unable to understand Jane's discounting of the murder or anything else she's talking about.

"You're confused because Janie has gotten used to speaking as though she's Claudia," I tell Dave.

"What?" he asks.

"She assumed Claudia's identity after Claudia's death and has been living as Claudia Hollings for the past six years."

"This is all a joke," Jane snaps.

"The murder was no joke to Claudia Hollings," I say to Jane. "I've checked the coroner's report. Claudia was killed in Ruthie's apartment." Even hard words like "kill" don't register on her face. For all I know, Jane can exude evasiveness and camouflage indefinitely. I'm hoping not.

"Where has Kurt Brewster been all these years?" Dave asks. "I figured he got arrested and was in jail somewhere."

"Kurt disappeared after Claudia's death and the police never found him," I explain. "Stuart Lilienthal was involved in the murder, too, in some way. Lilienthal still has a stake in covering up what really happened. He has threatened me, warned me not to look for Ruthie."

"I never met Stuart Lilienthal," says Dave. "My wife was always the one to take our daughter to see him. I used to smoke and Delilah wouldn't let me drive with Lisa in the car." He shakes his head to clear it and seems to have a thought.

"Lilienthal was Ruthie's boyfriend for a while," Dave says. "I know that for sure because Ruthie told me and she didn't lie. Lilienthal was nuts about her. What did he have against her that made him want to get her involved in some kind of murder plot?" Dave stops again as if to finish sorting the puzzle, then asks, "Who did Ruthie think was murdered?" I give Jane a chance to answer but she doesn't.

"Ruthie saw the body at the murder site and at the police morgue. She had to know it was Claudia. But she identified the body as Jane's. That's why the police didn't pursue Kurt Brewster very hard. He would have been a prime suspect in the death of Claudia Hollings, he had been seeing Claudia for two years. But the police thought they had a dead Jane Gold. There was only hearsay evidence from Ruthie and the supposed Claudia to connect Kurt Brewster with Jane Gold at all." I face Jane. "It hasn't escaped my notice that you are the main person who profited by Claudia's death. You inherited her life."

"I won't have you taking potshots at me and jeopardizing my business reputation." Jane speaks through teeth that lie edge to edge.

"I'm taping this, Jane, so it's clear to posterity that I didn't push you around." She purses her lips and examines the room more acutely.

"Why did you want to tell people that you're Claudia?" asks Dave, once again completely befuddled. Jane turns an incendiary eye on him. "You have so much more going for you than Claudia ever did. May she rest in peace," he adds.

"Some of the things Janie had going for her were troubles with her drug connections in L.A., bad debts, bad checks floating everywhere she's ever lived, and a questionable part in an unfortunate accident which happened to her father's business partner in Orange County." Jane advances toward me in a hostile manner, she uses fluent body language.

"I talked to someone this morning who knew you when, Jane. Detective Theodore Cochren in southern California. He's been wondering whatever became of Janie Gold. And while we're on the subject of Sam Kaplan, your father's late business partner, now deceased," I pause for emphasis, "let us not forget the untimely demise of Claudia Hollings. Or was it timely for some of you?"

My taunting finally seems to be stirring the Janie Gold about whom I have heard so many rumors. Mrs. Hammerstein on Poinsettia Court, Ottie Dresner, Marcia Finkle at the Temple, they all mistrust Janie's character and temper. I watch her sharply.

"You're stepping over the line, Eliza." She sounds overly familiar with my name.

"I can't believe this," breathes Dave. "Thanks for inviting me, Eliza, this is real dramatic."

"I'm going to find out what happened to Ruthie whether you help me or not," I steer things back. "You've got nothing to lose by leveling with me now."

"When my friend, Steve, finds out about you trying to intimidate me, I won't guarantee your safety," says Jane, her hands balled into fists. The aerobics instructor has forgotten that if the large and small muscles are extended, we feel more in control. "I have no interest in telling you anything."

"You have enough interest in me to have hired young Lawrence from the dance company to have me mugged. You have enough interest, if I recall recent history, to try to rehire Lawrence to do major damage to me. Why didn't you use the local talent? Steve only handles your top priority muggings? You probably split Lawrence's fee with your cohorts, Lilienthal and Rich Goldeen. So I hold you at least one-third accountable for injuring and threatening me." Dave looks more alert, by this time, than I have ever seen him.

"If you needed help, Janie," he says with concern, "you could have come to me." We both ignore him.

"Janie," I begin. A fracas at the entrance to the weight room interrupts us. Linden vainly tries to restrain someone whom he can't handle. A distinctive grey-clad figure, moving wildly, cuts across the room. I hear several voices behind him. Lilienthal lopes, at a crazy swift pace, toward us. I hesitate for a second, deciding whether to pull my gun.

Suddenly, Jane lets out a shriek of repressed laughter. She leaps around the table corner, grabs my shoulders, and shakes me. I haven't been assaulted in this way since I attended an elementary school where the tough girls used grabbing and pinching to demonstrate their power.

I weave, and now reach for my gun. But before I can get the gun free of its holster, I'm attacked. Lilienthal pounces on me and sinks his teeth into my upper arm.

Jesus! I hadn't known a human being could bite like an animal. Lilienthal's teeth will dislodge a large chunk of flesh when he pulls back.

A wave of water startles my skin. Better yet, the water shocks Lilienthal into loosing his bite. In agony, I think to myself—if only I'd worn long sleeves! Lilienthal screams hor-ribly as if mortally wounded by the water. He sinks to the ground, pawing at the wet spots on his suit and shirt. My vision, greyed by pain, clears enough for me to see Honor holding a janitor's bucket.

"Kurt Brewster," yells Dave, looking at Lilienthal. "What the hell are you doing here, you crazy bastard?" The doctor's eyes meet Dave's and then dart to me, slitty with anger. Lilienthal probably hasn't used the name Kurt Brewster for six years, probably disliked using it then.

Lilienthal springs from the ground into the air with all fours outstretched, some weird act of levitation. His fingers reach for me. No sane person could duplicate the unhuman tautness in his body. I try to manage my gun with my left hand. I hear Dave yelling, "Hey," impotently at my right ear.

A shot rings out before I find whether I can pull a trigger left-handed while being mauled. Lilienthal drops out of the air onto the ground and curls, grasping his arm and whining.

I kneel down beside Lilienthal to ascertain whether he's still a threat, pushing away Honor who wants to look at my wounds. He stares at me unblinking. When I can't stand to look into the gleaming brown eyes any longer, I haul myself to my feet. Lilienthal's whining grates on my psyche. I think I hear the word "flea" several times. When I look back down, he has closed his eyes and lies catnapping on the floor.

Dennis ambles toward me with a sympathetic smile, gun in hand.

"Thanks, Den," I say. "I'll pay you back later." He rubs my good arm for comfort, his gun ready for any unexpected move from Lilienthal. Honor thrusts her face several inches from my arm to inspect the bite and shivers.

Linden appears at the door, looking greatly perturbed. "Sutton," yells Dennis, "call the police." Linden turns and runs.

"We can use some backup here," says Dennis. "From what you've told me, we want the police to take Lilienthal and Jane away for us." Dennis keeps his gun pointed in Jane and Lilienthal's general direction. I experience a wave of relief that Dennis has made the decision to turn them in. I might have been tempted to hang onto them longer, for fear of eliminating any byway leading to Ruthie.

"I hope poor Linden can handle everything," says Honor. "He looks rattled. But I'm not leaving your side until you get medical assistance, Eliza."

We hear heated conversation from the entrance to the room. Rich shows up, late for his appointment. He views the disarray in the weight room. His facial expression lapses into a look of biliousness. When Rich notices the wounded Dr. Lilienthal prone on the floor, he bawls, "God Almighty. Stuart. Don't let them get to you."

Lilienthal lifts his head. Only Dennis and I hear him growl, "Rich Goldeen, you furball." Fresh blood spurts from Lilienthal's flesh wound. Dennis fetches an old undershirt from a cubby behind us, ties it around the bullet wound and pulls the doctor's fashionable sports jacket over it. Lilienthal resumes his wordless vocalizing.

Rich trudges toward Lilienthal, oblivious of anyone else in the room. When he sees Lilienthal's blood on the floor, he becomes overwrought. "You've ruined everything," Rich groans at me, reaching into his pocket.

Dennis, apparently thinking Rich might be going for a gun, draws, aims, and fires, winging Rich slightly. Dennis stands close enough to make sure his bullet goes high and to the side, stopping Rich but not really injuring him or anybody else. I can see a small tear in the shoulder of Rich's nubby plaid jacket. Eileen won't like this.

Rich seems to be having a hard time not crying. The man doesn't hold up well without Eileen or Dad beside him. Dennis doesn't look any more chagrined at being forced to fire on Rich than he did over Lilienthal. He took my word, obviously, that the two of them don't amount to much.

"I wasn't going to hurt her," Rich snivels. "I wanted to hold this." He reaches across his belly with his left hand. Dennis holds his gun ready. Rich extracts Eileen's blue rabbit's foot from his pocket. Dennis and I don't laugh.

Dennis says to Jane, "I'm not sure what all you've been up to but I'm going to appoint myself to keep an eye on you for now."

"You can't legally detain me," says Jane, but not in the forceful manner of which she is capable.

"I can legally ask you to step over here with me, while holding a gun for which I have a legal permit. We can discuss why you were so impolite the last time I saw you." Dennis really does hate rudeness. He moves away to take a position by the entrance.

Rich looks vulnerable and miserable. I disregard the holes in my arm and pull myself upright so that I'm looking directly into his eyes. "I know about your dealings with Lilienthal and Jane, Rich. I'll deal with you later, after I've settled things with Eileen."

"What does Eileen know? Oh, God, what will she think?" Rich looks like he might actually throw up. He loves her.

"Eileen doesn't know anything about the Claudia/Jane story or about who owns South Street Spa & Gym. I think it would be prudent of you to tell her." Rich blanches, fading to a paler green hue.

"Rich," I say, "right now, I'm not in great shape. Why don't you leave me be and go minister to your friend, Lilienthal, until the paramedics and police come?"

"Police? You've called the police on Stuart? You're insane," Rich cries.

"No, he's insane. Which probably means he won't get what he deserves for attacking me, harassing me, and acting as accessory, at the very least, to Jane in establishing a business using a false identity and taking advantage of a woman's

251
▲

murder. That's the beginning of the list unless one of them actually murdered Claudia Hollings."

"I don't know how I got into this," moans Rich. "She drove me to it."

"Eileen?"

"No. Claudia, I mean, Jane. I'm in all this trouble because of a woman who depises me." He looks over toward Jane, under Dennis' guard. When she notices him, she conspicuously changes her pose to illustrate that she has no connection with Rich and intends to stare into space, waiting for things to happen in her favor.

"Are you going to tend to Lilienthal or not?" I can't restrain myself. "It will be no sweat, he's a pussycat," I say and start to laugh. Rich stares at me. "You may quote me," I tell him. Honor knows I am starting to lose control.

"Eliza, you're lightheaded," Honor uses a nursy voice. "You'll have to excuse us, Rich." Rich gives us an automatic salute goodbye, his eyes on Dennis and Dennis' gun across the room. All in all, I've enjoyed Rich more just now than I ever have previously.

Linden, Dave Gray, and the gym employees who showed up when they heard the first sound of gunfire hide beyond the weight room doors. Jane, possibly afraid that one of us will shoot her too, remains still. Honor guides me toward Jane. I make a pitch to the understanding side of Honor's nature as we go.

"I have to talk to Jane, Honor. Now, while she's off-balance."

"You should be lying down," Honor states.

"Respectable detectives don't work lying down," I tell her, hoping she'll laugh. She doesn't. "Stay with me?" I ask. If I require her aid she's less likely to impede me.

"I'll stay by your side," she agrees.

"Just don't talk, Honor. I need to get information out of Jane. This is what I'm trained for." Honor gazes around the battlefield-like scene in the weight room with a certain amount of skepticism. "Please let me ask the questions."

"Don't get upset, I'll be quiet," she says soothingly.

We walk past Rich, crouching at Lilienthal's side. Rich has tears in his eyes, I don't know exactly why. Honor looks down at Lilienthal.

"He's not much of an arch-villain is he? He can't say anything intelligent. He can't even get up off the floor. Eliza, you don't look all that heroic triumphing over an adversary who won't get out of the fetal position."

"And a furball and a possible felon wearing a peach-colored leotard and skirt." I have another brush with giddiness and start to laugh.

"You have to contain yourself, Eliza," says Honor severely, "you don't want to let your bizarre sense of humor get the better of you until we're safe."

We move over, along the edge of the table, until we stand next to Dennis and Jane. Honor props me against the table. Accustomed to filling silence with social badinage, Honor says to Jane, "You must have inherited a hardier constitution than your sister." I guess she assumes the questioning, for which she will remain silent, hasn't started yet. Recognition dawns in Jane's eyes. She met Honor at Heavenly Bodies once before. People don't tend to forget Honor.

"I've made the most of my potential," replies Jane. People get used to spouting their accustomed platitudes. It will take Janie a while to metamorphose again and construct a new vocabulary. Maybe she'll be learning prisonese. I'd like to think so.

"Dennis, will you make sure Honor's brother has called for all the authorities and emergency personnel we need? I can cover the situation until you get back." He looks unsure that I can manage things in my condition but the bad guys around us don't look formidable at this point and he'll be right outside the room.

I maneuver the gun to my right hand. I couldn't shoot left-handed if my life depended on it. The gun's weight doesn't make the pain any worse than it was already. "I'll be okay for a little while. Thanks, Den."

Honor and I remain with Jane. Honor eyes my gun with disgust. She might use a weapon if the children or I were immediately threatened but she's not volunteering now just to save wear and tear on my injured arm. Jane, like Rich, follows Dennis and his gun with her eyes as he crosses the room.

"Jane," I say, jiggling my pistol slightly for effect, "I won't bring up the mugging to the police or mention Lawrence if you'll talk to me. I'm not going to leave you alone until you talk." I watch her weigh her ill feelings for me against a chance to get out of this more easily. She shrugs.

"I don't know where Ruthie is." She looks glad that she doesn't, happy to thwart me. "I haven't heard from her for six years. My parents moved to some place in New Mexico when they found out about the trouble I'd gotten into. Some of the problems involved friends of theirs. I told them I was going to disappear." I listen closely and catch a slight, old sigh. She continues.

"They hate my brother for giving up his religion. They decided they might die of disgrace. They're uneducated, old-fashioned people. So they changed their name. They hid all their assets from me and Jonathan. They told me that they never wanted to hear from me again." She shrugs again.

"They've never even told me what name they took or exactly where they live. They're dead to me. I'm dead to them. So is Jonathan."

"And Ruthie?" I urge.

"They probably took Ruthie with them. There was something wrong with her. She was upset about Claudia even though she didn't know . . ." Jane breaks and then recomposes her sentence. "Even though she didn't know Claudia that well." A silence.

"My parents wanted to hospitalize Ruthie. If she went outside during the day, she fainted. She was afraid of the sky. She cried all the time." Across Jane's face flits the first hard evidence of feeling I have seen in her, a trace of sadness.

"They wanted Ruthie where they wouldn't have to worry about what was wrong with her. What a joke. They were always sure that Ruthie would be the one to take care of them in their old age. She couldn't even sit up in bed unless the shades were down. I'm sure they took her with them. As far as I know, she's in a New Mexico mental institution or hospital." She glares at me, motionless, as if frozen by her cold family saga. I have to keep ice-fishing. I'm sure she knows more.

"I could call Lawrence in on this, Jane. And *my* friend who's hanging around out there looks trigger-happy today. We all want to see this wrapped up. We want to know what happened to your sister. Spill your guts about Ruthie. Now." I've tried to be ladylike but she asked for this.

Jane's breathing becomes audible, a sign that she may be going to crack. She folds her arms across her chest, an ungraceful defensive gesture that might be Jane Gold's own instead of one created for the second Claudia Hollings.

"A couple of people have told me what a hotshot you are but you missed a lead or two, didn't you?" she says.

"I haven't found the right one," I agree.

"What the hell?" Jane's voice becomes strident. She hates giving me what I want so she clenches the information in her mind for as long as she can. Honor and I wait out the pause, we've waited this long.

"The 'S' in G, S, H & L Corporation," says Jane. I remember the name which the "S" stands for from Rich's documents.

"Ruthie is using the name Saffarian?" I ask.

"No. But all those years ago, I wanted to know where Ruthie was in case I needed her. I was told I could send letters to her by writing care of M. Saffarian at some address in Peoria, Illinois," Jane discloses. "I don't have the address anymore. I destroyed it. I erased every trace of the Golds."

"Who is Saffarian?"

"An investor that Stuart solicited. I don't know anything about him, except that Stuart told me he could get letters to Ruthie by that route."

"Did you write to Ruthie?" I question.

An interval passes. "Yes. She was my sister, after all." Jane sounds enervated, sapped by her enforced candor.

"When did you last hear from Ruthie?"

"Never," Jane whispers.

"What?" I say. I don't know why I should trust her even though she seems to have folded in her hand.

"Ruthie never sent me anything. I haven't heard from my family for six years."

"Sorry," I say.

"I'm not sorry I started fresh. Maybe I'm due now for another fork in the the road." She speaks to herself as much as to us.

"Maybe you can go back down the road and get yourself," I suggest. Jane musters a wilting look and Honor puts an arm around my waist in case I wilt.

"That's all I know. You've stirred this up," Jane gestures at the scene around us, "for one letter of the alphabet. My sister has been dead to me for six years and it's just as well. Ruthie collapsed. The whole group of them collapsed and ran. I didn't run. I followed the plan I made the day Claudia died. I did what I wanted." We leave her standing by herself.

"If I had Jane for a sister, I'd wish they mixed babies up at the hospital the day she was born," mutters Honor when we're out of earshot.

I can't believe I neglected to ask, maybe it has become an afterthought. I whirl around, wincing. "Who killed Claudia?" I ask.

Jane turns toward me with no spite left to color her face. "I told Ruthie that I didn't want to know. And I don' ` Ruthie."

Time blurs. Blood runs down under my arm and my elbow onto the floor.

I am not going to do or say anything further to rub Lilienthal the wrong way. I don't need anything from him except that he never come near me again. Honor isn't as restrained.

I hear Honor interrogating Lilienthal about whether he has had a tetanus shot in the past five years. She asks him when he last brushed his teeth, which probably sounds crazy to everyone but me and the Suttons present. She wants to determine how much bacteria I might have been infected with. Lilienthal doesn't answer Honor, appearing to have no more language than a cat.

The police arrive. Dennis convinces them to take Lilienthal and Jane. Jane looks composed. She has probably reckoned that nothing overtly illegal can be pinned on her very quickly. She may be given the time to disappear and become someone successful somewhere else. I don't know her plan but I bet she already has one.

I take one last look at two evil people. I have noticed before that evil doesn't necessarily show. Lilienthal looks rumpled, bloody, but basically ready to step before the camera on a TV talk show. His tan skin glows with health, his suit speaks of wealth and good taste. Jane Gold looks like the prosperous businesswoman and athlete she constructed out of someone else's life.

On his way out the door, Lilienthal looks more pulled together. Perhaps with the police for an audience, he will revert to his celebrity psychiatrist facade for as long as he can. Honor leaves Lilienthal for the police and returns to my side.

"Lilienthal seems perfectly able to talk now," Honor reports. "I heard him tell the police that he wishes he never heard the name Ruthie Gold. But I didn't catch anything else he said." Lilienthal has a point. As I have noticed before, names have great significance for these crazy types. Lilienthal, and the rest, got away with their crimes and pretenses until Eileen called forth Ruthie's name out of the past.

Dennis, for some reason, persuades the police not to haul Rich away. He may have decided that he himself has dispensed enough justice to Rich Goldeen. Rich agrees to visit the Berkeley police voluntarily for questioning after he gets away from the hospital emergency room where he will have his graze attended to. Rich reports to me, glassy-eyed with fear. A faint tinge of pink stains the perimeter of the hole in his ugly sports jacket. His face entreats me not to sentence him.

256
▲

"I won't tell Eileen anything about you and Jane and South Street Spa and Gym until you get a chance to tell her yourself. Eileen wants you home. I think you'll find her to be easier to talk to than she used to be," I say to him. I don't elaborate and tell him about Eileen's medications and changes of heart. He has to figure those things out for himself.

Rich nods and backs away without a shred of pomposity. I don't know whether he's most afraid that the police will see him as an accomplice or that Eileen and his dad will turn on him because of his complicity. When last I see Rich, Dave Gray holds him up by his good shoulder and appears to be administering words of solace.

Honor mentions Dorothy in *The Wizard of Oz*. I don't know why, until I remember the bucket of water which freed me from Lilienthal's grip. She massages my temples with her long brown fingers which makes my heart swell with love for her. My upper arm starts to swell too.

An ambulance and a fire truck arrive for me. Linden, it turns out, panicked at the sight of blood and called the emergency services number with a garbled story about a cat. The call didn't get deemed top priority so they took their time getting here.

The troop of uniformed paramedics seems sincerely interested in how I could have incurred a psychiatrist bite. They want me to lie down in their van. I insist on a compromise: Dennis and Honor will drive me to the Alta Bates Hospital emergency room.

The attending doctor admits me to the hospital overnight, probably because I sustained my injuries in an unusual way. Two large furrows in my arm are carefully sewn back together by a staff plastic surgeon who makes jokes about what big teeth my grandma has. I'm installed in a sunny room with a glorious view of the Bay, the dinner doesn't taste bad and it's hot. Honor and Dennis show up after dinner both carrying irises. Honor has brought a vase.

After half a day spent watching people on television preview movies and prepare low-cholesteral meals, I am ready for conversation. I ask Honor and Dennis if they have figured out how Lilienthal came to arrive on the scene with his teeth bared. They tell me that Warren Siegel discovered Lilienthal this morning on our property. Lilienthal seemed agitated and told Warren he was going to be in a dog fight. He was going to get "that bad terrier." Lilienthal asked Warren if the children could come out and talk with him. He asked where I was. Warren became concerned and called Honor and Dennis.

"So how did Lilienthal find me if Warren didn't tell him?" I ask.

"Lilienthal didn't go to Heavenly Bodies to find you, he went to find Rich," says Dennis. "Rich's office gave him the address. If Rich hadn't been late for his appointment with you, maybe he could have controlled Lilienthal and prevented him from leaving this blotch on your formerly perfect flesh." Honor frowns. She doesn't find teethmarks humorous when they occur on the surface of a loved one.

"Rich couldn't have restrained Lilienthal," I reply. "Lilienthal had all the power in that relationship. And Lilienthal's obsession about covering up the messes he's made during the last six years, or more, was all focused on me at that moment. Cheer up, you guys. Lilienthal is probably in more trouble than we know about." Dennis and Honor exchange looks, which makes me wonder, but I want to tell them what I know so I don't stop to question.

"We know he dated Ruthie and then terrorized her," I begin the list. "He had an affair with Claudia Hollings, telling her his name was Kurt Brewster. The affair somehow culminated in Claudia's death. Claudia must have found him out. He may have killed her. He could have killed her out of passion, or fear, or by mistake." My visitors can't conceal another little look.

"Jane had enough evidence to pin on Lilienthal that he helped her become Claudia to keep her quiet," I continue with a sharp eye on Honor and Dennis. "He invested a lot of the initial capital to help her start a business. Lilienthal has always treated Jane as though he respects, or fears, her. He didn't play cat with her the way he did with Ruthie, and with me.

"Lilienthal wasn't afraid of Ruthie, though. Ruthie was in danger because she knew Lilienthal as Lilienthal. She could have put him together with his Kurt Brewster identity."

"You'd think that dimwit, Dave Gray, would have managed to figure the whole thing out," says Honor. "He was right there and it wasn't that big an apartment building."

"Dave Gray is who he is," I remind her. "He could have met Lilienthal in the elevator many times. But since he was introduced to Kurt Brewster and figured he knew him, he never questioned his presence at the building again. To be introduced to Dave is to be his friend for life."

"How does your buddy, Rich Goldeen, fit into all this?" questions Dennis.

"Rich and Lilienthal have had a business relationship for years," I tell him. "Rich recognized Jane Gold, soon after she assumed Claudia's identity. Lilienthal and Jane decided to keep him in line by giving him a reason to keep quiet. So they made him a partner in their business. Rich Goldeen wanted to establish himself as a businessman in some other sphere than his father's construction company so he grabbed the chance. They bought him.

"Lilienthal has created miscellaneous other problems for himself," I continue. "I know of at least one patient's mother, and possibly the patient herself, who he diddled with. The mother plans to sue. If I know of one, there have to be more patients he violated. And someone other than me must have realized that he's completely loony. He seems to have less and less control over the cat in his mind."

"I think a loony who has an M.D. and wears a suit is less likely to get put away than your average loony," says Dennis philosophically. "Although, when you're meowing, even a suit might not bail you out." Honor gives him a suspicious smile.

They know something I don't know. I'm not comfortable being prone while talking business and I hate being coddled.

"What's up, you two?" I demand to know.

"Honor doesn't want you getting excited. If you get up and run out of here without permission, she's going to kill me," Dennis says nervously.

"That's right," Honor agrees.

"What? I'm not going anywhere. Tell me."

"I got a tip when I was hanging out with the Berkeley Police earlier," Dennis says.

"Lie back, Eliza," Honor orders, leaving me frantic to find out immediately what they know that I don't. I lie back.

"Lilienthal cracked under questioning. Once he fell apart, he talked cat talk and did a major confession. He admitted that he murdered the original Claudia Hollings. I don't have any more details but the rest of the details are going to be good."

"No shit," I exclaim. "That's terrific. If I could get to him right now, he might give me everything he knows about Ruthie. The Berkeley police have got the pump all primed for me."

"This is why we weren't even going to tell you until tomorrow," Honor's vehemence extends to Dennis and me. "Don't you dare leave this bed."

"He's incommunicado until they've put him through psychiatric evaluation. I don't think you could get to him even if you tried," Dennis puts in.

A nurse opens the swinging door and leans in. "Eliza, there's a San Francisco police officer here to see you." She reads from a card, "Detective Philip Cologne. You get two visitors maximum on this ward. What shall I tell him?"

"I'll talk to him," offers Honor, standing up, "you've already had your share of police today, Dennis. And you'll be spending plenty more time with the Berkeley police, won't you? Or have you explained away shooting two people in the session you had with them earlier today?"

"I'm almost off the hook," replies Dennis. I rise up on my pillow with concern. Dennis waves me down. "No problem, Muscles. Ruthie's friends look so bad, I'm okay."

"Do you know what to say and what not to say, Honor?" I ask, too knocked out by current events and pain killers to take control.

"I'll tell him you were surprised at the shape of events today," Honor practices her statement. I am reassured. The cop won't be able to pin anything on me after a dose of Sutton rhetoric.

"Detective Cologne called Warren at the house earlier because you had an appointment with him," Honor tells me on her way out the door. "Warren says that Cologne thought he was going to make points with his department in San Francisco by locating Lilienthal. He didn't expect Lilienthal to be arrested and taken into custody in Alameda County. He's a disappointed man but I'll handle him." As soon as Honor leaves, I miss her astringent presence at my bedside.

"You know where Lilienthal is now?" Dennis laughs. "Highland Hospital, probably the psych ward. I hope they have a good veterinarian on staff."

I let Dennis read my get well cards from Linden and Lucy and Dave Gray, for diversion. Honor brought them. They all hope that I'll be feeling better soon, but Dave Gray feels sorrier for me than Linden and Lucy whose place of business I disrupted for hours this morning, I can tell. When Honor returns to my bedside, I avail myself of this opportunity to get her to hold my hand.

"Do you think Ruthie went with her family to New Mexico?" asks Honor.

"I don't know," I say. "I need to follow up on my 'S.' I worked hard enough to get it. I talked to my client on the phone a while ago. Eileen's main interest, aside from getting

Ruthie and her husband back, is in finding out why Lilienthal shaved Ruthie's kitten when he stole it and returned it to her door dead in a shopping bag six years ago."

"Why did he?" Honor has heard enough not to be surprised by Eileen's odd line of vision.

"The scarab mark was identifiable. He could have shaved it off the kitten for fear of being caught or for superstitious reasons. I don't know why and I may never get to talk with Lilienthal again. Eileen doesn't know yet that Rings the kitten wasn't actually dead."

"What?" asks Honor. Dennis isn't surprised. He got me the information I needed about Lilienthal's pets from the secretary at the doctor's San Francisco office.

"Lilienthal must have retrieved the cat when Ruthie put its body out for the garbage collectors. He kept the kitten alive all these years. It was Rings that Eileen found dead in her car the other day. Eileen thought that the dead cat was her Dutchess. That's because it was Dutchess' kitten."

"That means that Lilienthal is worse lately," remarks Honor.

"What do you mean?" I ask her.

"He killed a cat he'd taken care of for many years. He must have had a relationship with that cat."

"That's an ugly thought," agrees Dennis.

"Eileen will be hysterical," I say. "She'll take it better if I can furnish Ruthie at the same time."

"You will," says Honor. "You've eliminated 25 letters of the English alphabet. And besides, Ruthie must have gone to New Mexico. The person, 'S,' will give you the address."

"I don't believe that Ruthie went lamely off with her parents for a six-year rest cure."

"Why not?" Dennis questions. "She was pretty debilitated, wasn't she?"

"Yes. But I don't think Ruthie wanted anyone, including her parents, to ingest her. It doesn't fit her pathology."

"So where did she go?" Honor must be curious or she wouldn't be asking any further questions which might interfere with my bedrest.

"To play the piano in the Middle East?" I suggest. "I'm tracking her through someone named Saffarian. Ruthie was accustomed to conflict. I'm kidding, I don't know where she is. But I plan to be able to tell you in a few days. I have a tame case lined up for myself after I serve up Ruthie to Eileen. I want to be ready to start the new job next week." I am tired for a moment, a convalescent.

Honor heartily approves the pedestrian nature of the work which I'm moving onto, after Ruthie has been laid to rest.

Dennis leaves for a late dinner with Sharon. Sharon has sent her love to me. I send my love to Sharon. I meant to ask Dennis what that damn saying is, that a detective should live by. Honor remains sitting on the bottom of my bed.

"Will you be there when I get home?" I ask, the wounded gallant.

"I'm not ready," says Honor slowly. "I need more of a break from our life. The constant responsibility for details and the strain of worrying about you and your work has worn me down. I hadn't realized it, but I needed this time off."

I've always assumed that I carried the weight of our life together on my back.

"Some break, huh?" I say lightly. "What with the cat fight and my trip to Alta Bates? The next case will be ordinary, Honor."

"I haven't given up on you yet," says Honor, to offer me something. Honor stays until just before visiting hours end.

Right after she leaves, Warren Siegel visits in order to say goodbye and to fill me in on his part in the morning's adventures. Without his skill at locating people and making arrangements by telephone, I would have had no troops behind me when I faced Lilienthal and Jane. Two nurses hover over me to enjoy Warren's easy charm. He has brought me a card from the children. They've heard the whole story of how I landed in the hospital.

Annabelle and Jemmy have drawn pictures in felt pen of Honor and me in our kitchen at home, of themselves playing ball with me, and me looking everywhere for Ruthie. On the inside, I find an illustration of Ruthie, strangely, wearing her hair in long golden ringlets. The children have drawn Ruthie with a thin red smile and one eye closed as though Ruthie winks at me.

lie awake during the night with my arm throbbing. I feel miserable. A nurse would bring me a pain pill if I rang but the thought of the pill makes me queasy.

The information that Jane gave me plays through my mind. It's probably valid as far as it goes. But Jane doesn't care enough about her sister to have given Ruthie's fate any significant thought.

I give Ruthie some thought. What I told Honor off the top of my head feels true. Crippled by her troubles as Ruthie was, I can't believe that she would be willing to entangle herself with her voracious, commandeering parents. Ruthie resisted being eaten alive.

They move a comatose older woman into the bed next to mine around midnight. She whimpers as she lies there. One arm has fallen down beside her bed. I get up and tuck her arm under the covers.

I prop two pillows against the headboard and sit up. I feel better upright. The old lady at the temple in L.A. was probably right when she told Honor that Ruthie went north, north of L.A. She was right about the location of Ruthie's parents.

I open the drapes a crack and sit looking out the window at the night lights and the foggy bay until long enough past daybreak to call Eileen. When I reach her she has already been up for hours. She would like to see me sooner but she agrees to meet me at my office late this afternoon.

Warren Siegel left Annabelle and Jemmy with our neighbor, Nancy, this morning so that he could catch an early flight. I'm released and fetch them as soon as I get home. They spend the next hour demonstrating how thankful they are to have me back. I get the feeling that a morning with Nancy is not like a day at Disneyland or even as good as elementary school. The weather has turned grey and drizzly, which happens occasionally until summer brings perpetual sunshine to the East Bay Area, so I spend the day lying in my bedroom with a fire going in the fireplace. The children make popcorn, hot chocolate, and cottage cheese for lunch. Honor will pick them up at 3:00 p.m.

Honor calls at 1:30 p.m. to ask if the children can stay with me for another week. "Father is a terrible influence on them. And I'm afraid every time they say something cute that someone's going to write it down."

"Honor, I have an appointment this afternoon and I'm probably going to be out of town tomorrow and the next day." I can't conceal my exasperation.

"I'll come over and babysit any time you want," pleads Honor. Having Honor babysit would insure that she can't come after me when I'm out of town trying to wrap up business. I give up and let her have what she wants.

I sleep until 4:30 p.m. When I get up, I feel more pulled together than I have in two days. Honor arrives and begins scrubbing the kitchen counters and cleaning the stove even though our one-day-a-week housekeeper came four days ago.

I see Sarah Frybarger in her office when I arrive at mine. In light of Jemmy's chat with Sarah at Precious' party, I avoid her. Eileen arrives late. She looks pale and thin. The dark smudges around her eyes have grown to the size of saucers in a child's tea set. She hasn't bothered to train her hair into place.

"Rich would barely talk to me about the meeting you had with him. He said your friend shot him but he wouldn't say why. Rich was wounded. Wounded! And you too! Rich didn't know how you got hurt. It's just like a TV show—confusing." Eileen spills this out before I have a chance to seat her.

"I'm so sorry my friend unfortunately, and inadvertently, shot your husband. He was under the impression that Rich was pulling out a weapon. After that, I didn't get a chance to have the meeting with him. Before Rich arrived, Lilienthal got there and attacked me. Bit me, actually.

"Lilienthal has gone completely around the bend, Eileen, if he wasn't all along." I tell her some of what I know. Unfortunately, I still can't tell her what happened to Ruthie.

"I can't believe this. I caused all these people to go crazy just by hiring you. Even Ruthie's sister. I read the little piece about Stuart Lilienthal in the paper. 'Surfaced after a four-

264
▲

day disappearance.' 'Various charges,' my God. His mother is flying in from Chicago." She shakes her head and rubs both her eyes. The media hasn't even begun to collect the juicy material on Lilienthal.

"I found a magazine article about Dr. Lilienthal in Rich's study," says Eileen. "Dr. Lilienthal used to take care of stray cats and find them homes, when he was a boy. Who would have thought it?"

"Lilienthal has sheltered stray cats all his life," I tell her. "Did you realize that the cat you found dead in your car was Ruthie's kitten, Rings? That's why the cat looked so much like your cat, Dutchess. I wavered about whether to tell you but I decided you would want to know." Eileen looks stunned, maybe she didn't want to hear this.

"Lilienthal was also the one who injured Rings originally and the one who killed him the other day. Lilienthal experiences his most manic states occasionally, not all the time, even though he's officially off his trolley. He was obviously in bad shape when he killed the cat he nurtured back to health and kept as his companion for many years," I paraphrase Honor's insight. Fresh lavender tears fall as a memorial to Rings the cat.

"Lilienthal murdered Claudia Hollings, Eileen." I'm not going to appear to be very on top of things if I don't tell her this before it hits the newspapers. "He confessed to the police yesterday." Eileen looks less affected by this revelation than by the news about Rings the cat.

"What about Jane?" Eileen sniffles. "I really created a mess, didn't I?"

"I have a feeling that Jane is not crazy, just bad news. And you didn't bring this about. You're looking at the unfinished business Ruthie left behind, carried out by people Ruthie was lucky to get away from."

"Like me," says Eileen, who has grown more perceptive since I met her. "I wasn't a good friend to her. But I will be if I get her back."

"Eileen," I ignore her happy intentions, "I bullied a name out of Jane before I had her arrested—Saffarian, M. Saffarian. Stuart Lilienthal used funds from him to put together G, S, H & L Corporation which owns South Street Spa and Gym. I found him in only three phone calls."

"G, S, H & L? Rich told me this morning that he's the G. I couldn't believe that he has owned property without telling me. It all has something to do with her—Jane Gold." Eileen's face darkens.

"You can forget Jane Gold now," I say.

"Forget her? She tried to wreck my home. Of course, that was years ago but I don't think I can forget it. And she sent someone to mug you."

"How do you know that, Eileen?"

"Rich had drunk a few beers on top of his stomach medication so he let some things slip. He told me that before I even met you for the first time he was on the phone to her—Jane Gold. She bragged to Rich that if I did hire someone to find Ruthie she would have them stopped."

"Let's figure Jane Gold is over and done with," I reiterate.

"Who is the man you mentioned? The S?"

"He's a lightweight money man whose primary holdings are in a medium-sized corporation based in Peoria, Illinois."

"What does this have to do with Ruthie?"

"Hardly anything. Except that Jane was told she could get letters to Ruthie via Saffarian. When I talked to him this morning, I told him that Stuart Lilienthal is going down. I told Saffarian I would keep his name out of it if he told me what connection he has to Ruthie."

"Did he tell you where Ruthie is?" gasps Eileen.

"He had forgotten ever hearing the name Ruthie Gold. Six years ago, Saffarian went into a business deal with a college friend of his who hooked them both up with Lilienthal. In the course of the deal, Saffarian's friend asked him to be the front man. Saffarian's name appears on everything instead of his friend's. We're not talking about a business enterprise that would have been a big deal to Saffarian. By the by, Saffarian's pal asked if he would forward mail from his Peoria address. One of the people he agreed to send mail on to was Ruthie."

"Who is the friend you're talking about?"

"Someone you know. Geoffrey Lowe of Santa Barbara," I tell her.

"Antonia's husband? I don't get it." Eileen keeps on following the discussion without drifting off onto the shoulder of the road.

"I don't get it either but I want to fly down and meet with Antonia tomorrow," I break the news to insecure Eileen. "I talked to Antonia's husband a couple of weeks ago. I'm assuming that he was lying to me. He claimed not to have been in touch with Ruthie for six years but we now know he set up some kind of a link with her, after that time. You didn't get along with Antonia, Eileen, but is there anything you can tell me before I see her?"

266

▲

"Antonia? She's not going to be any help. She's slyer than anyone I've ever met. Her tricks made me look stupid in front of Ruthie, like I told you." Eileen looks more depressed than ever at the recollection of her relationship with Antonia.

"I want to work with Antonia instead of approaching her husband directly. Antonia's pregnant, she might not have the energy for games." Eileen begs me not to mention her part in the search for Ruthie and I assure her I won't.

"Eliza? Here's a check. You've earned it. Rich says you're going to have marks on your arm. I've included payment for all the hospital bills too." Eileen can't be faulted on her generosity. "I still want Ruthie. Maybe you can fake Antonia out and she'll tell you something. I want you to try.

"But you know what? I was thinking last night that I want Rich back more than Ruthie." Eileen faces me with a clear, candid look.

"You probably think Rich doesn't act nice to me. But he does, when we're alone. He tries to give me everything I want. He even wants me to have Ruthie now that I know about him and Jane and about the South Street Spa and Gym.

"His involvement with the Gym was what he wanted to hide. That's why he tried to scare me out of keeping you. Now Rich feels like his whole life is an open book." I hope Eileen has not misplaced her trust in Rich. Maybe she can trust her own judgment more now than she could before we went looking for Ruthie.

"This will work out for you, Eileen," I tell her. I have a feeling that I will leave Eileen a satisfied customer. "One last thing, Eileen. Why does Rich have an autographed copy of Newell Sutton's book?" I count on Eileen not to wonder how I know.

"Newell Sutton? He's one of Rich's favorite authors. Rich has modeled his business career on Newell Sutton's principles." By a miracle of training and restraint, I don't even hint at laughter. Eileen waves goodbye.

I call the Santa Barbara number and ask for Antonia Noyes-Lowe. A formal voice asks who I am. I tell the voice I am a friend of a friend from the past. The voice does not sound intrigued. After some time, a new voice, lively and lilting, says, "This is Antonia. What can I do for you?"

"My name is Eliza Pirex. I'm a friend of the Gold family. I've been given your name as a friend of Ruthie Gold's. I'm trying to locate Ruthie. Can I make an appointment to see you? Preferably tomorrow?" I don't know whether I should have constructed a more devious story in order to prevent Antonia from trying to foist me off.

"Do the Golds remember me? Ruthie would be shocked to find out that her parents ever paid attention to who her friends were. I heard that the Golds flipped out about family stuff and retired to somewhere," says Antonia in an exceptionally good-humored voice. "I haven't seen or heard from Ruthie for years," she continues. "We haven't stayed in touch."

"How many years?" I ask.

"I don't know exactly. Maybe I got a card a few years ago from somewhere she was visiting."

I don't react to her, the first person to admit having had contact with Ruthie in the past six years.

"The reason I'm calling," I say with measured calm, "is that I'm going to be in Santa Barbara tomorrow. I wonder if I could see you for a short time to talk about Ruthie?"

"I don't have much to tell. But so what? It sounds like a kick to talk about Ruthie." Antonia pauses. "We're putting an addition on our home so there's construction going on. But why don't you meet me here if you don't mind the disorder?" We agree to meet at 11:30 a.m. She gives me colorful directions to her home featuring unusual points of interest I will pass on my way, such as a gas station shaped like a seagull.

I call Dennis to assure him that I am fit to handle the Santa Barbara trip with less than full function in one arm. We concur that the potentially harmful characters in this drama have been marched off-stage and have lost their motivation for menacing me.

I get into Santa Barbara at 9:30 the next morning. The sun shines and the air seems perfectly clear. The San Francisco Bay drizzle fades from memory. I find a pleasant motel, the Galleon, with a white stucco front and a red tile roof. Every structure in the city seems to have Spanish-style architecture, all the buildings match, giving the place a clean, well-ordered presence. The seagull gas station may be an aberration out of Antonia's imagination, for all I know, or outside the city limits.

I drive out, past a sleazy student town near the city, and look at the University and the beach. The beach looks tarry. Eileen and Ruthie once got tar on their feet, I remember. I wonder if the residents of all those tasteful white houses in Santa Barbara wade out into that water and get blemished by petrochemical garbage.

I purchase a street index for the area. Antonia's house overlooks a large golf course, according to the map. I wind up the hills past increasingly pricy homes. Even the gas station made to resemble a truck-size stucco seagull employs color to meld tastefully into the environment.

I've spent more time driving to rich people's houses in the course of this case than in the last few years all together. I miss the older walk-up apartments with a few pieces of good oak furniture, or business offices with over-flowing grey metal filing cabinets, where I meet with most clients. I myself feel comfortable in those small, hot rooms from which ordinary people look out at the colossal dangers beyond. I drop the thought, downshift, and head further into the hills.

I pull up to the Noyes-Lowe residence. The site crawls with workpeople. Fresh building materials, neatly stacked, block the driveway. I park on the street and walk in. The house doesn't look as grand as others I've seen recently but I suspect that the location overhanging the golf course makes it a desirable piece of property.

I wander through the lumber to the front door where a well-dressed and freshly made-up pregnant woman opens the door when I ring the bell. She looks like every pregnant woman would like to look. Most expectant moms probably feel too tired, or don't have the money, to achieve the effect. Her stay at her mother's must have done wonders.

"I'm Eliza Pirex. Mrs. Noyes-Lowe is expecting me," I say, not leaping to the conclusion that this is Antonia, no longer assuming anyone to be who they should be.

"I'm Antonia Noyes-Lowe," she says smiling, radiant, "won't you come in?" I follow her inside through the foyer.

"I think I told you on the phone, I'm a friend of the Gold family." I pause, recalling how unlikely Jane Gold would be to call me a friend of hers. Jonathan may have liked me a little. But probably not. "I'm a private investigator. The Golds have asked me to locate Ruthie Gold's current whereabouts." At this point, if I were Antonia, I would ask me for a letter of introduction from the Golds.

I take out a photocopy of my license and hand it over to establish credibility. She reads carefully, brows knitted, and then bursts out laughing. "I love this," her voice ripples happily. "This is so Perry Mason. Can I get you something to drink? What do you drink? Beer?"

I don't quite know why she gets this much amusement out of me but I smile back. Maybe I should wink. "I'll have whatever you're having." I don't worry until too late that we might both be having beer. Antonia leaves me in a spacious living room with a view of golf carts toiling across an unnatural green. She returns soon with two glasses of chocolate milk.

"Ask me everything," she says, gulping her milk. "I wouldn't want to conceal any vital clue that might solve the mystery of the missing Ruthie Gold. Now would I?"

A practical thought inhibits her mirth for a minute. "How did the Golds lose track of Ruthie in the first place? When did they see her last?"

"When did you hear from Ruthie last?" I ask carefully, hoping she won't be cagey with me. Her face becomes thoughtful.

"Two years? I know it's been at least that long since I've known where to send a birthday card. Have the Golds been out of touch with her that long?"

"They must have lost track of her soon after that," I say, deciding not to tell her what I know. Why would Ruthie have corresponded with this one person out of all the people she knew? I'm going to find out.

"Where was she the last time you heard from her?" I ask.

Antonia's eyes dance. "Hong Kong, maybe? I just don't remember. She's bummed around everywhere, playing the piano." Ruthie may have played the piano well enough to make traveling money from her skill. Antonia's story isn't bad.

"Did you keep any letters or postcards, any pictures, from Ruthie?"

"Maybe some letters from when we were in college are stored at my mother's house. But I stopped saving anything once I got married. Life is intense enough without rereading it, don't you think?"

"Can you try to visualize the last postcard for me? Maybe we can verify that Ruthie was in Hong Kong by your memory of the picture," I encourage her.

Antonia seems delighted with the assignment. "Bridges? Rivers? And buildings with a Chinese kind of skyline," she says rapidly. I sigh. I can conjure up the image of Ruthie sitting on a piano bench in Asia, because I have a graphic imagination, but I hardly believe it.

"Do you remember anything special that she wrote to you? After all, it was the last time that you heard from her." Antonia beams at me before answering.

"Ruthie was happy with her music. Nothing special. I assume that she's been too busy to write, in the last couple years. You know how it is when you haven't seen someone for awhile. Your lives go separate ways. You don't feel the same

270
▲

need to sit down and communicate. Ruthie probably has new people in her life."

"Did she mention anyone?" I jump on her last statement.

"Not that I remember. I'm just guessing," Antonia replies sweetly. Her hands massage the baby.

We move into a word game. I pitch questions, trying to hone them down until they demand a definite response. Antonia deftly repaints my thinking about Ruthie's fate. She creates an impressionist portrait. Her laughter jingles from self-mocking to gay to ironic depending upon the material we cover.

Antonia's vision of Ruthie's life over the past years doesn't fit mine. Ruthie traveling to exotic foreign locales and winning people with her music. Ruthie playing new, more sophisticated music for the crowned heads of Europe and the nouveau-Westernized people of Asia and Africa.

Antonia appears deeply fascinated by me. She questions me, not about Ruthie but about myself. Each of my answers cause her to laugh, even the answers to such questions as, "What do your children tell their friends at school that you do?" (P.I.) and, "What was your last success in your work?" (discovered large sum of money got misplaced not embezzled). I try to restrain her questions so that I can keep badgering her about Ruthie.

Antonia definitely withholds something and whatever she withholds brings a sparkle to her eyes. This woman doesn't garble like poor Eileen but I can't get a grip on her story, the same sensation I have with my client.

I decide on a new line of inquiry but before I can bring the questions to light, a deep, jovial voice interrupts. "Who has my spider lured into her den? Toni will play with you until you're sucked dry, you know." A man who fits the description "beefy" walks forward with a springy stride, holding out his hand. He doesn't look like a professor of mathematics and I wonder if Eileen might have gotten his profession wrong. We shake hands. Grinning fatuously, he kisses the top of Antonia's head.

"This is Eliza," Antonia introduces me. "She's looking for Ruthie Gold. Remember? I told you yesterday. Eliza, this is my husband, Geoff." Geoff has probably put on weight and become redder of complexion since the period during which Eileen knew him. Eileen might be pleased to know that Rich Goldeen has held up better physically than Antonia's husband. Geoff looks at me with a curiosity which matches his

271
▲

wife's, maybe a touch of concern can be read into his expression.

"Geoff didn't know Ruthie well," says Antonia with her eyes fixed meaningfully on her husband.

"Honey," Geoff petitions, "the builders are going to be right on top of your head any minute. We could lose some plaster off this ceiling. They're going to cover the furniture in this room with drop cloths for a few days. Can you and your guest find somewhere else to play?" A booming laugh, unanticipated by me, issues from his chest. Life in this household must be very jolly.

Antonia turns her smile toward me. Suddenly an ecstatic look crosses her face as if she has decided on a forbidden indulgence.

"I know a cozy place to eat. I'm going to take you to lunch." She uses the same tone as Judy Garland and Mickey Rooney at the point in the movie when they said, "Hey kids! Why don't we put on a show?"

"Sure. It's nice of you to ask," I accept. I am surprised by the offer, but then Antonia does seem more captivated by my interview technique than most people.

"Where are you going?" asks Geoff.

"A cute place I've found downtown," replies Antonia gaily. She puts on a charcoal-grey lightweight wool maternity coat, perfect for late spring. I gauge that she spent $300 on a coat she'll wear for four months. I remember that at the end of Honor's pregnancy with Jemmy she wore the same two men's plaid flannel shirts over and over, on alternate days.

"What's the matter with the Clubhouse? It's good enough for you to eat there every day with me. I don't like you driving in your condition." Antonia responds with an irritated laugh. Geoff puts hands on hips.

"I'll drive," I say, lost in the jocular crossfire.

"She'll drive," says Antonia.

Geoff looks me over for a second time. He sobers and turns to his wife. "I wish you wouldn't push yourself, Toni. The baby's due in three weeks."

"Come on, Geoff. I'm having fun with Eliza, lots of fun. Be nice and tell me to have a good time."

"Have a good time," he says, resigned. Antonia opens the front door, waving to him.

Antonia directs me through sprawling white houses with tasteful addresses. We make our way past the outskirts of Santa Barbara's downtown. "It's an out of the way place," says Antonia, at this point. She gives orders to turn left or right.

Every time she forgets until too late to tell me where to turn and I have to backtrack, she chuckles. I start feeling exuberant myself, it's contagious.

We discuss what Antonia will name the baby. Toomuch Noyes. Highn' Lowe. Turnthe Noyes-Lowe.

By the time we pull into a parking lot, half paved, half unpaved, I am disoriented. I know we're not downtown or near the beach. The place looks like a diner or truckstand. A sign reads, "Joe's." I don't see the words "Eat At" anywhere.

I open the car door for Antonia and give her a hand. "I love the food here," she says eagerly. "It's the ultimate home-cooking. And they give you plenty."

I push through the swinging door with the diner's hours painted on the front. A sign asking that customers wear shoes and a shirt swings into my hip. Antonia grabs my arm and whispers urgently, "Eliza, it ruins my digestion to talk about business while I eat. Because of the baby, you know. Not one word about Ruthie until we're back in the car." I sigh. I seem to be here as an escort and fodder for Antonia's boundless amusement.

We enjoy a hilarious lunch. Antonia does seem to appreciate the food. She hurriedly forks up a hot roast beef sandwich with gravy, thick fries, milk, and strawberry cream pie for dessert. I have chicken pot pie. I skip the heavy bottom crust to make sure I'll be able to walk out on my own volition.

The waitress must be almost as pregnant as Antonia. She takes our order with a slight smile for Antonia. Her plastic badge reading, "Diane, I'm happy to serve you," rests at a horizontal angle above swollen breasts that blend into her belly.

"She and her husband, Joe, have owned the place for years," says Antonia, leaning back from the table. "When I was in college, I used to come here with friends. Joe's mom and dad ran the place then. It's homey, isn't it?" She giggles like a college girl. The waitress sends her a doleful glance.

I pay the check and Antonia leaves a handful of bills for a tip. We play riddle all the way back to Antonia's home. I try to trick her into producing some details about her correspondence with Ruthie. She draws a more and more colorful but fuzzier view of Ruthie's life as seen through infrequent postcards and letters. I pull up outside her house exhausted.

"You've been great," says Antonia, taking my hand and squeezing it. "You've made me feel more awake than I have in these weeks I've been sitting around waiting for the baby."

"Here's my card," I say. "Let me know if you think of anything that might help me locate Ruthie."

She interrupts. "I've already done more than I expected," she says, looking me full in the face and smiling from ear to ear.

"Send me an announcement when the baby's born," I say without knowing why. Who knows what this woman might go ahead and name the baby, to get a laugh?

I feel let down. I go back to my motel room and lie down. Do I need to start combing the world, asking if anyone has heard Ruthie playing the piano? I feel sure the answer is nearby, if I can just put the pieces together.

If not, I will go back and tell Geoff Lowe that I know the connection between him and M. Saffarian. I will try to push him a bit by revealing his business dealings with Lilienthal. I doubt that I can worry him much, he's only peripherally implicated, but a mathematics professor might not like me bringing any disorder to his life. He might admit his ties with Ruthie, to get rid of me.

I meditate during the afternoon soap operas. I read my notes. I commune with a golden conquistador, his foot on a rock, who hangs in a picture frame above a brown veneer desk in my room.

By 4:30, I have resolved the glitches in the day. I enjoy a warm, steady feeling in the center of my abdomen as if I have had a big shot of alcohol. I drive back to Joe's, by a more direct route which I map out in advance, hoping to arrive before the dinner crowd. I don't laugh once along the way. This time, I get a spot on the paved area of the lot. I push through the well-oiled door and make my way to a seat beside the jukebox near the counter.

The waitress and owner, Diane, brings a menu and flips it down in front of me. Her smock now sports sauce stains. She probably can't see them over her belly. She turns, about to disappear back behind the counter.

"Ruthie," I call. My ears ring.

"Me?" she answers, razor-voiced. Then she shuts her mouth. The mouth becomes a thin red line. I see that make-up and the last stages of pregnancy obscure Ruthie's face. The woman in front of me could have been spectacular in the past, probably was. One for Eileen.

Ruthie walks slowly to my table and lowers herself onto the padded bench on the other side of the booth.

"Who are you?" she asks.

"My name is Eliza Pirex. I'm a private investigator. I was hired by your friend, Eileen Goldeen, to find you. Because she misses you. No other reason."

Ruthie stares at me. We both know there are always other reasons.

"You haven't found me. My name is Diane Krantz now and that's who I am. You can ask my husband. Joe is the only friend in the world who really knows anything about me."

"How did you come to be here, Ruthie?" I ask.

"Call me Diane," she says. I feel abashed, as though my presence here testifies to a fundamental rudeness. A tall, thin man with a used apron tied around his middle appears at the end of our table. He clears his throat nervously. Diane forces a smile for him out of facial muscles rigid with tension.

"Honey, we got the rest of the set-up for dinner still to go." He speaks deferentially.

"Joe, this lady was paid by someone I used to know to find me. I've got to give her a few minutes and then I'll send her along. Sammy will be here in a bit. We'll have him start a few minutes early and we'll let him go early."

Joe gazes at me with meager interest, then his eyes revert to Diane. "I'm right here if you need me, honey," Joe says. He puts a gentle hand on her shoulder and she clasps her hand briefly over his. He nods and leaves, asking me one question only. "Any coffee for you?"

"No, thanks," I answer.

"We never talk about my past," Ruthie looses the words slowly. "Joe's not interested. The diner and our life together are all he cares about. And the baby coming, of course. He's easier to please than anyone I ever met." She turns to watch him sorting silverware.

A smile shaded with real affection and warmth causes me to smile in response. Suddenly, she looks different, not like the shell of a used-to-be charismatic person or the missing mythological Ruthie for whom I have searched. She looks like someone I don't know, a nice woman expecting a baby, smiling at the husband she cares about.

Diane looks back at me. She seems taken aback by my expression. Her smile was not for me.

I rake her face with my eyes. The skin looks lined, the jaw swollen with pregnancy and Joe's cooking. I judge, by the lines in her face, that her habitual expression must be frank and peaceful. My visit depresses her.

"How did you two meet?" I ask, speaking softly.

275
▲

"I came to Santa Barbara at loose ends. I tried staying with Antonia, but she pushed me to stay in contact with my family and friends. I was playing the piano to make money but I was never really good. Antonia wanted me to work at my music all the time. She wanted to keep me at her house so she could be a patron of the arts." Ruthie shakes her head, a scant, cynical motion.

"Finally, I took a waitress job here and Joe and I got married. We started running the place after his father, Joe Senior, died. That's all there is." She gazes at me.

"Why didn't Antonia say hello to you today?"

"She's not allowed to tell anyone where I am. She knows that perfectly well. She was playing with you. She can't help playing tricks, that's the way she is. I'll make sure she never does this again. I don't want Antonia having her fun at my expense," Ruthie replies.

"She didn't identify you to me. She did try to protect you."

"She used to be a friend," Ruthie unbends a little. "She brought you here to show you to me. I'm sure she thought I would be glad that people care about me and want me back. She can't understand."

"She told me a story about getting postcards from you, mailed from all over the world," I tell Ruthie.

"Antonia has always thought that I should invent travels and a career to ease the minds of my parents and the friends I left behind, and keep them at bay. She thinks that I do mail them postcards sometimes. But I don't." She stares into space once again.

"Diane, Eileen would like to see you."

Her face floods with terrible pain. I grind my teeth in shock. The intensity of that pain reminds me of Eileen's Ruthie.

"They'd all love to see me. We all love Ruthie, she flatters us so. She keeps our dirty secrets and never tells. We'd kill for her." Her facial muscles quiver and tears form in her eyes. She swipes at her face angrily until she has it under control.

"Diane?" calls Joe.

"I'm fine, Joe. Thank you." She signals him that she can really handle me. He signals something back.

"What happened before you left San Francisco, Diane?" I ask her. "I've been exploring your past for weeks now. I want to end my involvement with your personal history. I'd like to know what happened to you so I can put this to rest and have some peace." At the word 'peace' she straightens up, suddenly taller on the bench.

276
▲

"I see," she says. She shudders. We lock eyes for one long minute. With a shrewdness acquired since she stopped being Ruthie, she realizes she will have to buy me off. She'll have to talk to me, to get me to leave her in peace. She values peace.

"Diane, I don't want to upset you."

"You never do. But you all upset me to death until I met Joe. And none of you meant to." Diane's face stiffens as she makes the decision to speak. I now understand entirely the Ruthie phenomenon. It doesn't matter whether or not she used to be good-looking. The emotional intensity of the woman, even diluted by time, even turned off at the meter, could knock you down. There's some weird way I already feel that I want something from her, something just for me, not for Eileen, and I know better.

"You know about Claudia and about Stuart Lilienthal?" she asks. Her mouth purses as if the names leave a rotten taste.

"Some," I say.

"When Claudia found out Stuart was lovers with us both, using two different names, she asked to meet me at my apartment and she told me about him. Stuart found out she was coming. He came to the apartment in a rage. Claudia was threatening to talk to reporters, poor mousy girl. Stuart went crazy and decided to prove how much he despised Claudia and wanted me. He said to me, *'I'm going to snap her neck and chew her up. For you.'*

"'For you,' he said. Stuart ran out to the back porch and picked up a plane. When Claudia came out of the bathroom, he said, *'I want Ruthie, not you.'*

"'Ruthie, not you.' My name was the last thing she ever heard, my name came at her like the instrument of her death. Then Stuart took her hair in his fingers and hit her on the neck with that heavy tool. She fell and made some noise and crawled, trying to get away. Then she died. She never shut her eyes. Her eyes rolled around, and soon they dried out. He said, *'Don't call the police yet. I owe your sister, Jane, a favor. She did a favor for me.'*

"'A favor.' For my little sister who grew up as ugly as my life was. I let him do her a favor. He mentioned he was tired. My heart pounded that whole day like it would rupture inside my chest but he was tired.

"He didn't care that he had made me an accomplice to a senseless murder. I wasn't strong enough to do anything that might pardon me for my part in that nightmare. He said, *'We're in this together.'*

277
▲

"'Together.' He felt free to threaten me. The tool with his fingerprints lay right there on my floor. I could have used it against him. But he could have used it on me.

"He told me to leave the apartment for a while and then come back and call the police. He told me to identify the body for them. He ordered me to tell the police that it was my sister lying dead on the floor. I was to tell them that she had been threatened by a boyfriend I had never met.

"I left, I came back. He had cleaned off his fingerprints, wiped out every sign of himself from the apartment, and was gone. I sat with her until the authorities came. They took 35 minutes to get there because she was already dead.

"While I waited I made some phone calls. I told friends that I'd found Claudia dead. Claudia wasn't close to me when she was alive but she lay dead in my room. I needed to talk about her death. The last time I ever talked to Lilienthal, he said, *'Those people you called, tell them you were joking.'*

"'That I was joking,'" Ruthie repeats. "I never felt like playing the piano again," she adds. "He was not just insane, he was also evil and privileged, the most deceiving kind of monster."

"I'm so sorry," I tell her. "Lilienthal is in jail right now, he confessed to Claudia's murder and much more. He can't hurt anyone else."

"It's not my concern," she says. Her eyes grow harder, another door closes between me and Ruthie. "I wrote to tell Stuart I would soon be dead. He knew I meant it. And I told him to tell my sister, Jane, that I was going to die." A thin, painful sound whistles through her teeth.

"Maybe my biggest sin was freeing Jane from her name. Her name might have brought her to justice. She was dangerous. I should have taken responsibility for checking her course but there was too little left of me."

"Diane, they know about Jane now. She'll be sent someplace where they might be able to straighten her out." I hope I'm not being overly optimistic.

"I don't want to hear any more about it," Ruthie says in a dry whisper. I believe her.

I will soon make a difficult decision based on that belief.

"I'm working for Eileen," I reiterate, having not dared to make the decision yet. Ruthie looks at me with the most compelling dislike I have ever faced.

"If you're a human being, if you care about the child I'm bringing into the world, if you want to be better than some of them, you'll leave me for dead." Her new dislike of me, and her old convoluted hatreds, lend her words strength and dignity. She gives me no chance to respond. Ruthie rises. I have a feeling that no one will ever see her again.

Diane goes over to a sideboard. She picks up a package of napkins. She looks like someone who waitresses in a small diner.

Diane's husband starts to write the dinner specials on a chalkboard. At the top he writes, "Eat at Joe's." He doesn't notice me leave.

I return to the Galleon Motel. I lie back down on the bed, thinking about what to do with Ruthie's remains. I think about who might be accountable. Lilienthal traumatized and disillusioned her. A lot of people enjoyed the razzle-dazzle Ruthie show too much and grasped at her. Her family failed her.

But nobody punched her lights out. She flicked the switch herself. She likes living without all that electricity.

I go home. I talk to Dennis. He wants to know how Antonia led me to Ruthie. I explain the clues Antonia set. The musical career abroad of which nobody else knew. The downtown restaurant that was located a long way out of town. Antonia's failure to say even one word to a fellow pregnant woman whom she said she had known for years. Ruthie's middle name, "Diane," emblazoned in plastic on the waitress' badge. The fact that Antonia has always been a trickster.

Only Dennis, Honor, and the children know that no one did away with Ruthie, that Ruthie closed down the show. Dennis asks what I will tell Eileen. I call her, still not knowing.

"Eliza?" bellows Eileen. "I'm glad you're back. I have the best news I've ever, ever had. I'm pregnant. Rich has come back. His dad is even being nice to both of us because of the baby. I have everything I've ever wanted." Her words sound distinct and clear-minded. I sigh with relief.

"Congratulations, Eileen."

"Rich's dad is hosting a celebration dinner at the country club. For me." Her voice rings with joy.

"Another thing. You know how Rich smells like poison?" I had no idea that Eileen was conscious of Rich's toxic smell. "Now that Rich is going to be a father, his dad has given him a wonderful new office far away from the Plastics Department. He's beginning to smell normal and healthy."

She hasn't mentioned Ruthie yet.

"Eileen?" I say as softly as I spoke to Ruthie. "I've found out what happened to Ruthie."

"I can't believe it," Eileen gasps. I hope I can make her believe it.

"Ruthie passed away in Santa Barbara soon after she left here. I'm sorry, Eileen. She took her own life."

"Oh, God, Ruthie. She inspired us all." Eileen halts, dampened by this new evidence of the sorrow wrought by our ephemeral nature. Then she rallies. "You know what? The baby's middle name will be Ruthie. Or Gold if it's a boy. Rich and I want the first name to be after us. Little Rich or Eileen, someone who's really ours."

Jemmy says, "We knew you wouldn't tell on Ruthie."

Annabelle adds, "We'll never tell, either." And, being highly reliable children, they never do.

Honor points out, "This won't enhance your earning potential."

"It can't hurt my earning potential much. My fees are rock bottom already. I don't know how many people Eileen could have talked into employing me even if the case had been a dramatic success. How many people would take Eileen Goldeen's recommendation?"

Eileen, who now dreams regularly in color, calls back one last time to explain herself to me. "Rich says my need to find Ruthie was caused by hormones secreted by the fetus. He's read about this kind of thing." In spite of the outcome of the case, I feel as though I helped get Eileen what she wanted.

Doris Shipley calls. "I've made a small investment in a franchise opportunity for my friends, Pete and Eva. All of a sudden, they're too busy to come by my house. I need to find out how they're spending their time."

"Doris, you don't have enough net worth to finance what I would charge for my services," I tell her.

"I don't know why I called. You are a complete waste of money, Eliza Pirex. I hear rumors that the girl you've been running around looking for, like a chicken with its head cut off, has been dead for years." I hang up on Doris, secure in the knowledge that my new security system goes into place this week so that she will never again make herself privy to my business. I'll miss her but I can't afford the aggravation of keeping her in my working files.

Doris would love to know that I let Eileen recompense me royally. I feel I earned the money just as much as I earned the nicely sewn bite marks on my upper arm which make the skin pull tight when I raise my arm above my head.

Newell Sutton, unbeknownst to anyone at first, adds this case to one of his working manuscripts, *Tales of a Private*

Investigator: The Casebook of Eliza Pirex. He has been listening in on phone calls that Honor made from his house and eavesdropping on his grandchildren. The piece has a weak ending since Newell has no way to find out what happened to Ruthie and can only speculate. Honor has neglected to protect me from him, not being one to consider that I might be as vulnerable as the children and herself.

Our neighbor, Nancy, opens the drapes she has skulked behind and announces her engagement to Newell's son, Linden. Nancy has convinced Linden that the two of them were husband and wife in a former life and still have unresolved issues to work through. Newell Sutton offers to pay for premarital regression therapy.

Lawrence Taylor develops bursitis in his shoulder and wrist. Forced to abandon his career with Jazzmatazz, and having acquired an interest in crime and punishment, he takes the LSAT, a first step which, I'm sure, will lead him to a long tenure as a superior court judge or ambulance chaser, depending upon which way he gets nudged by circumstances. Bradley Evigan's trial results in a hung jury and the state treats him to a second one.

Dave and Delilah Gray win $180,000 in their suit on behalf of their daughter, Lisa, against Stuart Lilienthal, M.D. Lilienthal spends a great deal of his personal holdings on legal fees, psychiatric care, and public relations, but the Grays eventually receive a partial payment. Andy Beeson, Doris' erstwhile companion, gets convicted of second degree murder in the death of prostitute Lou Denny, and subsequently spends a great deal of time at Folsom Prison where he earns the nickname 'Friend.' Kains College fires Dwayne Blount for sleeping on the job.

For a few days, my existence and everyone else's feel precarious to me. What strings restrain anyone from cutting loose their identity on an uncomfortable day, and disappearing? Of all the Golds, only Ruthie's eclipse, out of all of them, caused much repercussion among other people.

I go to sleep one night fretting over the question. When I wake up, Golds no longer float through my mind. After all, most people are moored better than them, better berthed. I send partially fictitious notes to all parties interested in the fate of Ruthie and her family. When the Alameda County Sheriff's Department releases Jane Gold, pending trial, she too disappears without causing a ripple in the pool.

I cruise into a modest job, working for a medium-sized, bland business. I get home every day by 4:30 when the children get home from afterschool care. We finish eating the dinners that Honor left in the freezer before she left home. Jemmy and I cook hamburgers and macaroni after that.

Several Mondays later, Honor mentions, "Maybe it's time for me to come home." I smile into the telephone. "Don't say anything, Eliza Pirex, but I'm starting a writing project," she says. "I'm illustrating it myself. My book will speak to children who have been exposed to the public eye by a parent. I want to help children who have lived through what I have."

"Give me a few days to think about it," I want to tell her because I have suffered her imperiousness all these weeks. But I don't. I'm glad I can't see and smell her. I wouldn't even have the restraint to keep from snatching her into my arms. It turns out that some losses can be averted.

Dennis comes over that night after the kids go to bed, glum with marriage plans. We make ourselves strawberry daiquiris and take them out to the deck. "How's Sharon?" I inquire.

"She's in therapy. She needs to cope with her loss of freedom." Dennis stretches out on the chaise longue. He props his glass on the arm rest.

"How's Honor?" he asks.

"She's going to write a book for exploited children." Dennis and I both hoot at Honor taking up the pen.

"Dennis?" I ask drowsily. "What's that maxim about detective work that you taught me when I was apprenticed with you?"

"You mean, 'Keep trying even when you don't feel like it'?"

"That's it? Those are the words you gave me to live by?" I say, offended.

"What do you want? I'm an Oakland P.I., not your sensei." He takes a long swallow from his glass.

Up above, the city stars grind their gears a little as they make their orbit. Dennis and I drift lethargically under them. The children upstairs turn in their sleep to avoid bad dreams. And farther south, Ruthie, the vanished Ruthie, pivots on her spindle like a neon sign with its bulbs burned out.

It's closing time. Joe puts the cat out. The jukebox plays a last selection, piano music.

DIANA McRAE was born in Berkeley, California. She now lives in Oakland with her non-traditional family which includes children, Wilder and Jaslo. She has worked as a librarian, with the Alameda County Library System, doing information and outreach services, for many years. Though Diana has long been a freelance writer, *All the Muscle You Need* is her first novel. She is currently at work on a second mystery.

spinsters | *aunt lute*

Spinsters/Aunt Lute Book Company was founded in 1986 through the merger of two successful feminist publishing businesses, Aunt Lute Book Company, formerly of Iowa City (founded 1982) and Spinsters Ink of San Francisco (founded 1978). A consolidation in the best sense of the word, this merger has strengthened our ability to produce vital books for diverse women's communities in the years to come.

Our commitment is to publishing works that are beyond the scope of mainstream commercial publishers: books that don't just name crucial issues in women's lives, but go on to encourage change and growth, to make all of our lives more possible.

Though Spinsters/Aunt Lute is a growing, energetic company, there is little margin in publishing to meet overhead and production expenses. We survive only through the generosity of our readers. So, we want to thank those of you who have further supported Spinsters/Aunt Lute—with donations, with subscriber monies, or with low and high interest loans. It is that additional economic support that helps us bring out exciting new books.

Please write to us for information about our unique investment and contribution opportunities.

If you would like further information about the books, notecards and journals we produce, write for a free catalogue.

Spinsters/Aunt Lute
P. O. Box 410687
San Francisco, CA 94141